Praise for Harold Coyle

"Harold Coyle has been dubbed the Tom Clancy of ground warfare and it's easy to see why. He focuses on the grunts because no matter how fancy the weapons are, eventually the military has to send in men to hold new territory."

—*The New York Post*

"Coyle is a master at high tech suspense. He spins his story with such power that you're swept along to the climactic finish."

—Clive Cussler

"Nobody knows war like Harold Coyle and nobody writes it better."

—Stephen Coonts

"When it comes to good military thrillers, Coyle is as good as it gets."

—*Booklist*

"Coyle's attention to detail, his intimate knowledge of small unit fighting is remarkable."

—Thomas Fleming, *The New York Times* bestselling author of *Washington's Secret War*

"With writers like Coyle standing watch over us, who needs Bruce Willis?"

—*Kirkus Reviews*

BOOKS BY HAROLD COYLE

WITH BARRETT TILLMAN

AGAINST ALL ENEMIES

HAROLD COYLE

FORGE®

A TOM DOHERTY ASSOCIATES BOOK
NEW YORK

This is a work of fiction. All the characters and events portrayed in this book are either products of the author's imagination or are used fictitiously.

AGAINST ALL ENEMIES

Copyright © 2002 by Harold Coyle

A Forge Book
Published by Tom Doherty Associates, LLC
175 Fifth Avenue
New York, NY 10010

www.tor-forge.com

Forge® is a registered trademark of Tom Doherty Associates, LLC.

ISBN 978-0-7653-6386-2
Library of Congress Catalog Card Number: 2001058283

First Edition: May 2002
First Mass Market Edition: February 2003
Second Mass Market Edition: May 2009

Printed in the United States of America

0 9 8 7 6 5 4 3 2 1

. . . that whenever any form of Government becomes destructive of these ends, it is the Right of the People to alter or abolish it, and to institute new Government, laying its foundation on such principles, and organizing its Powers in such Form, as to them seem most likely to effect their Safety and Happiness. Prudence, indeed, will dictate that government long established should not be changed for light and transient Causes; and accordingly all Experience hath shewn, that Mankind are more disposed to suffer, while Evils are sufferable, than to right themselves by abolishing the Forms to which they are accustomed. But, when a long Train of Abuses and Usurpations, pursuing invariably the same Object, evinces a Design to reduce them under absolute Despotism, it is their Right, it is their Duty, to throw off such Government, and to provide new Guards for their future Security.

**FROM THE DECLARATION OF INDEPENDENCE,
1776**

A well regulated Militia, being necessary to the security of a free State, the right of the people to keep and bear Arms, shall not be infringed.

**ARTICLE II (COMPLETE TEXT),
THE BILL OF RIGHTS, 1787**

A little rebellion now and then is a good thing.

THOMAS JEFFERSON, 1787

Revolution is the locomotive of history.

KARL MARX

My Country, may she always be right. But right or wrong, my Country.

**INSCRIPTION AT THE
UNITED STATES NAVAL ACADEMY**

PROLOGUE

The sight of file after file of redcoated soldiers marching boldly onto the green was unnerving. Nestled between his fellow militiamen, a young New England farmer who went by the name of Ned Smith nervously shuffled about as he watched. Every so often he would cast an anxious glance to his left and right in an effort to gauge the response of his companions. Rather than offering some measure of reassurance, however, the sight of their grim faces and his company's pathetically thin ranks only served to heighten his apprehensions.

Never having been in combat, Ned had no clear idea what awaited them once the British had completed their deployment from a line of march into one of battle. What little his captain had been able to teach them during their musters on this very green did little to prepare him for the sights he now beheld and the sensations they were evoking within him. Never one to be shy about voicing his opinion, Ned wondered if it would make him look cowardly if he called out to his captain and asked if he thought it wasn't a good idea to stand down and disperse. In Ned's mind they had pushed their defiance as far as they dare. To linger here in the face of such overwhelming odds would be foolish.

Yet stand their ground they did. Silently the band of militiamen waited. Across from them the rhythmic tromping of marching feet mixed with the rattle of muskets and gear, stirring the chilly morning air and blood of all present. Every so often this muted cacophony of noise was punctured by crisp commands barked by stern-faced English officers. With machinelike precision the solid phalanxes of the King's troops responded by wheeling about this way and then that in preparation for the pending contest. While few of the rank and file expected they would need to do more than present their muskets and make ready to fire in order to chase away the rabble across from them, none doubted that they would prevail.

This confidence came not from arrogance, but from a simple appreciation of the facts, the same facts that Ned Smith was so keenly aware of. This was not the streets of Boston, where roving mobs felt free to hurl taunts and insults at a handful of British soldiers standing their posts. If it came to it, this would be their sort of scrap, a stand-up fight, the sort they had been trained for. Given a chance to play this little drama out to its conclusion, there was not a soldier present who doubted that they would prevail. The only regret that some entertained as they waited was that they would not be given a chance to do so. They would be held back, as they always were, from meting out the just punishment the wretched colonial rabble deserved. After having endured the outrageous treatment that they had been exposed to for so long, all felt the urge to set the record straight and put the colonials back in their place.

Standing before a collection of men who were his neighbors and friends, Captain John Parker was at a loss for words. He found himself unable to muster up a pat response, or find a witty saying that could ease the apprehension that he shared with men he had gathered together in defiance of the orders issued by officers of the King. In time, he knew he would have yield to the regulars now assembled before him. But he was determined to do so only at the last possible moment, and only after making it clear that they were simply giving ground, and not the principles which had compelled them to make this stand.

Behind Parker, Ned Smith waited with growing concern. Though he could feel the shoulders of his companions on either side rub his as they shuffled about nervously, the young farmer felt very much alone. Absentmindedly, he fingered his weapon's lock as he watched, waited, and prayed.

Ned was no stranger to this piece. He had used it to slay many a squirrel, and, when the occasion presented itself, a rabbit. These little forays beyond the neatly plowed fields of his family farm had been, for him, an enjoyable break to the monotony of daily chores that made those who farmed here as hardy and tough as the land they tended. Whether he sallied out on his own or in the company of friends, the excitement of hunting his prey, and putting his skills to a test, never failed to bring joy to what would have been an otherwise drab and uneventful existence. Perhaps that was why he answered the call by the local militia captain. The militia company was, for Ned, an adventure, a chance to shed the last vestiges of his childhood and stand with the men of his community, for the first time, as an equal.

While such whimsical goals had sufficed to get him into the ranks then, Ned was quickly becoming aware that it would take more than that to keep him rooted to this spot as he watched as untold numbers of tall grenadiers marshaled before him. This was no longer a game that was being played out by radical politicians. It was no longer a pleasant diversion from the drudgery of farming the rocky plot of earth his father had willed to him. This was a serious matter. These were soldiers of the King, the finest musketeers in the world. Everything from the bayonets that caught the glint of the early morning sunlight to the cold, hard expressions worn by the soldiers who made up the long red ranks told young Ned Smith that trouble was but a hair's breadth away.

On either side of him stood his fellow militiamen, men who had been encouraged by their community leaders, families, and peers to stand up for what they had been told were their rights. Now, like Ned, they stood there in silence, arranged in what passed for a line of battle. Each and every one of them watched the swift, precise movements of professional soldiers arrayed before them. Everything about the English, from the ominous sight of their unsheathed bayonets, to the solid ranks that seemed to stretch across the green and beyond, made Ned and his companions painfully conscious of their own vulnerability.

"They're like a machine," the youth muttered to no one in particular. "They'll sweep us aside like so many cinders."

An older man, a grizzly coot dressed in a homespun vest and a coarse muslin shirt, leaned on his musket as if it were a walking stick. He surveyed the scene before them through narrow, squinted eyes. "They're just as nervous about this as we are," he stated bluntly. "See," he indicated with a nod toward the far end of the green, "how their officers are circling and wandering about."

"Well," a gruff voice replied, "their officers may be a bit uneasy, but watch out for their lads. Have you taken note how they eye us with the contempt of Boston thugs. Mark my words, they're spoiling for a fight, lads."

While the gruff voiced militiaman's statement may not have held true for all of the King's men, it certainly summed up Private Robert Johnston's attitude. Like so many of his companions, he was growing impatient with his own skittish officers. Worked up into a near frenzy by the tensions that had been building up, Johnston stepped out of ranks and began shouting oaths for all he was worth. Like many of his mates he ignored his officer's threats to cease yelling and stand to attention. He was tired of standing in ranks like a great bloody statue, forced to endure everything from taunts to stones thrown at them by damned colonists like those across the way without being allowed to respond. "Look at 'em," Johnston hissed as he thrust his fist out toward the line of militia, some sixty yards away. "They stand there, armed to the teeth, in clear violation of the King's law, and dare us when they know there isn't an officer in our regiment with the backbone to give the order." Glancing at a young subaltern doing everything he could to shove the men of 4th Regiment of Foot back in line, Johnston grunted. "I don't know who disgusts me more, our own officers who shy away from a real brawl like a spring virgin or those damned hooligans who call themselves patriots."

Johnston's companion, a pale, thin fellow named Martin who was also enflamed by the moment, didn't respond to his comrade's comments. Instead, he contented himself with fingering the musket held close to his side as he eyed the gaggle of militiamen gathered opposite them. All that stood between these lines were a handful of mounted British officers who rode between the two lines of armed men in an effort to defuse the situation. Finally, Martin spoke as he eyed a particularly nervous looking colonist who appeared to be backing away from the fray. "One good volley," he finally muttered menacingly. "Let us hit with one good volley and we'll end it right here."

With a grunt, Johnston nodded his agreement. "Aye, that we would. Let 'em see a bit of their own blood spilled. Perhaps that'll make 'em a bit more mindful of the King's law."

"If not the King's law," Martin snapped, "at least we would teach the bastards a bit of respect for his troops."

Shifting his weight from one foot to the next, Johnston was about to hurl a volley of fresh insults when their lieutenant, his face as red as the scarlet coat he wore, passed before him. Sword drawn, he pushed Johnston on the chest with his free hand and shouted. "Hold your place. Keep silent and hold your place, or it'll be the cat-of-nine for you." Without another word, the young officer continued down the ranks until he stopped in front of another offender and repeated his threat. With a sideward glance, Johnston looked at the officer, then over at the rebels. For a moment, the musketeer weighed the merits and risks of continuing with his taunts. Only after considerable thought and the memory of the drummer's lash biting into his flesh did Johnston relent. The release of his pent up anger and frustrations, he concluded, was not worth the punishment. So Johnston pulled himself erect, tucked his musket into his side, and contented himself with watching the confused scene unfold before him in silence.

If it were a simple matter of numbers and demonstrated abilities with weapons, or logic and common sense, this strange confrontation would never have occurred. The armed men who eyed each other across the flat expanse of village green were, after all, Englishmen. Both were ruled by the same King. They shared a common language. The institutions and practices that governed their day to day life had sprung from the same roots. In times gone by, they had fought a common foe under the same banner.

Yet Ned Smith and many of his fellow New Englanders no longer saw themselves and the King's men as fellow countrymen. Slowly, almost imperceptibly at first, the English soldiers who closed Boston to all commerce had been transfigured into something else. Rather than guardians, they had become intruders, men from a foreign land sent by a distant government to deprive Ned and his fellow New Englanders of their rights and their liberties.

Of the many issues that had propelled these two armed bodies to assemble across from each other in the cold dawn light, there were but two that compelled the militiamen to stand their ground as long as they did, and the English soldiers to seek battle without a hint of hesitation. For the militia, the sight of the redcoated troops on the ground which they called their own brought home to them the harsh reality that the issues of freedom and liberty were no longer abstract thoughts bantered about by rebel rousers in Boston's public houses. The agents who possessed the will and means to deprive them of both were there before them, but a stone's throw from their own front doors. While each of the militiamen knew they could capitulate and escape with their lives, all understood that the price of doing so would be surrendering the freedoms and right they had come believe were God given.

There was nothing abstract at all about the forces that propelled the regulars. They represented the King. Every English law and every English institution was on their side. As the duly appointed defenders of the King and Parliament, it was their lot in life to follow his orders and enforce the laws of the land. They had been dispatched not to judge right or wrong. Nor were they there to listen to the grievances of the provincials. The soldiers had come across the Atlantic for no other purpose than to carry out their orders and put an end to all resistance, by whatever means. And the means upon which they relied was not a judge's gavel or a lawyer's petition, but a Tower musket, caliber .75 equipped with an eighteen inch triangular bayonet.

With their own men properly deployed and, for the moment, in hand, mounted British officers rode up and down between the opposing lines. "Disperse," they repeated angrily, spitting out their word as they grew frustrated with the lack of response. "Disperse, you damned rebels, and be gone."

Though it was all but impossible to take his eyes off one mounted English officer who loomed before him, Ned managed to glance to his left and right. Like him, some of his companions were clearly intimidated by the English officers and the solid wall of regulars standing behind them. Twitching and shuffling about in their loose formation, Ned saw more than a few glancing back over their shoulders as if they were making sure there was nothing that would impede their flight if it came to that. Others, however, seemed totally unmoved by the overwhelming might that was arrayed before them. Holding their muskets at the ready, those men simply stood stone cold still, carefully eyeing anything that they perceived to be threatening, which, for Ned, was everything.

Slowly, it dawned upon Ned that they were in an impossible situation, one in which there was no good outcome. If they simply obeyed the King's officer, turned their backs and went home, they would have to face the humiliation and criticism of friends and fellow militiamen. That would have been hard for young Ned to live down, especially after all the bold talk he had bantered about in the tavern. Humiliation, however, could be survived. Standing their ground, as many a crowd had done before in Boston, and hoping that the English would back down, might not. The English, after all, had their pride, too. They had their masters to whom they must answer. What if today was the day, Ned asked himself, if they said, "enough of this" and fired. And if they did, then what? What would he do? What would become of their homes, their families?

Where, the young man wondered, had any of the fine gentlemen of Boston addressed *that* in their fine speeches? Why weren't they here? Why, Ned asked himself, was he there in their stead?

That there were others who agreed with Ned's assessment of the situation was obvious. After delaying as long as he dared, their own commander began to make his way down their line. Though nervous himself, Captain Parker at least retained the presence of mind to face the fact that there was nothing that they could accomplish by standing their ground any longer. Even from sixty yards, it was quite obvious that the ordinarily well disciplined English musketeers were in an ugly mood. With no hope of reinforcement, and ever mindful that the men under his command were his friends, neighbors, and their sons, Parker gave them the order to disperse. To Ned, already on the verge of quitting the field, this was sound advice, advice which he fully intended to follow.

The efforts of the mounted officers riding back and forth along the rebel line seemed to be having an effect when, from somewhere off to one side, a single shot rang out. A quick sweep of the rebel line by every English officer, mounted and afoot, failed to detect any telltale signs of smoke drifting away from it. Leaning forward, despite frantic threats from his officer, Johnston glanced down their own line in an effort to see if he could discover the source of the shot.

He was still looking when, to his surprise, another shot rang out, right next to him. Jumping, Johnston's head spun to his left where he laid eyes on his companion, now enshrouded in a cloud of gray smoke. With an ease borne of long hours of drill and training, the man was bringing his musket down to reload. "DAMN YOU ALL TO HELL!" Martin shouted as he reached behind with his right hand to fish a fresh round from his cartridge box. Then he looked over at Johnston. "Well," he roared. "You're always griping that we're never allowed to take our measure against those bastards. Here's your chance, man. Take it now or never utter another word of complaint to me."

Johnston was still staring dumbly at Martin, considering what to do, when several more men in the ranks around him brought their pieces to bear on the rebels and fired. Though he hadn't heard an order to fire, Johnston didn't much care. Finally, he realized, he could do what he had wished he could do for so long. He could lash out and strike a telling blow against a foe that had, for so long, taunted them with impunity.

With the steady, measured steps that were second nature to him, Johnston brought his musket up to his shoulder, pointed it at the group of men who were, under the King's law, as much an Englishmen as Johnston himself. But this little legal nicety didn't matter to Johnston. Not in the least. With great deliberateness, he locked the hammer of his musket back into the full cocked position, steadied his piece, and pulled the trigger.

The crack of musket fire was deafening. Even on the ground, where Ned lay, the sound was the most awful noise he had ever heard. For the longest time he stayed there, wondering where he had been hit. It took young Ned a moment before he realized that he hadn't been shot. Only then did he slowly begin to look about. To his front, the English line was half masked by billowing clouds of smoke their own firing was creating. Off to his right he watched as several of his fellow militia gamely tried to return the English fire. Feeling embarrassed by the fact that he was cowering instead of standing tall and bold, Ned turned his eyes away to the left.

This, however, brought him no relief, for his eyes were met by the sight of Robert Munroe, lying but a few feet from him. Munroe, with blood pouring freely from an ugly wound, was motionless. Closing his eyes, Ned began to whisper the Lord's prayer.

Only the sound of feet scampering all about him by caused Ned to open his eyes. This revealed a most horrible sight. Individually and in pairs, English soldiers, with their bayonets leveled, were rushing forward. To Ned it seemed as if their own officers were trying hard to restrain them, to hold them back. Whether this was so didn't matter to Ned Smith. In a single swift motion he was up, on his feet, and fleeing. What consequences the events he had just witnessed would have on him, on his family, and on his tiny community of Lexington did not matter at that moment. All that was important to Ned was that he put as much distance between himself and the vicious regulars who had brought death to the community in which he had been born.

CHAPTER 1

Making his way around the corner, Dale Stoner didn't bother scanning the row of buildings that loomed up on either side of him like the walls of a sheer, gray stone canyon. The heavy afternoon traffic, which always starts earlier on Friday afternoons, covered the floor of this drab man made valley. The streets and roadways, populated by office workers and corporate professionals streaming out of the city for home demanded Stoner's full attention, even though their forward progress was more akin to a creeping glacier than a roaring river.

By nature a cautious man, Stoner drove with both hands on the wheel, keeping an eye out for inattentive drivers and lane jockeys. When threatened by one of these hazards, Stoner would maneuver his oversize delivery van out of harm's way with an ease and grace that had earned him the respect of his fellow drivers and supervisors. That this praise did not translate into bonuses or pay raises did not bother Stoner any more. Nor did he mind the extra hours. The work, though tedious and routine at best, kept him from dwelling on his problems, most of the time. But not always.

Despite his best efforts, Dale Stoner couldn't keep his mind from wandering back to the chain of events that had led to this day. In high school, it hadn't been his aspiration to be a delivery truck driver. It had just happened, just like the First Gulf War, and his estrangement from his own family. Before those tragic events he thought he had it all. He believed that he knew what was right and what was wrong, that there were people who loved him and upon whom he could depend. But then the war had come and nothing was ever the same again.

Stoner had loved being a soldier. The camaraderie that

grew out of shared hardships, the sense of purpose the Army gave him, and a comfortable illusion of security the peacetime military generates was worth the low pay and hassles that had gone with the job. He was just starting his second hitch as a combat engineer in the beginning of August 1990 when Iraq invaded Kuwait. Together with his companions, Dale Stoner swallowed whatever personal fears he harbored and sallied forth to meet his sworn obligations. Like millions of Americans had done in the past, Stoner was ready, able, and willing to defend his nation and his fellow countrymen. At a time when so many other Americans had nothing else but profit margins, net worth, and capital gains on their minds, he was out there, on the edge, doing things other men only dreamed of. Yet, despite years of training, Dale Stoner found he was unprepared for what happened to him.

A sudden blur in his sideview mirror alerted Stoner to a danger, more perceived then understood. With a shake of his head, his attention snapped back to the task of driving his van. It took Stoner a moment before he was able to focus on the potential hazard. There, in his right sideview mirror, Stoner spotted a road warrior coming up from behind, scooting about from lane to lane in a small metallic blue German import in an effort to beat imaginary foes. As he watched in his oversized mirrors, Stoner saw the little blue import cut in front of a white Japanese four door. The driver of the Japanese car, trying to enjoy a cup of cappuccino while jabbering on a cell phone and driving, was caught off guard by the sudden appearance of the metallic blue car in front of him. Stoner could clearly see the driver of the white car panic as he let go of his cup, grabbed the wheel with both hands, and swerved without looking. This set in motion a chain reaction that disrupted numerous phone calls and caused fellow drivers to spill drinks and or spew globs of late afternoon snacks all over their pinstriped suits and silk blouses.

Having triumphed over the white car, the driver of the metallic blue car set his sights on Stoner's oversized delivery truck as he began to maneuver into position to pass it on the right. Patiently, Dale Stoner did nothing as he watched the metallic blue car draw near. Confident of his ability to pass the lumbering van, the driver of the metallic blue car took one hand off the wheel and reached down to grab his cell phone. Stoner could see that the driver was a young, clean-cut, professional type, wearing a crisp white shirt, a nondescript tie, and sunglasses like those favored by aviators. There was no way, Stoner thought, that this character had served in the Gulf, or Bosnia, or Kosovo, or anywhere else. The closest this geek had gotten to the First Persian Gulf War had been on his television. With that thought in mind, Stoner watched and waited as the metallic blue car continued to close.

Stoner's patience was rewarded. Just as the front fender of the metallic blue car pulled even with the rear bumper of his truck, the driver of the car turned his head to search for something on the passenger seat. Seizing the moment, Stoner flipped on his right hand turn signal and jerked the wheel of his truck a tad to the right. He didn't intend to move over into the other lane, for in truth there wasn't any room in the traffic to do so. He just wanted the other driver to think he not only wanted to do so, but was, in fact, in the act of doing so.

The ploy worked. The flashing turn signal and the unexpected motion of the big delivery truck caught the driver of the metallic blue·car off guard. Panicked, he threw his phone over his shoulder, brought his free hand onto the steering wheel, and gave it a hard pull to the right. In an instant, the metallic blue car was up and over the curb. Unnerved and shaken, the driver struggled to control his car as the hard plastic bumper of his overvalued import glanced off not one but two parking meter poles, leaving a gash that would more than eat up his collision deductible.

Though he would have liked to slow down some in order to savor his small victory over the forces of ignorance, Stoner's turn was coming up. After having allowed himself the indulgence of becoming distracted from his task, it was time to concentrate on making his way safely to the left.

Deftly, he nudged his large truck over into the left-hand lane, made his turn, and continued on to his target.

As he approached the Federal building and made for the driveway marked "deliveries," Stoner tried once more to piece together how this nightmare had all started. Perhaps it had been during the air war when nightly SCUD alerts sent them scrambling into poorly built bunkers where they sat in the dark silence, masked and covered head to toe in chemical protective clothing, wondering what was to become of them. Or it could have been the day his platoon made its way slowly along the road north of Kuwait City that the media had dubbed "The Highway of Death." Even the mere thought of that experience conjured up memories of sights and smells that still haunted him to this very day.

Bringing his truck to a stop, Stoner sat quietly in his seat for a moment and thought. Given a chance, he could have dealt with any of those nightmares, singularly or together. If only he'd been allowed by his Creator to keep his health, Stoner was sure that he could have held things together, to have soldiered on and keep both his sanity and family. But like countless others, he was denied that opportunity by the onset of a series of nebulous and ill defined conditions that eventually became known as Gulf War syndrome.

It crept into his life slowly, unnoticed at first. For him it was like an unending bout with the flu. He was never really outright sick, but neither was he free for more than a few days of misery that alternated between sweats and chills. First the military physicians, and then those at the VA after he was medically discharged, explained away Stoner's continuous ill health with any number of theories, none of which solved his problems. Even his own wife, worn thin by his continuous complaints, did little to help. "Dale," she'd scream at him in frustration, "it's all in your head. You've got to pull yourself together. Forget about the Gulf and get on with your life." And though he tried, tried with all his strength, he found he was unable to overcome either his chronic illness or those terrible visions that he kept locked away inside where no one could see them or be hurt by them.

As bad as his separation from his wife was, the unkindest cut of all came in the fall of 1996 when the Department of Defense, after denying the existence of Gulf War syndrome, suddenly announced that yes, an unknown number of soldiers *had* been exposed to chemical agents during the Gulf War. To Stoner the admission that some of the illnesses experienced by Gulf War veterans could have been related to service there, after the government had denied any connection between the two for so long, was a breach of faith. Hadn't he done his part? Hadn't he fulfilled his obligations to his duly appointed superiors and the people of the United States in the belief that they would, if necessary, support him in his time of need?

The memory that no one had done a dammed thing to help him provided the last spark of anger he needed to carry him through the next hour. Like vets from the Vietnam War, Dale learned the hard way that those whom he thought he was protecting and serving wanted nothing to do with the human wreckage left in the wake of war. People such as the arrogant young professional who had been driving the metallic blue German import had their own lives to live, narrow and self-centered lives that left little time for those who had shouldered the rifle when duty called and suffered for their efforts.

Once on the loading dock, Stoner dropped the hydraulic gate, opened the rear doors of his truck, and climbed in. Mechanically, he began loading the heavy-duty four-wheel cart. As he had done so many times before in his mind, Stoner stacked the boxes made to hold five thousand sheets of copier paper in a predetermined order. Carefully he placed the boxes he, himself, had packed in the center of the cart. A small arrow, all but unnoticeable unless you knew what to look for, pointed outward on one side of the box lids. These would all be stacked in the center, four high, and surrounded by boxes containing real copier paper.

In silence Stoner completed loading his cart, watching out of the corner of his eye as an increasing number of Federal employees used his van as cover in their effort to slip out a bit early. It was no accident that Dale had selected this particular hour and weekday to make this "special" delivery. He had been here during this time of day before and noted how everyone, from the most senior judge in the building to the lowliest clerk in the mailroom, was in a hurry to finish up his work and leave. Stoner not only expected this outbound traffic, he was counting on it.

Carefully he eased the heavily burdened cart down the aluminum ramp. From here on in it was all a matter of luck and following through. After closing and locking the door of his truck, as he did every time he left it unattended in a public area, Dale pushed his cart up to the double doors of the Federal building.

"Someone doesn't like you," the security guard at the entrance called out by way of a greeting.

Stoner struggled with his load, forced a smile and nodded. "Oh, I don't mind," he replied. "This is my last delivery."

The security guard returned Stoner's smile as he looked over the cart full of copier paper. "Know what ya mean," he responded with a halfhearted sigh. Nothing showed on the scanner as Stoner passed through the security checkpoint with his cart. Nor did any expression of concern, fear, or anticipation betray a man who had, by now, put aside any doubts. Used to seeing Dale Stoner deliver tons of copier paper to the Federal building week after week, the guard didn't bother to check the invoice or make any effort to poke through the boxes that seemed to be precariously close to toppling off Stoner's cart. Having done as much of his duty as he felt necessary, the guard went back to keeping one eye on the small portable TV he kept in his enclosed booth and let Dale make his way to the basement where the central supply room was.

Any second thoughts that were trying to worm their way into Stoner's consciousness disappeared when the doors of the elevator opened. With a grunt he gave his heavy cart a jerk to get it moving and maneuvered it into the elevator.

After pressing the button for the basement, Stoner closed his eyes and started to take deep, slow breaths. He didn't open his eyes until the elevator stopped. As if synchronized, his eyes opened as the doors of the elevator separated. With a heave, he shoved his cart out into the hall and began to make his way down the long, dimly lit basement corridor.

The idea for his plan had come to him not long after making a delivery, much like this one, late one afternoon months before. Alone, and in a hurry to be finished with his paperwork, the manager of the supply room had pleaded with Dale to have a heart and wheel his cart into the main storage area. "Drop the stuff off wherever you can find a spot," the frazzled Federal employee had explained to Stoner. "I'll sort it out on Monday. I just want to clear my desk and get out of here before the traffic gets too bad."

Left alone in the basement of the building that day, Stoner had noticed that the room, used for storage of office supplies as well as unused furniture, had no walls. Most of the building's main support pillars for the left half of the building, encased in concrete, stood exposed in one cavernous room. How easy, he had found himself thinking, it would be to drop this place. With a little bit of C-4 and det cord, Stoner was confident that he could bring at least half of the building down upon itself, just like a house of cards.

That this thought had stayed with him long after he had left that day didn't surprise him. Stoner had been in and out of that building on many an occasion on other business. He had wasted hours traveling from one Federal agency to another in an effort to eke out some sort of justice from a government that had turned its back on him. More than once he had stormed out of an office after being rebuffed by a pasty faced bureaucrat who was unable, or unwilling, to deal with him in a manner that he, Stoner, thought a disabled veteran deserved. More than once he had driven away from this very building wishing he could blow them all to kingdom come.

It didn't take much before his fits of anger began to

transform themselves into a idea, and then action. Perhaps, he told himself as he made his way down the corridor, it had been only natural to come up with his plan, given his training. He had already sketched out a rough concept in his mind before he attended his first militia meeting. By that time, he was interested only in working out the details, not the reason or even the target. Dale Stoner had no intention of becoming a member of a group known as the 5th Brigade. They were only interested in beating their chests, and playing soldiers. He, on the other hand, had a purpose in life. The former combat engineer was intent on exacting his revenge from a government that no longer represented him or millions of other hard working, honest citizens like him. Armed with motive and the technical expertise his years of active duty had bestowed upon him, all Dale needed was the means.

When he pushed his way into the outer office, the employees charged with receiving and storing all the supplies used in the building were gathered there, waiting for their work day to come to an end. Stoner made it a point to bang his cart against anything he could in the office crowded with desks and shelves. Out of the corner of his eye he caught a glimpse of the man in charge rolling his eyes at the sight of Stoner. "Jeez," the supervisor sneered as he looked over Stoner's load. "Why didn't you wait until we were halfway out the door before delivering this stuff?"

Bringing his cart to a stop before responding, Stoner wiped some sweat from his brow, then smiled at the chubby old coot. "Sorry 'bout that. Yours was the first one they loaded at the warehouse and, I'm sorry to say, last off my truck."

"I'm honored," the chief supply clerk shot back.

"Well," Stoner added quickly, "if it makes you feel any better, I'll take it back there myself and unload it. I know where it goes."

Stoner's offer was greeted with smiles all around. The men and women who normally would have been left the task to unload the boxes off Stoner's cart onto their own and then haul them into the main storage area, all turned to stare at their boss who sat at his cluttered desk, considering Stoner's offer. With the heightened state of alert that every April 19 brought to every Federal facility having passed without a single incident, the chief supply clerk saw no harm in sidestepping proper procedures, again. Stoner's quiet blue eyes, framed by a bland, clean, expressionless face, didn't look anything like one of those crazed maniacs. He could be trusted. After all, he had done this sort of thing before.

Quickly altering his scowl into as decent a smile as he could manage this late on a Friday afternoon, the chief supply clerk waved Stoner on. "Well, sure. If you're willin' to put that stuff away, I'm willin' to let you do it."

With sighs of relief, the other supply clerks went about finishing up the last bit of work they would need to clear before they left. With a free rein and an open door, Dale Stoner gave his heavy load one mighty heave in order to get it moving again. By the time he had disappeared into the main storage area, the busy Federal employees replaced any thought of him or his cargo with other, more pressing concerns such as home, family, and what was for dinner.

Stoner hadn't bothered to study architectural engineering or common construction techniques. Nor had he made complex calculations as to size and shape of his charges. Instead he was content to rely on simple guesswork, common sense, and years of training and practical experience. Only in his choice of explosives had he taken his time. Trained as a combat engineer, Stoner took pride in his skills and found great enjoyment in solving the technical problems he faced. From the beginning, he had ruled out a fuel oil and fertilizer bomb like that used in Oklahoma City. It would be, he figured, too bulky and difficult to move about in pieces. Besides, law enforcement agencies were tracking the sales of large quantities of ammonium nitrate and dynamite too closely. No, he told himself when he recalled the image of the room full of pillars.

What he needed were explosives that were precise, yet portable.

His original idea of using C-4 and det cord was not at all practical. To obtain that sort of thing would have meant stealing from the military. Anxious to avoid exposing himself to the chances that such a theft would entail, he held that as a fallback position only. It was much better, he reasoned, to manufacture his own explosives using common chemicals. That's what had led him to the 5th Brigade. If anyone knew how to fabricate explosives, they would. So late in the fall he had attended a couple of their meetings. He had even gone out on "maneuvers" with them once. Unfortunately, he had found himself disliking the whole lot of them. While he had heard the term "Cox's Army" before, he had never known what it had meant until he spent time with the 5th Brigade. A maneuver with that mongrel organization was the military's equivalent of a bad hair day. For weapons, the "soldiers" of the 5th Brigade carried everything from high powered sports rifles to old military weapons that looked to be more dangerous to the owner. Only the wild diversity of physical appearance and stature of the members of the unit surpassed their strange assortment of weaponry. With the exception of three or four former soldiers, the unit of the 5th Brigade Dale fell in with was composed of fat men well past their prime or boys trying hard to make noises like men. In disgust Stoner had left that group and, for a short time, despaired of finding a suitable explosive for his project.

In the end, the solution to his problem was delivered to him via the World Wide Web. While browsing the Internet on a friend's computer, Stoner had stumbled upon the formula for an explosive called RDX. With a force one hundred and fifty times that of TNT, a modified version of RDX could be molded like C-4 into a shaped charge. That stuff, Stoner thought, would be ideal for cutting through the concrete and steel pillars that he often visited in his dreams. Like a slow burning fuse, Dale Stoner's trail of Biblical justice was ignited.

• • •

On this day he had no need to pause or survey the cavernous store room. Stoner had already worked out the details, in his mind, time and time again. So he was able to go quickly from pillar to pillar. At each of them he brought his cart to a stop, removed one of the boxes with the small arrow from the center of the stack, and placed it on the floor, right up against the pillar at its base with the small arrow pointed at the pillar. Around each of these boxes he piled the boxes of real paper. While this would do little to direct the blast, since the hollowed out, inverted cone shape of his explosives would already do that, Stoner felt that it just might help the blast along, if just a little.

He didn't have enough explosives for all the pillars. He knew that beforehand. To compensate for this, he selected those that stood in what he thought was the center of the building. At the base of each of them, he placed one of his homemade shaped charges, setting it so that each of the detonations would blow in, against the pillar and toward the middle of the building. Not only would this collapse the pillars inward, but the force of each of the devices would converge in the center where it would be vented up and through the floors above. If the loss of the supporting pillars didn't bring the floors above down, then the gaping hole left by the upward blast might.

Placement went quickly since there had been no need to set individual fuses. All the tinkering and experimentation needed to make them function properly had all been painstakingly worked out well in advance. The actual setting and initiation of the fuses had been done the night before, when he had connected the small, battery operated alarm clocks to the model rocket engines he was using as primers. All of these items, as well as the ingredients for his explosives, had been purchased over the months from supermarkets and department stores. Unlike the Oklahoma affair, none of his purchases were of such a quantity that they would attract attention. Nor did he buy everything at once. Like the crippling series of illnesses that robbed him of his health, then his family, and finally his dignity, Dale Stoner took his time.

• • •

When he was finished and he had said his farewells to the crew of supply clerks who hadn't managed to slip away early, Stoner made his way back to his truck. There he abandoned his cart and took a brown paper bag and a letter from the passenger seat. Re-entering the building, Stoner made his way though the crowd, out the front door into the bright late afternoon sunlight. Slowly he walked down the wide steps of the Federal building to the street. He weaved a crooked path through people coming and going until he reached the bank of mailboxes that sat along the curb. Dale looked at the letter he had carefully prepared, addressed to the Veteran's Administration. Revenge, he knew, would have no meaning if the people from whom he was extracting it didn't know what they were being punished for. So he had put down into words, as best he could, the reasons that had led him to the course of action he had chosen. "As hard as I try," he explained in his letter, "I can not find a single person in the Army, or the Government it defends, responsible for what it has done to me and others like me. So I must mete out my punishment against the entire Federal government, and those who work for it. I pray, deep down inside, that my actions, regardless of how horrible and despicable they may seem, awakens someone's consciousness to the wrong that this government has done to 'We, The People.' "

Without a second thought Stoner dropped his letter into the mailbox, turned, and reentered the Federal building. Making his way through the crowd, he took a seat on a bench in the lobby that he judged would be right over the spot where the force of the blast from all his little devices would meet and then go up as they sought to vent their destructive power. Opening the brown paper bag, Stoner took out a sandwich he had made that morning and began to eat as he waited for his appointed time.

Ironically, the bench he sat on faced an Army recruiting office. For him that office represented the start point for a journey that had proven to be long and tiring. All the lies had started there. The promises of an education, of an exciting career, and the respect of his fellow countrymen had been heaped upon him like so many brightly colored junk mail catalogs. He had believed it, all of it.

But like the leaves of a tree, each of those promises had withered, died, and fallen away. Those exciting and wonderful assignments overseas never came his way. Instead, Dale went to Fort Hood, Texas, a place he found was far closer to purgatory than paradise. Nor had he been able to take advantage of any of the educational benefits he had so desperately wanted. Such things were only dreams for soldiers assigned to field units. Still, he had adapted to the reality he found and made do with a life that, while perhaps not ideal, had at least been comfortable while he had been in the Army.

"Comfort," Stoner thought as he stared at the door of the recruiting office. Now there was a word he hadn't been able to use in years. The skin irritations, the achy joints, the late night sweats, and the nightmares all conspired to rob him of a physical comfort that was now as alien to him as were the men and women who hurried on past him. The loss of his wife, in part due to his declining health, but mostly as a result of the building rage he found he was no longer able to control, denied him the emotional comfort that could have seen him through all the physical aliments that had become the norm for him. But above all else, it was his inability to find the comfort that comes with knowing that someone cared, that someone was doing something to help him. Denial, procrastination, and a steady outpouring of lies and half-truths concerning the illness that had ruined his life was simply too much to handle. It was this reneging on the promise that "we look after our own," that pushed Stoner over the edge. If this building had been the beginning of his long, cruel journey, it was fitting that it also be the end.

Frank Bowman and the rest of the new shift of Engine Company 3 didn't need to be told by anyone that something terrible had just happened. Even five blocks away, the force of the explosion shook the very foundation of their midtown fire station, knocking pictures off the wall and rattling every window in the place. Without comment or hesitation, the men and women of Engine Company 3 and the ladder truck that shared the building slammed their half filled cups of coffee down on the nearest flat surface and made their way purposely to their trucks before the first alarm came in. Above the tramping of sock clad feet across the concrete floors of the bay where the pumper stood, the voice of the central dispatcher rattled off the names and numbers of fire and emergency units that were being dispatched as well as the location of the emergency. Few of the members of Engine Company 3 paused to look at each other when the words "explosion at the Federal building, 122 East Main" blared from the speakers. Yet each and every man and woman, struggling as they pulled on heavy, oversized boots, yellow jackets with broad silver strips, and visored helmets, saw the same image in their minds. The scenes of Oklahoma City were too well etched in their collective memories for any of them to discount that possibility.

With an ease that belied the difficulty of the task, Bowman maneuvered the pumper truck of Engine Company 3 down the last few chaotic blocks leading to the front of the Federal building. Having been totally absorbed by the task of driving the mammoth vehicle, Bowman was unprepared for what he saw when he finally had a chance to glance up at the massive Federal building. To be trained to deal with something did not mean that you were truly ready to come face to face with the harsh reality of such an event. Awed by the smoke and flame that bellowed from shattered windows and gaping holes where a solid marble facade had been, Bowman didn't realize that he had run up onto the curb until the huge front bumper of his truck began to bowl over and crumple the row of postal boxes that stood before the building. Slamming on his brakes Bowman brought his pumper to a halt, throwing his fellow firefighters forward. Even after regaining their balance, it took them all a moment to absorb the shock of what they were seeing before springing from the cab of the truck to begin the task of laying hose.

Finally, it was their lieutenant who snapped them out of their awed trance. "Okay," he stated in a flat, unemotional voice, "we have a job to do." With that, Bowman and his companions went into action. As they did so, Bowman found that it was difficult to ignore the multitudes of victims who wandered about all over the street and plaza. Most were stunned, dazed, and choking from the smoke. Alone and in small groups more could be seen staggering out through the rubble that had once been a building's lobby. Others who had escaped the inferno earlier were rolling on the ground or thrashing about in pools of their own blood. Through this throng of victims, the men and women of Engine Company 3 struggled forward with their heavy hoses and tools to attack the flames that were leaping out to greet them. Sorting the dead from those who were wounded or simply stunned was someone else's responsibility. Bowman and his companions belonged to an engine company, charged with knocking down the roaring blaze that was climbing the shattered building with alarming speed.

When all was set the firefighters on the nozzles cut loose and began to attack the sheet of flames rolling across the pile of rubble before them. With drilled precision, they began their advance, leaving teams of EMTs in their wake to deal with the casualties. This task was complicated, somewhat, by the streams of dirty water that began cascading down over the bloody debris strewn steps of the building. When this water had finished its task of quenching the fire, the warm, dirty water wound its way out of the shattered building and into the street. Along the way, it passed over and around the bodies of the dead, the wounded, and the dying. From there the water, now tinted red, ran through the crushed mailboxes, carrying with it into the gutter and down a storm drain the letter that contained Dale Stoner's confession of guilt and his feeble justification.

CHAPTER **2**

LEXINGTON, VIRGINIA · MAY 11

Taking his time, Scott Dixon turned his back to the shower head, letting the streams of hot water cascade over his shoulders, then down his spine. Placing his hands on the wall of the shower, he eased himself forward, permitting the jets of near scalding water to pound their way downward until they were pelting the small of his back. For Scott, long tormented with back problems, this was a treat, a genuine luxury to be enjoyed whenever possible, for as long as possible.

Indulging himself was not something that came easy to the senior Army officer. As the commanding general of the 4th Armored Division and post commander at Fort Carson, Colorado, Scott found he had precious little time to enjoy much of anything remotely personal. What made this sorry state of affairs even more annoying was the fact that the United States was still enjoying its longest period of "Peace" in the past half century. With each passing year he found himself complaining more and more to his wife of ten years. "For crying out loud. I'm a general officer, lord master of all I survey. I should be able to come and go as I please."

Jan Fields-Dixon, an energetic and hard working professional herself, never gave Scott an inch. "Well, me lord," she'd remark sarcastically, regardless of where they were or who they were with. "If you're so tired of the Army, why don't you quit? I could always use a good wife to take care of the home and all the little chores I simply don't have time to deal with."

Going along with the act, Scott would throw his hands up in the air. "No respect. I don't get any respect. Who do I look like, Rodney Dangerfield?"

Jan, of course, knew whom, or more correctly, what she

had married. Not that she was ever given a chance to forget. As a television journalist, she had covered everything from wars to sexual misconduct in the military. All too often she found herself in the awkward position of having to file reports that did not show the Army at its best. Scott, a career soldier, never said a word to her about anything she did professionally despite the fact that he was often the target of close scrutiny and, on occasion, pressure because of her stories. That he allowed her to continue, without comment, never ceased to amaze her. Jan had seen far too many colleagues lose spouses over conflicts of interest that were far more trifling than the ones she and Scott routinely faced. So it was not without good reason that she often found herself thanking her lucky stars that she and Scott somehow always managed to see their way through every tempest and road block that going against conventional wisdom threw at them.

This inconvenience was, of course, a double edged sword that cut into Jan's career just as deeply as it did Scott's. Many of her fellow journalists, biased against the military, saw Jan as little more than a mouthpiece for that institution and all it stood for. More than once she had seen her stories criticized not for what they said, but simply because she was perceived as nothing more than "the dutiful little wife of a professional Neanderthal." Such attitudes, and the need to move about the country, left Jan to face hard decisions as to what her true priorities were, time and time again.

Deciding that he had burned as much time as he dared, Scott turned the shower off. It never ceased to amaze him how Jan had made their marriage work while maintaining her own professional dreams and personal dignity. Even now, just hours before his oldest son was to graduate, he could hear the television in the other room blaring as she did her best to keep her finger on the pulse of the latest development of the day's hot news story. Anxious himself to hear if anything of value was being released to the media, Scott leaned over and pushed the bathroom door open a smidgen.

"That's right, Katherine," a serious, monotone male

voice responded to a question Scott had not heard. "The people here are most impressive in the manner in which they are handling the situation they faced." Scott found himself chuckling. Whoever was doing the yakking on TV definitely wasn't talking about the FBI.

"The militiamen used tactics taken right out of our own military's manuals," the speaker continued.

"Then it's safe to assume," a female voice asked, "that some or all of the assailants had military training."

"Oh," the expert du jour responded with great confidence. "There's little doubt about that. Many militia units actively recruit former military. After all, they are better trained, disciplined, and more physically sound than your average American male. What better way to obtain the skills and experience you'll need in a conflict with the Federal government," the expert asked rhetorically, "than to utilize the very same soldiers that government itself has trained? It's sort of like what the Confederate States did when they seceded from the Union in 1860."

This analogy made Scott wince. He hated it whenever "subject matter experts" used historical references incorrectly. There is no comparison, Scott found himself muttering, between the Southern Confederacy and the current militia movement. None.

Finished toweling off, Scott walked out to where Jan was sitting before the television, watching it intently. As was her habit, she had showered, done her hair and makeup, and dressed first so that she could avoid dealing with the steam and mist that always lingered in the bathroom after one of Scott's long showers. Even though he always offered to go first, she seldom accepted the invitation. Besides, on days like this, it allowed her to spend more time catching up on the news while Scott dawdled in the bathroom.

Her interest was less on what was being reported than on how it was being done. The host of her own news show as well as a stringer for World News Network, Jan was forever looking for new ideas, new approaches, and even new faces. That she wasn't impressed with this particular journalist was obvious. Her eyebrows, scrunched together in the center, forced her eyes into narrow slits and left small furrows across the bridge of her nose.

"You're going to mess up your makeup if you keep screwing your face up in that expression," Scott remarked in an effort to get her attention.

Jan ignored his remark. Instead, she threw her hand out toward the television. "Look at that!" she proclaimed. "Who in the world do they have producing this travesty? The Marx Brothers?"

Pausing a few moments to watch the tube, Scott tried hard to discern some difference between what he saw on the television before him and any number of other shows he found himself forced to watch. After deciding that there was no real difference, Scott shrugged. "Looks okay to me," he finally announced.

"Okay?" Jan exclaimed as she took her eyes off the set and looked at Scott for the first time since he had emerged from the shower. "Scott, put on your glasses, for God sakes. This 'show,' not to mention the twit who's hosting it, is an embarrassment."

With another shrug, Scott turned and walked away. "If you say so."

When Jan didn't return his taunt, or even take note of the fact that he had been standing next to her stark naked, he realized that she was too caught up in what was being said. As he went about dressing, Scott cocked his good ear and listened.

"Spokesmen for the FBI have repeated their claim that their perimeter, after multiple penetrations, is finally secure. The chances of any reinforcements reaching the members of the 5th Brigade are, according to the spokesmen, nil."

"While everyone has been criticizing the FBI's handling of this situation," the host asked when the expert was finished, "why hasn't the Wyoming National Guard taken a more active role?"

"That is simple," the expert stated as he sported a smirk and leaned back in his seat. "Such cooperation apparently has never been offered. The commander of the Guardsmen here, a Colonel Tinselly, takes his orders from the governor of Wyoming. The governor, in turn, has taken every opportunity to restate his position that this is a Federal matter. Until state laws are violated, he has no quarrel with the besieged militiamen."

"Bullshit," Scott muttered as he stood before the mirror and knotted his tie.

"Hush," Jan snapped.

"In the second place," the expert droned on, "we must not forget that the men and women of the National Guard are part time soldiers, not professionals. They were brought together for one specific task, to establish an outer perimeter designed to keep the curiosity seekers away from the FBI operation. They are not trained to handle the type of law enforcement operation that the FBI is currently engaged in."

"Double bullshit," Scott shot back in response.

"Scott Dixon," Jan hissed. "Keep quiet, or I'll smear your brass with my fingers."

This caused him to smile. She really knew where to hit a guy. Finished with his tie, Scott stepped over to the closet and took his dark green blouse out. The ribbons, decorations, badges, rank, and other insignia made it heavy, far heavier than the average man's jacket. But Scott didn't mind the weight. He never had. As he carefully slid his arms down the sleeves, he watched himself in the mirror. Each and every one of those items that added so much weight meant something. Every ribbon signified an achievement, an event, or a period of service. Some were "give me's," ribbons representing medals that everyone who served in a theater or had put a certain amount of time in received. Others, such as his Purple Heart, were very, very personal. And one, a simple powder blue ribbon with a sprinkling of tiny white stars, meant more than all the others combined.

Finished, Scott looked himself over. When he was satisfied that all was in order, he walked over to the television, snapped it off, and stood before Jan. "Hon," he said solemnly, "it's time."

On any other day Jan would have protested. But not today. Today was a special day, one of those pivotal days that mark the end of one stage in a person's life and the beginning of a new one. For Scott it would be deeply emotional. Today Major General Scott Dixon, a man who had endured much in his life, was about to suffer one of the greatest pains a parent was asked to endure. Today Scott was going to watch his oldest son graduate from college and enter into a world that Scott had, for so long, fought to make safe.

THE VIRGINIA MILITARY INSTITUTE, LEXINGTON, VIRGINIA · MAY 11

From his seat on the speakers' platform, Scott looked out over the graduating class. Though he tried hard not to, his eyes always came back to one face in the crowd of bright young cadets enduring their last ritual. That face, bearing more of a resemblance to Scott than he would ever admit, was beaming. Nathan Andrew Dixon, Scott's oldest son, surrounded by his classmates, was looking back up at Scott.

With both father and son overwhelmed by the emotions of the moment, it took a third set of eyes, those belonging to a trained journalist, to put the scene in perspective. Sensing the mood of the assembled graduates, their parents, and the faculty and staff of VMI, Jan Fields-Dixon could not help but pull out a small pad she always carried. Balancing it on her lap, she discreetly scribbled her thoughts as they came. "It is a meeting of generations. Upon the dais, aloof and perhaps a bit world weary, sit the older generation. They face a generation that will, in time, replace them. From below, the eyes of bright young men and women look up into the eyes of their elders, their mentors, their heroes. Those longing gazes are returned emotionlessly by old men who see in the fresh young faces before them the faint shadows of dreams they, themselves, once cherished. Between the two lies the great gulf of time and long journeys through a troubled world that scarred and maimed them while, paradoxically, it has nurtured their sons and daughters and fostered their hopes and aspirations."

Always curious about everything his stepmother did, Scott's second son looked over to see what she was writing. With a smile, he poked Jan in the arm with his elbow. "Dad's not going to be thrilled," he whispered, "that you're referring to him as an old man."

Jan smiled as she closed her notebook and returned it to her purse. "Your father has always had difficulty dealing with reality."

Unable to suppress his laughter, the younger Dixon let out a hoot that caused everyone around him, including his own mother, to turn and give him angry, annoyed looks. Though Jan didn't embarrass easily, she did turn an appropriate shade of red while reaching over with her right hand and slapping her stepson's hand hard enough to give an audible snap. This quick administration of justice was enough to satisfy the other parents gathered to watch their sons and daughters graduate. When they had turned their attention back to the address being delivered by the superintendent of the Institute, Scott's second son leaned over and whispered in Jan's ear. "Do you suppose he's prepared any remarks?" Then, he added with a smirk, "Or is he winging it, as usual?"

This annoyed Jan. Scott never seemed to prepare his speeches beforehand. "What happens," she asked him in frustration once after her admonishments to him to write something down had been stonewalled, "if you get up there and nothing comes to mind?"

Scott, ever cavalier about matters that he considered trivial, smiled. "Well, as I see it I would have three options," he replied quickly. "First, I can tell a war story. Folks always expect that from an old broke dick soldier like me. Second, I can tell them a dirty joke. Old cavalryman are not expected to have any couth what so ever, so I wouldn't be disappointing anyone. And third," he concluded with a flourish, "I can tell them a dirty war story that's funny, which would please everyone."

An attitude such as Scott's was unnerving to Jan. Having been a journalist her entire adult life, she prided herself on the amount of preparation she put into each and every story she did. She demanded the same from those who worked for her. So Scott's snide response was always met with a cross expression, a swipe of her hand across the top of Scott's head, and the same comment. "You are the most annoying man I've ever met."

Unmoved by Jan's performance, Scott would flash a grin that went from ear to ear, scoop up his second wife in his arms, and squeeze her until she screamed to be let go. Before he did so, he would quickly bend over and smother her in passionate kisses that, more often than not, led to a long night of passionate lovemaking during which Jan would forget about her efforts to change her husband's slovenly habits.

While a quick kiss would often suffice to solve intramarital disputes on the subject, it did little to solve Scott's current problem, which was what, exactly, *would* he say to the multitudes gathered before him. As this was a graduation, a joyous occasion for graduates, their parents, and the faculty and staff alike, his speech needed to be uplifting and positive. That it needed to have a message was a given. A speech without a message, after all, was little more than a collection of words thrown out and left to scour the countryside on their own in search of an idea to unify them.

But what message, Scott thought as he looked down at Nathan, would be meaningful and relevant to my son and his peers? For a moment, he thought back to his own graduation from the Virginia Military Institute. It had been another world that had faced him when he sat there waiting to leap up onto the stage to snatch his diploma from the hands of the superintendent. Even during Scott's four years as a cadet, the world had changed. He had entered VMI together with four hundred brother rats knowing full well that they would leave that place and go to a distant country known as Vietnam to fight a war that fewer and fewer of their fellow countrymen seemed to understand.

Fate and diplomacy had been spared him that trauma. In its place, however, he had entered a military that was shunned by its own countrymen. Scott became part of the wreckage of an army that was unsure of itself. Only the threat of "The Evil Empire" held that Army together through the troubled seventies. Eventually a handful of gifted leaders who managed to maintain their focus on what was important and a bold commander-in-chief emerged to make the United States Army a force to be reckoned with.

That evil empire was gone now, or at least defanged for the moment. In its place, there was no single, unifying foe with which to threaten the graduates of Nathan's class. There wasn't even a national goal or agenda. Scott had grown up with the challenge of Kennedy's race to the moon, LBJ's Great Society, and the Civil Rights movement, too. And though the world seemed to be on the brink of something monumental, something important, Scott had no idea what that "something" was. When he discussed this very issue with close friends, it became apparent that everyone was at a loss to describe where, exactly, the world they were living in was headed. Like survivors of another planet cast away in a strange new land, they were all searching for a new direction, a new cause to guide their footsteps.

Looking around at the faces of the young graduates, Scott was suddenly reminded of other young faces that were now little more than memories. While most were still alive, pursuing their own careers in a world they had helped mold, others had fallen along the wayside, victims of that long, arduous march that had brought him to this place. Surely, Scott told himself as he realized that the superintendent of the Institute was already launching into his introduction of him, he could not go in front of all these eager young graduates with such dark, foreboding thoughts setting the tone of his subject. No, Scott told himself. He would need to find a theme fitting for the occasion. It was his duty as the commencement speaker, and duty was something that Scott Dixon understood.

• • •

"General Dixon's faithful and loyal service to our nation," the superintendent declared briskly as he swept on to the conclusion of his introduction, "both in peace and in war, is an inspiration to us all. Ladies and gentlemen, graduates and guests, I am pleased to present Major General Scott Dixon."

Scott didn't really hear the applause. Nor was he very conscious of his actions as he stood and walked slowly to the podium where he shook the hand of the superintendent. Grasping the podium to steady himself, he thrust out his chin and looked out over the heads of the audience at the outline of the distant mountains that protect the Shenandoah from the outside world. As he gazed at those hills, he collected his thoughts as quiet returned. Only when all was silent did Scott lower his eyes and sweep the audience with them as if he were inspecting troops during a grand review.

"Ordinarily," Scott began, sporting an impish grin that he shared with his oldest son, "I would open my remarks with an off-color joke. Unfortunately my wife's in the audience." He paused long enough to allow a few people in the audience to chuckle. "You see, with Jan, I'm faced with a real problem. Not only is she my wife, she is also a journalist. As a member of the fourth estate, she would duly castigate me for my political incorrectness and insensitivity to whatever group or faction bore the brunt of my humorous remarks. But it's in her role as my wife that she'd really heap on the righteous hellfire and damnation for being so crude and tasteless. So, in line with our Commander in Chief's policy of preserving domestic tranquillity at all costs, I will skip the joke and cut right to the chase."

Shifting his stance at the podium, more as a signal that he was in the process of changing mental gears than anything else, Scott prepared to deliver his main address. With a measured pause, he once more surveyed those before him.

"For the first time in our lives our worlds, those of the graduates of this class and their parents, will come together. From this moment on we will live in the same reality, the same time and space. What comes tomorrow will be determined by what we, together, do today." Pausing briefly, he let those words sink in. As he did so, Scott moved back from the podium, bowed his head as if catching his breath, then prepared to continue.

"Until now we have lived in very different worlds. As parents we have always been the caregivers, the providers, the chief judge and magistrate, the ruler of the roost, the defender of the domestic realm, the lord and master of all we surveyed. Ours has been a role of dominance tempered with love and teaching, honed by experience. You, the offspring, the prodigy, the next generation, have been little more than objects of affection that needed close attention, careful handling, continuous monitoring, and tutoring as to the ways of the world. Many times we have not played our respective roles very well. All too often we, the parents, were distracted by other concerns or desires and were neglectful of our God-given duties. Perhaps, on occasion, we proved to be too zealous when it came to ensuring that you adhered to rules we had set down and were not as caring and understanding as we should have been.

"On the other hand you, the child, often proved to be uncooperative. As living, breathing creatures yourselves, you often changed in ways that we didn't quite comprehend. You headed off in directions we sometimes did not approve of. Frequently maturity, in body and mind, came long before we parents were able to finish the vital task of imparting to you the wisdom that you needed in order to deal with the ever expanding world you found yourself adrift in. Like two shadow boxers we have struggled and grappled with every issue and situation imaginable as you fought us for your independence and we endeavored to ensure that you had the skills, the discipline, and the knowledge to use that freedom wisely and justly."

Again, Scott hesitated, as much to collect his own thoughts as to give the audience a chance to consider his remarks so far. "That we have come to this place, today," he continued, "is evidence that we have somehow survived that trying process in fairly decent shape. And while I do not mean to infer that we parents are going to disown you graduates the moment that the superintendent hands you your diplomas, I am here to say that our relationships will never again be the same. You see, from this point forward, we shall march into the future side by side. While we may not be equals, we will be coworkers, tasked with the awesome responsibility of shaping and responding to the events that this world is waiting to throw at us. For the first time in your life, you, the graduates, will have your hand on the throttle of the engine that will pull us all forward into the future. It is for that reason that this ceremony can be called, with equal accuracy, a graduation and a commencement. You are, after all, graduating from the status of a dependent to that of a full citizen who has mastered basic skills and knowledge and is ready to take on the responsibility of your own life. At the same time, you are commencing a new life, one which is nothing like that which you are leaving behind. But regardless of how you view this joyous occasion, it is a time of coming together. Our two generations, for so long separated by views, by tastes, by physical age and ability are, from now on, committed to face the world and whatever it throws our way together."

The balance of Scott's address conveyed the usual admonishments to the graduates to set themselves the highest goals they could and pursue them with all their might while remembering that they were humans, living in a world peopled by other humans like them. He tried to temper his "give it all you got" message with warnings that they needed to live full and healthy lives all along the way. And though, when he finished, he had no idea just how much of what he said was heard in the way he wanted it, the rousing ovation at the end at least signaled that what he had said was appreciated.

After all the speeches, awards, and ceremonial duties had been completed, Nathan Dixon's class rose as a single body, for one last time, and let loose with a thunderous cheer. And then, before any of them knew what they were doing, it dispersed forever. Nate, as he was called, took as much time as he dared to shake the hands of fellow classmates, embrace several with fierce bear hugs, and bid a few special friends fond farewells that would have been emotional had they lingered. It was a wild and jumbled time for Nate, a fitting end to the four long and arduous years spent exiled to a small college nestled in the mountains of western Virginia. Though he was glad to be done with it, deep down inside Nate knew this place would always be a part of him. His father had warned him of that. "Your years here at VMI, Nate, will be unlike anything you've ever experienced, or will ever experience again. You'll alternate between loving it and hating it, sometimes on the very same day. But let there be no doubt about this. No matter where you go, no matter what you do, it will always be a part of you. Whether the memories and experiences you carry away from here are good ones or bad will depend on how you choose to embrace this institution." Then, after looking over his shoulders first one way then the next to make sure no one was near enough to hear, Scott Dixon leaned forward and whispered in his son's ear. "Do yourself a favor, lad, and don't take this place too seriously. Remember, God is on the side of the person with the best sense of humor."

Taking that advice to heart, Nate Dixon had wandered through four years at VMI, spending as much time in trouble as out. From his first day there, he had been marked as a nonconformist who could not resist speaking his mind. While a member of the cadre was instructing Nate and his fellow rats, or freshmen, on how to fold and properly store socks so that they were all neatly lined up, Nate had watched in utter amazement. When the cadre finished and asked if there were any questions, Nate raised his hand and, straight faced, asked, "Isn't that being a bit anal?"

Had it not been for his personality and ability to see the brighter side of even the most depressing situation, Nathan would have been broken by the extra duty and "special" attention a few renegade upper classmen had heaped on him. Only after his rat year was at an end did Nathan discover that many of the upperclassmen actually went out of their way to find him in the hope of getting a good chuckle out of what he said. Thus a reputation had been created, one that Nathan strove to build upon during the balance of his cadetship.

That his time at VMI was coming to an end was a bittersweet experience to the young man. Unlike his former life, lived in the shadows of a father who always seemed to be larger than life, Nathan's success at VMI had been his own. He had come here as just another face among many and managed to succeed. And though he appreciated the fact that it was his parents who were making this education and experience possible, he took great pride in the fact that his academic achievements, not to mention notoriety, were all his.

Above the cacophony of conversations and adoration that rose from the gathering of families, friends, and cadets, Nathan heard Jan's voice. "Nathan, over here." Looking about, he caught sight of a hand fluttering above the heads of the crowd. With a mixture of gentle shoves and taps, always followed by a polite "thank you," Nathan made his way to where his mother, his younger brother, his roommate, and his roommate's parents were gathered. As he joined the small cluster, Jan asked, "Have you seen *the general*?"

Jan seldom referred to Scott as "the general." When she did so it was usually a sign that she was annoyed with him or found herself in the midst of a situation that she was anxious to get away from. In this case it was the latter. Though Nathan and Ronny Goldman had been fast friends, in and out of mischief for their entire four years together, Jan could not stand Arthur and Rita Goldman. Arthur Goldman, a prominent trial attorney from New York City, had political aspirations and an ego to match them. To Jan he always came across as too friendly, too quick to please whomever he was with. Having to spend too much of her professional time dealing with politicians, the last thing she wanted to do was associate with a congressional wannabe during her free time.

"So," Arthur continued where he had left off when Jan

had abruptly turned away from him to flag down Nathan, "then you don't think the FBI has done enough as far as the latest bombing is concerned?"

Jan, angered that Arthur would even bring such a subject up on a day that was supposed to be one of celebration, was a bit sharper than usual with Arthur when she responded. "What I said, Art," she replied, using a nickname she knew he despised, "was that either they've got nothing at all, or they're holding their cards awfully close. Either way, we're not getting anything new from anyone in the government, which is making a lot of folks nervous."

Never one to shy away from a good fight, Arthur Goldman smiled. "Why is that, Jan? Ratings dropping?"

Having trained herself to resist reacting emotionally whenever someone was pressing her button, Jan took in a deep breath, flashed her award winning smile, and cocked her head to one side. "There are very real concerns, among average men and women in the country, in regard to their safety and security. One attack on a federal building can be written off as a bolt out of the blue, a fringe element that can't possibly affect the nation and its citizens as a whole. But two, *that's* a different matter. After all," she asked in an innocent tone, "doesn't the thought that you might be there, in person, for the next bombing, give you pause every time you enter the lobby of the Federal Court House to file a brief on behalf of one of your clients?"

Arthur was able to shrug that question off with an easy smile, especially since his law office used messengers and legal assistants whenever they were required to conduct business at Federal facilities. "We cannot let ourselves live in fear," he finally responded. "That is exactly what these people want."

"Well," Jan countered, "I'll be a lot happier when 'those people' are afforded the chance, either voluntarily or otherwise, to tell a jury of their peers what their druthers are."

On this note Scott, coming up behind Jan, reached out and grabbed his wife's arms and squeezed them. "Well, if you asked me, I'm about ready to get out of this uniform and go celebrate."

Pleased that the cavalry had arrived to save her, Jan

broke free of Scott's grasp, turned, and threw her arms around his neck. After planting a kiss on his cheek, she leaned forward and whispered in his ear, "For God sakes, Scotty, beam me out of here!"

Looking up at the false smile Arthur was sporting, he greeted the attorney with a nod, then whispered to Jan using the best Scottish accent he could manage, "I'm doin' the best I can, captain, but the engines won't take much more of this."

While Nathan drove his grandparents and his brother back to Natural Bridge along Interstate 81 where they would all meet and have dinner with the Goldmans, Jan and Scott took the slower, scenic route along old U.S. 11. Scott was enjoying the lushness of Virginia's mountain greenery while Jan, not at all thrilled about the prospect of spending more time with Arthur and his latest trophy wife, tried hard to think about something pleasant. Scott finally broke the silence when he muttered absentmindedly about the landscape that seemed to engulf them. "I'm going to miss coming here to visit Nathan. Though I never would have guessed he'd pick a place like VMI, I'm glad he did."

Shaking her head, Jan looked over at Scott and forced a smile. "Yes, it has been nice."

Glancing out of the corner of his eyes at his wife, Scott looked at Jan as she started to withdraw into her own thoughts. "Did Arty get you that upset?"

"Oh, it's not Arthur, that dear, dreary fellow, so much as it is the subject he keeps harping on," Jan explained.

"The bombing," Scott threw in. "Yes, it's been getting to you, hasn't it."

"It's not so much that," Jan went on. "This story is different than any other terrorist story we've covered. It refuses to go away. It just keeps hanging there, like all the unanswered questions it raises. Try as hard as I might, I simply cannot convince my bosses at the network that we need to move on to other, more important issues."

"Such as?" Scott ventured.

"Such as the President's inability to dodge the charges that Congress keeps getting hurled at him."

Scott, trying to make light of Jan's concern, smirked. "We'll, if you ask me, I'll take a good old home grown bombing over political mud slinging on the six o'clock news any day of the week."

Jan gave Scott a dirty look. "How can you be so cavalier about something like that? People were killed."

Though annoyed by Jan's attitude, Scott knew he had made a grievous tactical error and tried to extract himself. "Please, Jan," he pleaded. "I'm not trying to make fun of the bombing. Lord knows, I'll be glad when they catch the bastards. I'm getting tired of passing through every sort of security check, short of a cavity search, whenever I enter my own headquarters."

Jan sighed, realizing that she had been too sharp with Scott. "With luck, the FBI will find a lead somewhere and we'll be free to go about our business."

Laying his hand on Jan's thigh, Scott gave it a squeeze. "Well, with one son launched and sent slipping down the ways and the other just a few years behind, luck is something I think we have plenty of."

Placing her hand on his, Jan smiled. "I suppose you're right. We have to be thankful for what we're here to celebrate."

"Yes we do. Even if it means enduring dinner with the Goldmans."

Pulling her hand away, Jan gave Scott a dirty look. "General Dixon, I warn you, don't get me started."

Raising his hand as if he was prepared to fend off an attack, Scott pulled away from Jan. "Oh, yes, missy, so sorry missy. Please don't hit this poor soul. I sorry, missy."

Unable to hold back, Jan laughed. Though she had just lost a son, Jan was pleased that she would always be surrounded by the outrageous Dixon humor. "Driver," she commanded, "pay attention to the road and don't call me missy, or I'll . . ."

"You'll what?" Scott snapped.

Reaching out, Jan laid her hand high on Scott's thigh and gave it a gentle squeeze. "I'll show you later, dear sir, when we're alone."

CHAPTER 3

Evening came early along the eastern face of the Rocky Mountains. The sun, well along on its daily journey to the west, was blocked by the towering mountains long before last light of day gave way to the star studded night sky. During this protracted passage of day into night, long shadows chilled the barren foothills that gave way to the sweeping plains farther to the east. Even now, as spring struggled to overcome the last, desperate days of a long, hard mountain winter, the view, from any spot in this lonely part of the country, was spectacular.

But few of the Federal agents clustered in the folds of earth that made up the foothills of North America's greatest mountain chain took note of how the setting sun splashed the sky and high, thin clouds with stunning hues of crimson, pink, and yellow. This was especially true of Special Agent Ben Branson. Following the same worn footpath he had been using for the past ten days, his eyes darted over the landscape, not searching for hints of the coming spring, but seeking out any sign that the militia members his teams had run to ground here had moved. His dedication to his profession and the task at hand blinded him to any other thought or sight that did not contribute to the swift and successful completion of the operation he was in charge of.

Stopping at each of the twelve positions that dotted the landscape manned jointly by members of his team and U.S. Marshals, Ben Branson greeted their occupants with little more than a nod. As he climbed down, or up as each particular position required, its occupants would step aside to permit Branson free access to the rampart that overlooked the militia compound. Each of these positions were more or less the same, a ring of sandbags augmented by a foxhole carved out of the rocky soil. Few efforts were made to camouflage them. In addition to protecting the FBI agents and U.S. Marshals from direct observation and fire from the besieged, the ring of bunkers were meant to intimidate the renegade militiamen. Each collection of sandbags and dirt thrown up about the silent ranch reminded them that they could not hide from the omnipresent gaze of the Federal government.

Once at the front of the position, Branson would plant his elbows upon the sandbags, lift a pair of binoculars that always hung about his neck, and begin to carefully study the clusters of outbuildings, sheds, and the weather-beaten house before he lost the last of the day's fading yellow light. As he did so he made a mental picture of every detail, every scrap of wood, discarded oil drum, and pile of rubbish. In the morning he would do the same, matching what he remembered from the night before to how everything lay at that moment. If anything was out of place, if something had been moved, he would have one or more of his teams focus all the high powered optics, scopes, video cams, and still cameras on the site in question in order to examine it in excruciating detail. Only when his experts were able to convince him that the alteration in the landscape was accidental or totally innocent would he relent and allow his men to return to duties that had now become routine.

Behind him the senior U.S. marshal for this operation, Kyle Millner, looked out over the same scene Branson was studying so intently. When he was satisfied with his cursory inspection, Millner grunted. "Ben," he whispered in a voice that never failed to betray his southwestern origins, "if I was one of those good ole boys down there, I swear I'd sneak out every night and move things about, just so I could watch you and your boys flutter around out here every morning like chickens in a hail storm."

Branson took a moment before he replied. Only when he was finished searching every nook and cranny of the seemingly deserted ranch did he honor Millner with an answer. Even then he did so without taking his eyes away from his binoculars. "Kyle, if those 'patriots' had a sense of humor, do you think we'd be here?"

"Oh, be real, Ben," Marshal Kyle Millner scuffed. "Just 'cause they believe in something as strongly as they do doesn't mean they're not human."

This time, Branson did lower his binoculars and turn to face his companion. His gaze was hard and uncompromising, the sort that made it clear that Branson would brook no disagreement, no response. "You forget, Kyle, I saw what these people did. I was there, sifting through the rubble, looking for clues while rescue teams were still poking about right next to me collecting body parts in plastic bags." Narrowing his eyes until they were but slits, Branson nodded his head toward the old house and sorry collections of structures. "They're murderers, Marshal Millner. Criminals and murderers. They threw away whatever claim they had to being regarded as members of the human race the day they bombed the Robert Dole building. And even if they did try to do something funny," Branson added as he went back to his nightly inventory of the ranch before him, "I don't think I'd notice. No sir, I doubt if I'd be able to find even a shred of humor in anything they did."

"You're a hard man." Millner snorted. "Hard and stubborn."

This time, the fading light fell upon a wicked little smile. "Well, Kyle," Branson responded as he pushed himself away from the stack of sand bags, "that's why I'm here."

Behind a rise not far from the militia compound sat a cluster of trailers, tents, armored personnel carriers, and four-wheel drives of every description. Except for the hum of generators or the purr of an idling diesel engine, or the federal agents shuffling from the mess tent to the trailer that served as the command post and briefing area, the place was silent. Not much needed to be said. The men and women of the night shift knew what was expected of them. The team leaders from the day shift had no new developments to pass on to them. Even their stock of jokes, stories, and good-natured banter had been exhausted. All that remained for the FBI agents and U.S. marshals to do was check their weapons and night vision devices, grab one last cup of coffee, and head out into the gathering darkness for another long, chilly night on the perimeter.

Pausing outside, Ben Branson watched the night shift go by without comment. A tough and dedicated professional, Branson didn't feel there was any need for him to play cheerleader. Each and every man and woman under his command was a professional as well. He maintained his focus on the task at hand and expected each of his people to do likewise. Single-minded devotion to his duty guided every action and every decision Branson made. "If a man knows what he's about," he told a friend once back in Washington, "and has confidence in his training, equipment, and his teammates, what's the point of wasting my time with pep talks and morale building sessions. We go in," Branson explained, "do our job, and bask in whatever glory there is to be gained in this job *after* the bad guys are locked up or in the coroner's loving care."

Upon entering the crowded trailer that served as his operations center, Branson paused and looked about. Directly in front of him were two maps. One was a standard topographical map of the surrounding area covered with various symbols. In the center were red markings representing the buildings and positions where members of the 5th Brigade were holed up. In a tight circle around them were a string of blue triangles, numbered one through twelve, indicating the location of the FBI observation posts. Farther out, mostly along the roads and trails leading into this site, other blue marks showed the checkpoints and roadblocks manned by the state police and Wyoming National Guard. Under Branson's immediate control were his own FBI antiterrorist team, reinforced by an FBI hostage rescue team and U.S. marshals. They controlled the inner perimeter and had the task of resolving the standoff with the militiamen. The Wyoming state police and National Guard, each commanded by a senior officer of their own, were charged with keeping the media, curious onlookers, and sympathizers away from the FBI operation as well as providing backup. The journalists didn't like being held at arm's distance any more than the state police liked playing the heavies, responsible for keeping them out. But this was Branson's show and the last thing he wanted to do was to give the members of the 5th Brigade any more publicity then they had already garnered out of this standoff. "They'll have their day in court when they come out," he told a pool of journalists at a rare interview. "Until then I ask that you have a little faith in your government and let us do our job."

That his men and women would eventually prevail was never a question in Ben Branson's mind. He had the manpower, the technical expertise, and determination to see this through. Moving over to the right, to where his small desk sat covered with phones, radios, photos, and an assortment of manila folders, Branson was accosted by a young five foot, two inch woman who held a clipboard and wore an expression as determined as Branson's own.

"Sir," Special Agent Angel Raymos shot out in a tone that was as hefty as her one hundred ten pound frame would permit. "Here are the updates from the Bureau and the tactical summary."

Branson looked at the young, energetic woman for a moment. Dressed in jeans and a flannel shirt, only her blue jacket with the large block letters "FBI" on the back told anyone that she was one of his. "Special Agent Raymos, as important as those things are, even more critical, at this particular moment is . . ."

"I know, I know," she lamented as she lifted a steaming cup of black coffee that she had been holding in her left hand. "Your hourly fix of caffeine."

Branson smiled as he took the cup. "You'll go far, pilgrim. You'll go far."

Besides being the most diminutive FBI agent on site, Raymos was also the newest. Fresh out of the academy, Branson snapped her up as he was throwing together his team for this mission. His official explanation for asking for someone so new to the agency was that it would be good to "blood" young agents in this sort of thing as quickly as possible. "With these standoffs becoming more frequent," he explained to his superior, "it's important that we expand the pool of agents who have experience in handling them."

Every one of Branson's old hands, however, knew that Raymos was brought along not so much to learn the ropes as to serve Branson as a personal assistant. Not that they blamed him. Even the other women on his team appreciated the fact that an agent with Branson's seniority and responsibilities needed someone to keep the little things at the ops center squared away. But Raymos was there to do more than tend to Branson's personal needs. The majority of her time was spent fielding the endless series of phone calls. Even more important to Branson was the need to have someone sift through of all the incoming information and package it into a useful product. "The curse," Branson told her in the beginning, "of the information age is information. What I need from you each and every day is not a massive data dump. Any moron can do that. What I need is a person who can stick her hand into a bunch of goo, that a moment before was a pile of faxes, and know what to do with them."

After savoring a long sip, Branson made his way to his desk, plopped down in his seat, and leaned back. Raymos waited till he was settled in before she started. "The afternoon update from the agency is pretty much a repeat of this morning's. The prime suspect, the delivery man named Stoner, is still at large. Two more survivors have placed him at the scene. One, a woman, followed him out of the building, claiming that he even held the door open for her and smiled when she thanked him."

"Well," Branson sneered. "That was right neighborly of him, wasn't it."

Raymos, endeavoring to impress Branson with her professionalism, nodded politely but continued with her summary. "The forensic people have found plenty of residue from the Composition 1, or RDX that he mixed in his own bathroom, but no other fingerprints other than Stoner's anywhere in the house except on the literature he had from the 5th Brigade."

At this, Branson brought his feet down to the floor, spun his seat around, and looked at a cluster of photos posted on the wall behind his desk of known and suspected members of the 5th Brigade. Bold red checks in the upper right hand corner of three of the photos identified those members of the 5th Brigade whose fingerprints had been found on printed material and books Stoner had left behind in his house. "How come I don't see any new ones, Special Agent Raymos?" Branson asked as he returned his seat to face his assistant.

"That's all they could find. And according to the agent I spoke with this afternoon, that's all they expect to find."

Branson folded his hands on the desk, cocked his head to one side, and thought about it. Then, he leaned back in his seat again, bringing his still folded hands up onto his stomach. "Well, three's going to have to be good enough."

"It should be," Raymos added, "since two of them are in there."

"We think," Branson corrected her. "There are two of them in there. We're still not sure how many of the little ass wipes we've got cornered yet. Ten days," he sighed. "Ten days, and we still don't know." After thinking this over a moment, Branson took another sip from his cup, then nodded. "Continue."

"The spokesman and lawyer for the militia in Cheyenne continues to claim that his group had nothing at all to do with the bombing. He stated that the members of the 5th Brigade are willing to cooperate with the investigation, but not while the Federal government continues to, quote, hold a gun to the heads of innocent patriots who have no other interest but to see justice meted out against those who violate God's holy commandments, unquote."

Snickering, Branson shook his head. "Gosh, where have I heard that before?"

Not knowing if this was a serious question, Raymos hesitated a moment before she tried to continue with her report. "I have an answer back on your inquiry concerning . . ."

Branson raised his hand and waved her off as he would an annoying child. "The rest can wait till after I get something to eat." Looking past her, he caught sight of Kyle Millner, clustered with several of his people at the other end of the trailer. "Kyle," Branson shouted above the noise of the trailer. "You ready to get something to eat?"

Millner raised his hand. "In a minute." Then he went back to discussing whatever it was he was sharing with his fellow marshals.

While he made his way to the door, Branson looked around, noticing that something was missing. "Where's all our friendly National Guardsmen?" Branson asked Raymos, who was following him to the door.

"Their colonel called this afternoon after you had left for your rounds, and informed their liaison officer that all members of the Wyoming Guard would eat at one seating at their own mess. According to him, when they tried to serve in two shifts those who ate with the second one were always getting cold meals. So Colonel Tinselly passed the word that they would all be served at the same time."

"Great," Branson roared. "Just great. Do me a favor, will you and check the patches on their BDUs the next time you see one of 'em. I want to make sure they're on our side."

Not sure if her boss was being serious or simply joking, Raymos simply smiled. "There is one more thing," she added, almost as an afterthought, "that I *really* need an answer on."

Pausing, Branson sighed. "Yes?"

"The Bureau insists that we hold another briefing for the media here, tomorrow if possible."

Branson's expression became tense. "Tell them that's impossible since the Bureau has failed to provide me with a public affairs officer, as I have requested every day since I got here. Explain to them that I have neither the time nor inclination to answer insipid questions from a group of pasty faced liberals who get paid more for their looks than for their brains. Tell them that it doesn't matter what I or anyone else out here tells them since their networks see absolutely no need to report what is actually going on, only what sells."

Realizing that he was ranting, as was his habit every

time the subject of the journalists was brought up, Branson paused. In an effort to extract himself from his tirade gracefully, he shrugged and sported the best smile he could muster. "Please inform the folks in Washington, if you would, Special Agent Raymos, that nothing here has changed from the last time we spoke with the members of the press. If they want to do a story on this, I suggest they save themselves the trip and instead use last week's file footage."

"I tried to explain that to them but, unfortunately, no one bought it," Raymos explained "Perhaps," she ventured, "if you called personally and explained it to them, they'd listen."

Anxious to get something to eat so that he could start his nightly rounds, Branson shook his head. "No," he announced triumphantly. "I have a better idea. You'll handle the briefing."

In shock, Raymos's big brown eyes flew open. "Me?"

"Yes, you. The folks from our friendly neighborhood media pool as well as the PR guys back at the Bureau will love it. You're young, female, Hispanic . . ."

"Puerto Rican," Raymos stated quickly, as she always did whenever the honor of her heritage was put in question.

"Yes, even better," Branson continued, taking Raymos's rebuke in stride. "You're Puerto Rican, bright, articulate, and, dare I say without sounding patronizing or offending anyone anyone's politically correct feelings, quite lovely."

This last remark brought a blush to Raymos's cheeks. Embarrassed, she averted her eyes. "Are you sure you want me to do this?" she asked after she had managed to regain her voice.

"Listen, Angel, I know it's a dirty job but . . ."

"Yes, I know. Someone's got to do it."

Branson was just starting to chuckle when he and Raymos were joined by Millner. "This a private joke, or can anyone join in?"

"No joke, I'm afraid," Branson explained. "Special Agent Raymos here has just volunteered to brief our friendly journalists' pool tomorrow."

Millner made a quick sign of the cross, as if he were blessing her. "May God go with you, child."

Like everyone else, Raymos liked Millner. It was hard not to. Though his reputation would have made the old time lawmen of the west green with envy, he had the personality of a teddy bear. With her clipboard, Angel Raymos gave Millner a poke in his bulging midsection. "I may have to take your grief, Marshal, but I don't have to tolerate your blasphemy."

Turning to Branson, Millner started to push the senior FBI agent out the door. "Quick, partner, let's get out of here before her hot Latin blood begins to boil."

"Puerto Rican," she corrected him as the two men fled into the darkness and made their way to the mess tent. "I'm Puerto Rican."

From his perch on the lower slopes of the mountain, Thomas Jefferson Osborn watched the comings and goings of the people in the FBI base camp through his binoculars. Unlike the compound where the members of the 5th Brigade were holed up, neither the FBI nor the National Guard made any effort to conceal their locations. This would make things easier for him, he thought, as he eased himself back down into the gully where his people waited.

Once he was down in the gully he had been using for concealment, he looked over the huddled figures who had followed him this far. Dressed in army surplus camouflage fatigues, they watched Osborn's every move wide-eyed as they clutched their weapons. When he had called the three separate cells that made up what was known as the 2nd Battalion seven days ago, fourteen of the seventeen belonging to that group showed up. After explaining to them that they were going to go south to rescue their brothers of the 5th Brigade, that number dropped to twelve. Four days of intensive last minute training and two rehearsals further reduced their ranks to ten. When it came time to pull out of their camp in northern Idaho, nine climbed into their trucks and four-by-fours. Now, the question that rattled through his mind as he prepared to issue his final instructions was whether or not the seven who had made it this far had the balls to go that one last mile. *Well,* he told himself as he pulled his old canteen from its faded OD cover, *now's a good a time as any to find out.*

As he took a long, slow sip from his canteen, he looked over his "command." Of those who had come down from Idaho with him only one of them, other than himself, had been a member of the armed forces. Known simply as Lou, this man appeared to be the most dedicated, most hard-core of the lot. He even surpassed Osborn himself in his devotion to the Cause. Yet it was exactly for this reason that Lou made Osborn uncomfortable. He was, even for Osborn, a bit too fanatical.

None of the others could be accused of that, Osborn thought, as he tightened the cap back onto the canteen. The two brothers, Tom and Rob, were nice enough fellows and talked a good line. But that was all they seemed to be interested in doing. Even the Kid, a boy who had just celebrated his sixteenth birthday, put both of the brothers to shame when it came to marksmanship and savvy in the field. Given a few years, Osborn thought, the Kid would be dynamite.

The other three were all middle-aged men Osborn didn't much care one way or the other about. They'd do what they were told and would serve the Cause. Nothing more.

If there was one bright spot in this whole affair, it was the quality of their weaponry. When asked to lead this effort, Osborn had been given a carte blanche as to arms and equipment. Knowing full well that his numbers would be small, he realized from the beginning that fire power would be needed to compensate for the small numbers he had anticipated. So he asked for two M-60 machine guns, the old style M-16A1 that was capable of full automatic, and a high caliber .50 sniper rifle. When Osborn was told by a gun shop owner in Pocatello, Idaho that he could have the M249 5.56mm squad automatic rifle instead of the older 7.62mm M-60 machine gun, Osborn had demurred. "I want something that has some hitting power and range. The Hog is an impressive gun, especially when viewed from the beaten zone."

Feeling that there was no point in delaying the inevitable, Osborn took in a deep breath, looked at his assembled followers, and went over the plan one more time. "We move out in four teams, just like we rehearsed. Lou, you and the Kid have the farthest to go. So you'll leave first. We'll give you thirty minutes from the time you leave to get set up. At the end of that thirty minutes, open up with your M-60 on the FBI compound. What you nail down there doesn't much matter. Just raise as much hell as you can. Confusion and chaos is your sole purpose in life."

Even in the dark, Osborn could see a sinister smile light up Lou's face. *Yeah*, Osborn thought to himself, *I picked the right man for that job*. Turning next to the two brothers, he reminded them that they would follow him and one of the older men. "When I give you the word, you two will split off to the right and continue to move along the slope of this mountain until you're overlooking the Federal position I marked on your map as Alpha. Once you hear Lou and the Kid open up, wait five seconds before you begin shooting. I'm hoping the Feds will pop up out of their holes like a pair of prairie dogs to see what's going on and give you a good target. If they do, take your time and aim before you shoot."

"And what do we do," Rob asked, "if they don't oblige us and stick their necks out?"

"Well then," Osborn responded sarcastically, "I guess you'll just have to pepper their hole and make sure they don't change their minds and come up looking for the two of you."

Not waiting for a response, Osborn turned his attention to the older men named Jordan and Albert. "The two of you will stay here. The post you're after is just down there," Osborn indicated pointing along the gully. "You won't have any problem finding it. Like the brothers, wait until you hear Lou and then keep your marks from interfering with the breakout."

When the two grim faced men nodded that they understood, Osborn turned to the last member of his undersized squad. "You and I have the hard part. We have to get up close and personal with the Feds in position Bravo and take them out. Once we've done that, I'll make my way down to where the boys in the 5th Brigade are and lead them out through the hole we've made in the Feds' perimeter. The success of our entire mission," Osborn stated blandly as he shifted his attention to the others in the group, "rests with the ability of those assigned to keep the Feds at position Alpha and Charlie suppressed and unable to interfere with the evacuation of the compound. I'm hoping that Lou and the Kid will be able to create enough pandemonium with their leaders that we'll be in and out before anyone at the FBI base camp can respond."

Flashing his wicked smile as he had before, Lou patted the machinegun he cradled in his arms. "You won't have to worry about that."

With a wary nod, Osborn continued. "We've come a long way since our first maneuver. During that time we've lost a lot of good men at Ruby Ridge, Waco, and West Texas, men who stood their ground alone and outnumbered. Men who fought for what they believed in. Well, it's time for us to stop dying alone under the guns of a government that has abandoned the Constitution and the people it was written for. Starting right here, right now, we're going to serve notice to the Federal government that we'll not let our brother patriots be picked off one by one. We're going to show them that they cannot go about the country, killing off God-fearing Americans, whenever someone has the courage to stand up and disagree with them. Keep that in mind," Osborn concluded as he stood up and took up his M-16, "those people out there besieging our brothers are the real traitors. They're the ones who chose to turn their backs on the Constitution and its laws. So don't hesitate to do what our forefathers had the courage to do."

Finished with their meal, Ben Branson and Kyle Millner dallied in the warm, well lit mess tent and chatted over the next day's activities as they sipped coffee. Except for a group of three off duty U.S. marshals seated in one corner, Branson and Millner had the mess tent all to themselves.

Outside, the only noise that interfered with their quiet conversation was the steady hum of generators and an occasional vehicle as it went about tending to any one of a variety of housekeeping chores.

The reactions of Millner, a long time veteran of Federal service who had been in his fair share of tight spots, and Branson, who was rated as one of the Bureau's top field men, to the sudden long, high pitched burst of machinegun fire that ripped through the night air were hesitant. Trained to assess the situation and formulate a plan before making a move, Ben Branson sat bolt upright in his seat, looked about, and tried to determine if the firing was coming from his perimeter or the militia's positions. Millner, aware that something was terribly wrong, was up and out of his seat, headed for the entrance before Branson saw he was gone. "Get off your dead asses," Millner yelled at the covey of marshals gathered in the corner, "and follow me."

Only when a second, long, staccato burst began to rip through the mess tent did Branson slip from his seat. Bent over double, he made his way past the rows of empty tables and headed for the opening at the end of the tent that Kyle Millner had already gone through with his fellow marshals in tow. Ignoring the crisp, sharp sounds of bullets as they flew blindly through the green canvas tent, smashing whatever happened to be sitting in their line of flight, Branson pressed forward. He fought the urge to throw himself onto the ground and its relative safety. Instead, he focused his entire attention on the flaps of the tent, left partially open by the last of Millner's men. Like a ball carrier charging for an opening in the opponent's line, Branson aimed his head for the gap and kept going.

Branson had no idea what he'd find once he was out of the mess tent. From the sounds of confused voices and scrambling feet all around him, he knew things were bad. He had already figured out that the fire raking the area was coming from somewhere outside their perimeter, not from within. He also realized that there was no return fire, which indicated that whoever was firing the machine gun had the upper hand. That meant that whatever it was they wanted to do, they were probably doing it. Branson was just turning his mind to figuring out what he would do, running for all he was worth toward the ops center as he did so, when his feet snagged on something in his path. With his mind distracted and the forward momentum of his own body too great to arrest, Branson flew headlong through the air.

The impact brought him, and all organized thoughts he had, to an abrupt end. Despite the fact that he didn't normally curse, Branson let loose a string of oaths as he struggled to push himself up out of the mud in which he had landed face first. Though it hurt to do so, he lifted himself up on his hands and twisted his body to see what he had stumbled on. Still night blind, it took Branson several seconds to realized that the mound his feet and legs were draped over was the body of one of Millner's marshals. This revelation came as something of a shock. His men, men he was responsible for, were being cut down. And there he was, flat on his face doing nothing.

On the other side of the perimeter, where Osborn had chosen to make his penetration, things were going far better than he could have ever hoped. The two brothers, in particular, had been lucky. Just as Osborn had predicted, two heads popped up out of the pit when Lou's first burst ripped through the still night. Delighted with this, both brothers grinned at each other before laying their cheeks against the stocks of their rifles and letting fly with a withering hail of gunfire. A scream, sounding more like a dog's yelp than a human's cry of pain, told them that at least one of their marks had been tagged.

"All right!" Rob yelled as he let up on his trigger, looked up over the sights of his rifle. When he saw no sign of their victim or any motion coming from the direction of the Feds' hole, he reached up, switched his rate of fire selector from full automatic to semiautomatic, then took up a good firing position again. As he had in their rehearsals, once their initial volley had achieved its desired effect, Rob kept up a steady fire in order to pin the Feds down.

• • •

In the pit designated Alpha by Osborn and Number Three by Ben Branson, a very confused and frightened FBI agent crouched low and pressed up against the wall of sandbags that surrounded him. Though he could hear the sound of bullets whining overhead, and occasionally smacking against one of the exposed sandbags that ringed the pit, Special Agent Anthony Hope paid them no heed. His whole attention was riveted on the body of his partner, Special Agent Elizabeth Shoeman. In the faint light thrown off by the half moon, Hope could see the streams of blood running from the hole one of their assailants' bullets had drilled neatly into the side of her head. While uninjured in any way himself, the sight of a fellow agent dead at his feet was all that was necessary to take him out of this fight.

Farther around the ring that had kept the men of the 5th Brigade captive, the two older members of Osborn's small force found themselves engaged in a spirited fire fight with the U.S. marshal and the FBI agent occupying observation post Number Five. Neither of these Federals had exposed themselves long enough for Osborn's men to get a clear shot. And when the militiamen had opened fire, their initial volley had been wild and wide of the mark.

That's not to say that they were being ineffective. On the contrary, the two middle aged patriots were doing exactly what they had been sent out to do. They were keeping the Federals at Position Charlie busy and unable to do anything to help their companions at Bravo.

Stopping only long enough to look to his left and then to his right to make sure that there was no fire coming at him from the positions he had designated as Alpha or Charlie, Osborn shifted his feet about in pit Bravo in an effort to find some firm footing. The bodies of the two men who had occupied it had been reduced to a tangled heap of lifeless arms and legs, making it difficult to find solid ground to stand on. When he did, Osborn placed his hands on the top of the sandbags, gave himself a boost up and out of the front side of the pit. Once there, he squatted on the edge and looked back down into the bloody pit at his partner. "Keep your eyes and ears open. If someone comes at you from any direction other than the ranch, shoot them."

"What if he's one of ours?"

Anxious to be off, Osborn snapped back, "Then he fucked up and he deserves to be shot. Now, shut up and stay here." Without another word, Osborn was on his way toward the silent cluster of buildings that had, for so long, been the center of Ben Branson's world.

If there was one part of the entire operation that Osborn had misgivings about, it was this part. He had no sure way of knowing if the besieged men of the 5th Brigade knew of their plan. He had been told that they would be warned. But he had also been cautioned that this was a warning only. "It wouldn't be wise," his contact had told him, "to tell them too much. All they need to know is that someone will be coming."

Even as he approached the first building of the compound, Osborn was still unsure how best to make contact with his fellow militiamen. To shout out while he was still approaching might draw attention to himself from a Federal at another, unsuppressed observation post. Yet creeping right up to the buildings where the members of the 5th Brigade were holed up could be just as dangerous, for they might mistake him for an FBI agent using the confusion as cover.

In the end Osborn didn't need to do anything. Even as he was making his way carefully forward, trying hard to decide what to do a low, menacing voice called out. "Halt!"

Instinctively, Osborn stopped dead in his tracks. "Don't shoot," he whispered as loudly as he dare. "Tom Osborn, of the Idaho 2nd Battalion. I'm here to lead you boys out of here."

For a moment, there were no sounds, other than the steady pop, pop, pop of M-16s and the rattle of Lou's machine gun in the distance. Finally, after what seemed to be an eternity, Osborn saw the barrel of a gun emerge from the shadow of one of the buildings. Slowly the image of the barrel was joined by an arm, then a dark figure as his challenger stepped closer to examine Osborn. Only when the militiaman of the 5th Brigade was satisfied that Osborn was who he claimed to be did the militiaman lower his weapon. "It's about time," the low, gravelly voice snapped. "We were wondering if there was anyone up in Idaho who had the balls to put their money where their mouth is."

Relieved beyond all measure, Osborn began to breathe steadily again. "Well," Osborn responded, "I'm here to tell you, we're as good as our word. Now, get your stuff together and get a move on. We don't have a hell of a lot of time."

Time was a commodity neither leader felt he had enough of. Making his way to within a few feet of the trailer that served as his ops center by rushing from the cover of one stationary vehicle to another, Branson found himself unable to complete his journey when he was within arms' reach of the front door. Resting against the side of a National Guard armored personnel carrier parked haphazardly in the center of the crowded base camp, Branson watched as another stream of machinegun bullets ripped along the aluminum side of the trailer, sending sparks into the air whenever a round struck a piece of solid metal. Though there were still lights on in the trailer, he saw no sign of any activity coming from it. Dear God, he found himself praying, please let there be someone alive in there calling for help.

Unable to do anything, Branson looked away from the trailer and around the still brightly lit compound. Why, he found himself asking, hadn't anyone thought of killing all those damned flood lights? Then, he realized that even he was not sure if there was a single switch that would cut all the lights that were making him and his people such easy targets. Yet despite this crippling handicap, some of the FBI men and women, and U.S. marshals, were taking their chances and returning fire. Most, with nothing more than their personal handguns, fired into the darkness where the angry flashes of the devastating machinegun could clearly been seen. Twisting his head about, he looked up at the armored personnel carrier that was providing him protection. For the first time he became painfully aware that in his travels from the mess tent to his present spot, he had not seen a single Guardsman. Only then did he remember what Agent Raymos had told him. All of the Wyoming Guardsmen were in their own compound. While this annoyed Branson, he could not ignore the positive side of the colonel's arrogant display of self-importance. Perhaps they were not under fire. Perhaps the Guardsmen were coming, like the cowboys they were, galloping to the rescue.

From a site little more than a mile away, Colonel Matthew Tinselly of the Wyoming National Guard, assigned to assist the FBI, watched the one sided fire fight between the FBI compound and the lone militia machinegun. Around him his officers and NCOs crowded together while they waited for his orders. But no orders came. As the minutes ticked by, and the effective fire that held the FBI and U.S. marshals at bay showed no sign of diminishing, some of the Guardsmen began to grow restless. Finally the major serving as Tinselly's ops officer turned to his colonel. "Sir," he announced after clearing his throat. "Shouldn't we dispatch a relief force of some type? I don't think it would take much to get around behind that machinegun and . . ."

"And what?" Tinselly snapped. "Get our men killed, too? Bullshit," he snorted as he answered his own question. "Don't you think they expect us to do that? Don't you think that there's at least a half a dozen of the bastards lying out there in the dark, waiting for us to come charging out of here like the goddamned 7th U.S. Cavalry to save the day?"

The major, recoiling under the colonel's tirade, stepped back.

"Of course they do. That's why I'm going to hold back until the situation clarifies itself. Besides," Tinselly added slyly, "our assistance hasn't been requested. If those people down there really needed our help, don't you think the phone would be ringing off the hook?"

The major, unwilling to endue more verbal abuse, bowed his head. "Yes, sir. I imagine they would be calling us."

Satisfied that he had made his point sufficiently to allay any suspicions about his complicity in the affair, the Guard colonel went back to observing the efforts of Idaho militiamen as they worked to free men who had always counted Colonel Tinselly as one of their own. It took all the Wyoming colonel's strength to keep from muttering, "Give 'em hell, Idaho."

The dawn that followed the long, bitter night brought no relief to Ben Branson. Though he tried not to look as he came out of his shattered ops center, his eyes always managed to wander over to the row of black body bags lined up alongside the trailer. Most of the people who had been on duty in the ops center when the attack had begun were now lying there, silent and dead. Special Agent Angel Raymos, barely causing a crease in the bag she occupied, was among them.

So too was Kyle Millner. The bulging stomach that had been the butt of so many jokes stood out, even when covered by the slick black waterproof bag that kept his remains safe from the early morning chill. The sight of these bags, more than the temperature, caused Ben Branson to shiver. Millner didn't belong there, Branson thought. The old cowboy should be sitting with him in the mess tent, enjoying a cup of coffee as they sorted through the day's upcoming business. Branson closed his eyes and tried hard to picture the U.S. marshal's ruddy face, shrouded in steam rising from a cup of coffee held more for the heat it gave off than its drinking pleasure. But there would be no coffee shared in that tent this morning. Not by Millner, not by anyone. It would take hours to clean up the bloody mess in there where the wounded had been taken, when it was all over, to receive first aid.

At least, Branson thought as he turned to walk away, those stains would eventually be washed away. How long, he wondered, would his memory retain the sight of body bags lined up next to the trailer, or the thought that he had, somehow, been instrumental in filling them?

CHAPTER 4

When we consider the framers of the Constitution, we must take into account *their* view of the world, not ours." Pausing, Dr. Edmund Fallner scanned the students before him as he allowed this point to sink in. "Most of the men who met in Philadelphia in 1787 were trained in the classics. These leading Americans, the political elite of their day, were men who were desperately trying to cobble together a nation based on principles and ideas that their world had not seen practiced in centuries, if ever. Not only were they searching for solutions to issues that they themselves had been forced to wrestle with, but they were trying to anticipate problems that they could imagine. In drafting a document that would define the government of the United States and against which every law would be measured, they did not trust the judgment of others, just as they did not trust others to define for them the rights and obligations of their new nation's citizenry."

Pausing again as he moved out from behind the protection of his lectern, Fallner leaned on the podium and put one hand in his pocket. Gesturing with his other hand, he continued. "It should not be surprising that men like Jefferson, Adams, Washington, Hamilton, and the rest viewed themselves as modern versions of the ancient Roman patricians. *They,* the educated, the wealthy, and the successful, were *born* to rule. It was not only their *right* as they saw it, but their *duty* to do so. Unlike the huddled masses who were ignorant of the great works of Aristotle, Locke, Rousseau, and Hume, Jefferson et al, had a firm grasp of what these men were saying, or so they believed."

From her seat in the second row Nancy Kozak listened. She had long ago laid her pen down in order to concentrate on what Fallner was saying. As quickly as each new thought came in, Nancy's mind took the idea, ripped it down to its bare essentials, examined it for a moment, then filed it away in her memory as useful, or discarded it as pure drivel. Trained by years of service in the Army, Nancy Kozak still had difficulty seeing shades of gray. Everything in her world was either black or white, right or wrong. As a graduate student, Nancy's approach to dealing with what Fallner said was ideal.

"Jefferson, Adams, and their peers shared many traits with ancient Rome's republican patricians," the professor of history stated. "Both groups believed that they had civic duties that only they could discharge. Both had a fear of the masses, whom they considered fickle. And both had a love for the law, which they considered to be supreme and incontestable. So it is to the traditions of the Roman Republic, which many of our founding fathers saw as being pure, that they turned for a model, and not the corrupt, easily manipulated English system that they had so recently broken with."

As was his habit, Fallner pushed his wire framed glasses back up the bridge of his nose and looked around. This motion was more than a subconscious idiosyncrasy. It was a means of announcing to the class that he was about to discuss a subject near and dear to his heart. To his students it was a signal that their right to freely express their opinions on the subject being considered were, for the next few minutes, suspended.

"Unfortunately," Fallner began, "our new system was flawed at its very inception. Take Thomas Jefferson. In this man, long held to be the intellectual father of this country, we have the epitome of the hypocrisy that characterized most of his peers. Anyone who compares what this man said and wrote with the life he actually lived cannot help but see that he was a far better preacher than he was a practitioner." Again Fallner paused to allow his students to chuckle at what he considered funny. But the class before him didn't crack a smile. Normally a good number of his students would let out a nervous chuckle, or even halfhearted laugh, but not this class. Whatever control he had once exercised over them, whatever power he had once possessed to sway them had been lost, months before, when he had allowed himself to be bested during heated classroom discussions by one of his own students. Even now he couldn't help but glance over and warily eye that student, wondering when she would interrupt his lecture and present him and the class with an alternate viewpoint.

From her seat Nancy Kozak returned Fallner's cold stare. He was challenging her, she concluded. His bold statement was bait. He was presenting a view of history which was so outrageous, in her mind, that it could not be ignored. Not yet ready to comment, as she always did whenever he tried to show that America's mythical heroes were nothing more than lying, self serving little men, Kozak held her tongue.

When his traditional antagonist did not rear up and challenge him, Fallner continued. "On one hand," he stated as he held out his right hand for emphasis, "Mr. Jefferson writes a declaration which states that all men are created equal. At the same time, however," throwing out his left hand, palm up, "he not only continues to hold onto the slaves he has, but acquires more. Yet even today, we are forced to listen to supposedly educated people who continue to claim that Jefferson was a great man."

If Fallner's remark about "educated people" had been an effort to discourage her from launching into a defense of Jefferson, it failed. Nancy Kozak was too savvy to be dissuaded by such a ploy.

Though he tried hard not to, Fallner glanced over at Kozak with the same anticipation one feels when eyeing a vicious neighborhood dog. He hated adult students, hated them with a passion. They came into the course with preconceived ideas, unprepared and unwilling to accept his views as gospel. Young students, those yet to be contaminated by the world, were far easier to manipulate and persuade.

The professor of history continued even as he braced for the response he knew would come. "Like so many of his contemporaries, particularly those from the south, Mr. Jefferson was more than willing to talk the talk of democracy but never quite managed to get the hang of the walk. Though he had resolved during the Revolution to free his slaves, he never found the courage to do so. Conventional wisdom and a keen eye for a good deal when it came to cheap labor seem to have stayed his hand until his death."

Unable to hold back, and seeing an opening, Kozak let loose. "Professor Fallner, isn't that the point? Thomas Jefferson was a prisoner of his time, his culture, and his society, just as we are of ours. To have gone against any of them would have left him isolated and unable to serve his country in any capacity."

With the battle now open, Fallner abandoned his notes, leaned one elbow on the podium, and faced Kozak. "Ah, well, that's just my point. We have these men, Jefferson included, throwing up this facade of democracy while, at the same time, working hard to enshrine institutions that limited the franchise to themselves and a handful of fellow patricians. With one breath they declare that all men are created equal. With the next, they allow slavery to continue, restrict voting to those who owned land, and permit only men the right to participate in the machinery of their newly created republic."

Leaning over her desktop, Kozak assumed an aggressive posture. "Like his contemporaries, Jefferson was just that, a man. None of them were gods. There wasn't even a demi-god amongst them. Chosen or self-appointed, they were leaders, mortal men faced with creating a form of government unlike anything that had ever existed before. While their intentions might have been noble, they were wise enough to face the harsh realities of their times and the world they lived in. To have held out for a utopian form that encompassed every aspect of radical political thought of the day would have condemned their entire enterprise to failure. The framers of the Constitution were, after all, answerable to their constituents, people who held certain beliefs to be true and sacred. Our founding fathers understood that if the document they were drafting was to have meaning, they would have to forge a compact between themselves and those who had sent them to Philadelphia. It was those people, after all, who would have to open their pocketbooks and spill their blood for the nation that was being created."

"So, Ms. Kozak," Fallner stated triumphantly as he stood upright, glanced at the clock on the wall, and smiled, "you believe that the continuation of slavery was justified, that political expediency can excuse a person from doing what is morally correct."

Fighting the anger she felt welling up in her, Nancy Kozak brought her two hands together on her desk, squeezed them tightly, and responded carefully so as not to betray anger. "As difficult as the concept may seem, especially when discussed in the sterile halls of an institution divorced from the realities of the real world, there are times when people have to pick between the lesser of two evils. To have pushed for the exclusion of slavery and the total enfranchisement of all adults, men and women, in the late eighteenth century would have condemned this nation to obscurity and failure before it was even born. Jefferson and his contemporaries were, above all else, rational men who understood the world they lived in and their fellow citizens. That, sir, is more than I can say for those in positions of authority today."

Assuming that Kozak's last remark was a slight, Fallner was about to respond when the buzzer signaled the end of the hour. As one the class began shoving books and binders into bags and backpacks, preventing Professor Fallner from responding to Kozak's impertinent oratory. Pleased that she had managed to get the last word in, Nancy looked directly at Fallner and smiled. The professor merely stood at his lectern, thinking all sorts of horrible and unkind thoughts that did not conform to the liberal image that he was so careful to cultivate.

Once in the crowded corridor Helen Swanson caught up with Kozak. "As always," Helen shouted in an effort to make herself heard over the noise of hundreds of disjointed conversations and the shuffling of feet, "you got to old Foulner again!"

Nancy laughed, as much at the mutilation of the man's

name as at her minor triumph. "I just can't help it," she explained as they followed the flow of students toward the stairwell. "He throws out ludicrous statements and all but dares me to respond."

Helen laughed. A mother of three, she was returning to graduate school after an absence of many years. "Sometimes he reminds me of my former husband. Not only was he always right, the mere idea that someone, especially a woman, disagreed with him was unthinkable."

"Well," Nancy replied jokingly, "thank God *I've* never known anyone like that." This comment caused both women to laugh.

While still battling their way through a mass of students, Helen ventured a word of advice. "As much as it can be entertaining to play with him in class, it doesn't pay to piss off the professor. In the end he's the final arbiter of who goes on and who fails. I was a teacher far too long not to be tempted to abuse the power that the grade book gave me."

Having already considered this, Nancy shrugged off Helen's warning. "He's too smart to fail me," she explained. "His course is a prerequisite for Professor Turnbull's. If Foulner fails me he faces the agony of spending another semester with me in his class. No," Kozak reasoned as she paused to watch her step as she began to descend the stairs. "He'll pass me. And he'll do so with a good grade just to be rid of me. The man's little more than a jellyfish, capable of inflicting an annoying sting every now and then but with absolutely no backbone."

This caused Helen to let out a loud and unladylike guffaw. "Nancy," she called out as they rounded the turn at the landing and started down the next flight of stairs amid a herd of fellow students, "you're too much. I don't know what I'd do without you."

Kozak smiled. She too didn't know what she would have done without Helen. They had begun the fall semester feeling totally out of place in an environment foreign to them both. Helen, in the process of divorcing her first husband, had latched onto Nancy for both support and comfort. Nancy responded by befriending the thirty something woman and accepting her warm invitations to join her small family whenever she could. This helped ease Nancy's transition from an aborted military career into civilian life. During quiet, reflective moments, when Helen's children were in bed and the two women were alone in a cluttered living room that reeked of family and togetherness, Nancy would often turn to Helen and tell her how in debt she was to her for the kindness and understanding that she had shown her during a most difficult period. Helen, giving Nancy the same patient smile she had used when speaking to her own children, downplayed her role. "I've done nothing special," she explained, "except provide a sympathetic ear and a warm hand to hang onto when you asked."

For Nancy, so used to standing alone in a world that often proved cold and unfriendly, this had been a blessing.

As the two women were about to part company in the parking lot, Helen paused. "Up to anything special this weekend?"

Knowing this was Helen's preamble to an invitation for a home cooked meal followed by a video, Nancy shook her head. "I'd love to, but I can't."

Though she knew Nancy wasn't seeing anyone at the moment, Helen nevertheless took the opportunity to kid her. "Hot date?"

Nancy rolled her eyes and she walked backwards in the direction of where she had parked her car. "No, nothing like that," she explain. "Just the opposite."

"Oh," Helen replied with a laugh. "It's your time of month."

"Yep!" Nancy beamed. "I get to play weekend warrior with the boys."

Helen sighed. "I really respect your dedication, but I don't envy you."

"Well," Nancy shrugged. "It's a dirty job, but someone's got to make the coffee."

With a laugh, Helen waved to Nancy. "I'll sleep safely tonight knowing that the defense of Idaho is in your capable hands."

"Go home Helen," Nancy chided her friend as she

laughed, "I think I hear your kids. It's either that or the local SWAT team is running a hostage rescue drill."

HEADQUARTERS, IDAHO NATIONAL GUARD, BOISE, IDAHO • 19 MAY

Every time she entered the office of Plans, Training, and Operations, Lieutenant Colonel Nancy Kozak felt as if she had come home. Though still very much an outsider here, the familiar sights, sounds, and smells of a military head-quarters awoke feelings of purpose and pride that were still very much a part of her. There was none of the abstract or theoretical that so dominated her day-to-day labors at the university. What she did here affected real people. Come summer, when most of the units of the Idaho Guard mustered for their annual two week training, they would benefit from the long hours Nancy put in ensuring that the proper ammunition was on hand. It was a thankless job, as anyone who ever had to deal with training management could attest. Still, it allowed Nancy to keep in touch with the real world, one populated by people who lived real lives. Even more importantly, it permitted her to hang on to the one thing that had always been of paramount importance to her, the Army.

It had not taken her long to find that one could not simply turn one's back on an organization such as the Army. A decorated veteran, Nancy had participated in the First Gulf War as well as a few minor conflicts here and there around the world. Quickly she had discovered that her experiences and achievements in the military were not only of little concern to the very people she thought she had been defending, but all too often, a source of problems for her. "Have you ever stopped and wondered," Helen told Nancy when the two of them were discussing their lack of a serious love life one night instead of studying, "how intimidating it has to be for a man to know that the woman he is dating is not only trained to kill, but has been afforded the opportunity to do so?"

Nancy, who up until her resignation had associated almost exclusively with other military types, had never much given that particular aspect of male and female relationships much thought. Naively, she looked at Helen wide-eyed. "Do you really think that makes that much of a difference?"

Not realizing that Nancy was being deadly earnest, Helen reached out and patted Nancy on the hand as she laughed out loud. "Kid, you're a hoot!" she roared. Though Nancy would have liked to have corrected Helen's misconception, she let the matter drop. But she hadn't forgotten it. Instead, Nancy kept her thoughts to herself as she tried to reconcile her past and live in the present while struggling to find a future for herself.

That was where the National Guard came in. In many ways it was a crutch, a place where she could be her old self without fear of isolation or the need be overly careful about what she said. That did not mean that she could totally drop her guard. For even though the members of the Idaho National Guard wore a uniform with a "U.S. Army" tape sewn over the right breast pocket, they were not the same United States Army Nancy had served in. No Guard unit, Nancy realized, would ever be like the regular Army.

"You've got to remember, Colonel, this is the Idaho National Guard," her superior, Colonel Victor Simonson, cautioned her when she started working as a training officer. "Though we are a leg of the 'One Army' concept, our primary duty and responsibilities lie here, in this state, and with the people of Idaho. Unlike the active Army we are directly linked to the community we serve. Those people out there are our friends, our neighbors, our employers and employees." Stopping, Simonson turned, looked out the window of his office, and waved his hand waist high in a sweeping motion. "The people we serve are the very people you meet every day in the convenience stores, on the highways you pass coming and going from here, in the college you're attending. When the floods sweep away everything they own, or the snows overwhelm a locality's ability to deal with them, or a group of prisoners feel their civil rights have been violated, those people depend on us to help them and protect them. Keep that in mind, young woman, if you expect to get along in this headquarters or anywhere else in this organization."

Reaching her small cubicle, Nancy set her laptop on her desk, opened a lower drawer, and dropped her purse into it. When she had been on active duty she had seldom carried a purse. Not only had it been impractical, but it would have been totally contrary to the image she was always struggling to maintain. But here, perhaps because of her change of lifestyle or simply because she had grown used to carrying one around, Nancy found herself becoming attached to her plain black shoulder bag.

With a tap of her combat boot, Nancy shoved the drawer closed, forgot about that trivial feminine accessory, and sat down to collect her thoughts and redirect them into a military frame of mind. She started by shuffling through the papers and files that had found their way into her "In" box. Randomly mixed in with notices about changes in Guard benefits, news about upcoming events, and strongly worded admonishments by the headquarters commandant advising staff officers to improve the appearance of their workspace or tighten up on how they wore their uniforms, were new requests for training ammunition, the monthly status report of pending requests, and advisories on suspended or condemned lots of munitions. Without bothering to even give the administrative notices and directives a second look, Nancy separated them from her reports and requests and tossed them into the wastepaper basket.

From behind her, at the opening of her little cubicle, a gruff voice interrupted her sorting. "You know, a lot of time and taxpayers' money were expended to generate all that paperwork you're so casually disposing of."

Without having to look, she knew that Master Sergeant Theodore Valineski had caught her. Allowing a smile to crease her lips, Nancy swiveled about on her worn gray chair and faced Valineski. Of all the people in the office, Nancy felt most at ease with the old master sergeant who was universally known as Teddy by officer and enlisted alike. From her first day as a member of that headquarters, Valineski had made her feel welcome, a feeling that was still a rarity. Laying the half sorted stack of papers in her lap, Nancy leaned back in her chair. "Teddy, believe me when I tell you, I know exactly how much effort is wasted, I mean expended, in coming up with this, ah . . ."

"Bullshit?" Valineski replied.

"Well, that's not the first word I would have selected to describe it, but it is an excellent choice."

"Not to mention applicable," Valineski added as he leaned against the wobbly office partition.

"Yes, well, be that as it may. The truth of the matter is, if I went through every notice, directive, and non-training related piece of paper that came across my desk, I'd need to spend a second weekend a month in this office just to do all the work I failed to finish because I was reading that, ah . . ."

"Bullshit."

"Yes," Nancy responded. Then, changing her voice until she sounded like Lily Tomlin, she added, "And that's the truth."

The heavyset master sergeant chuckled. "Well, it may be the truth, but it's all part of the game. And speaking of that, I came by here to inform you that there'll be a briefing of all headquarters personnel at oh nine hundred hours in the main conference room."

Letting her smile disappear and shoulders droop, Nancy looked over at the clock suspended from a twisted wire hanger on the partition. "Damn!" she exclaimed before looking back at Valineski. "What's this earth shattering briefing about? Remedial training on the proper method of boot blousing?"

When Valineski answered, there wasn't a hint of humor in his voice. "Counter terrorism measures. Seems the attacks on the Federal buildings have gotten some folks mighty concerned, especially since no one's been fingered for it yet."

"Yes," Nancy responded glumly. "I suppose questioning the usual suspects hasn't produced any leads."

Straightening up in preparation for going to the next stop in his rounds, Valineski shook his head. "That's what seems to be giving everyone the willies. If they could come up with a reason, or a group, I imagine everyone could make whatever adjustments they needed to for protection and get on with things. But with this just sort of hanging out there, unanswered, well . . ."

Changing the direction of the conversation, Nancy leaned forward. "Teddy," she asked slowly. "Have you been following what they've been saying about the Wyoming Guard colonel who was in charge of the troops supporting the FBI at the siege that went bad?"

Before answering Valineski looked over his shoulder, as if he was checking to see if anyone would hear his response. When he did look back at Nancy and answered, he did so in a very low voice. "Who hasn't been?"

"Do you think that colonel held his men back intentionally?"

The expression on Valineski's face as he considered his answer reminded Nancy of the same look that soldiers accused of mischief affect. It was, she thought, as if Valineski was trying to figure out what answer would be appropriate for her.

When he finally did select what he considered an appropriate response, it was very noncommittal. "I don't know," Valineski mumbled. "I wasn't there. You of all people should know how hard it is to pass judgment on something this far removed from the scene. It's like being a Monday morning quarterback. Who knows what you would have done in that spot?"

Understanding that the master sergeant had no intention of answering her question, Nancy accepted Valineski's response. "Okay, thanks. I appreciate your thought."

Neither Valineski or Nancy said another word as Valineski walked away. Now pressed for time, Nancy returned to the business of sorting out her piles of work without giving the subject of the upcoming briefing, or of the incident in Wyoming, another thought.

CHAPTER 5

Through the window that faced east, a faint hint of light could be seen as it began separating the great American plains from the vast western skies. Soon the tips of the jagged peaks of the towering Rocky Mountains would be illuminated by a sun still hidden below the horizon. Unable to sleep any longer, Jan Fields-Dixon reached out and placed her hand gently on her husband's bare chest as she enjoyed the birth of a new day.

Snuggling closer to Scott, Jan watched while the night sky slowly faded into pale shades of blue. She loved this time of day. It was a wonderful, magical time, a time when she was free to enjoy the privacy of her home. Safe and warm between the crisp, clean sheets, she could let her thoughts wander freely while enjoying the presence of a man she loved like no other person she had ever loved before. On occasion, when Jan was in a playful mood, she would slowly arouse Scott's passions into frenzy wild enough to make Scott forget that he was a general officer with schedules to keep and duties to perform. Mostly, though, she lay quietly next to him as he continued his slumber, enjoying the tranquil peace that smothered her soul like a cozy, warm comforter on a cold winter night.

From the nightstand, the harsh buzz of the alarm shattered Jan's serene reflections. Nimbly, she reached across Scott and mashed down the off switch. Scott, roused by Jan's movements more so than by the piercing noise, grunted and snorted like a bear roused from hibernation before his time. His first efforts to speak were utter failures, ending in disjointed sounds that reminded Jan of garbled German. Scott was more successful in prying his reluctant eyelids open. While Jan slid back into the crook of his arm, he looked about the room. "It's still dark," he muttered as if he were making a deathbed declaration. "What time is it?"

"Early," Jan responded as she ran her fingers along his chest. "You can sleep for another half hour. I've got to go in early today."

"Better you than I," Scott murmured before he rolled over, gave his pillow a tug, and slipped back to sleep.

Having lost the moment, Jan quietly slipped out of bed and threw on an old worn bathrobe Scott had taken from an Army hospital. Like a cat making its morning rounds, she quietly crept through the house toward the kitchen. While passing the den she heard a rhythmic thumping, punctuated by labored breathing. Peeking in she saw Nathan, his feet shoved under the sofa, lost to the world as he knocked out sit-ups as quickly as he could. Rather than break his concentration Jan finished her trek to the kitchen, where she fixed a pot of decaf for herself and regular coffee for Scott and Nathan.

Now that she was up, Jan was ready to get going. Unable to wait for the coffee machine to run its full course, she pulled the decanter out and shoved her empty cup into the stream of fresh, hot coffee. She ignored the drops that splattered about, hissing and bubbling as it burned off as soon as it hit the hot plate. Instead, she watched patiently as her cup filled. When she had enough, she pulled her cup away and replaced the decanter in a single, swift motion. After dumping artificial sweetener into the cup, she started to make her way back to the bedroom to dress.

When she passed the den a second time she saw that Nathan had changed positions. He was now pumping himself up and down, doing more push-ups in one session than Jan had ever done in her entire life. Fascinated, she stopped, leaned against the doorway, and watched for a moment. Like Scott, she was very proud of the way Nathan had turned out. In a day and age when so many young people were wandering about in a mental fog, or were so self centered that they were unbearable, it never ceased to amaze Jan that she had helped raise a child like Nathan. That she had never given birth to her own still tugged at her heart. Even now she could feel a pang of regret over that fateful decision as she watched Nathan's ramrod straight back go up and down in cadence with his breathing.

Only when he was finished, and had dropped his knees to the floor to rest, did Nathan pick his sweaty head up and take note of Jan. Flashing her that smile that had always been one of his greatest assets, Nathan greeted her. "Up kind of early, Mom."

"Not as early as you," she replied before taking a sip of coffee.

"Well, I've kinda gotten into the habit of being up before the sun," he chirped while he rearranged his legs and arms until he was sitting. "Though I don't think Fort Benning is going to be all that much of a challenge, I'm not taking any chances. You know how those airborne infantry types think."

This made Jan laugh. "No, thank God I don't. I've had enough to handle trying to decipher the random thought patterns of an old cavalryman."

Nathan joined Jan as she chuckled. "Dad's not so hard to figure. All a tanker needs is a whiff of diesel fumes, some grease on his hands, and a motor pool full of oversized dinosaurs and he's happier than a pig in . . ."

"Nathan!" Jan snapped before he could finish. "You're not in the barracks anymore."

Though he stood a good head taller than Jan, he blushed and sheepishly hung his head low. As he looked up to apologize as was his habit when admonished in this way, Jan couldn't help but recall the sight of the small, sandy haired boy who was always in trouble for minor offenses. That she was about to lose that child hurt her as she had never been hurt before.

With a shake of her head, Jan flashed a warm smile. "Well, I don't know about you or the General, but I have a big day and I must be going."

Rather than give his mother a smile, Nathan's expression turned to one of sadness. "Mom, do you think Dad will ever forgive me for choosing Infantry over Armor?"

Jan knew this was a sensitive subject between the father

and the son. Nathan, concerned that he would never be able to measure up to his father's achievements, had opted for a path that would avoid such comparisons. Walking over to where Nathan sat, Jan placed her hand on Nathan's sweaty back and gave it a gentle, comforting rub. "Your father loves you very much. And he's proud of what you've achieved."

"I couldn't go Armor, Mom," Nathan explained plaintively, though he had no need to do so. "I just couldn't. Everything I did, every achievement of mine would be measured against his. As bad as it is being the son of 'General' Scott Dixon, it would be a million times worse if I were a tanker, too."

Bending over, Jan planted a kiss on the top of Nathan's sweaty head. "Your father understands that better than I think you give him credit for."

Looking up, Nathan finally managed to summon his impish smile. "Thanks, Mom. Now, go out there and give 'em hell."

With a smile on her face, Jan walked away, waving her free hand as she did so. "Yeah, yeah. I know. And don't take any prisoners." She was about to add, "You're just like your father" before she disappeared around the corner but caught herself in time.

The drive to her office in Denver was good for Jan. It allowed her to slowly rearrange her thoughts, letting the peaceful tranquillity of domestic concerns slip away and those of work come to the fore in a gradual, unhurried way. The scenery all about her, mountains to the left, rolling plains to the right, helped. Only the antics of other drivers harried by schedules that always seemed to be too tight or stress that knew no end intruded as Jan thought her day through. Slowly, methodically, she laid out a mental plan of how she would deal with her own duties and responsibilities, while steeling herself to deal with whatever unforeseen crisis fate was waiting to throw in her way.

There had been a time when Jan would have scoffed at the very thought of commuting back and forth to the same office and the same job, day in, day out. As a star journalist for the World News Network, she had once viewed the entire globe as her office. From the Middle East, to the Far East, with occasional stops in Europe whenever there was an international hiccup there, Jan had dashed about, bringing the latest breaking news to America. Even after her marriage to Scott Dixon, she had managed, somehow, to juggle her career, his career, and a love affair that never seemed to fade.

Yet, after making the move to Colorado two years prior, "following the flag" as Jan called it, she had been offered the opportunity to scale back and host her own one hour show. To everyone's surprise she had taken it. When asked why, not even Jan could explain it then. Only now, as she maneuvered her car into the parking lot of the local Denver station from which her show originated, could she look back and explain what had caused her to throw away a lifestyle and career that many thought of as being glamorous and exciting for a home nestled in the foothills of the Rockies.

She hadn't even finished crossing the threshold of the station before the tranquillity of Jan's early morning slumber and her leisurely drive into Denver evaporated. From across the room, a producer shouted out to her. "Jan, five minutes. I need a bit of advice." Trying hard to hide her annoyed look, Jan made for the communal coffee pot and began drawing a cup of coffee without responding to the producer. Though this producer had no connection at all to her show, people who worked in the newsroom at that station were always seeking her opinion or advice on various matters.

Ann Warren, who did research and background work on developing stories for Jan's show, saw Jan and made straight for her in an effort to get to her before the producer did. With a nod of her head, she signaled Ann to meet her in her office. With that taken care of, Jan turned to face the producer. "James," she stated firmly as she raised her hand and started moving briskly toward her office, "unless the Martians have blown up the White House and you have video of it, I don't think anyone cares what your lead story is."

"But Jan," the producer pleaded as he pursued her, "I really could use your expertise and judgment. The jury in the Henderson case could come out with a verdict any minute. Do I cut into regular programming and announce it, or wait until a regular news update?"

Pausing at her door, but only for a second, Jan looked the producer in the eye. "James, use your judgment. Keep an eye on the other networks. The instant you see them cut into their regular programming, jump in yourself. Okay?"

Happy to have been given a decision that took him off the hook, the producer left with a smile on his face, leaving Jan free to go into her office and begin the task of preparing for her show at noon.

"Okay, Ann," Jan asked before she even reached the sofa on which Ann had settled. "What do you have for me on Governor Thomas that I don't already know?"

The thirty something Ann Warren was more than the news department's token lesbian. A former congressional staffer, Ann had cultivated sources and contacts that would have made the CIA green with envy. Jan didn't much care whether these sources were part of Ann's circle of friends or traditional arrangements that people in high places delight in developing with key members of the media. Ann delivered grade A material in a timely manner. For Jan, that was all that mattered.

Ann's inside political contacts were especially critical when they dealt with characters like George Oliver Thomas and his efforts to thwart a growing effort to revise the Constitution. As a popular governor, Thomas had managed to recreate a coalition of other conservative governors, senators, and congressmen in an effort to curb what he saw as an erosion of states' rights. Through the use of guile and persuasion, charisma and bare knuckled politics, the native of Idaho had managed to become a force on the political plains of America. With a power that far exceeded the mandates of his office, he managed to block every effort that came out of the nation's capital that he felt was intrusive or violated the spirit of the Constitution. His influence had become so pervasive, it was rumored that before the Senate Judiciary Committee voted for a candidate for the nation's Supreme Court, the chairman of that committee had called a recess in order to call Thomas and consult with him on the matter.

"We have tons of material," Ann started as she picked up a one page bio from the stack of file folders she had on the table in front of her and handed it to Jan. "In a nutshell, Governor George Oliver Thomas, popularly known as GO Thomas for his 'go get 'em' attitude and campaign slogan, was a very successful entrepreneur before he was elected governor of Idaho as an Independent."

"That," Jan snapped, "is old news."

"Well," Ann continued, unperturbed by Jan's sharp response, "what is less well known are rumors concerning his ties to right wing militia groups."

This caught Jan's attention. "For years now both journalists and disenfranchised politicians from the left have been trying to make that connection," she quipped as she settled down onto the sofa. "What do you have to offer by way of proof?"

Ann smiled. "Documents from the Attorney General's office." Pausing, she watched Jan's reaction, pleased that she could still manage to get a rise out of a hard case such as Jan. Continuing, Ann connected the dots. "At the heart of the business empire Thomas built are various franchises and businesses that are run by people he hand picked. In turn these men have been quite careful when selecting their employees."

Sipping her coffee, Jan looked into Ann's eyes, suspecting that she was building up to something. "Okay, go on."

"Several years ago, before our man GO stormed onto the political stage a third echelon staffer at the FBI made a startling discovery. While compiling a list of known or suspected members of militia units in the west and northwest, he began to notice that a disproportionate number of them worked for companies or businesses that were either wholly, or partially owned by our Mr. Thomas."

"Circumstantial," Jan countered, "at best."

Ann didn't waver. "It gets better. This staffer did more than match names. He compared the organizational charts of those militia units with the hierarchy of Thomas's various enterprises."

Excited now, Jan couldn't hold back. "Don't tell me, they matched."

For the first time Ann permitted herself to smile. "While not true for every business interest GO Thomas owns, it was determined by the Justice Department that this connection was more than coincidental, especially since the one franchise in which this was most pervasive was a chain of gun shops."

Though excited, Jan managed to throttle back her enthusiasm. "If this is all true," Jan stated as she leafed through the material Ann was handing her, "the FBI, and the powers that be inside the Beltway, would have leaked this during Thomas's race for governor." Pausing, she looked up at Ann. "You know how much the establishment hates seeing a political outsider win a race, even if it is in faraway Idaho."

"Though my source didn't say so," Ann explained, "she alluded to the fact that they tried, but failed to make a connection. Not long after the matter was dropped, every file concerning the investigation disappeared. Even more interesting is the fact that everyone who had been working on the case at the Department of Justice and FBI was transferred to such wonderfully diverse places like Anchorage, Alaska, and Barstow, California."

"While this is disturbing," Jan responded, "what's so unusual about this case? After all, we've seen this sort of thing in Washington for the past eight years. Besides, if neither the Department of Justice nor the FBI found anything before and were willing to let the matter drop, what's changed?"

"April 25th and the aborted FBI siege in Wyoming. Embarrassed, the FBI has resurrected every investigation they've run in the past few years involving domestic terrorism and the militia movement. That includes the one they had conducted on Governor Thomas. Though the FBI is being far more circumspect than they were before, in an effort to avoid being tagged as political storm troopers for the Administration, they are, nonetheless, going forth."

"And how," Jan asked as he looked her research assistant in the eye, "did you hear of this investigation if it is suppose to be so circumspect?"

"I came across the first hint of it on the Internet," Ann explained. "I followed up by making some calls to people I know in the Justice Department."

"The usual sources, I suppose?" Jan asked smiling.

"Better than that." From her stack of papers, she pulled a fax. "This is a copy of a Federally ordered wire tap I was sent by an old friend."

Grabbing the fax, Jan scanned it in an effort to discern if it were genuine. After determining that it was, she looked back at Ann. Though she tried to be liberally minded as her profession dictated and her peers expected, Jan could not help but wonder if this "source" was one of Ann's old Washington lovers.

Ann went on, "Even though he has moved into politics, he's continued his habit of hand selecting his subordinates. He's known as the kingmaker in Idaho. Even at county and town level, politicians in that state consider his nod of approval the single most critical element of their campaigns."

Ann paused as Jan scanned the bio before her. When she reached the section that addressed his service record, Jan smiled. "Oh, he was a Hog driver."

Ann, who had prepared the bio, made a face. "A what?"

Catching herself, Jan smiled as she glanced over to Ann. "He flew A-10s when he was in the Air Force and during the First Gulf War."

Not quite sure what an A-10 was, but satisfied that Jan was impressed by that tidbit of information, Ann let the matter drop as her boss continued to scan the bio. "Okay," Jan said as she placed the bio off to one side for future use. "Next."

Next Ann opened a file folder containing several news stories she had copied from newspapers. "Mr. Thomas's PR people were quite obliging about providing us with information. They faxed us most of this material here. Together with what I was able to dig up, you have just about everything you'd need in case you have the insane urge to start a local chapter of the 'I Love GO' fan club."

Jan looked at the stack and shook her head. "Ann, I want to interview the man, not marry him."

A woman who pursued a quiet life with her domestic partner, Ann forced a smile before she continued. "Our man is not content with just being a local hero. He uses every opportunity to make his views known wherever he can find a forum even when what he says is not what the people want to hear," Ann pointed out as she shoved a copied news story in front of Jan. "This is part of a speech he delivered to the Christian Foundation."

"For an American to stand up and claim that he or his group represents the only morally acceptable standards for this country flies in the face of our national heritage. This country was founded on the principles of religious freedom and religious tolerance. Thomas Jefferson, who gave us our Declaration of Independence, felt that his Declaration of Religious Freedom, adopted by Virginia, was his greatest achievement."

Jan smirked. "I'll bet that just tickled the members of the Foundation."

"On the contrary," Ann replied while Jan scanned the balance of the article. "The news piece states that he was given a fifteen minute standing O when he was finished."

When Jan put that article down, Ann handed her the next one. "This one, I felt, pretty much summed up his views on social programs and such."

"Don't tell me, he's somewhere to the right of Adolph Hitler and Attila the Hun when it comes to welfare," Jan jokingly asked.

Caught up in her job, Ann missed Jan's effort at humor. "No," she responded flatly. "Quite the contrary. If you didn't know any better, you'd think he was a socialist. Here, listen to this. 'Corporate America has forgotten that its single greatest responsibility is not to its shareholders who seek only monetary gain, but to the people of this country who have made the corporation's very existence possible. The business community has a duty to its employees and the community those employees live in, to preserve and serve this country's two greatest assets, the American worker and their communities.' "

Fascinated by the portrait Ann was creating, Jan raised an eyebrow as she took the copy of the news story. "It sounds as if Mr. Thomas is running for sainthood."

"Perhaps," Ann countered quickly. "Here," she injected as she went through her stack of photocopied pages, "listen to this." When she found the article she was looking for, she pulled it out and started to read. "The political system, as it now exists in the United States, has been corrupted beyond redemption. Neither I, nor any other American with a lick of common sense, can trust our federal government to reform itself or the way it conducts its affairs. In 1796 George Washington, the man who presided over the gathering that wrote the Constitution himself, said, 'The basis of our political system is the right of the people to make and alter their constitutions of government.' While there is a growing chorus of special interest groups who claim that the time has come to do just that, I believe the solution to the problems we face today can be found in the document that has guided this nation through times more troubled than those we now face. Rather than discarding our current Constitution, I believe our salvation lies in returning to its original meanings, as laid out by our founding fathers. Let us stop using that document as an engine for social engineering and instead, employ it as they meant it to be used, as a means of curbing the abuses of government and protecting the freedom of the people."

"Well," Jan remarked as she reached out and snatched the copy of the news story from Ann's hand when she was finished. "While not exactly a popular view, the Governor's statement does not justify initiating a new investigation into his affairs."

"Wait," Ann all but squealed in excitement as she flipped through her stack of photocopied articles. "It gets better." When she found what she was looking for, she pulled it out of the stack, ripping the paper a tad in her haste. "This quote was given to a reporter for a Boise newspaper, the *Idaho Statesman*, during the big to-do over the various militias that were forming in the northwest a few years back. 'With few exceptions, the principles upon which these militias stand are sound and justified. After all, the revolutionary movement that took this nation out of the British Empire and put it on the road to independence was based on militia organizations that were, in concept, little different from some of the better militia groups that have recently sprung up around the nation. Were it not for the manner in which the leaders of these militia movements went about promoting themselves and their beliefs or carrying out their programs, more people, people disenfranchised by the excesses and abuses of the Federal Government, would support them. Eventually, I believe the day will come when a man on a white horse shall come forth and lead this nation through the dark cynicism that pervades our Federal government and lead the American people into a new era of greatness. When that day comes, he may well do so supported upon the bayonets of the militia movement.' "

"Well," Jan commented dryly, "from saint to revolutionary in less than five minutes. Quite a record."

Ann nodded in agreement. "Yes, particularly when you consider that he has done just about everything he admonishes others to do. He likes to describe himself as a force upon the plain. Not only is he hyperactive when it comes to implementing his ideals in the business community and in the politics of his home state, but also in the communities wherever he has a major business concern. It seems there isn't anything that he isn't involved in. The Coalition of Governors for States' Rights and Constitutional Law is an excellent example of his efforts to translate his views and beliefs into action."

"Does that include," Jan asked, half seriously, "fomenting a revolution?"

"Well, that's yet to be determined. But there is something you should be aware of," Ann quickly added.

"What's that?" Jan asked, her mind already working on the possibility of getting portions of her interview on national television.

"Just before he started his campaign for the governorship of Idaho, he made a concerted effort to expand his business holdings in two states in particular."

Pausing, Jan looked at Ann, knowing that her assistant was leading up to something.

"Those states are Kansas, home of the Bob Dole Federal Building and . . ."

Jan lifted her hand to cut her off. "Let me guess. The second state is Wyoming."

Ann's smile was all Jan needed as confirmation.

To protect herself from being accused of misleading a guest she intended to pounce on by being friendly before one of her interviews, Jan made it a rule not to associate with guests beforehand. Even in the last few minutes before the cameras went on, as she sat opposite her guest on the small studio set, Jan busied herself giving directions to staff members waiting in the wings or pretending to study notes she kept on her lap but never used. GO Thomas, however, simply refused to be ignored.

"I would like to take this opportunity, Mrs. Dixon," he stated in a deep, resonating voice, "to thank you for this chance to appear on your show."

Jan looked up at Thomas, surprised at hearing him use Scott's last name and not Fields. As befitting a professional woman Jan used her maiden name at work to demonstrate that she was still an independent entity. "Well," she replied in a halfhearted effort to make light of the compliment, "it was either you or the monkeys from the zoo again."

Thomas chuckled. "I hope it doesn't turn out that you regret not using the monkeys."

Though she was tempted to reply that she hoped he didn't have the same regrets in a few minutes, Jan held her tongue.

"One minute, Ms. Fields," the producer called out. Jan

glanced up at a monitor and saw that a commercial was running over the air. Sitting up, she gave her shoulder length hair a quick toss before staring at the camera as she waited for the red light to flash on.

As if activated by the same impulse, Jan began as soon as her cue illuminated, telling her that her lead-in was over. "Yesterday on this show," she stated without any preamble, "we discussed the investigation into the bombing in April of a Federal building in Kansas, as well as the breaking of the FBI siege in Wyoming last month. Like many of us, our panel of experts on domestic terrorism are concerned that the FBI seems to be no closer to making any arrests in connection with those investigations."

A signal from the director cued Jan that the camera, until now showing only a close up of her, was about to switch to another camera covering a wide view that included both her and GO Thomas. Shifting her gaze from the first camera to the second with impeccable timing, Jan continued without missing a beat. "With us here today is George Oliver Thomas, better known by his friends as GO Thomas and, as of last year, Governor Thomas of Idaho. An outspoken critic of the Federal government, Governor Thomas has made it his life's work to promote states' rights and support groups that advocate radical reform of the Federal government." Taking her eyes away from the oversized camera lens, Jan looked at Thomas, gave him a perfunctory smile, and started right in. "Governor Thomas, thank you for taking time out of your busy schedule and joining us."

Flashing a smile that lit up his boyish good looks, Thomas nodded. "I cannot tell you, Ms. Fields, what an honor it is to be here with you today. I have always been a great fan of yours and an admirer of your husband's achievements."

For a split second Jan was caught off guard. With a nod and a shy smile, one that Ann felt robbed her of the force of her opening, Jan acknowledged Thomas's compliments. Quickly regaining her balance, Jan struggled to get back onto course. "How is it, Governor Thomas," Jan stated pointedly as she leaned over the arm of her chair and looked directly into GO's eyes, "that you, a decorated veteran, a successful entrepreneur, and the governor of Idaho, have become the object of a federal investigation concerning terrorism, and in particular, the bombing of the Bob Dole Building last April?"

Leaning back in his chair, GO Thomas smiled. If he had been caught off guard by Jan's stinging question, his demeanor didn't show it. "As you know, Ms. Fields, since the Clinton years it has become quite fashionable for the President to use Federal agencies to investigate and intimidate his political opponents. The fact of the matter is, were I not the object of at least one Federal probe, I'd worry that I was not being effective."

Despite her best efforts, Jan found herself joining Thomas as he chuckled.

"At heart," he continued, "I am, after all, just an ordinary citizen, exercising his right to make a living, serve his community, and express his opinion as guaranteed by the Constitution. That the Attorney General and the FBI has somehow managed to connect me to mass murderers is astonishing to me."

His use of the term, "mass murderer" while smiling threw Jan. GO Thomas saw this and pressed on. "You see, Ms. Fields, all my life I have done what I believed was right for my country and its people. I chose to serve my nation at a time when doing so was not in vogue. Like your own husband, General Dixon, I rallied around the flag when so many of our peers were doing their damnedest to burn it. I didn't do so just to be different. Rather, I did so because I believed in what it stood for. That," he said with a self-assured smile, "was a decision that I am still quite proud of."

Pausing, GO Thomas relaxed a bit as he leaned back in his seat. "My dedication and commitment to those ideals, Ms. Fields, didn't end with my tour of duty in the Air Force. When I left the service I took the principles of duty, honor, and country that had been drilled into me by my parents and the service into the business world." Dropping his smile, Thomas leaned forward across the arm of his chair and looked Jan straight in the eyes. "And do you want to know something, Ms. Fields? I found that high moral and ethical standards *do* have a place in business."

Sensing that she was losing control of the interview, Jan seized the first question that came to mind. "If that were all you were doing, what would cause the federal government to suspect you of terrorism?"

Thomas paused a moment while he gathered himself, like a fighter preparing to strike out. When he was ready, he allowed himself to ease further back into his seat and resume his innocent smile. "Well, Ms. Fields," he stated quietly as he waved a hand in the air, "the only thing I can conclude is that while exercising my freedom of speech, I have made comments that some folks in government found a bit disquieting. If that, and my habit of upsetting the political establishment by promoting states' rights and local rule are grounds for suspicion, than I suppose I am guilty."

"In the past few years," Jan shot back, "you have been accused of supporting and promoting philosophies that are shared by many right wing militia movements."

For the first time Thomas's face hardened a bit as the ends of his infectious smile turned down a tad. "Ms. Fields," he replied with a noticeable lowering of his voice, "I have fought for this country before and will gladly do so again for no other reason than I happen to love this country. Like your husband, my oath of commission commits me to defend the Constitution of the United States, against all enemies, foreign *and* domestic. While I do not support the methods or some of the radical views held by many of the unorganized militia movements in America today, neither can I turn a deaf ear to the problems about which they, and other responsible Americans, are trying to warn us."

"And those problems are?" Jan asked as she tried to conceal a self-satisfied smile.

With the flood gates thrown open, GO Thomas spent the next ten minutes delineating not only the problems he felt needed to be addressed, but also his views on how best to solve them. He ended his discussion of these issues by bluntly warning that a failure to do so would, in time, lead to a confrontation. "This country stands," he stated as if he were a preacher delivering a moral lesson from the pulpit, "at a crossroad. If wisdom prevails, and leaders with foresight and conviction come forth, we can reform our national institutions from within, painlessly, justly. Otherwise," he warned, "we will face a crisis unlike anything that this nation has been witness to since the War Between the States. Of that," he concluded, "you can be sure."

"And how, Governor," Jan asked as innocently as she could manage, "do you see that happening?"

Thomas gave Jan a kind, fatherly smile. "The same way most revolutions start. A man with a clear vision of the future will ride forth. In his wake the honest, hard working people of this country who have been alienated by a Federal government run by political elites will rally to his standard and follow."

Though tempted, Jan held back from asking the one question that begged to be ask, namely, if George Oliver Thomas, Governor of Idaho, was that man.

CHAPTER 6

When he was given the choice of how he wanted to enjoy his last evening at home before departing for the Infantry Officers' Basic Course at Fort Benning, Nathan Dixon opted for a small, family dinner at home. That their son had selected this option came as no surprise to either Jan or Scott. Having been a cadet himself, Scott understood the desire to seek out and enjoy every opportunity to be with one's family. So Scott made no effort to dissuade his son. On the contrary, he all but applauded the decision. Given their respective careers, both he and Jan leaped at any excuse to skip out early and enjoy a quiet evening at home.

Of course, once the four parties who made up the Dixon household gathered around the table, quiet was all but nonexistent. Nathan and Andrew Dixon had been raised by two strong willed parents who were in the habit of openly exchanging their ideas and views. So it was natural that their boys would grow up feeling that they, too, were free to contribute their own opinions and comments. This resulted in conversations that wandered about without direction ranging from serious discourse on world events to light hearted exposés, to downright ludicrous debates on subjects that were sometimes pointless but always entertaining. Though the occasion was a solemn one, this evening's fare proved to be no different.

"It's just been incredible," Jan kept repeating as she served up a steaming bowl of pasta shells covered with thick, spicy tomato sauce. "It's like someone turned on a light in a room full of cockroaches. Everyone's just scattering for cover."

Nathan, the author of that evening's ample, if simple,

dinner, looked over. By way of response, Scott rolled his eyes. "Mom," Nathan asked plaintively, "could we skip using any analogies that include cockroaches until *after* supper?"

Before Jan could reply, Scott added, "*Well* after, if you don't mind. And only if I'm not in the room."

Jan, caught up in her own excitement, looked quizzically at Nathan, then Scott. "Oh, well," she finally replied, "I had forgotten how squeamish you big manly men are about such things."

Nathan growled. "Being faint hearted has nothing to do with it, Mom. It's just that I've been enjoying a break from having to share my dinner with those ancient orthopterons."

"Prehistoric, Nathan," Scott corrected his son, as he had done so often during his life. "I believe it is more correct to consider them to be prehistoric. Ancient is normally associated with the period that begins with the early Egyptian kingdoms and ends with the fall of the Western Roman Empire."

Amused, Jan looked at the two of them, then at their second son, who was busy spooning heaps of sauce covered shells onto his plate. "Aren't you going to wade into this debate?"

Not bothering to look up as he scooped out another helping of pasta, Andrew shook his head. "I'd be a fool to go up against those two. They're a combined arms team now. Everyone knows you can't beat Armor and Infantry when they're cooperating."

Jan laughed, ignoring Scott and Nathan, who were now actively debating the age of the aforementioned insect. "We don't have to worry about that, now, do we. After all, when was the last time you saw those two cooperating?"

"I heard that," Scott snapped as he glanced over to Jan. "That's going to cost you."

Jan smiled sweetly. "Well, if you persist in continuing this ridiculous discussion, it's going to cost you your dinner."

Looking over at Nathan, who had turned his attention

to prying the bowl of pasta shells from his brother's grip, Scott noticed that it was already half empty. "Hey, hey, there, lieutenant," he shouted as if he were on a parade ground. "There are other people waiting to eat here. Let's not forget that this isn't a mess hall."

Nathan looked up at Scott, and then Jan. "But Dad, sir," he replied jokingly. "Andy and I are doing you and Mom a favor. After all, it's a well established fact that as people grow older, their metabolism slows down. Since you're unable to burn off one hundred and thirty fewer calories per day with each passing year, you both face the danger of an increase in girth if caloric intake is not diminished appropriately."

Jan laid her hand on Scott's arm. "Scott, dear. I think we've just been counseled."

"Counseled," Scott snapped as he looked at Nathan. "I'll counsel you later, boy." Then, with a grin, he added, "but not until after you pass me that bowl of pasta."

Nathan sat up straight in his chair and pulled his chin in until there were wrinkles of skin showing before he pushed the pasta shells across the table to Scott. "Yes, sir, General, sir. Right away, sir."

With a nod, Scott smiled. "Ah, now that's more like it, lieutenant." Turning to Jan, he flashed the boyish smile that Jan had fallen in love with so many years before. "Now, dear, you were saying."

"Well," Jan started, but not before giving Nathan a wink, "as I was *trying* to say, since my interview with Governor Thomas, everyone in Washington is running around like headless chickens."

"Oh, great," Nathan moaned. "From nasty, disgusting insects to freshly decapitated poultry. Gee, I can't wait to hear what our discussion over dessert is going to be."

"You hush," Jan snarled as she gave her stepson a gentle tap on the arm, "or there'll be no dessert for you." Then she turned her attention back to Scott, who was more interested in scraping a little extra sauce from the bowl than in what his wife was saying. "As I was saying," Jan continued, "everyone connected with the investigation of GO Thomas and the administration is busy seeking cover."

Looking up from his plate, Nathan smiled. "Everyone, that is, except you, Mom. I've seen your face on the news every half hour, on the half hour."

This caused Jan to smile. Yes, she thought to herself, this one story had managed to catapult her back into the national spotlight for the moment. It had, in the twinkling of an eye, brought her an offer from her old boss at World News Network back in Washington, D.C., to go up to Boise and head the team they were sending out into what he referred to as fly over country.

"You're the perfect person for this one, Jan," he told her over the phone. "You're now seen as a westerner, so you have that perspective down pat. You're also nationally known, so you've got instant credibility. Besides, I think this Thomas guy likes you."

That GO Thomas had been more than accommodating to her throughout the fifteen minute interview was noted by everyone who reviewed the tape. There was even some talk by those who were now her competition that she and Thomas had scripted the entire event. Were it not for her impeccable reputation for integrity, much of what transpired in the studio of a local Denver TV station would never have drawn the national attention her piece was still commanding.

Of course, none of those who were trying desperately to explain away Jan's extraordinary interview with GO Thomas suspected the real reason this man of great wealth and power had catered so readily to a TV personality. Only a handful of people within GO's own inner circle knew of his weakness for independent, tough-minded women. To GO, Jan was as close to his ideal woman as he could imagine. She was determined without being pushy. Confident, yet lacking all appearance of arrogance. Beautiful, yet approachable, almost longing to be touched. That she was happily married didn't much matter to a man who reminded all around him of his own peculiar spin on the teachings of their Savior, Jesus Christ. "Forgiveness without sin," he liked to explain after failing to meet his own high standards, "is meaningless."

From across the table, Scott took note of the distant look

in Jan's eyes. Though it was both fleeting and totally missed by his sons, Scott could tell she was up to something. That it involved her work was certain. Once presented with an opportunity, Jan was transformed into a zealot of the worst kind. She would not be able to let go of the issue at hand until she had dealt with it in the thorough, professional manner for which she was noted. Until that time Scott knew it was best just to leave her alone.

Instead, he turned his attention back to his meal. He never did much like the military wives who pined at home while their husbands were away or made busywork for themselves by intruding into the lives of other military families or their community. Whatever this new crusade of hers was, Scott knew it would be good for her.

Besides, Scott saw a chance to benefit from Jan's new crusade. With a commander's conference coming up in a few months he needed to decide on a topic that was both relevant and thought provoking. The issue of domestic violence, so long a concern for traditional law enforcement agencies, had been almost totally ignored by the Army. It was time, Scott thought as he toyed with the pile of pasta shells on his plate, to do what he could to change that. For Scott, like Jan, relished the challenge of taking on issues that conventional wisdom endeavored to avoid.

When dinner was finished, Scott rose from the table. Without a word, he gave Jan a nod that Nathan took to be a prearranged signal. Jan smiled. Turning to Nathan and Andrew, he invited his two sons to join him in the den. Both boys looked at each other. When their father was out of earshot Andrew leaned over and whispered to his brother, "Looks like another Dad lecture." Knowing that he would be the subject of whatever topic his father was about to launch into, Nathan said nothing as he stood to follow Scott.

Once the three Dixon men were seated in the den, Scott looked down at his oldest son and smiled. "Nathan," he stated in a friendly, conversational tone, "you can relax. There'll be no Dad lectures tonight." Both boys let out a short, nervous laugh. "Nor will I burden you with any more pearls of wisdom. God knows you'll soon have more than enough of those heaped upon you at wonderful Fort Benning." This time, only Nathan chuckled.

Then Scott's expression changed. Turning, he walked over to the mantel of the room's brick fireplace. Reaching up, he grasped the ancient Scottish broadsword that had been in the Dixon family for generations. Bringing the sword up almost against his chest, Scott slowly came back around, faced his sons, and took two steps until he was in front of Nathan. In a solemn tone, Scott recounted the history of that weapon, and its significance to them. "It's hard to say with certainty," Scott started slowly as he looked at the sword he held, "how long this sword has been in our family. When Ian McPherson, the first of our line to come to this country in the late 1740s, wrote of this sword, he referred to it as ancient. His grandfather, who had used it in the Scottish rebellions of 1715 and 1719, gave it to Ian at age fourteen when he left home to fight for the Stewarts in 1745. He used it to good effect, he claimed, at Culloden. Ian brought the sword to America where he carried it during both the French and Indian War and the Revolution. Upon his passing the sword was claimed by his oldest son, who carried it through the balance of the Revolution and wore it, if his account is to be believed, at Yorktown in 1781."

Scott paused, looked over at Andrew, then back to Nathan. "Since then this sword has been passed on from generation to generation. Over the years it became less and less a weapon and more and more a symbol for the members of our family. When Patrick McPherson died in Cuba in 1898 without a son the sword went to his daughter, Sarah McPherson-Dixon. And though she was a woman, she served as best she could as a nurse with the AEF in the First World War. She kept the tradition alive by seeing to it that her oldest son, my grandfather, was given the sword at the appropriate time. As she did so she told him that she hoped that he would never have to take it up in the defense of our nation. She told him she had not raised him to become a soldier. But she reminded my grandfather

that neither had her ancestors. Tied to their adopted home-
land and possessing a dedication to duty that the Mc-
Phersons and Dixons could never seem to ignore always
compelled them to take up the sword in the nation's time
of need. When my father was given this sword his mother
reminded him that freedom was a strange gift, one that
required the recipient to risk everything from time to time
if he hoped to keep it. It was because there has always
been a McPherson or Dixon willing to do so that we are
free."

Pausing, Scott looked down at the sword, lifting it ever
so slightly as if he were inspecting it from hilt to tip. Then,
his haunting gaze fell upon his son. "It is time for me to
pass this on," Scott said as he held the sword before Nathan.

For a moment, Nathan looked down at the gift he was
being offered. The pitted piece of steel before him had
been made ages ago by Highland craftsmen unconcerned
with ornamentation but with a keen eye for utility and
strength. It lacked any hint of frills or thoughtless flour-
ishes. Yet it was a religious icon to his father. One of the
worst beatings Nathan had ever received as a child was
the day he and a friend had taken the sword down from
its coveted perch and dragged it out into the yard to play
army. Throughout the years, he had endured, at regular
intervals, lectures on the significance of the sword. And
now that sword, held before his eyes like an offering from
the heavens above, was being passed on to him.

Across the room Andrew watched in relief. Like Nathan,
he had been subjected to the numerous "talks" on family
traditions, duty to one's nation, etc, etc, etc. He fancied,
as he sat there listening and watching, that he knew it all
by heart and imagined Nathan did, too. Yet there was a
difference between his view of that sword that did much
to define the difference between the brothers. Whereas the
stories behind the sword's history fascinated Nathan and,
in no small way, served to drive him toward his chosen
career, Andrew had always viewed the sword and the occasional lecture that went with it as little more than part
of being a member of this particular family. "Some fami-

lies," he once told Jan in confidence, "have legendary characters held up to them to be revered. Others brag about notable figures. The Dixons, well, we have Dad's rusty old sword, a worthless heirloom that couldn't even open a can of tuna."

While Jan had laughed at the remark, she had understood its meaning. Though he loved his father, Andrew wanted nothing to do with the Army. Whenever the subject came up he was fond of saying that he had devoted enough of his life following the flag, just as Jan had since her marriage to Scott. Andrew had no intention of continuing the practice. So it was with great sense of relief that his older brother, Nathan, was being anointed by their father, as a true believer worthy enough to receive the McPherson sword. Equally pleasing to Andrew was that his brother accepted both the weapon and the role as the defender of the faith and the keeper of the family's traditions.

Only after great reflection did Nathan take the sword from his father's hand. When it had passed from father to son, the son held it at arm's length, looking at it as if he were viewing it for the first time. In truth he was seeing this symbol with new eyes as he felt the power and the weight of the lineage that this sword carried as he never had before. When Nathan finally looked up at Scott, the son smiled. "I really don't know what to say," he stammered.

Scott said nothing as he looked into his son's eyes and prayed, deep in his soul, that the day would not come when this child would ever have to pay the ultimate price that his choice of vocation might demand. He prayed that some day, years from now when he was gone, Nathan would have the opportunity to pass the sword on to a son of his own.

POCATELLO, IDAHO · JULY 7

While the Dixon clan was reflecting upon their duties, others were preparing to fulfill theirs.

From their van two men watched the front of the gun shop that sat cattycorner from them. Sweating, as much from his nervousness as the heat, Special Agent Tim Werner squirmed about in his seat. He toyed with the idea of removing the windbreaker he was wearing. But every time he was on the verge of doing so, Werner would drop that idea. While it was bad enough that their muted red delivery truck literally stuck out like a sore thumb, the sight of one of its occupants dressed in a bulletproof vest would have made their identity and purpose even more obvious. Of course, the idea that they could sit parked on the street as they were for as long as they had without being noticed was laughable. Yet Werner and his partner, Albert Zimmerman, weren't laughing.

With darkness falling and traffic in this part of town trailing off, without any sign that the owner of the gun shop was about to appear, the likeliness that their stakeout had been compromised was becoming all but impossible to deny. Given the background of the individual they were waiting to arrest, and the incident in Wyoming two months prior, the two agents in the van knew that anything could happen.

As the special agent in charge of the Boise field office, Tim Werner had tactical command of this operation. Nervously he looked at his watch. "Five minutes," he announced. "We wait another five minutes. Then we go in."

Without comment, Special Agent Albert Zimmerman looked at Werner, then back at the door of the shop that was clearly displaying the "Closed" sign. Without making any effort to hide his actions, Zimmerman lifted a small radio to his mouth. "Stand by," he announced. "We go in five. Repeat, we go in five."

Like the other agents scattered about the area waiting for the shop owner to emerge, both Werner and Zimmerman had misgivings about the arrest they were about to make. Until the previous afternoon John Doherty had been only one of a dozen suspects that the Boise field office had been keeping tabs on as part of the investigation concerning the militia attack in Wyoming. With all the patience of a general preparing for battle, Werner had built his case against them slowly, methodically. Though he was as anxious to nail the bastards who had gunned down his fellow agents as anyone else, Werner was a chess player who appreciated the value of planning, preparation, and timing. When the trail of the Wyoming killers led to Idaho, Werner and his agents began the meticulous task of marshaling evidence against the suspects, monitoring their movements, and keeping track of who they met. In this way the number of people Werner's agents had been able to link to the Wyoming affair had doubled. It was Werner's hope that given the time, he would be able to piece together the entire puzzle and deliver them all up as a package and crush the organization that supported them.

His systematic and meticulous investigation, however, had been brought to a screeching halt the previous day by a phone call from the head of the Bureau itself. In a rather one-sided conversation, he explained to Werner that a number of people in the Justice Department had been spooked by Jan Fields's interview with the governor of Idaho. It was felt that if a simple reporter in Denver could dig up enough information about ongoing investigations to make that sort of connection, then the work of Werner's office and other task forces across the nation was in danger. Rather than watch their suspects scatter and go to ground, a decision was made to pick up those they had a case against and work from there.

While logical, the snap decision made in Washington, D.C., left precious little time for the agents in the field to organize themselves. It gave them even less time to coordinate with state and local law enforcement agencies. This last part was a particularly thorny issue for Tim Werner since he had done nothing to apprise his counterparts in Idaho of his activities. He felt the risk of compromising his investigation had been too great to do so. This assessment was driven home when one of the initial suspects turned out to be the son of a senior state police official. That they had discovered this before asking for assistance caused Werner and every agent involved in the investigation to breathe a collective sigh of relief.

Now, however, as Werner sat in the van watching the

minute hand of his watch race to the appointed time, he was having second thoughts. There would be hell to pay when the head of the Idaho state police found out after the fact that the FBI had been conducting a major investigation on his turf without being informed. Years of goodwill and close cooperation would be swept away. But it was too late to worry about such things, Werner told himself. Nor was that the most pressing concern he had on his mind at that moment as he glanced up at the gun shop.

John Doherty, and the gun store he ran, had come under surveillance after three of the Wyoming suspects had been observed frequenting the shop. Added to Werner's growing list of targets, it was quickly discovered that Doherty, a former Navy SEAL, was a member of the same militia group that all of the Wyoming suspects belonged to. With the cooperation of the ATF and the FBI's center in West Virginia, Werner was able to obtain a listing of the shop's inventory. This listing quickly showed that a large number of weapons in Doherty's shop had no place in a recreational hunter's gun safe. "There are national liberation organizations," Albert Zimmerman mused after seeing the inventory, "that would cream their jeans if they had an arsenal like this." While no direct connection had yet been established between Doherty, weapons he sold, and the Wyoming raid, Tim Werner was convinced that it was only a matter of time before his people would come across something that would tie them together.

Even with the prospect of putting his hands on some of those weapons looming before him, Werner was beginning to have second thoughts about storming the gun shop. It had been over an hour and a half since they had seen a hand flip the sign in the window over from "Open" to "Closed." In four weeks of surveillance, without fail Doherty had emerged within thirty minutes of that, making this suddenly change in routine ominous.

Glancing over at his superior, Special Agent Zimmerman couldn't help but notice the concern that creased Tim Werner's face. "Why don't we back off here," he suggested, "and have the team at his home pick him up?"

Werner looked over at his fellow agent, but said nothing. They had gone over all their options the night before when they had been planning the arrest. Since they were dealing with a felon suspected of being armed and dangerous establishing the possibility that there could be gunfire, Werner had made the decision to take Doherty in the commercial district where an inordinate number of strangers would not be noticed and at a time when there would be few civilians around. The plan, as envisioned then, called for Doherty to be apprehended after he had left his shop, locked the door, and was alone on the street with nothing more than the 9mm automatic pistol he carried. "Even if he does make an effort to resist," Werner had stated, "he'll be outgunned and in a position where the chances of collateral damage will be all but nonexistent."

Over the handheld radio that Zimmerman held, agents stationed around the store began to check in as the deadline expired. Rather than answering, Zimmerman continued to stare at Werner. "Well?"

Convinced that his reasoning for making the arrest here, away from the active neighborhood where Doherty lived with his wife and three children, was still sound, Werner shook his head. "We're going in," he announced. "Pass the word."

Though he disagreed, Zimmerman didn't hesitate. Even as he reached over to open his door, he mashed down on the push-to-talk button of the radio. "We're going in."

From vehicles and alleyways eight FBI agents sprang into action. Among them they had enough weaponry to take on a small army. Moving swiftly, they took up positions that covered every known exit from the gun store. Only after all teams had reported in that they were set did Tim Werner lift the bullhorn he held and call out from behind the front of the van he had been waiting in. "John Doherty, this is the FBI. Come out with your hands on your head."

For several anxious moments the agents surrounding the shop held their breath as they waited for Doherty to emerge. When he failed to materialize, Werner repeated his demand. "John Doherty, we have you surrounded.

There is no escape. Come out slowly with your hands on your head."

Again there was no visible response. As the seconds grew into one minute, and then two, Werner's fear that he had blundered by pressing this action grew.

Next to him Albert Zimmerman was becoming unnerved by the lack of response from the store. "He isn't in there," Zimmerman stated as he continued to aim his shotgun at the door of the shop. "The bastard has given us the slip."

Too committed to back off or admit defeat, Werner shook his head. "No, he's there. He's just waiting for us to come after him."

Turning, Zimmerman shouted, "He's not there, damn it. We blew it!"

Angered as much by the possibility that he had screwed up as by Doherty's refusal to come out, Werner grabbed the radio out of Zimmerman's pocket. "French," he called over the radio, "fire a round of gas into the shop."

While Special agent Ellen French gave Werner a "Wilco" and prepared to fire a canister of CS gas through a rear window of the store, Zimmerman glared at Werner. "You're making a big mistake, Tim," he warned.

"We have our orders," Werner snapped.

"Isn't that what the Nazis kept claiming at Nuremberg?" Zimmerman countered.

Already unnerved by the turn of events, Werner wasn't in the mood for arguments. "Shut up," he commanded, "and cover the front door."

Without another word Zimmerman complied. Together he and Tim Werner watched the front of the building for any sign of Doherty. For fifteen minutes they watched and waited. They waited when the smoke detectors broke the early evening silence as the CS began to fill the building. They watched as a faint orange glow appeared on the other side of the store door. They were still there, with their weapons held at the ready, as the first fire engine came thundering down the street in response to the automatic alarm that had been tripped by the growing fire.

By then even Tim Werner was convinced that their suspect had somehow managed to elude them. Yet, he dare not take any chances. With the history of members of militia units displaying behavior that was both irrational and unpredictable, Special Agent Werner could not risk that John Doherty was still in there, ready to die for his beliefs. Having already made too many miscalculations that night, Tim Werner was unprepared to make any more. Leaving one man to cover each of the exits, he quickly mustered the bulk of his task force on the main street well away from the front of the shop. There, they waved down the approaching fire engines and, to the surprise and shock of the firefighters, held them back.

While local officials bitterly argued with Werner and his agents, the gun shop erupted into flames. Above the pop-pop-pop of small arms ammunition going off, bystanders, drawn to the scene, could hear oaths and curses being exchanged between local officials hell bent on doing their jobs and federal officials equally determined to keep them at arm's length until they were sure that there was no longer any danger to them.

Among this growing crowd of on lookers stood two men. Both wore dark glasses and baseball caps pulled down low. "I'm going to miss that place," John Doherty stated dryly as he watched the flames from his store leap over the space between it and the building next to it.

Sporting a grin, his companion slapped him on the back. "I've got the feeling our friends in the Justice Department aren't going to give you the chance to miss it."

Looking over at Thomas Jefferson Osborn, Doherty nodded. "No, I guess not. Now, if you don't mind, I'll take you up on your offer of a beer. Odds are, it will be the last one I'll be enjoying for a while."

Osborn shook his head as the light of the flames lit his toothy grin. "Why of course, John, of course. Anything," he added, "for a patriot."

CHAPTER 7

Each day started pretty much the same way. George Oliver Thomas would awaken from his slumber long before the NPR hourly news began to blare from the clock radio that sat on his nightstand. No one rushed into his room to deliver his morning paper or coffee. No one crept about while he slept to lay out his wardrobe for the day. As he had since he was a child of five, he got out of bed, staggered into the bathroom, washed his face, brushed his teeth, and dressed himself.

Even when he emerged from his bedroom suite, his staff kept their distance. Only when he was entertaining an idea that wouldn't keep or had heard something on the radio show he wanted more information on would he summon an assistant. Even then, GO Thomas suffered the presence of this person only long enough to pass on whatever information he wished to be acted upon while he was exercising.

When he entered the country kitchen of the governor's mansion there was no cook standing by, ready to prepare whatever GO asked for. He saw no need for one that early. As was his habit, he poked around the neatly organized, well stocked cabinets until he found something that appealed to him. Usually it was a packet of instant apple-cinnamon oatmeal or some simple boxed cereal. With a banana and a tall glass of orange juice, this passed for his breakfast. While quite mundane and terribly repetitious, Thomas found this quiet, almost ceremonial opening of his day to be relaxing and, in a strange way, reassuring. To him it was a constant in a world where so much changed so fast. It gave him a sense that while he had been asleep and out of touch with the rest of mankind for six hours, the world he knew was still there, waiting patiently for him.

It was only now that variations were allowed to intrude on his morning routine. If his mind was fired up by a new idea or if a solution to a problem was right there, all formatted and packaged in his mind, GO would leave the kitchen and head for the part of the house that served as his personal office. Passing through an otherwise innocuous door that appeared no different from any other one in his personal residence, GO Thomas would step from his secluded domestic world into the heart of a state's government.

Yet even here, the decor and the appearance of the people manning this small office didn't come close to reflecting what popular culture and business practices of the day dictated. Instead of establishing an air of formality, aloofness, and authority that bordered on the impersonal, GO Thomas's personal office had all the quaintness of a living room. To many entering this place for the first time the tranquil, disarming sense that such a setting evoked was unsettling.

On other days, when there was nothing that demanded his immediate attention, Thomas would leave his kitchen and head for the rear door. There, in a small anteroom, he would slip on the appropriate footwear, select whatever outerwear he would need to brave the weather, and head off into the early morning air. A short walk took him to a public park.

Were this a few years earlier, GO Thomas would have broken out into a slow, steady run that he would maintain as he wound his way along the well manicured gravel paths of the park. Age and premature wear and tear on his body, however, prevented him from doing so. GO had weak ankles. While they were not bad enough to be considered crippling, they served to remind him that he was getting on in years and that his body was beginning to serve notice that it was time to slow down a bit. Still, GO did not give in completely. He walked at a brisk pace until he felt sufficiently limber. Normally, this was at the one mile mark at the far end of the park just before the trail looped around and began to wind its way back. Here, if all was going well, GO would break into a slow, deliberate jog. His goal was always to keep running until he reached his start point a mile away. Sometimes, when he was well rested and felt razor sharp, he made it. Of late, however, he didn't. Not only were fifty-two years of hard work, service to his country, and commitment to his community taking their toll, but the concerns of the state of his beloved country weighed heavily upon him.

Regardless of his pace, he often used his time alone in the park to look back on where he had been, what he had achieved, or where he was headed. The state troopers detailed to accompany the governor knew enough to keep their distance while, at the same time, remaining close enough to intervene should there be any attempt made on his life.

By any measure his life had already been a full one, though not exactly the one he had originally set out to live. Like all baby boomers, George Oliver Thomas found the society that he lived in bore no resemblance the one that had raised him. Little of his childhood world seemed to have survived the years. Even in Idaho he had watched the world of his father slowly peeled away like an onion, layer by layer, until nothing of substance seemed to be left. Whether it was the nightly images of napalm consuming the lush green landscape of Southeast Asia or the faces of angry black youths rampaging through their own neighborhoods, the visions that flashed before GO's young eyes when he was still a teen had left deep impressions on him that guided his every step. Those remote yet very frightening views of his world, together with the specter of his peers holding their own academic institutions hostage while revolutionaries like Che Guevara worked to bring third world countries into communism's loving fold, left little room for complacency.

That his generation would be called upon to fulfill some greater purpose as his father's had been was expected and anticipated. But unlike the men who had marched off in the forties to fight foreign dictators who were inherently evil, GO Thomas and his peers faced issues that were not as black and white. Theirs was a complex world, a world that seemed to be spinning out of control. They inherited a society that possessed no strong leader or great cause powerful enough to pull them together. Instead, each was left to thrash about in search of a cause that he or she could believe in. Everyone of GO Thomas's generation had to pick which path they would travel in an environment of racial, political, and social upheaval. They had begun their adult lives at a time when they could only comprehend black and white. Even now, as GO tucked his chin down and broke into a slow trot, he saw that there had been no easy choice, no way of knowing what was truly right. In the end, they had all followed the path on which their feet had already been well planted. In the end, they carried on, as best they could, the American traditions that fitted their particular personality and circumstances.

For GO it was college, the Air Force, and, ultimately, his father's business in Idaho. He didn't have to go to Vietnam as every one of his flight instructors and squadron commanders had. He escaped the trauma of having the stench of burnt human flesh branded in his memory until the First Gulf War.

But that brief experience had been more than enough. It had been a wake-up call, one that served to rock him from the long slumber he, and so many of his fellow Americans, had fallen into. In the late seventies, GO had left the Air Force just in time to partake in the unprecedented prosperity of the eighties. Using his father's Idaho business as a base, he created a network of franchises which were unrelated and wholly unimpressive when viewed from Wall Street. From three furniture stores and two gun shops located in Boise, Twin Falls, and Pocatello, GO Thomas built himself an empire based upon these franchises as well as several small scale manufacturing ventures. There had been no grand, guiding plan that drove this expansion. The only thing unifying GO Thomas's sprawling business concerns was Thomas himself and his personal ethics, ethics that included a belief in the supremacy and sanctity of the community, the church, and the United States of America. "The community is the heart and lifeblood of our nation," he personally admonished each of his senior business managers. "The church is the soul and conscience of the community. And America is a quilt upon which each community is attached, patch like, to all the other communities to form one complete nation, stretching from coast to coast, unified and interconnected. Every patch, each community must be cared for in order to ensure the future and well being of all."

It was only in the wake of the First Gulf War, where GO had served proudly with his Air Force Reserve A-10 squadron, that he came to the understanding that his view of the world was not shared by his fellow corporate chairmen. The global economy, embraced by so many American business leaders and politicians, frightened GO. He saw his beloved Idaho, a state he had worked so hard to protect from the ravages of a cut and slash economic boom, threatened by forces that he abhorred. Though his exploitation of the information age permitted him to run his vast and varied business concerns from the comforts of Idaho, the wild west atmosphere of cyberspace and borderless business world that it made possible loomed as a great, faceless threat in GO Thomas's psyche. "It is a boogie man to me," he confided to Fran Merkawitz, his personal assistant. "The new world into which we are so rapidly rushing is like the darkness under a child's bed. Though the child is told that he has nothing to be afraid of, he still lives in fear every night because the child sees and feels things that his parents can't."

As Thomas pushed himself in a vain effort to eke out a few more yards, he could almost feel the nagging doubts that he harbored over the future of his country. Unable to go on, he slowed and lapsed into an easy walk. For several minutes he ambled on, staring up into the cloudless morning sky as fat beads of sweat formed on his forehead before starting their downward race along the sides of his face. A few made their way down through his thick blond brows until they were stinging his brown eyes. Exhausted from his vain effort to beat one mile's worth of track, GO wiped the sweat from his eyes. With a shake of his head, he looked about, enjoying the last few moments of solitary peace he would have until he closed his bedroom door some time around ten P.M. that night.

What little joy he derived from his run on this late summer morning was further diminished by the prospect of the coming day. This would be the day when a Federal judge in Boise would hear arguments concerning a change in venue for the militiamen accused of planning and executing the May raid against the FBI in Wyoming. Though it was clearly a Federal case, the manner in which the FBI and the Justice Department had conducted its investigation of the men, their arrests, and their prosecution to date was considered an affront to many in Idaho. From the state's Attorney General, to the average citizen, there had been ceaseless cries of outrage over the incident. This was particularly true in Pocatello, where a fire started by the FBI during one of their arrests had resulted in the loss of an entire city block.

Thus far Thomas had been able to stay clear of the fracas, save for an occasional speech in which he condemned the FBI and the Justice Department. Under his state's constitution and Federal law, there was nothing he could do other than use the incident as political capital. How long this "hands off" policy would last depended on where the defendants were to be tried. Polls in Idaho showed that an overwhelming majorty of the people wanted to see the trial held in Boise, where the men could be judged, according to one radio talk show host, by their peers. Montana, while not quite home, came in a close second.

Those cities were not where the U.S. Attorney General wanted to see the trial held. Her preferences were San Francisco, home of the Ninth Circuit, or Seattle. Either would provide a jury pool that would be more sympathetic to the Federal government's case. When word of this made its way into the media, Governor Thomas was put on notice by many who had supported him in the past that such a decision, unopposed by him, would not sit well with them. His own Attorney General was quick to remind Thomas that his failure to make a stand would be politically disastrous. "When it comes to state's rights and an overly intrusive Federal government," the State Attorney General pointed out, "you've talked a good case. Now it's time to pony up."

What his Attorney General expected him to do was beyond him. Stopping at the end of the track, GO looked up into the pale blue sky. Closing his eyes, he took in a deep breath and held it. The weather was changing, he told himself. The warm, easy days of summer were coming to an end. All he had to look forward to was a long, cold season of storms and dark, gray days. Opening his eyes, Thomas exhaled. Something would come to him, he told himself as he marched back to the governor's mansion. This was not the first storm he faced, he reminded himself. Faith in himself, and his acute sense of timing when it came to seizing an opportunity, had always come through for him before. He was confident that this crisis, if it came to that, would be no different.

For the army of journalists, TV crews, and reporters who had descended upon Boise, the lack of activity by the state's outspoken governor and the delay in making a decision concerning where the trial of the Idaho Six would be held was intolerable. "I can't understand it," Jan complained to Scott in one of her nightly calls to him. "For the briefest of moments Boise, Idaho, the Potato Capital of the world, has the nation's full and undivided attention. And yet no one, not even the county sheriff, is willing to take advantage of all this free publicity."

"Did you ever think," Scott asked innocently over the phone, "that perhaps folks up there just aren't into having their business splattered over every TV screen?"

"Well, I don't know what the hesitation is, but the lack of a story is starting to make most of the journalists up here cynical."

Seeing an opening, Scott blurted out, "Gee, I didn't know there was a difference between an ordinary journalist and a wee bit cynical one."

With nothing concerning the investigation to report on and Thomas keeping his own counsel, the gathering of journalists was doing what journalists and commentators do when there's no real news to report; they began to interview each other or wander about, generating stories. One news team from Atlanta found it charming that GO Thomas's staff occasionally followed their noon news briefing with a free barbecue picnic in a nearby park. The Governor himself, though reluctant to make any firm statements concerning the Federal government's handling of the case involving the militiamen, was more than willing to demonstrate his skills as a chef and host.

This did not mean that there was nothing going on. While the people of Idaho went about their daily routine, officials and civic leaders on both sides of the issue were busy behind closed doors. On the fourth floor of the First Interstate Bank in Boise, the FBI was hard at work. There Tim Werner and his special task force were trying to patch together a case in a state where cooperation, at all levels, had all but evaporated. At the Federal Courthouse on the east side of town, Federal prosecutors and members of the Justice Department based in Boise worked and reworked their case for a change in venue against their better judgment. Like the governor of the state in which those men and women lived, they used every trick in the book as they procrastinated in the hope that something would come up and save them from having to make a decision that they knew would generate a firestorm. In the governor's mansion Thomas's staff held meeting after meeting with groups from across the state as well as representatives of states where governors dedicated to GO's states' right movement held sway, trying to find out who they could depend upon if the courts decided to move the trial and the governor took action to prevent it. And in the dens and living rooms of private citizens, concerned patriots gathered to make their plans.

Finished counting the cases of caliber .50 four-in-one linked armor piercing machine gun ammunition, Nancy Kozak decided it was a good time to take a break. Those on her detail addicted to the habit were dying for a cigarette break. Releasing them with a curt "Take ten," she waited until they had scampered outside before allowing herself to relax. Spotting two short stacks of crated 5.56mm ball ammunition left haphazardly in the center of the floor, Nancy wandered over to them. Placing her clipboard on the taller of the two, she used the second stack, consisting of two crates, as a seat. Leaning forward, she placed her hands on her knees, and closed her eyes. Taking in a deep breath, she drew in a lungful of stale bunker air and held it for a moment. The simple knowledge that she was surrounded by tons of crated small arms ammunition, together with the feel of her lightly starched BDUs and the odors of the bunker brought back memories. In a world where duty, honor, and country were little more than words, she found herself longing for the days when she had lived and worked with men and women who had dedicated their lives to those principles.

It had taken her a long time to come to the realization that she had made a mistake in leaving the service. What had been sound, reasonable arguments for resigning her commission then now seemed to her well-ordered mind little more than excuses to escape a terrible dilemma she had found herself in. Opening her eyes for a second, she looked down at her left hand.

Of all her mistakes, it was the absence of a ring on her fourth finger that she found herself dwelling on more and more. Her failure to aggressively pursue a soul mate had never bothered her much before. At age twenty-two, when she had accepted her commission as a second lieutenant in the United States Army, marriage was the least of her concerns or interests. Becoming a first rate officer and launching a career in the armed forces were all that she cared about then. Marriage, if anything, would have been a detriment to her dreams and ambitions.

That's not to say that Nancy Kozak lived a celibate life. During her years on active duty she had met more than a few fellow officers who were, to her, both appealing and available. Some found that they shared this attraction, leading to everything from casual affairs that provided little more than physical enjoyment to a few that almost went the distance. But in the end things never seemed to work out. Twice the transfer of one or the other to a new posting sounded the death knell of what could have been a wonderful, long term relationship. Once, Nancy's promotion below the zone well ahead of her year group soured an otherwise eager beau.

Drawing in a deep breath, Nancy looked up at the crude concrete ceiling of the ammo bunker in an effort to keep a tear of self-pity from streaking down her cheek. As difficult as it had been for her to maintain a steady relationship with a man while in the service, she found that it was near impossible on the outside. In all her wildest fantasies, she had never stopped to consider that most men were intimidated by her. While it was true that she could dress down an errant subordinate with the best of her male counterparts, it was equally true that she could be friendly, understanding, and rather compassionate. None of those qualities, however, were given a second look by a date as soon as they found out that she had been an officer in the Army. A few of her male friends tried valiantly to ignore this side of Nancy Kozak's character. Few, however, were able to forget that she was a woman whose views were, as one uncharitable bastard once pointed out, "more macho than John Wayne in his prime."

Looking around once again, Nancy studied the silent boxes of ammunition and explosives sitting patiently in this bunker, awaiting the day when they would be issued out for use in a training exercise. Her life, she thought as she wiped her eyes, was pretty much like that. Without a career or a mate to help her along, she was waiting, waiting for someone, or something, to come along and save her from her own, self-imposed limbo.

From behind her the voices of the soldiers who were assigned to assist in the inventory could be heard as they came through the open door of the bunker. Specialist Chester West, with a booming voice and western drawl, dominated. As was his habit, West was working hard to convince another of the party that he was right. "There simply is no way in hell, I tell you," he thundered over his shoulder as he came through the door, "that the FBI, the CIA, or the Secret Service are going to find anything on our boys. T'ain't no way, I say."

The object of this verbal barrage, Private David Tillman, followed West through the door with head bowed and shoulders slumped forward. "All I said," Tillman offered in his own defense, "was that things don't look too good for the six militiamen."

"Well," West countered as he came up to where Nancy now stood, "it would be one hell of a serious mistake to count them down and out while GO's in the governor's mansion."

Behind their two companions came the rest of the detail. Staff Sergeant William Lightfoot, the NCO in charge of the others, ambled in using the slow yet purposeful manner with which he did everything. His no-nonsense approach, a trait of his Nez Perce ancestry, made working with him a pleasure and earned him the nickname "Chief." Following in Lightfoot's shadow was the fourth member of the detail, Specialist Fran Meranno. Better known to everyone in her National Guard unit as "The Mouse," Fran Meranno was a plain, soft spoken single mother of two who used her Guard pay to stave off creditors who always seemed to be camped out on her doorstep.

When all four of Kozak's small detail were reassembled before her, Specialist West turned toward his companions. "The colonel here is an educated woman who's been out and about in the world," he began. "Let's ask her what she thinks the chances are that the Feds are going to have their way and ship our boys off to California for trial."

West's statement was little more than a ploy meant to delay the start of serious work. In truth Kozak wasn't much in a mood to do any more counting and moving of boxes and crates that day herself. With less than an hour to go before she'd have to dismiss them for the day, she saw no point in going on. The ammunition, she reasoned as she looked about quickly, would still be there waiting to be counted when they met to drill again.

Besides, Nancy was truly intrigued by what these men and woman thought about the current situation in Idaho. After all, they represented a far better cross section of the people of Idaho than the students and faculty of Boise State. It would be, she thought, refreshing to hear their opinions.

Smiling, she gave Sergeant Lightfoot a wink. "Well, seeing how we're not going to be able to get on with the inventory until we resolve this earth shaking crisis," Nancy announced in as serious a tone as she could muster, "let's take a seat and see what everyone thinks about it."

Sensing a postponement from the drudgeries of work, West smiled. "Now that's what I'm talkin' about."

Arranging themselves in a semicircle, each of the Idaho National Guardsmen followed Nancy's lead and pulled a box of small arms ammo over to sit on. "I'm a relative newcomer to these parts," Nancy announced as an introduction to the discussion. "So I'd like to hear your thoughts on the what's been going on between the Federal government and its efforts to try the militiamen accused of the Wyoming raid elsewhere. Do any of you seriously think the Governor is going to become involved in defending the militia groups, and, by doing so, endorse the latest bombing of a Federal building?"

As was his custom, Chester West spoke out first. "The way I see it, what happened in Wyoming and Kansas has nothing to do with what we're talking about," he stated emphatically. "The men the FBI arrested and the Feds want to hang are decent, God fearing Christian patriots.

Does anyone here, for one minute, think that they would have a fair trial in San Francisco?"

Without preamble, Sergeant Lightfoot dryly added, "Last time I checked, the people of that city were Americans. What makes you think that they'll see the law any different than we would?"

With crimson cheeks, West turned on Lightfoot. "They may be Americans," West countered, "but they're not our kind of Americans. They don't understand what it means to stand up and fight for what they believe in. They're all pussy faggots there. All they're interested in is porkin' each other in places where the sun don't shine."

"Obviously," Lightfoot snorted, "you haven't heard of Haight-Ashbury."

In an effort to cool the anger that was visibly on the rise, Nancy turned to another member of the group. "Private Tillman," she asked, ignoring the glares being exchanged between West and Lightfoot. "You work in one of the companies owned by GO Thomas and where one of the accused also worked. What do you make of all the fuss?"

Tillman was a shy man by nature. Embarrassed by the fact that he was being required to say something, he looked nervously at his peers before answering. He paused to clear his throat before he started. When he did, he was almost apologetic. "I can't say I know much more about what's going on other than what I've heard on the news and what folks say. I've worked for the man going on five years before he moved into the governor's mansion. During all that time, I've never personally laid eyes on Thomas. Nor have I met a bona fide militiaman, at least, not that I am aware of."

"Surely you have an opinion on this issue?" Nancy Kozak interjected when it became obvious that Tillman was trying to say as little as possible.

"Oh, I don't think I do," Tillman responded. "I work, I get paid, and I have a job that has pretty good benefits." He paused and looked at Nancy. "About the only thing I really feel strongly about is my vacation time." Everyone laughed at this, giving Tillman the courage to go on.

"I guess what I'm trying to say," he continued on a serious note, "is that from where I sit, GO Thomas is no better or no worse than any other politician. Sure he speaks his mind. And I guess if the Federal government tries to pull a fast one on those boys the FBI have in custody, he'll do everything he can to see they get a fair trial. But other than that, as far as I'm concerned, he's just another rich guy who has more money and time on his hands then he knows what to do with."

With a new target for his anger, West turned from Sergeant Lightfoot to Tillman. "He gave you a job, didn't he?" West thundered. "I mean, this state was headed down the tubes when GO Thomas took over his father's failing business. If it hadn't been for him, we'd all be a whole lot poorer."

It was Fran Meranno's turn to chime in. "That's what he'd like us all to believe, you know," she told West. Then, looking at the others, she continued in a tone that let everyone know she was anything but a fan of GO Thomas. "Far as I'm concerned he's no better than any of the politicians in Washington, D.C., that he's always criticizing. Look at who he's always hanging out with. He all but financed his own campaign this last time, not to mention doing the same for better than half the folks in the State House."

"So what?" West countered. "He's interested in supporting good people who'll stand up for those values that have made this country what it is. He's looking out for our interests since we can't do it ourselves."

"Our interests?" Meranno all but shrieked. "Who died and appointed him God? Who is he to stand there on television and tell me and every woman in this state that we have no right to have an abortion simply because it goes against *His* conscience." Quickly turning to Nancy, Fran Meranno continued to drive her point home. "If he had his way, I'd have three waiting for me at home, instead of just two."

This roundabout confession caused a bit of a stir among her fellow guardsmen, one which she didn't seem to notice as she continued. "You've heard him. Every time he gets on the subject of family values he always manages to find a way to blame everything from global warming to continental drift on the fact that children don't have a mother who is willing to stay home and carry out what he calls 'their God given duties.' Or he lectures us on how young girls who seek abortions are misguided souls who should have been given more training in living a moral, Christian life instead of sex education. I mean, excuse me, but as far as I'm concerned GO Thomas is nothing more than another egotistical male who's full of himself. Maybe if he had a wife and a few teenagers of his own to deal with he'd be singing a far different tune."

For a moment, there was a stunned silence as Meranno finished, folded her arms, and looked about, almost daring anyone to challenge her statements. When she was satisfied that there was no one present who was willing to do so, Nancy turned to Sergeant Lightfoot. "You came back to Idaho after having served here and there in the Marine Corps for eight years. What you think of all this?"

The full-blooded Nez Perce, who still sported his close cropped Marine style haircut even after being out of the Corps for almost two years, didn't answer at first. Instead, he stared at Nancy Kozak, giving her the impression that he wasn't going to say anything. Then, suddenly, he spoke, as he always did, in a deep well-measured voice that put Nancy in mind of a menacing rumble one might expect from an volcano on the verge of erupting.

"It is all, Colonel, much ado about nothing," he stated flatly.

West, who always made fun of the way his well-read sergeant spoke, hooted. "Will you listen to that. Much ado. Gee, I love it when you talk dirty, Sergeant Lightfoot."

Ignoring West, Lightfoot went on. "It seems to me the government's efforts to pin the bombing and the raid on the six militiamen they have is little more than an effort to create the illusion that they are doing something meaningful. While every rational person in this country hopes the FBI does find those responsible for the murder of innocent people and bring them to justice, I doubt if they will find any of them hiding here in Idaho under Thomas's bed as some in Washington would have us believe."

"Oh, I agree," Nancy found herself stating before she even realized that she had committed herself to a point of view. "But what about GO Thomas himself? What do you think of him, as a person?"

Before responding, Sergeant Lightfoot lifted his right arm and looked at his watch. "I think," he stated deliberately as he lowered his arm, "that it's time we get on with this inventory, ma'am."

Not sure if his concern was motivated by his dedication to duty or simply a desire to dodge the question, Nancy nodded. "Yes, Sergeant. You're right." Standing up, she lifted her clipboard off the ammo box it had been sitting on and looked down the long list of DODAC numbers and the names of various munitions they represented that still needed to be counted. "Okay, we're finished with the caliber .50," she stated more to herself than her detail. "We don't have enough time to do the 5.56 ball, but there's no reason why we can't do the 7.62mm four-in-one link and still finish before your evening formation. What do you think, Sergeant Lightfoot?"

Without a hint of expression, the sergeant nodded. "Well, ma'am, you're the colonel. If you say that's what we're going to do, then by God, that's what we're going to do."

Without any further thought of GO Thomas, the FBI, the Idaho Six, or anything outside the confines of the musty ammo bunk, Nancy Kozak and the tiny detail of National Guard soldiers went about their duties.

CHAPTER **8**

One of the duties Major Brad Underwood was charged with was knowing where the key members of the division's command group were at all times. As the secretary to the general staff for the 4th Armored Division he maintained their schedules and how they could be reached, whether they were on the post or off. While there were many within the 4th AD who considered themselves to be essential, his list was restricted to Major General Scott Dixon, the division commander; Brigadier General Frederick Ivey, the assistant division commander; Colonel Bob Felden, the Chief of Staff; and Lieutenant Colonel Joseph Brown, the division G3. Since the names of the brigade commanders didn't appear anywhere on Underwood's officer evaluation report, they didn't make the cut.

Tall, clean cut, and displaying a confidence that bordered on arrogance, Underwood was an infantryman by training and a staff officer by nature. He looked and carried himself in much the same manner as his contemporaries who made a living off the daily crap game known as Wall Street or bought and sold power and influence in the crowded corridors of the Capitol building as lobbyists.

Entering his office using the quick, short steps that staff officers often use when going about their duties, Underwood made a sharp turn to the right. He avoided a collision with a spec four only because she stepped back at the last minute when she saw him coming. He slowed his pace only when he reached the chief of staff's door. Sticking his head through the open doorway, he rapped lightly on the wooden frame. "Sir," he announced as Colonel Felden looked up from the staff paper he was busily marking with a red pencil, "all the principals are in place."

Felden threw down the pencil. "Do we have an ETA on Iron Horse Six?"

Underwood flashed one of his self-confident smiles that Felden always saw as a smirk. "Five minutes, sir."

"Very well, I'll be right there." Felden didn't bother to remind Underwood to make sure that there were two cold diet colas waiting for Iron Horse Six at the conference table. Underwood knew better than to overlook such an important item.

Iron Horse Six was Scott Dixon's unauthorized radio call sign. Official call signs were a series of randomly selected letters and numbers that changed daily. These call signs, along with other important signal and command and control information, were complied in a pocket size booklet known as the communications electronics operating instructions, or CEOI. Since the bulk of the information in a CEOI was classified, it had to be locked up and accounted for when not in use. American soldiers, who were no different from any other soldiers throughout the world or the ages, often found it bothersome to draw their CEOIs when going out to the field for a quick training exercise. Even when they did have their assigned CEOIs with them, it was sometimes a nuisance to look up or use the proper call sign, especially when the call signs changed at midnight or in the middle of a tactical situation. In those cases many a commander and soldier found it easier, and quicker, to use their unofficial call sign to identify themselves or call another station whose authorized call sign did not immediately come to mind.

Often these call signs had historical significance, referring to a unit's nickname. The 4th Armored Division was known, throughout the Army, as the Iron Horse Division. Hence Scott Dixon, the commander, was Iron Horse Six, the number six being used exclusively to identify commanding officers. Colonel Felden was Iron Horse Seven, the assistant division commander, Iron Horse Five, the division G3 Iron Horse Three, and so on. Sometimes the unauthorized call signs were changed by a particular commander to fit his personality or that of his unit. This was true in the case of the Division Artillery commander,

Colonel Peter Wilder. Given the nickname "Wild Thing" at West Point, he carried it around like a badge of honor. When he came to the 4th Armored, the division staff began to refer to their counterparts on the Div Arty staff as the Wild Bunch. The name stuck, leading to the adoption of Wild Thing Six for Colonel Wilder. Unfortunately for the division staff, Peter Wilder saw his nickname as more than a mere handle. It was an image both he and his staff endeavored to live up to.

Even now, as he and the other colonels who commanded the brigade-size components of the 4th Armored waited for Iron Horse Six to make his entrance, Peter Wilder was making his presence known. "You know," he called out to no one in particular as he poured himself a cup of coffee, "if half my battery commanders could achieve the same degree of synchronization that the CG and his wife always seem to pull off, I'd be the hottest damned artillery commander since Napoleon."

"Well," Bob Felden responded as he entered the room and made for the table where both Wilder and the coffee were, "you'd definitely be the shortest one since Bonaparte."

Spinning about to face Felden, an aviator, Wilder smiled. "Remember, Bob, it's speed and accuracy that matters, not the size of the projectile."

From the conference table the commander of the 2nd Brigade, Larry Fisher, chuckled. "Well," he announced to the assembled senior leadership of the division, "if what Pete's wife says is true, Wild Thing strikes out on everything save speed."

This brought a general round of laughter from everyone in the room save Clyde Emerson, commander of the 1st Brigade. It was one of his units training in the field that Scott Dixon had been visiting. Though he had confidence that the commander of the unit was doing what he was supposed to, no one ever knew for sure. After all, it was almost a truism that general officers had an innate sense of timing when it came to visiting a unit just when it was entering the throes of a major crisis.

As if to prove that point, a voice from someone near the door yelled out, "Atten-*tion!*"

Making straight for his seat at the head of the conference room, Scott Dixon paused only long enough to shed his web gear and helmet before pulling out his chair and plopping down. "Be seated, people," he snapped as he reached out instinctively for the can of soda that sat on a small tray before him.

In the process of resuming his seat, Clyde Emerson asked, in a rather offhanded manner, "How was your visit with 2nd of the 13th?"

Dixon paused, looked up from his soda, and made a face. "We'll talk about that later."

This was not good. Had all gone well, Scott would have responded with a compliment or a bland observation. But the words "we'll talk about that later," had the same impact on Emerson that a child in school would feel if his teacher told him, "see me after class." Dixon's quick, unemotional reply to Emerson's inquiry had a sudden, chilling effect on the assembled officers. The old man was in a bad mood.

Seeing that it was best that they press on with the commander's conference as quickly as possible, Bob Felden leaned forward, opened the folder before him, and started speaking. "The topic for today's discussion is the use of military force against domestic threats." He paused so as to permit everyone seated at the table an opportunity to open their own folders and focus their minds on the subject at hand. "The Army has, in the past, been used to resolve domestic disputes, disturbances, and violence of varying intensity and complexity. The most extensive use of American military power to deal with an internal crisis was, of course, the Civil War."

From the far end of the table, a voice that betrayed its Alabama origins interrupted. "Or, if you please, the War of Northern Aggression."

Scott Dixon, looking up from his folder, stared at Colonel John Battle Gordon, commander of the 191st Brigade, Alabama National Guard. As the commander of the division's round out brigade, Colonel Gordon was invited to every commanders' conference. That he had chosen to attend this one was no accident. "Aggression," Scott stated evenly, "is often a matter of perspective."

"In the case of Southern independence," Gordon replied, "the label of aggressor is a fit and proper one when discussing the collection of bandits and malcontents your Mr. Lincoln called armies. Their use to deny the southern states their right to secede from the Union was illegal and unjustifiable."

Scott smiled. "Ah, yes. The Tenth Amendment."

Gordon returned the smile. "Exactly, sir. Since the Constitution did not mention the act of secession one way or the other, and the Tenth Amendment specifically gave the states all rights not enumerated as belonging to the Federal Government in the Constitution, it was well within the prerogatives of the southern states to leave the Union. Given that, Lincoln's use of federal troops to suppress southern freedom was illegal. And given the fact that the first shots were fired in a southern state at soldiers of a foreign power that refused to withdraw when asked, I'd say aggression is an apt term."

Raising his hands in mock surrender, Scott chuckled. "Sir, I assure you, I am not here to refight a war that will be discussed and debated long after we're all dead and buried." Dropping his hands to the table, Scott leaned back in his seat. "What we are here to look at, however, is a subject that could be as divisive to us as the breaking up of the Union was to our forefathers."

In a single, swift movement, Scott sat upright, folded his hands on the table before him. "As part of our commissioning oath we pledged ourselves to defend the Constitution of the United States against all enemies, foreign *and* domestic. While it is very easy and desirable from a professional standpoint to focus on dealing with foreign threats, we would be remiss in our duties if we ignored our responsibilities when it comes to enforcing the laws of our nation within our territorial borders, even if that means a confrontation with our fellow Americans."

Scott let this thought hang in the air for a moment. Looking about at the table he could tell that he had the attention of everyone in the room. Of course, when you're the commanding general, you come to expect that. But the intense stares that met his quick gaze told him that there was a genuine interest in today's topic. That much of this was due to his own wife's recent story about the difficulties in Idaho didn't matter. What was important was that his senior commanders were already thinking about a topic that they would not have ordinarily considered relevant. That, in itself, justified the time taken out of the busy schedules of his senior leadership.

"Throughout our nation's history," Scott continued briskly, "the Army has been called upon, from time to time, to do exactly that. At times those duties were distasteful. Sometimes they were controversial. While individuals elected to do otherwise, never has the Army, as an institution, failed to perform its duty."

Again Scott paused to allow his points to soak in. Though his commanders' roundtable discussions were intended to promote open and freewheeling discussion and thought, Scott felt that it was important to set the tone of the discussion and make it clear where he personally stood. Some of his commanders, such as Larry Fisher, would never permit themselves to stray too far from the "official" party line. He had a habit of crafting his comments so that they conformed neatly to Scott's opinion. Clyde Emerson, on the other hand, would go out of his way to find a position that was diametrically opposed to Scott's "official" view. It was not that Emerson was a renegade or contrarian. Rather, he liked to make Scott and his staff work to defend *their* positions. This was not all bad. Every now and then Scott found that in the process of doing so he discovered flaws in his own initial thinking that had not been self-evident. So Emerson's position as the "loyal opposition" was both respected and welcomed.

"Today, perhaps more than ever," Scott went on, "we face the specter that the United States Army will be called upon to support the enforcement of national polices or laws that other Federal agencies are unable to handle. Just this summer we were witness to a situation some people in Washington and the media still claim cried out for just such a commitment. Ever since Waco there has been an escalation of violence against the Federal Government by various factions that cannot be ignored. While the FBI and other federal agencies have managed to rise to the challenge thus far, we cannot assume that they will always be able to do so."

Relaxing slightly, Scott unfolded his hands, looked down at the first sheet in the package that sat before him, and picked it up. "As the chief has already mentioned, the topic for today's roundtable discussion is the use of the Army to combat domestic violence. To kick things off the G2 is going to look at the theoretical threats that could prompt the national command authority to commit us to a domestic confrontation."

On cue Felden nodded to Lieutenant Colonel Gary Olson, the division's G2, or intelligence officer. Olson quickly moved to the front of the room with his back to a rear projection screen. From the room behind the screen an NCO turned on the projector and flashed the first slide up on the screen that showed the division's patch with the G2's motto. "Good afternoon," Olson announced, remembering to leave off the word gentlemen in deference to the aviation brigade's commander, Colonel Kristin Parkman.

"Historically," the G2 stated in a tone that was a bit too loud and overbearing for the size of the room, "the United States Army has been called upon to deal with a variety of domestic situations, ranging from disaster relief to armed rebellion. While it is impossible to predict what domestic missions the Army, and this division in particular, might be called out to perform, we can categorize these potential missions by type."

This last statement alerted the sergeant manning the overhead projector to flip to the next slide. "What you see here is a list of missions, ranked by severity or, if you wish, intensity." The G2 paused, giving the assembled audience an opportunity to study the list now being projected on the screen or look at the paper copy that had been included as part of their "carry away" packet. Not everyone had one of these packets. There were a number of straphangers and lower ranking minions arranged along the walls of the conference room. A few had come early enough to secure chairs. Those who hadn't, squatted Korean style or leaned against the wall. Some had come to back up their respective commanders. Others were there simply to get out of their own offices and away from the mounds of paper work that always seemed to plague staff officers.

"We'll start with the least controversial and most likely tasks that we would be called upon to perform and work our way up the ladder of intensity." A new slide popped up, listing only one of the items from the previous list. "At the lowest level," he stated, pointing at the screen, "we have emergency relief. By far this sort of activity is, from a public relations standpoint, the most attractive. The use of the armed forces during the 1906 San Francisco earthquake, relief assistance following Hurricane Andrew, or the search and rescue effort after Mount Saint Helens erupted are but a handful of examples of this sort of mission. In each case the nature and amount of military effort varied. In most emergency relief taskings the armed forces are required to provide logistical support to replace or supplement a damaged civilian infrastructure, as we did in response to Andrew. Sometimes it's our specialized equipment and communications, as in search and rescue, that are needed. In the case of the San Francisco earthquake, the skills of Army engineers were required when it was decided to stop the spreading fires by blowing up buildings to create a firebreak. In almost all disasters in which the armed forces were involved, the military played a key role in the maintenance of law and order. In a few instances, such as the forest fires that ravaged the west several years back, all that we were called upon to provide was bulk manpower and transportation.

"Next," the G-2 went on as a new slide came into view, "the Army has been used as an instrument to enforce Federal laws or mandates. President John Kennedy's celebrated use of the 101st Airborne to enforce federally mandated desegregation in Mississippi is an example of this sort of mission. While the mission was clear, focused, and, from a moral standpoint, necessary, it put the officers and men of the One-Oh-One in direct confrontation with fellow Americans who were against that policy. Here we see the potential for open conflict."

Clyde Emerson cleared his throat, indicating that he had a question. "What differentiates the duties of an MP during disaster relief and this type of law enforcement?"

The G2 looked at Colonel Emerson for a moment as if to determine if his question was a real one or if he was simply trying to trip him up by disrupting his prepared briefing. When Emerson continued to stare at Olson straight faced, the G2 decided that 1st Brigade commander was being quite serious. "Scale of the confrontation, organization of the opposition, and the underlying motives for the confrontation," Olson answered. "Usually troops policing an area after a disaster are confronted with individuals or small groups intent on taking advantage of the disarray and over extension of the normal community police force. The opposition are little more than thieves, intent only on personal gain. In the case of Mississippi, however, the opposition was an entire populace, the white southerners, who were against the imposition of federally mandated law."

Irked by this last comment, Colonel Gordon spoke out. "May I remind you, ladies and gentlemen, that not all white southerners supported the racist who stood that day in an effort to deny their fellow Americans an opportunity to an equal education. While I was just a child at the time, I can clearly recall my daddy standing up before the congregation of our church and calling for his fellow Christians to look into their hearts and seek the moral high ground."

"And how," Scott asked as he swiveled his chair to face Gordon, "did your daddy's fellow parishioners respond?"

Colonel Gordon's face grew red as he struggled to hold back his anger. Only when he was in control did he dare speak. "While I am sorry to say half of the congregation walked out that day, half stayed." Turning, he looked at into the eyes of the G2. "All I ask is that you temper your comments, sir, to reflect the reality of the times, not the mythology of today's politically correct view of history."

For a moment the G2 was unsure how to respond. In

the end he chose to ignore Gordon's comment and press on. "Ah, well, yes," he stammered as he sorted his briefing notes in his hands absentmindedly. When he was ready, he started again. "The next level is where we first see physical confrontation being a likely outcome." On the slide were the words "Civil Disturbance," followed by examples which included race riots and labor disputes. Casting a nervous glance back at Colonel Gordon, the G2 began to elaborate on this topic. "Throughout our nation's history the federal government has made it a point to allow local and state law enforcement agencies to deal with civil disturbances. On occasion however, the magnitude of the disturbances has overwhelmed the capabilities of local governmental agencies to deal effectively with them. In those cases, federal forces were called in to augment local agencies. One of the largest and bloodiest examples of this sort of employment was the draft riots in New York City in July, 1863. Troops from the Army of the Potomac, with the mud and blood of Gettysburg still on their uniforms, were dispatched to that city to end days of violent rioting in which Irish laborers lynched Negroes and burned government recruiting offices."

"Good move, Gary," Colonel Wilder threw in. "The Irish are always in season if you're looking for a minority to pick on."

Having sensed the tension, Bob Felden saw a chance to lighten the mood. "Well, Pete," he called out to Wilder, "that's because you micks are always so bloody annoying."

The officers at the table let out an uninhibited laugh. The minions lining the wall were more guarded in their response. Smiling, Scott nodded for the G2 to continue.

"Further up the scale," the G2 continued as a new slide flashed on the screen, "are small scale or very localized rebellions or uprisings. One of this nation's first major domestic crises was the Whiskey Rebellion in western Pennsylvania. The ink wasn't even dry on our new Constitution when farmers in the area around what is today Pittsburgh banded together to defy a tax on liquor. While the Federal government had no real army of its own, it did federalize several state militia units to march out and restore order.

Another example of a local rebellion that required the use of Army troops was the great Mormon campaign of 1857. In a war without battles, Colonel Albert Sidney Johnson marched the largest gathering of Army troops since the Mexican War from Fort Leavenworth to Salt Lake City to prevent the Mormons from leaving the Union. The ironic part of this particular episode, of course, was that Johnson would be killed at Shiloh, less than five years later, leading troops fighting for another government intent on leaving the same Union he had once defended. In both the Whiskey Rebellion and the Mormon Uprising a simple show of force was enough to cause the rebels to back down without any appreciable bloodshed."

"Which brings up a couple of excellent points of discussion, gentlemen," Scott suddenly stated while motioning to his G2. "You can take your seat, Colonel Olson." With a befuddled look on his face, the G2 realized he had been dismissed. Turning to his senior commanders, Scott took over the direction of the discussion.

"The first point that has relevance to this discussion," Scott started as he looked down at his empty can of soda on the table and slowly turned it, "is that a person's loyalty and duty can, depending on the situation, shift." Without taking his hands off the empty can, Scott peeked up at the expressionless faces staring at him intently, waiting for him to commit to a definite train of thought before commenting. "As you saw on the G2's first slide, the last category on his list was civil war. In 1860, the United States Army had roughly one thousand commissioned officers. All of them had taken the same oath of office. All shared the same hardships and hazards that the frontier Army of that day was noted for. With few exceptions all were graduates of West Point. In the years preceding the secession of South Carolina they shared everything. Yet," Scott went on, raising his voice slightly as he lifted the can a few inches and slammed it on the table, "when the Southern states started leaving the Union, this band of brothers broke up. Approximately one third went south, while a goodly number of those who remained with the colors left the regular Army and ran, as quickly as they could, to their home states where they took commissions in a grade several times above the rank they had previously held."

"While that is true," Colonel Kristin Parkman asked in a firm yet respectful tone, "do you think that we would be faced with the same situation today?"

Scott smiled as he looked at the commander of his aviation brigade. He could always depend on Colonel Parkman to kick things off. Known as Gun Slinger Six, Kristin was a trained attack helicopter pilot who never hesitated to commit her units to battle or verbally shoot down an errant subordinate. "By a simple show of hands, how many of you in this room," Scott asked by way of response, "are registered members of the President's political party?" Throughout the room, only two hands went up hesitantly. "Okay," Scott continued, "how many belong to the other party?"

This time the hands of well over half the commanders and straphangers shot up. "Okay, thank you," Scott replied after he saw that his audience had gotten a feel for itself. "As you can see, for one reason or another we do not share the views expressed by our commander-in-chief."

"That doesn't mean," Larry Fisher intoned, "that we wouldn't follow his orders. If the President pushes the button, we go. It is what we have pledged ourselves to do."

"While I am sure you are all cock sure what you'd do in a national emergency that pitted Americans against Americans," John B. Gordon stated, "I cannot say that I could blindly follow our commander-in-chief." Shifting a bit in his seat so that he was slouched down, Gordon threw his hands out, palms up. "After Albert Sidney Johnson, Bobby Lee was the most respected man in the United States Army. As the Southern states slipped away from the Union, he stood by the oath of office. That is, until his home state, Virginia, left. Always an honorable man, perhaps the last genuine gentleman this nation was to be graced with, he agonized over his solemn oath of commissioning. Yet, as hard as it was for him to go against an oath he had sworn before his God and country, the specter of raising his hand against the state that he and his forefathers had called home was even more frightening. In the end he came down on the side of his native state. Though he had proudly served his nation, it was Virginia that he considered home."

Gordon paused as he moved about in his seat, as if uncomfortable with what he was about to say. With his face screwed up, he looked straight at Scott. "Let there be no doubt in your mind, sir, which side of the fence I would land on if the President called upon the men and women of my brigade to take up arms against their brethren."

Scott wanted to say, "I rest my case," but felt that such a mundane statement would miss the point. Instead, he simply acknowledged Colonel Gordon's pronouncement with a nod and continued on as he looked into the eyes of his senior commanders. "Do not be so quick to decide how, exactly, you would meet such a moral dilemma," Scott stated. "What is clear here, in this comfortable room surrounded by like-minded people, may not be as crystal clear when you find yourself face to face with the real thing."

While Scott reached for his second can of Diet Coke, Timothy Bates, the commander of the division's support command, coughed before throwing out his question. "Perhaps this may be a bit presumptuous, but as we discuss this topic, does the general have a particular contingency in mind?"

Scott looked up. He knew the situation in Idaho was on everyone's mind, especially after his own wife aired an incredibly damning expose on the FBI and the hostility that had arisen from its actions in Idaho. It was just a question, he had realized when he had walked into the room, of how long it would be before one of his outspoken commanders brought that particular question up. "It was the Wyoming affair that prompted me to propose this subject as an item to be covered in a commanders' conference," Scott replied slowly as he pulled the tab on his can of soda. "Any thoughts that the timing of this discussion and events in Idaho are anything but coincidental are dead wrong. After all," Scott went on, leaning back in his chair and sporting a smile, "anyone who has seen firsthand how Jan and I coordinate our affairs at home would know we could never achieve this degree of synchronization in a million years."

This brought a ripple of laughter and, Scott hoped, an end to any such thoughts. "Now, where was I?"

Bob Felden leaned over to whisper in Scott's good ear. "You were about to elaborate on a second point."

Scott threw his head back. "Ah yes," he called out in his best John Cleese imitation. "I have two points to make. No, three, three points!"

With the mood lightened, Scott led his senior officers into further discussion of the topic, a topic that he, if the truth were known, was quite uncomfortable with himself.

From his perch behind his commanding general's seat Major Brad Underwood considered the subject. The idea that he would ever be called upon to choose between his core beliefs and his loyalty to the Army had never dawned upon him. He had always assumed that both he and great men like GO Thomas would always be on the same side. It was unsettling to this young officer to think that he could be called upon to march north, with an Army he so loved, to fight a man who stood for everything that he believed in. While other straphangers hung on every word and thought that their seniors were tossing back and forth, Brad Underwood turned his well-disciplined mind to a problem that he had no clear answer for yet.

CHAPTER 9

It is a display of power that few Americans ever witness. It's not meant to be a show of force. Nor is the daily ritual staged in order to convey a message to potential foes. It's just PT, the Army's acronym for physical training. Yet anyone who has participated in these morning excursions understands that it is more than a toughening drill. It is the only time during the day when the entire body of a combat division functions as one. It is the only time when the naked might of an airborne division, its soldiers, can be seen unencumbered by the high tech weapons and gadgets that make the modern American Army such a deadly foe.

The sounds, the image, even the smell of this collection of infantrymen, artillerymen, aviators, engineers, signal troops, staff officers, and combat commanders putting their bodies through the paces create a beast unlike any other. As with a creature in a science fiction novel, the individual pieces of this unique animal appear every morning as if by magic and assemble themselves. Then, guided by an unseen force, the animal begins to move. From the front of barracks and headquarters buildings all over Fort Bragg, the blocks that make up this combat division spill out into the streets and roads of the post. Slowly, they pick up a steady, methodical pace. Even on days when brigades and battalions do not form and run as units with their commanders and staffs at their head, the component parts of those organizations still merge together to create an enormous serpent that winds and twists its way through the predawn darkness. The rhythmic slapping of ten thousand pair of running shoes echoes off the silent buildings that line the streets. Cadence, called by senior sergeants, provides the heartbeat that keeps the twenty-thousand-legged beast moving forward, always forward, together and in step. To call this spectacle anything but awe inspiring would be to do disservice this holiest of holy airborne rituals.

Yet even more takes place as the beast of many hearts and minds moves along. To anyone whose sole experience with masses of people is the jostled and harried crowds found at every corner of eastern city streets or sporting events, it is difficult to appreciate how a daily drill that packs soldiers into a dense moving horde of sweating humanity can be a positive and enjoyable experience. Yet even those who view the morning run as a necessary evil cannot escape the sense of being part of an organization that has a common goal, a single purpose. Though each soldier is an individual, as individualistic as the Army permits, the morning run serves to renew their allegiance to their comrades and their unit. It provides an opportunity to forget about everything that exists out there, beyond the confines of the formation and surrender one's self to a group, a unit, a collective force. In a society fractured by racial, political, social, and economic diversity, this sensation of being part of something bigger than themselves is a unique experience that few will ever enjoy again once their time with the colors is over. For unlike the very nation they are expected to defend, everyone present knows exactly what he or she is doing and exactly where they are going, something that many of their counterparts in "The Real World" will never be able to claim.

Not every soul has the privilege of losing himself in the teeming masses plowing forward with the determination of a swarm of locusts. Like a hundred other young company commanders, Captain Andrew King stood out in front of his command. His only companion was a tight lipped guidon bearer who carried the light blue, swallow tail flag bearing crossed model 1842 muskets that was the emblem of the infantry.

Like his guidon, King's isolated position was symbolic. At twenty-six he was the "old man" or commander. On this run, as on all runs, he was expected to set the pace and to guide the unit. This role, of course, did not end when the morning's PT was over and the great beast melted away into ten thousand tiny pieces. While he could not lead every activity that the soldiers of his company engaged in during the balance of the day, he was still expected to be the guiding force for the young men and women who comprised Company A, 3rd Battalion of the 517th Airborne Infantry Regiment.

Modern warfare demands that company commanders like King be thinkers and planners as well as leaders. Companies that used to fight in formations that packed soldiers in shoulder to shoulder now fought over frontages that extend up to a thousand meters, sometimes more. Even platoon leaders, the officers who serve as the links between the company commander and the rifleman on the killing edge, seldom find themselves in a position where they can physically see more than a handful of their own men. Under such circumstances it is critical that every soldier in the company understand that Captain Andrew King is there, directing their efforts, if not in body, then in spirit. So it was important for Captain King and his peers to seize every opportunity to physically lead in order to firmly establish that idea in their soldiers' minds.

Andrew King, nicknamed King Andrew by friends and detractors alike, didn't much mind the isolation that comes with commanding a company. As the oldest of four, he had learned at an early age to give orders and assume a responsible role over his younger, less capable siblings. When his mother, a woman who had found herself abandoned by every man she ever thought she loved, gave up her attempts to find security in marriage, she allowed Andrew to became the "man" of the house.

This sad state of affairs probably saved King from a fate many of his peers shared. Like them he lived in a household run by a mother who worked at two, and sometimes three, menial jobs in order to eke out a substandard living on the edge of Kansas City's own unique version of an urban ghetto. Unlike his own father, he did not abandon his family. Nor did he join a gang as his boyhood friends urged. Instead he threw himself into the task of caring for his two brothers and one sister while applying himself ac-

the hope of securing a scholarship to a col-
far from the mean streets of home.

se of action, one which seemed so wise for
one so young, was not without its price. As with too many
African-American youths who apply themselves academi-
cally, this decision cost him dearly. Without the relative
protection of a gang, Andrew found himself in a strange
middle ground, a no-man's land, alone. There he lived by
his wits, sustained by the slim hope that somewhere, up
ahead, in the hazy and uncertain future, his efforts would
be rewarded.

In his senior year, they were. Almost by chance he received an appointment to the United States Military Academy at West Point. While the Army had never really
figured into his plans as a child, the opportunity to attend
college absolutely free was too good to pass up. So he
grabbed the brass ring when it came his way and never
looked back.

Within the Army King found the sense of self-worth and
security that had eluded him in his earlier life. Rather than
be scorned for his scholarship, he was applauded. Instead
of having to defend his decision to stand up for his mother
and siblings with his fists, he was praised. And, as he assumed a role of leadership in the corps of cadets, then in
the small peacetime Army itself, Andrew found himself on
familiar ground. He was, in so many ways, home every
time he walked into a barracks. Now, as the commander
of an airborne company, Andrew King found that he had
a new family.

Like every family, this one had its problems. When he
assumed command of his company, King inherited an executive officer and two platoon leaders who had been
trained by his predecessor. That officer had commanded
with a light touch that bordered on casualness. Despite the
fact that the unit performed well in the field, it left much
to be desired while in garrison. It was for this reason that
Andrew King had been given this particular company. His
mandate, handed to him by his battalion commander during his initial briefing, had been to "put some starch" into
Company A.

There is a truism in the Army that states that a unit will never have a better commander than the last one they had. Within two weeks of his arrival Andrew King had earned the dislike, and in some cases, hatred, of almost every man in A Company. But Andrew didn't much care what his soldiers thought. He had a job to do and he intended to do it. His soldiers, each and every one, were volunteers, first for the Army, then for the airborne. Though they bitched and moaned, they complied. They lived secure in the knowledge that sooner or later either they or King would leave Company A due to normal rotation, ending the misery that was being visited upon them by a man they considered to be little more than a martinet.

Dissension among the rank and file is one thing, something King had learned to expect. But not from his officers. Unfortunately for King and these officers, this was the first time that he had actually commanded other officers. As a company executive officer, he had on occasion assumed command of the company he was assigned during tactical exercises or when the CO went on leave. But that was different. Then he had been little more than a place keeper, a temp. Now, however, he was "The Man." He made the polices for the company. He set the pace and tone of the company. He established the standards each and every soldier under his command were expected to live by while on duty. And he punished those who did not live up to them.

But there is far more to being a company commander than simply training the soldiers and officers of a unit so that it could execute its assigned mission. A company commander has to do more than educate his young platoon leaders. He has to carefully nurture them, using a variety of skills and techniques that range from psychology to simple common sense. At times a company commander must play the big brother, helping his younger, inexperienced sibling overcome the many trials and tribulations the Army throws at a junior officer. At other times, the Old Man has to become the wicked stepfather, whipping the errant lieutenant into shape. All of this requires a deft hand and a keen sense of judgment and timing that is, unfortunately, all too rare in twenty-six year old captains. In Andrew King, it was totally lacking.

This shortfall quickly became obvious when King came to blows with the officers he inherited from the former company commander. Those young and ambitious professionals, men who had been used to having their own way in how they ran their platoons, didn't like King's heavy hand. Frequent "discussions" between himself and his lieutenants were cut short by Andrew declaring, in a firm and uncompromising manner, "Look, I don't care how you did things before. I am in command now and you'll do it my way. Is that clear?" While this did have the desired effect of ending debates, King was peeved about having to employ this tack. It did little for unit esprit and cohesion, twin pillars that often make or break a unit in combat.

As King led his company that morning, he concluded that it was critical that he grab the second lieutenant newly assigned to him from the get go and train him properly. What he would say, and how he would deal with Second Lieutenant Nathan Dixon when he reported for duty that morning, was very much on Andrew King's mind as the creature with twenty thousand legs pounded its way through the chilly North Carolina dawn.

Throughout the tortuous ordeal known in the Army as processing, two hard facts kept slapping Nathan Dixon in the face everywhere he went. The first was that his experience as an Army Brat had done little to prepare him for life in the Army. Though he had begun to suspect as much while attending the Infantry Officer's Basic Course at Fort Benning, it wasn't until he reached Bragg that he suddenly discovered how precious little he really knew about the organization he had committed body and soul to. Of course he was familiar with the sights, the sounds, and the comings and goings of military types. He could rattle off the terms and acronyms like a veteran. And he had a knowledge of tactics and military history that was far superior to that of the majority of his peers.

Yet Nathan had not been "in" the Army. Up until recently he was, like Jan, simply associated with the Army. Even his four years at the Virginia Military Institute and six weeks of ROTC summer camp had not prepared him for the psychological shock of walking into the headquarters of the 11th Airborne Division as a second lieutenant. He could almost feel himself being drawn deeper and deeper into an organization that, on the outside, appeared familiar, yet was turning out to be totally alien. By the time he finished with the centralized inprocessing at division, he carried his paper work as if it were a death warrant rather than his ticket to the future.

Feeling the need to recoup before reporting to the battalion he was assigned to, Nathan made his way to the main post exchange for lunch. Perhaps, he thought, everything would look a whole lot better after he had choked down a PX burger and Coke.

That hope, however, was quickly dashed. He hadn't even managed to bite into his burger before a sergeant first class came up to the table to where Nathan was seated. "Excuse me, sir," the sergeant blurted out. "I noticed your name tag and couldn't help but wonder if your father is 'The' Scott Dixon."

With his burger suspended midway between the table and his mouth, Nathan looked up at the NCO. The sergeant's innocent question reminded him of the second cruel truth that had dogged him all morning. He was not just another newly minted butter bar, fresh from the Fort Benning School for Boys. He was the son of a general, a famous one at that.

After setting the virgin burger back in its greasy paper wrapping, Nathan wiped his hands on the small napkin that disintegrated between his fingers, leaving tiny shreds of paper stuck to them. Standing up, he looked at the NCO for a moment before sheepishly responding with a meek, "Yes, I am."

The sergeant's response was similar in every way to those that he had experienced all morning. First, a broad grin, made broader by the fact that the person asking Nathan could relax in the knowledge that he had not made a fool of himself by asking the wrong person. Then, the inquisitor's right hand would shoot out toward Nathan. As they shook vigorously, the person would state that he or she had served with his father here, or there, or during a particular crisis or war. In the case of this sergeant, it had been the First Persian Gulf War when the man had been a private and Scott a major in the same tank battalion. Then the platitudes would flow. These ranged from polite and proper, "He is the best there is," to "He was a damned fine officer and a hell of a tanker."

In the beginning, Nathan would try to respond to each of these intrusions with something original, something profound. But as this ritual was repeated time and time again, he restricted his response to a nod and a mumbled, "Yes, indeed he is."

Like many of soldiers who had known Scott Dixon, this sergeant first class made two statements that irked Nathan. The first was to the effect that he had heard the son of Scott Dixon was being assigned to the division. This bothered Nathan. Nathan, like many sons, was anxious to move out into the world on his own, free of his father's influence. To discover that this was all but impossible in such a small, tightly knit organization such as the Army was discouraging. Nathan had hoped to enter the Army and his first troop assignment without his father's rank and reputation hanging over him like the sword of Damocles. That this would not be possible was quite disheartening.

The second, and equally annoying statement that many a potential well wisher presented to Nathan was the sincere hope that Nathan would prove to be "half as good" as his father had been. Whether the officer or enlisted man addressing Nathan was making this assessment based on previous experiences with the newly commissioned sons of general officers or they were merely heaping more praise on Scott Dixon didn't much matter to Nathan. By the time the sergeant had made his appearance, Nathan was starting to regret not taking his brother's suggestion that he use Jan's last name instead of Dixon.

"What unit are you going to?" the sergeant asked politely.

"Company A, 3rd Battalion of the 517th Airborne," Nathan snapped.

For a moment, the sergeant thought about Nathan's response. Then, his eyes narrowed as his expression grew somber. "Captain Andrew King is the CO of that outfit, isn't he?"

Tiring of this, Nathan took an exaggerated glance down at his unviolated hamburger before he replied. "Yes, I think so."

The sergeant shook his head. "In that case, sir, best of luck." Turning, he started to leave, but then paused. "Sir, watch your six," he added quietly over his shoulder.

Nathan, who was in the process of resuming his seat, didn't have a chance to ask the sergeant what he had meant by his remark before the man disappeared in the noontime crowd milling about at the serving counter. Whether this was a good omen or not didn't much bother Nathan at the moment. His fate, he figured, was pretty much cast in stone. All that remained for him to do was to get on with it.

Like a character in a Joseph Conrad novel, Nathan Dixon made his way down the divisional structure toward his ultimate goal. At each level he became more aware of how much he stood out from the soldiers around him. It was more than the simple fact that they were in BDUs, faded to perfection from years of field use and repeated washings while he wore his dress greens that were all but bare of ribbons and qualification badges.

There is an easy confidence with which the paratroopers carried themselves. It comes from the knowledge that they have done things which are radically against human nature, such as throwing one's body out of a perfectly good airplane or the willingness to place oneself in harm's way on short notice. This self-assurance translates itself into a swagger, a swagger that permeates everything they do, from the manner in which paratroopers walk to the way they talk. It even taints their view of the world, for everyone now falls into one of two handy, well defined categories. Those human beings who had the courage to have trusted their life to a few hundred square feet of nylon and suspension cords were fellow "sky troopers," men and women who had made the grade. Everyone else would, ever after, be a "leg," a term applied to anyone who didn't quite have "the right stuff." While even the most hard core paratrooper knew that "legs" were necessary, they were tolerated as one would put up with an annoying pet.

It was that cool, devil-may-care attitude which unnerved Nathan. For him, it was like being a Rat at VMI all over again. Memories of being surrounded by upperclassmen screaming in his face kept welling up from that place in his mind where all such nightmares lurk. While his conscious mind kept telling him that the soldiers of the 3rd Battalion of the 517th Airborne had better things to do than point at him and talk about the new spit-shined 'cruit lieutenant violating their tight-knit little world, Nathan longed for the opportunity to ditch his greens and slip into a set of BDUs. At least then, Nathan figured, he would be less conspicuous.

But a simple change of uniform would do little to change the fact that he was a brand new second lieutenant, traditionally an object of contempt and pity in the United States Army. Old Army names like "shave tail" or more modern terms such as "butter bar" were some of the nicer words used to describe second lieutenants. Every officer, starting at the grade of first lieutenant and going all the way to the chief of staff, as well as every enlisted man, had their own particular second lieutenant story. Most of those stories portrayed the most junior of junior officers in the worst possible light. And though few needed additional embellishments, for second lieutenants do have a habit of doing the most peculiar things, everyone took great pains to dress their tales up as much as their command of the English language permitted them. Having been brought up in a military family, Nathan had heard more than his fair share of second lieutenant stories from his father and his father's friends. In those days, Nathan had found them funny and entertaining. Today, as Nathan recalled some of the more outrageous tales he had heard over the years, he realized that he was now vulnerable to becoming part of that collection. Suddenly he found he was not at all amused.

The real trial for Nathan began when he reached his battalion. Thus far everywhere that Nathan had visited on post had been administrative offices or higher headquarters, places that Nathan, as a second lieutenant of infantry, would have little call to visit. As a platoon leader his world was the battalion and company area. Except when he was in the field, he would come to this place practically every day for the next two to three years. Even when the training schedule did not demand it, Nathan knew the place would draw him in, as it had pulled his father away from him when he was a boy and couldn't understand that the Army was more than a job.

Making his way to the adjutant's office, Nathan was directed to take a seat in front of a clerk's desk. That he was in a combat unit was obvious even from the appearance of the clerk. While those at division and brigade had been properly dressed and had their hair trimmed well within regulations, the clerk before him now sported a severe buzz cut that left each individual hair standing upright, as if at attention. The clerk's BDUs were obviously starched despite a prohibition against the practice. There was little doubt, Nathan thought as he watched the clerk thumb through his paperwork, that the clerk's boots could be used as a mirror.

Young Lieutenant Dixon was still sitting there, answering questions and filling in the nine thousand seven hundred and eighty-fifth form of the day when a loud bang, like a door being kicked open, reverberated throughout the building. Lost in his own thoughts Nathan all but jumped out of his seat, jolted by the noise into a sudden flashback to his first days at VMI. With a shake of his head Nathan regained his composure and previous posture as quickly as he could. As he did so he noted that everyone in the office, including the cool and collected clerk who had been preparing more forms for Nathan to fill out, was frozen in place with one ear cocked, waiting for whatever came next.

From the hall outside the office, a raspy voice bellowed. "*ADJUTANT!* Get me Captain Cockran, *NOW!*"

From an adjoining office a voice Nathan assumed belonged to the adjutant called out in response as the tromp of boots stormed down the long hall. "Do you want him on the phone or in your office, sir?"

The angry footfalls stopped where Nathan guessed the door of the adjutant's office opened into the corridor. Through the open door that connected the adjutant's office to the one he was in, Nathan saw a helmet fly across the room before it smacked into a wall with a loud thud. "*In my fucking office, Captain,*" the helmet thrower responded in an irritated voice that echoed throughout the building.

The senior clerk, a sergeant first class, let out a sigh of relief and whispered, "Thank God he missed the window."

The clerk in front of Nathan, now reassured that he was not going to be the object of the intruder's wrath, leaned forward over the pile of forms closer to Nathan. "That, sir, is Lieutenant Colonel Norman Blackwell, the battalion commander. He must have been displeased with the inspection of the rifle range Cockran's company is running." Easing back in his seat, the clerk paused a minute before returning to his incessant paperwork, watching with glee as Nathan's apprehension about the coming interview with his new battalion commander multiplied by a factor of ten.

He didn't have long to wait. After making a call to B Company, the adjutant gingerly stuck his head around the corner into the open doorway that connected his office with that of the battalion commander. While the clerks around him threw themselves back into their work, Nathan strained to hear the exchange between the adjutant and commander. "Sir," the adjutant choked out, "Captain Cockran isn't in right now. First Sergeant Pruit isn't quite sure where he is. But," the adjutant hastened to add, "he promised he'd find him most ricky tick and send him up here."

At first there was no response. Nathan could all but feel the anger radiating from the battalion commander as he struggled to regain control of his temper. As with so many other things, the sights and sounds of this sort of tantrum were familiar to him. Often his father, frustrated by a bad day, would storm home where he would transfer his anger from a deserving target to his own children. Scott Dixon never meant to do so, Jan often told them. "Your father is a passionate man," she would explain to a young boy whose only concept of passion was love and affection.

Finally the raspy voice mumbled something that Nathan didn't quite hear. Watching, he could see the adjutant's shoulders visibly relax despite being well hidden by the baggy BDU shirt he wore. "Sir," the adjutant continued while still exposing only his head in the open doorway, "while you're waiting for Captain Cockran would you care to talk to our new lieutenant? He's right outside."

In Nathan's mind alarms sounded as he held his breath and waited for the response. "No, please no," Nathan found himself praying. But luck was seldom an item second lieutenants were issued in any appreciable quantity. From the open doorway through which the adjutant peered, came a disgruntled "Sure, why not."

Not waiting to be called forth, Nathan stood up and slowly began to make his way through the first open doorway. As he did so Nathan was amazed by how closely his feelings of dread and apprehension matched similar feelings he had experienced in the past. It had been this way when he had been a small child, called to task by his father for smacking his younger brother with a baseball bat. There was no difference between his feelings now and those he had when he went off to his high school principal after it had been discovered that Nathan and his friend had fed a program into one of their teacher's computers that forced the poor teacher to endure several minutes of military marches before he could do anything on it. And of course, answering numerous special reports to the commandant of cadets at VMI for public display of affection always managed to generate a level of fear and loathing that was most uncomfortable.

Pulling back from the entrance to Colonel Blackwell's office, the adjutant informed Nathan of the obvious. "The battalion commander will see you now, Lieutenant." There was no missing the relief in the adjutant's voice.

Stopping at the doorway as he had been taught, Nathan rapped on the doorframe and waited to be called into his superior's private lair. The first thing that struck Nathan as he moved forward until he was but three feet in front of the battalion commander's desk was the proliferation of maroon and gold banners, pennants, and other regalia. Even as he snapped his right arm up into a crisp, regulation salute, Nathan could not help but think things had just about gotten as bad as they could. His battalion commander was an Aggie, a graduate of Texas A&M.

Stepping from the shadows of the doorway, where he had hung the field gear he had been wearing on a rack neatly, Colonel Blackwell slowly made his way to his seat. As he did so, he eyed Nathan up and down. From his position Nathan did likewise, as best he could. Blackwell was a tall man who gave new meaning to Nathan's definition of lanky. What hair he had was close chopped to the point where the widow's peak dipping down into his forehead was all but invisible. There was so little of the stuff that Nathan could not tell, for sure, what color the man's hair was.

"Take a seat, *Lieutenant*," Blackwell barked, all but choking on the word lieutenant as if it were a bone stuck in his throat. As he did so Nathan looked into the colonel's eyes. Everything about the man, he quickly concluded, was lean and mean. From the narrow, almost hawkish-looking face to the cold, steady gaze Blackwell returned stated boldly that he was a warrior.

For the longest of moments Blackwell stared at Nathan. Not knowing what to do or say, Nathan returned it. Was this, Nathan wondered, some sort of trial of wills? Was he waiting for me to blink, or flinch, or divert my eyes? If it was, the young officer concluded, he would not give the old man the pleasure of breaking first. As he had learned to do with his father, Nathan allowed his eyes to narrow, just slightly, to show that the flame of passion and determination burned within his heart just as brightly.

Having seen many a lieutenant come and go during his

eighteen years of service, Norman Blackwell knew a winner when he saw one. Allowing one corner of his lips to curl up a tad in what passed as a smile for him, Blackwell allowed himself to ease back in his seat. "I know you're not going to want to hear this, Lieutenant Dixon, since I'm sure you've been hearing it all day, but I greatly admire your father. He's a warrior. A no frills, cut the bullshit and get the job done honest to God warrior. How he ever managed to make it to general in today's Army has never ceased to amaze me."

While it was obvious that the colonel's statement had much more meaning packed into it than he probably intended, Nathan listened politely and nodded. "Yes, sir," he responded when he couldn't think of anything better to say.

Again, there was a momentary silence as Blackwell looked Nathan over. Then the colonel leaned forward, placing his forearms on the desk before him and resting the weight of his upper body on them. "That having been said," he stated slowly in a low, rumbling tone that reminded Nathan of prelude to a Wagnerian opera, "I have no intention of measuring you, one way or the other, against your father. You, lieutenant, will stand or fall on your own merits and abilities. As long as I am in command of this battalion, it will be your performance and not your father's past achievements or current rank that will determine if you have a future in *my* Army."

Though he was unsure if the colonel was expecting a response, Nathan felt obliged to give one. "That, sir, is what I expect."

Again, there was a slight quivering at the corner of the colonel's mouth as it struggled to smile. "Good," he announced. "You're going down to A Company, Captain King's unit. He's a good man and a tough character. He'll push you to the limits."

What exactly Blackwell meant by this escaped Nathan. But whatever it portended, it didn't sound very comforting. After another long pause, the colonel leaned further forward until he was all but lifting himself out of his seat. "You're being given 3rd Platoon, I hear. That's Sergeant

Gandulf's platoon. It's a good platoon. Don't fuck it up."

After having been lulled into a sense of security, this last statement rattled Nathan. "Don't fuck it up?" This was the single most important pearl of wisdom his battalion commander could give him? Don't fuck up a platoon?

Nathan's mind was still reeling from this shock when he heard the adjutant's voice from behind. "Sir," the staff captain whispered, "Captain Cockran is in my office, awaiting your pleasure."

Without a glance or a nod Blackwell acknowledged the adjutant, then turned his attention back to Nathan. "This battalion, like all airborne battalions, has a tough mission," he stated as he stood up and extended his right hand toward Nathan.

Jumping up from his seat, Nathan took the colonel's hand. "Well, sir, I'm ready."

Grasping Nathan's hand in a viselike grip, Blackwell pulled the young lieutenant forward a bit. "You better be," he whispered menacingly before he let Nathan's hand go. With that he dismissed his newly assigned officer and turned his mind and attention to dealing with one of his captains as only a battalion commander knows how.

After the interview with the battalion commander, Nathan's introduction to "King Andrew" was a breeze. From the moment he stepped into his company commander's office, Nathan could sense that this officer did not possess the same commanding presence that Norman Blackwell had in abundance. It was more than the tone of voice in their stilted conversation. Blackwell had paused several times when he had talked to Nathan. But those pauses had been for effect. The numerous interludes in conversation with Captain Andrew King, however, seemed more from a lack of forethought than intent.

Unlike the battalion commander, King took great pains to explain what his expectations of Nathan were. "You have great deal to learn," King pointed out several times, "about handling soldiers. This isn't VMI, or West Point, or Texas A&M. All too often the troopers you'll be leading think they have a better idea, or what is or isn't important. I am the company commander," King stated crisply. "I obey the colonel's every order and, in turn, when I give an order I expect you to hop-to, salute sharply, and execute that order without question, without hesitation. Is that clear, Lieutenant?"

Nathan resisted the urge to smile. He had heard this all before, first from his father, then from his cadre at VMI. He was beginning to wonder if this statement, like so many others, was not carefully inscribed on a sacred stone tablet entitled "The Maxims of Army Leadership" that was hidden away where the passing of time and sunlight never intruded. Of course Nathan knew that an order was an order. Of course he understood that when a company commander said jump, the only question that would be tolerated from a platoon leader was "how high?" So he let this part of the protracted in-briefing by his company commander make its way in one ear and, just as quickly, slip out the other.

The rest of this first meeting between Andrew King and his new platoon leader covered a lot of ground. During a monotone monologue, King tried to address everything. The status and strength of the unit, the daily routine of A Company, the training cycle they were currently in, and a brief discussion on what to expect by way of exercises in the near future were all touched upon. "Our plate," King pointed out after doing so, "is quite full. So I expect you to hit the ground with both feet and at a full run."

For some reason, Nathan felt at ease with his new company commander. Not because he sensed a budding friendship. Nor was it out of respect. Rather, the feeling that he had little to fear from this man began to slowly make its way into Nathan's conscious mind. While King looked every bit the company commander and spoke the words Nathan had come to imagine a company commander would use, King radiated a sense of uneasiness. Whether it was just this particular situation he found himself in or if the man truly was not comfortable with his position as a company commander was hard to say. Only time would tell if King was as good as Blackwell had made him out to be.

In the meantime, Nathan had other concerns and issues to deal with. There was the task of meeting his platoon, no small thing for a newly minted "butter bar" intent on making the best possible impression on the men he was expected to lead. But first, before all else, Nathan was determined to shed his dress greens and break out a set of BDUs as quickly as possible. Only then, when he had made himself a less conspicuous target, would he be ready to train and maintain in a manner that would be befitting, and expected of, the son of Scott Dixon.

CHAPTER 10

Ted Lahowitz didn't budge when Ellen French opened the passenger door of the plain white late model Ford. "Are you going to help me or what?" Ellen called through the rolled down window as she struggled to balance the two cups and bag she held.

Ted made no efforts to come to her assistance. Instead, he merely looked over at her. "As I recall," he replied in a high pitched tone that bordered on being sanctimonious, "there is a Bureau policy that governs this sort of thing. It states, if I remember correctly, that members of different genders are prohibited from doing anything extraordinary or different during the performance of duties simply because the gender of their partner is different. That, it seems, could be construed as sexual harassment."

"Screw you, Ted," she snapped as she looked down to see if the coffee in her hands had stopped slopping about after her long walk from the convenience store. When it had, she placed one cup on the roof of the car so she could open her door.

"I hope you realize that's prohibited by policy, too," Ted said, without stirring from his slouched position.

"You can be such an asshole when you're on stakeout," Ellen muttered in a disgusted voice as she turned to sit while keeping the coffee from spilling.

Feigning surprise, Ted Lahowitz recoiled. "Why, Special Agent French, I am shocked! I am simply trying to protect you from becoming victimized."

"Bull," Ellen sputtered as she settled in and set the cups of coffee in the cup holders. "You're bored, just like me, and have nothing better to do than bust my chops."

"Ellen," Ted replied using the same exaggerated manner he had before, "I thought you would be thrilled sitting out here, in suburbia, watching the comings and goings of a suspected terrorist?"

"If I wanted to waste my days sitting in a car," Ellen mumbled as she pulled the lid off her cup of coffee, "I'd stay home and play chauffeur for my own kids." Then she looked up, out the windshield of the car at the small two bedroom cracker box belonging to Louis Garvey and a local mortgage company once owned by GO Thomas. "He still hasn't come out this morning?" Ellen asked before carefully testing the temperature of her coffee by taking a small sip.

"Nope," sighed Ted as he settled back into a more comfortable position. "Unlike our fearless leader, Captain Queeg, Mr. Garvey varies his routine."

"Captain who?" Ellen asked as she sipped her coffee and watched the house.

"Captain Queeg, the commanding officer in Herman Wouk's book *The Caine Mutiny*. Are you telling me you never heard of it?"

Ellen looked over at Ted. "Why? Should I have?"

"Well," Lahowitz replied incredulously, "*The Caine Mutiny* is only the most famous novel of World War Two."

In a tone that reminded him of his wife's response when she was unimpressed or uninterested in something he was discussing, Ellen responded with a short, crisp "Oh."

"You don't get it, do you?"

Ellen looked up. "No, I really don't."

"Well," Ted started, shifting his weight so that he faced his partner, "it's the middle of World War Two. There's this Navy warship . . . ."

"Was there another type of warship in World War Two?" Ellen asked playfully.

Ignoring her barb, just as he did with his spouse, Ted continued. "They have this captain, Captain Queeg, who's a real zero. He's a real marionette who does nothing but make life for his ship's company and their officers absolutely miserable."

"I see," Ellen responded in a silly, exaggerated female voice as she watched the house.

Undeterred by her efforts to make fun of him, Ted went

on. "Well, when Captain Queeg finds out that he's unpopular, he retreats to his cabin every chance he gets, just like our own, jolly special agent in charge. When he does come out Queeg always takes the same path to the bridge or the ward room in an effort to avoid contact with his crew. The crew, in turn, kept that part of the ship spotless while leaving the rest of the boat go to hell."

"Unlike some people I know, I keep my desk straight even though Tim Werner doesn't bother walking by there."

The words, "well, of course, you're a woman," were on the tip of Ted's tongue but he managed to keep them in check. Instead, he twisted in his seat a moment while he thought of another retort. "My desk is functional," he mumbled.

"Ha!" Ellen exclaimed. "So is a toxic waste site."

Finding himself becoming agitated by his partner's attitude, Ted was about to give her a good "what for" when Ellen sat upright. "Our man is on the move," she snapped as she watched Garvey walk out of the house and head for his well-used blue pickup.

Ted looked at his watch. "Where do you think he's headed? He's not due in at work for another two hours."

"Could be he was called by the school about one of his children," Ellen ventured.

Shaking his head, Ted watched their suspect slide in behind the wheel. "No. We would have been alerted by the boys monitoring his phone." When Garvey pulled away from the curb, Ted started his own car, checked the rearview mirrors, and started to follow, making sure that his departure was smooth and easy, so as not to arouse too much suspicion. "Give the office a call," he ordered. "Let them know we're on the move and alert the backup team."

Though she was already on the phone Ellen replied with a crisp, "I'm on it."

For a while the two special agents followed the blue pickup as it made its way along Broadway into Boise. As each of his normal stops slipped away into the rear view mirror, both Ellen French and Ted Lahowitz perked up. "Give a call and have them double check his calls," Ted ordered as they made their way along.

Ellen shook her head. "The monitoring team has already confirmed that the last time he was on the phone was last night, when he signed on to the Internet. Maybe this trip was triggered by an e-mail."

Now it was Ted's turn to shake his head. "Yeah, well, you're probably right. Whatever got him going, let's hope he's finally leading us to someone that really matters. I'm getting tired of watching him."

"Oh boy," Ellen exclaimed mockingly. "Then we can go back and join the rest of the boys and girls from the office sitting outside the governor's mansion as he and the media make fun of our surveillance there."

Ted looked at Ellen and chuckled. "Well, at least they eat better out there. I hear tell that after July Fourth the quality of the food GO's staff brought out to our people actually improved."

Ellen smiled as she poked her finger into the soft layer of flab that protruded over Lahowitz's belt. "Maybe that's why you were assigned to the night watch."

Before he could reply Ted noticed that the blue truck slowed as it approached the Federal building on West Fort Street. The smirk that he had been sporting was instantly transformed into a frown. "What the . . ."

When he saw the truck pull into the drive leading to the security checkpoint Ted was faced with a tough decision. He could come to an abrupt stop and let Ellen dismount to follow their man on foot, or pull up behind the truck now stopped at the security guard's booth. Unsure of what to do but faced with the need to do something fast, Ted slowed the car and swerved off the main street, blocking the driveway leading to the Federal building. "Ellen, get out and see where he's going."

On the phone again, Ellen didn't respond to his command. Instead, she listened to the voice on the other end until it was finished. Clicking the OFF button, Ellen looked over to Ted. "Well, we know where he's headed."

Confused, Ted looked over at his partner. "Oh?"

"The judge is about to announce his decision on the question of venue for the Idaho Six."

Ted shook his head. "When did they find this out back

at the office? No one told me this morning about this."

Ellen paused. "No one in the office was informed until just a few minutes ago."

Pausing a moment, Ted considered this bit of information. "Didn't you say that our boy made no calls, or received no calls after he signed off the Internet at 10:30 last night?"

Flustered at being asked this at a time when she was trying to get out of the car and take off in pursuit of Garvey, Ellen snapped, "That's right. No calls, incoming or outgoing and no Internet."

"That means he knew last night," Ted exclaimed in utter amazement. "He knew this was going to come down and when it was going to happen hours before we did."

Finally understanding, Ellen looked back at her partner. When the shock of this revelation finally passed, she shrugged her shoulders and sighed. "What can I say. This is Idaho."

The scene in the hall outside the courtroom was utter pandemonium. A throng of cameramen, sound techs, and photographers milled about in front of the closed doors protected by a pair of harried Federal marshals. Pulling her badge from her purse, Ellen flashed it in one hand as she used the other to push her way through the throng. At the door she came across a marshal wearing a disgusted look on his face. "Sorry, ma'am. This is a closed session. We're under instructions to admit only those with official court business."

Ellen thrust her FBI credentials in the marshal's face. "FBI. I have business in this court," Ellen bellowed out in order to be heard.

Though he was tempted to deny her access, several journalists heard Ellen's announcement and began to press forward in an effort to engage her in an interview. Seeing that he could stand fast and face being crushed by a gaggle of frenzied reporters or let the woman in, the marshal opted for self-preservation.

Once inside, Ellen collect herself. Looking up after

smoothing out her skirt, she searched the room for the man whom she had been following for months. Not surprisingly, everyone that mattered in Idaho was there, including the Governor's personal assistant, the state's attorney general, and the head of the state police. Seated in the row behind this assembly of officials was her man, Louis Garvey. Just how he had managed to make his way past the Federal marshals intrigued Ellen, as well as the question why he had chosen that particular place in the courtroom to roost.

Putting those concerns aside for the moment, Ellen scanned the courtroom. At the front of it, standing inches away from the judge's bench, was Kevin Duke, the high profile lawyer who was representing the Idaho Six. He was consulting with the judge in private. She also noted that she was the only FBI agent on the scene. Stepping aside, she found a seat, fished out her cell phone, and began to make a call to the office to report.

Another spectator who was seated behind Ellen leaned forward to shush her as she tried to fill her boss in. Angered by this, Ellen turned around to tell the person trying to hush her where she could go. When she saw who it was, however, the special agent checked herself. It would not be in the best interest of the Bureau at a time like this to piss off Jan Fields. After exchanging glances with the nationally renowned journalist, Ellen settled down to listen to the proceedings.

While the harried Federal attorney cooled her heels at the table reserved for the prosecution, the judge and Kevin Duke conferred in whispers. "Your honor," Duke repeated, "my clients are pawns."

Placing his hand over the mike before him, the judge nodded. "I fully understand that the decision I am about to hand down has all sorts of political ramifications." Then, sheepishly, he looked into Duke's eyes. "Kevin, I did the best I could."

This did little to calm the attorney for the accused. "Frank, you know as well as I do that the people of this state are not going to let their own be carted off to Seattle to be tried in a community noted for its liberal leanings."

"Kevin, it's Seattle. The Attorney General was pushing for San Francisco."

Duke shook his head. "If you ask me, Seattle is no better. Hell, you might as well ship my clients off to Tiananmen Square and let the Chicoms run them over with tanks. In the end the results will be the same."

Tiring of Duke's argument, the judge shook his head. "The decision has been made. Now, if you would please go back to your table we can proceed and be done with this."

Duke stepped back, but could not resist the temptation to get the last word in. "I'm sorry to hear you say that, Your Honor," he stated in a voice that could now be heard throughout the courtroom. "I do hope that you and those folks back in Washington bear in mind that we, the people of Idaho, as well as every self-respecting American concerned about his Constitutional rights, are far from being done with this."

Even before the judge's gavel slammed down to bring the session to an end, the assembled journalists were off their marks and in a race to get their stories out. With her cameraman and sound tech following in her wake, Jan Fields picked her way through the press of reporters, spectators, Federal officials, and miscellaneous individuals who had the bad luck of being on that floor of the federal building at that moment. Knowing that she would be live on national television within minutes, Jan ignored everyone, including her own crew, as she made for the queue waiting at the bank of elevators. Her mind, as it always was at moments like this, fixed on the sights and sounds of the events she had just witnessed and how she would package and present them to the American public.

Through this jumble of thoughts a feeling that the story here in Idaho was far from over began to manifest itself in Jan's conscious mind. The strident statement made by the attorney for the Idaho Six had been little more than a poorly veiled threat. That his sentiment was shared by the state and local officials who had been present was obvious as they made no effort to hide their outrage over the decision handed down. Though their responses were a tad more guarded, none bothered to hide their disappointment or disgust during the pandemonium that had brought the proceedings to an acrimonious end. No, Jan found herself saying over and over as she waited for the elevator, this is just the beginning. What occurred in the courtroom, she told herself, was but another skirmish in that bitter struggle between those who stood for states' rights and the containment of the Federal government and that government itself. That much was obvious. What was not clear was how, and where, the next act of this drama would be played out.

When the elevator doors opened, she was swept along with the crowd into the elevator. Like her there were a number of journalists anxious to get out onto the courthouse steps where they would find a spot and shoot their stories. After shifting her shoulders about until she had established her own comfortable space in the crowded cab, Jan looked up, like everyone else, to follow their descent.

Suddenly, from somewhere in the dark recesses of her mind, an image leaped forth into her consciousness. It was a picture, a still photograph of a shattered elevator cab like the one she was in lying twisted and partially covered by rubble of a building ripped apart by a terrorist's bomb. Though she couldn't recall whether it was from Oklahoma's Murraugh Building, or the World Trade Center, or the last Federal building to be hit, she clearly remembered the debate over whether it should be used in a news story or not. Some felt that the image of a bloody arm hanging listlessly from doors jarred partially open by the impact of the elevator's fall was too intense for TV audiences. Others chided the more squeamish, reminding them that they had used images that were far worse before. "Remember what they say," one particularly cavalier individual admonished. "If it bleeds, it leads."

Jan had remained aloof from the discussion. Not because she didn't have an opinion. Rather, she had found herself mesmerized by the photo. She found that she had to keep reminding herself that the photo had not been taken in Tel Aviv, or Bosnia, or Colombia. The photo had been in her own country, in a building very much like many a one she and her loved ones often visited. While she had faced danger in the past, the idea that such things could occur in the very city where she lived, or that a wanton act of terrorism could take from her people she loved and cared for in the blink of an eye rattled her in a way she had never been shaken before.

Suddenly Jan found herself gripped by panic. The idea that the next arm hanging out of a demolished elevator could be hers overwhelmed her. Glancing about at her fellow riders Jan wondered what she would do if a bomb suddenly went off in this building. Nothing. There would be nothing that she could do. She would die right there together with this random collection of strangers. Instead of being a star journalist she would simply become the next victim, part of another tangled pile of mangled body parts left for a rescue worker to find, sort, tag, and bag.

Nervously, Jan shifted her weight from one foot to the other, subconsciously trying to push her way forward as if being close to the door might somehow get her out of this terrible danger sooner. Jerking her head up, she looked to see what floor they were on. *No!* she found herself thinking. *We're going too slow. Too slow.*

When the elevator stopped on the second floor to discharge some of the passengers, Jan couldn't take it any longer. In desperation she squeezed herself between two men in front of her and slipped by her own crew. Dumbfounded by her unexpected and irrational flight, the cameraman watched Jan as the door of the elevator closed between them.

For a moment she just stood there. As beads of sweat began to drip down her brow, Jan stared at the outer doors of the elevator trying hard to regain her composure. While she was still in a Federal building and, in theory, no safer here than she would have been in the elevator, somehow, just being free of the press of people in an enclosed space made a difference. Was this, she finally found herself thinking as she felt her pounding heart begin to slow to its normal rhythm, what the terrorists are after? Is this the sort of fear and panic they are seeking to sow in the hearts and minds of their fellow Americans? *Why?* she wondered. *Why did they want to do this to us? To me?*

After what seemed like an eternity, she found she was able to move, and Jan turned away from the dreaded elevator. As she made her way to the stairway, she found that she could not escape the irony of this incident. After so many years of being exposed to violence all over the world, Jan realized that she had finally come to feel true fear and panic in the country that had always been synonymous with safety and security. A land that was her home.

CHAPTER 11

Slowly Tim Werner passed his razor under the faucet, flushing away the shaving cream and accumulated stubble. With more effort than it should have taken, he looked up at the face in the mirror before him. The dark circles under the eyes and pale, gaunt expression belonged to a man who had been beaten down and humiliated, not a special agent in charge of a field office. Mechanically lifting the razor to his face, Werner took a few short, quick strokes. He was used to having his way. He was a man that his superiors turned to when they had a case no one else could handle. As he eased the razor across his chin Werner found himself asking where he had gone wrong. When had he lost control of this investigation? He even began to wonder if had ever been in control.

The answers to those questions were no real mystery to him or anyone else privy to the politics that had been driving the case. Hampered by oversupervision from the Bureau and unrelenting pressure applied by the Justice Department, Werner had never been afforded the opportunity to establish a coherent methodology with which to pursue his investigation. The order to arrest those suspects prematurely that his agents had been following only accelerated the unraveling of a case that was already teetering on the edge of failure. The massive fire that had accompanied the arrest of a gun shop owner in Pocatello and the release of Louis Garvey, a man known to head the most notorious militia unit in the state, due to a lack of evidence only served to make things worse.

Within days of arresting the militiamen who were being referred to by the media as the Idaho Six, every man and woman in his office had become the target of vandalism and harassment. From slashed tires to pigs' heads impaled on stakes planted on the front lawns of their homes, Werner and his fellow agents in the Boise office had been under siege. By the end of the first week those agents who could do so had sent their families out of state in an effort to keep them out of harm's way. After two weeks the entire administrative staff of the FBI's field office in Boise had quit or applied for indefinite leave. Were it not for the fact that the Bureau had sent replacements in from the Washington office, Tim Werner's investigation of the militia movement in Idaho, hamstrung as it was, would have come to a complete and screeching halt.

Not that he had been able to make any progress of late. Even before the last embers of the fires in Pocatello had died, cooperation from state and local officials had ceased. The reams of advice sent to him daily from Bureau head-quarters on how to proceed only tended to make matters worse. Rather than pursuing vicious criminals, Werner and his people had become virtual prisoners in an unde-clared war between the Federal government and the people and state of Idaho. What had started as a difficult case had become an unending nightmare.

Finished shaving, the bewildered agent in charge cleaned his razor under the running water. Without cere-mony he splashed hot water over his face to clear away the last traces of shaving cream before turning his back on the miserable wretch in the mirror that greeted him every morning.

Well, he concluded after carefully checking his car in an effort to determine if it had been tampered with during the night, at least this sorry chapter in his life would soon be over. Once the Idaho Six had been turned over to the FBI's hostage rescue team flying in that morning, and whisked away to Seattle, he would be permitted to quietly close down his investigation here and return his office to normal operations. How he would accomplish that in the face of the animosity that was sure to linger was a good question. The only thing Werner was sure of was that the legal attaché position in London, England that he had been in line for was no longer his for the taking. He was even beginning to wonder if he'd be retained as a special agent in charge. The way he figured it, as he aimed his car toward the heart of Boise in the predawn darkness, they wouldn't leave him in Idaho for very long once the dust had settled. After an appropriate amount of time he'd be shipped off to either a training or an administrative posting at the Bureau. There, in a backwater job with nothing but a desk to supervise, he'd be permitted to serve out his time until retirement, if he was lucky.

He was still mulling over these depressing thoughts as he made the turn into the underground parking garage of the First National Bank Building where the FBI officers were when he found his path blocked. At first he didn't quite know what to make of the black and yellow wooden barricade that sat smack dab in the middle of the entrance ramp. Only when a state trooper stepped out of the shadows and tapped on the car window did Tim Werner snap out of his momentary brain lock. Shaking his head, Werner rolled down his window. "A bomb threat?" he asked without thinking.

With his face frozen in a tense deadpan expression, the state trooper asked Werner for identification. "Special Agent Werner, FBI. What's going on?"

The trooper didn't answer. Instead he straightened up, took a quick step back away from the car, and brought his right hand up till it rested on the butt of his pistol. "Sir," the trooper commanded, "please keep your hands in sight and get out of the car."

With his growing sense of confusion giving way to anger, Werner stared at the trooper for a moment. "Do what?"

Like ghosts rising out of the morning mist other troopers began to gather in the shadows behind the one confronting Werner. With his legs spread shoulder width apart and his weapon half drawn, the lead trooper repeated his demand. "Sir, for the last time, get out of your car."

For the first time Werner appreciated just how precarious his position was. Slowly opening the door of his car he climbed out, taking great care to keep his hands in full view at all times. Though the anger he felt welling up was damned near intolerable, a voice of caution from the back of his mind kept whispering that he was still in Idaho. Here, the voice reminded him, the accepted rules of law and order that he had spent a lifetime enforcing did not always apply.

BOISE INTERNATIONAL AIRPORT, BOISE, IDAHO • EARLY MORNING, OCTOBER 30

The Air Force transport rolled through the darkness down the taxiway to the area where Air National Guard aircraft sat. There the transport would be guided into a slot assigned to it by a ground handler. Once parked, the FBI hostage rescue team would be free to off-load their vehicles in the relative security of this isolated portion of the airport.

Standing next to the aircraft's loadmaster at the rear of the aircraft, the head of the hostage rescue team, Special Agent Keith Brown, yawned as he waited for the ramp to be lowered. Like the rest of his men he had spent most of the flight fast asleep. Somehow, escorting six prisoners from Boise to Seattle just didn't seem to be all that demanding to men who were trained to deal with world class terrorists and certified wackos. Lacking any prospect of imminent danger, Brown had found it all but impossible to get himself or his people pumped up for this operation. Everyone who had someone waiting at home for them had advised their domestic partners that they would be home for dinner. "We collect the dirt bags in Boise," Brown informed the men and women on his team, "drive them out to the airport, load 'em up, and hustle them off to Seattle."

While he was not a man who took any of his assignments lightly, Brown knew a sleeper when he saw one. So his mind was on everything from the next day's training schedule to the lecture he'd deliver to his rebellious fourteen year old that night as he rubbed his eyes and listened to the whine of an electric motor lowering the ramp.

The booming voice magnified many times louder than it needed to be by a bullhorn came as a shock. "Attention hostage rescue team," the voice thundered. "This is Major Joshua Campbell of the Idaho State Police. Come down the ramp with your hands over your heads."

Stunned, Brown dropped his hands from his face. Bug eyed, he found himself staring into the glaring headlights of a dozen police cruisers pointed at the tail of the Air Force transport. Behind him other members of the team dropped what they had been doing and began to gather around him to see what all the commotion was about. Unprepared for this sort of reception, Brown desperately tried to sort out the situation that he faced. "You out there," he shouted as he held his hand up to shield his eyes from the lights. "I am Special Agent Keith Brown, Federal Bureau of Investigation. We are here to . . ."

"We know who you are and why you are here," the voice boomed back.

"Then you realize that you are interfering with the transfer of prisoners as directed by the Department of Justice of the United States and the Ninth Court of Appeals," Brown retorted as loudly as he could in a vain effort to match the bullhorn assisted state trooper.

"By order of the governor of the sovereign state of Idaho," Campbell bellowed in return, "I have been instructed to take you and your men into protective custody until such time as arrangements can be made to return you to wherever it is you came from."

"What the hell is going on, Keith?" a voice from behind him called out.

"It seems," Brown finally stated, "we're going to be late for dinner."

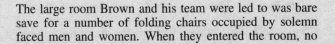

The large room Brown and his team were led to was bare save for a number of folding chairs occupied by solemn faced men and women. When they entered the room, no one made the slightest effort to greet them or explain what was going on. No longer able to control his rage, Brown exploded. "Who the *hell* is in charge of this goat rope?" he demanded after the last of his team had entered the room and the door slammed shut behind them.

From a corner of the room a man sitting alone, with dark circles under his eyes and a gaunt expression, lifted his head and looked at the newcomers. "I guess I am."

Like a Marine drill sergeant lighting into an errant recruit, Brown stormed across the room, screaming as loudly as his voice would permit. "You guess? You guess? What in Jesus, Mary, and Joseph's name is going on here? What in the hell is happening?"

With the calmness of a man who had fallen as far from grace and power as a man possibly could, Tim Werner looked up at Brown, who now stood towering over him. "Welcome to Idaho," Werner stated blandly. "Have a seat and stay awhile."

BOISE, IDAHO · EARLY MORNING, OCTOBER 30

With her crew crowded around her in their van, Jan Fields watched the live feed they were getting of the Federal officials and FBI agents being hustled down the ramp of a commercial airliner in Las Vegas, Nevada. "Do you think that there is a Biblical message in this?" Ito Saitama, the sound tech, ventured as they watched.

"What do you mean?" Jan asked without taking her eyes off the monitor.

"Well," Ito explained. "Maybe this is Governor Thomas's way of telling the FBI and Department of Justice to try their luck elsewhere."

Angela Carter, the cameraman, not generally known for her humor, managed to crack a smile. "Somehow, I think a man like GO Thomas wouldn't miss that sort of connection."

Jan didn't say anything. Instead she leaned back in her

tiny seat and shook her head. She was still upset that some-how a story like this unfolded just blocks away from the hotel where she was sleeping without her knowing it. "You're slipping, old girl," she whispered to herself as she caught a glimpse of Special Agent Tim Werner.

"What was that?" Ito asked, perking his ears up.

"Oh," Jan replied with a wave of her hand as she finally tore her eyes from the monitor and swiveled the chair to face her companions. "I said, you're both forgetting that it takes more than an order from the governor to close down the Federal building and expel all officials and agents of the Federal government from Idaho. There's a lot of people who have to be willing to put their butts on the line for something that is more than your average everyday run of the mill political grandstanding."

"Political grandstanding?" Angela shot back. "Are you trying to tell me that this is nothing but a stunt?"

The sound tech laughed before asking Jan if she thought the governor had lost his mind, a question many people across America were asking themselves that morning.

Jan didn't need to think before responding. She had al-ready managed to sort out the political landscape of the story she was covering long before this slow motion train wreck had occurred. "Idaho is far too small for a man like Thomas or the agenda he has been promoting. Somehow I have the feeling that he expects to walk out of the ex-ecutive mansion here in Boise two years from now and right into 1600 Pennsylvania Avenue. By making a radical statement like this he not only locks down the popular support of the people who have come to fear or resent the power of their own government, he stands to win those who have been praying on bent knee for a national leader who had the gonads to stand up for what he believed in. In the twinkling of an eye he has gained national recog-nition as a man of action, unafraid to confront a system many feel has run amuck."

"Well," Angela added, "if it was a bold political state-ment he was trying to make, he seems to have succeeded."

"Calling this a bold political statement," Ito quipped, "is like saying the Japanese bombing of Pearl Harbor was simply an expression of their displeasure over American foreign policy."

"Oh, come on. What happened this morning was not a declaration of war," Angela chided her coworker. "While I think it's more than a stunt, I doubt if this will go any further than an exchange of tersely worded phone calls and the usual exchange of political bombast and heated rhetoric. Within two weeks all the talk show hosts will be back to talking about the O. J. trial and who killed JonBenét."

"Well, let's hope you're right," Jan stated as she forced herself to put a check on her imagination. *After all,* she told herself as she turned back to watch the TV monitor and await instructions from the World News Network center, *I now have two people that I need to worry about if things get really stupid.*

THE GOVERNOR'S MANSION, BOISE, IDAHO • MORNING, OCTOBER 30

After mashing the button on the remote that controlled the small TV he kept in his office and chucking the remote onto his desk, GO Thomas spun about in his seat to face his Attorney General. "Tell me again how it is that you somehow got it into your head that you didn't need to call me before you staged this little disaster?"

From his seat Attorney General Thomas Jefferson Osborn shrugged. "There wasn't much time from when we received confirmation that the transfer was about to go down and the arrival of the FBI team from Quantico. As it was we barely had enough time to scrape up the units we needed in order to cover all the bases."

Thomas made no effort to hide the incredulity he felt over this lame excuse. "Tom, how many times have I told you that you can't bullshit a bullshitter."

Mustering up his best righteous indignation, Osborn shot back without hesitation. "We had no choice, GO. The only thing we would have accomplished by contacting you before this went down would have been to destroy your ability to deny that you were part of it."

Jumping out of his seat, Thomas slammed his hand down on the surface of his desk. "For Christ sake! I'm the governor of this state! I'm suppose to be in charge here!"

In response Osborn also came to his feet. "Then start acting like it, by God."

For a long, tense moment the two men glared at each other. Only after the heat of the moment had passed did Thomas look away. "You're right, Tom. As always, you're right."

Doing his best to hide the satisfaction he felt, Osborn relaxed his stance. "You better believe I'm right about this. After all, there has not been a more clear cut case of abuse of power by the Federal government since Reno snatched that little Cuban boy away from his relatives in Miami and sent the poor little wretch back to Castro. And while that was a slap in the face to every freedom loving American, to stand by and do nothing while Federal agents swooped down on your own state to haul away six of its citizens while an appeal over the issue of venue was still pending before the Supreme Court would have been disastrous to our cause."

Slumping down, GO Thomas brought his arm up onto the arm of his chair and rested his head in his hand. "This is not going to go well for us, you know. The national media will eat us alive. Together with the White House they will tie us to the bombing in Kansas and that incident in Wyoming. Everything we've worked for will be swept away."

Osborn smiled. "I've told you, GO, there is no way the FBI or anyone else can tie a single citizen of this state to either of those events. You've seen my report on the investigation I chaired."

Looking up at his Attorney General, Thomas shook his head. "You know as well as I do that the truth does not matter. It's what people feel to be true that counts. If there is one thing that those people in Washington have managed to do over the past ten years it's been to train the American people to ignore the facts."

"That may be so," Osborn responded. "And the timing may not have been our choice. But there it is. We either step up to the plate like men or step aside and let the redcoats march across the green and take what's left of our freedoms and the last of our dignity."

Spinning about, GO Thomas turned until he faced a portrait depicting the Battle of Lexington. "Do you suppose those men knew what they were starting that morning, or where their efforts would eventually lead them?"

Knowing that he had won his case, Osborn's smile grew. "Unlike those brave lads, I dare say we are better prepared to capitalize upon the opportunity that our foes in Washington have handed us."

Looking over at Osborn, Thomas felt a sudden chill. He was unsure whether it was due to the manner in which his Attorney General had referred to their fellow Americans as foes or the wicked little smile he was sporting. Whatever the reason, Thomas opted to say nothing. This was no time to begin to entertain doubts about the cause he had worked so hard to promote or the people he had chosen to help him achieve it. Faith, trust, and courage would be needed to see them through this.

Then, sensing that he had stumbled upon an idea around which he could fashion an address to the people of Idaho, GO snatched up a pen from his desk and scribbled those words down. Finished, he picked up the pad he had written on and stated them out loud. "Faith, trust, and courage."

Still smiling, Osborn nodded his approval. "I like that. I like that very much."

BOISE, IDAHO · AFTERNOON, OCTOBER 30

Unable to concentrate on her studies Nancy Kozak tossed aside the history book she had been struggling to read and picked up the remote to her TV. The news program that flashed up on the screen appeared to have picked up where it had left off an hour before when she grown weary of listening to witless news commentators and talking head experts rehash the events of that morning over and over and over again until even a dedicated news junkie like her could no longer tolerate it. Within five minutes she had had her fill. Getting up from the sofa, she marched over to the TV, hit the OFF button, and turned on her CD player. While she wasn't exactly in the mood for Celtic music, anything had to be better than listening to late breaking news that was eight hours old.

As the haunting melody of an Irish lament filled the room, the middle aged graduate student wandered about like a caged lioness. As unsettling as the events of that morning were to her, even more bothersome was the fact that she was not in a position to do anything about it. In the Army she had been a player, a participant who was always ready, willing, and able to respond. Even when a crisis popped up that didn't concern the United States, Nancy had felt some comfort knowing that simply by being in uniform, she was serving a useful purpose. Now, however, she was a no one. She was simply another spectator standing on the sidelines of history watching and waiting as others moved and shaped the world she lived in.

So when the call from her colonel came, she all but leaped at the opportunity to answer the call to the colors. Any thought that she was being sucked into the ever expanding storm that threatened the very foundation of the nation she so loved was, for the moment, conveniently forgotten. Never having been a good spectator, Nancy wanted to be a participant, not a pawn. As one of her old Army mentors was fond of saying, "There are only two kinds of people on the battlefield, killers and targets. Which are you?" Those who knew Nancy Kozak never had to ask her in which category she placed herself.

At the state headquarters Nancy didn't even have an opportunity to make it to her cubicle before she was whisked away to Colonel Simonson's office. "Have you been brought up to speed on what's been going on?"

With a look of confusion on her face, Nancy held her hat and purse out before her. "Sir, I haven't even laid eyes on my desk yet."

Pausing, her superior looked over at the purse and hat. Looking up, he shook his head. "No," he mumbled absentmindedly, "I guess you're not quite on board."

Nancy smiled. "Oh, that's okay. I imagine the situation isn't too hard to figure out."

Without another word, Simonson turned and walked behind his desk where he slumped down in his seat. As he did so his expression clouded. "I wish I could be as confident."

Nancy let her face assume an appropriate expression of concern as her arms dropped to the side and she waited for the colonel to continue.

"As a first move," Simonson started as he rotated his seat slowly around until he was looking out the window, "the President attempted to federalize the National Guard here in Idaho. The state adjutant general, of course, politely declined the mission, stating, and I quote, 'I have but one master, and one duty. My master is the governor of this state, and my duty is to defend that state and its people.' With that, he hung up the phone and issued orders that no one was to respond to any orders, instructions, or reply to any requests for information from anyone connected with the federal government or the media."

"So where does that leave us?" Nancy asked when the colonel's pause stretched out longer than she was comfortable with.

Spinning his seat around quickly, Simonson looked up at her. "It leaves you out at the ammo point at Gowen Field. You're to pull your detachment together as quickly as possible, beat feet out there, and secure of that facility as best you can."

"And after that?"

Simonson hesitated, rubbing his hands together as he thought for a minute. "Who knows," he finally admitted. "Perhaps nothing. Maybe, a serious case of sanity will break out and everyone will back down."

"If not?" Nancy pressed.

Standing up, Simonson wiped his hands on his trousers and stared at Nancy. "Colonel, I want you to keep a lid on the place. No one is to draw any ammunition without a written order from me. Is that clear? I have a nasty feeling," he added quickly, "things are going to get stupid around here right quick. I'd hate to see our people, or anyone else for that matter, running around armed to the teeth. Somewhere, someone is bound to do something unsmart. That, you can be sure of. There's not much I can do to stop them. But I can make damned sure the wrong folks don't get their hands on the good stuff."

Her superior didn't need to explain any more. While she had been shedding her civvies and breaking out a set of freshly laundered BDUs, she had managed to catch glimpses of the news. One of the more troubling reports was filed by an old acquaintance, Jan Fields. Besides interviewing the usual suspects, Jan Fields managed to find the leader of one of Idaho's most notorious militia groups, a man by the name of Louis Garvey. When asked by Jan what he and his group intended to do, the self appointed militia leader puffed out his chest and faced the camera head on. "We'll do anything necessary," he stated proudly, "to protect the sovereign rights of this state and its people. Anything."

So it wasn't the nature of the threat that worried her. Rather, it was the question regarding her authority. "If that's the case, sir," Nancy asked in an effort to extract as much guidance from her superior as possible, "what are the rules of engagement?"

"Rules of engagement?" Simonson asked rhetorically. "Colonel," he said as he leaned over his desk, supporting his upper body on his outstretched arms and knuckles. "Do whatever you need to do to keep all unauthorized personnel away from that ammunition."

"Who, sir," Kozak pressed on, "is authorized to draw ammunition?"

Growing angry, more from his own perceived impotence than from her questions, Simonson snapped. "As far as you and I are concerned, no one is. Understood?"

Coming to attention, Nancy saluted. "Understood." Knowing that there was nothing more to gain there, she smartly pivoted about on her heels, just as she had in the old days, when she had been serving with the best, and marched out of Colonel Simonson's office. She had a mission. Her orders were clear and, at a time like this, quite sensible. Now all she needed to do was gather her forces, organize them to do as she was ordered to, and make sure that they understood as clearly as she did the importance of their task.

FORT BRAGG, NORTH CAROLINA · EVENING, OCTOBER 30

Standing next to the doorway of the barracks, Sergeant First Class Michael Gandulf watched as the members of 3rd Platoon, Company A, 3rd of the 517th Parachute Infantry scramble by. Every so often he'd shout out, "Move it, people. Move it."

Outside, where the company stood parade, young Second Lieutenant Nathan Dixon watched men he didn't even know yet form ranks in front of him. Like him, they were decked out in full field order with weapons. Unlike him, they were completely at ease, not only with the way they were turned out, but with the organized pandemonium that had engulfed the entire battalion.

For the moment Nathan had nothing to do. Following his father's advice he was letting his NCOs do those things that they did best. While he was always given a rousing "Yes, sir!" whenever he said something Nathan appreciated the hard fact that he was not quite ready to handle his forty-plus paratroopers with the same degree of confidence and firmness that his NCOs could. During a lull in the frenzied activities, Nathan had pulled his platoon sergeant off to one side and asked if he could take care of things until they reached the green line. The platoon sergeant, who had seen many a second lieutenant come and go in his time, looked back at Nathan. "Sir," he announced without expression or any hint of disrespect in his voice, "I was planning on doing just that." Only after he saw what he took as hurt on Nathan's face did Sergeant First Class Gandulf reach out and place his hand on his platoon leader's shoulder. "Sir, I know where you're at. So don't worry. Me and the squad leaders will take care of you." With that the platoon sergeant excused himself, turned, and started chewing out one of their troopers who was wandering past them in a daze.

In the center of the battalion area, as Nathan watched his sergeants execute their assigned duties with an air of authority that Nathan envied, Lieutenant Colonel Blackman was casting a wary eye his way. When Blackman caught sight of Captain Andrew King he called that officer over to where he stood. "Is young Dixon ready for this?" the colonel started while the two were still saluting.

Andrew King was taken aback by his commanding officer's question. "Yes, sir," King responded, surprised that his commander would ask such a question. "Of course, he is."

Blackwell looked down at his junior company commander. "Of course?" Blackwell snapped. "Why 'of course?' I don't think you fully appreciate what we're being asked to do. Weren't you paying attention at the briefing?"

Offended that his superior could even entertain such a thought, Andrew King drew back. "Sir, I understand completely what we're about to do."

Blackwell snorted. "Well, then you're way ahead of everyone in Washington."

Shocked that his superior would denigrate their national leaders at a time like this, Andrew King didn't quite know what to say. Taking note of his subordinate's confusion, Blackwell's expression changed. "You're wondering how I can stand here, a leader who expects his troops to hop to and literally jump when I say so, and speak so disparagingly of our political leaders."

"Yes, sir," Andrew replied hesitantly.

Blackwell's face recast itself into an expression that betrayed the anger he always felt when discussing the matter. "Since the end of the cold war it has become a matter of habit," he stated in the low growl that was his signature, "to throw the military into situations that it has no business being thrown into by people who have no idea of what they are doing. Whether it be a quagmire like Somalia or a painful, lingering sore like Kosovo, presidents who have never shouldered a musket or lifted a finger in the defense of their country somehow imagine that they have the wisdom and intelligence necessary to weigh the risks and make informed decisions about when and where to place this nation's sons and daughters in harm's way. They rely on advisors and political appointees who have acquired their military expertise in the lecture halls of Harvard and Duke. They listen to military experts dredged up from the bottom of strategic think tanks ensconced in plush offices. And to lead the armed forces, they appoint generals whose primary qualifications are their adherence to the political correctness of the day and their ability to prove that they have impeccable mating habits."

By now, Andrew King was regretting having questioned his commander. Blackwell, ever a passionate man, was in rare form. The early evening darkness made his menacing expression even more sinister and threatening.

The battalion commander waved his hand in the direction where their soldiers were assembling. "I hope you appreciate the fact that it is those soldiers who pay the price if the well briefed plan we have just received goes astray. It will be young Dixon and his men who will have to sort out the mess created by our national leader's missteps and errors in judgment. And," he paused as he lowered his voice, "when it's discovered that the task we've been assigned is beyond our means, it'll be you and young Dixon who'll have to zip the body bags closed and write the letters home."

Embarrassed, Andrew King lowered his head to avoid his colonel's gaze. "Sir," he finally managed to state when he felt an appropriate amount of time had elapsed. "I am sure that Lieutenant Dixon is ready."

Blackwell, who had been doing his best to suppress the dark memories of a failed raid that had left the streets of Mogadishu littered with the corpses of his men years before, looked down at King. "You better be, Captain," he stated sharply. "Because if you're as wrong about Dixon as I suspect the man in the White House is about this mission, then it'll be you who'll have to face his father."

CHAPTER **12**

The young second lieutenant of infantry wasn't troubled by weighty thoughts of what might happen. Nor was he troubled by brutal images like those that plagued his battalion commander, for the younger Dixon lacked the memories of past wars that all veterans carried with them like an uncomfortable rucksack. Instead Nathan found himself swept along by the rush of events, a wide eyed innocent caught up in a world that he found both fascinating and exciting.

Everything was as he had imagined it would be. All around him soldiers armed to the teeth scurried about in a manner that was hasty yet purposeful, confusing yet productive. At key points commanders and staff officers were very much in evidence, standing erect as they watched and directed the marshalling of troops and equipment. In the staging areas they roamed through their units with a casualness that belied the concerns that furrowed their brows. With all the poise of a well rehearsed actor, these officers took care to stay out of the way of those who were moving things along while doing their best to instill an air of confidence and determination in the men and women they were responsible for and led.

Working side by side with the officers, yet clearly on their own and in a manner very different from that of their superiors, were the noncommissioned officers. These men were also executing their assigned duties with a single minded deliberateness that could not be swayed or denied. Even for one as inexperienced as Nathan, it was easy to see that it was the sergeants, young and old, who were pulling things together at the squad, platoon, and company level. For all his training, for all his mental preparation, it was only now that Nathan Dixon came to appreciate just how much he still had to learn about this Army that he belonged to. Equally clear to him was that it would be his sergeants and the soldiers whom they led, pulled, and kicked all the way from the barracks to the Green Line at Pope Air Base who would provide him with that education.

As if he were reading his platoon leader's thoughts, Sergeant First Class Gandulf went out of his way to make sure that he kept Dixon in motion and headed in the right direction. "Sir," Gandulf would say when he or one of the squad leaders caught sight of a senior officer headed their way, "If you have a moment, sir, 1st Squad is ready for your inspection." Or he'd shove a copy of the platoon's manifest in his face, asking loudly as he did so, "If you don't mind, sir, would you look this over?" In this way the veteran platoon sergeant kept his new lieutenant out of harm's way and, as best he could, taught the young and inexperienced officer what being an officer was about.

Of course Gandulf couldn't be everywhere all the time. He did, after all, have things that needed to get done that didn't require an officer or were best done without an officer present. When he and the squad leaders were off doing sergeant things, Nathan Dixon was left to his own devices.

There had been very little that Nathan needed to do to prepare himself or his personal equipment. Like all new officers he had sat alone in the middle of his apartment floor putting his gear together and combat packing it the very night it had been issued. Everything, right down to the spare underwear and socks secured in plastic food storage bags, was ready and waiting long before he received the phone call alerting him. And since he was an officer and expected to be squared away, he didn't have to endure the spate of pre-combat inspections that his men went through, first by their squad leaders, then by Sergeant Gandulf, followed by Nathan, and, finally, by Captain King.

It was during these awkward moments that the young platoon leader found himself staring at the riflemen of his platoon. They, in turn, unabashedly returned his stares, looking up from the ground where they sat nestled upon their equipment in reclining positions that looked more comfortable then they really were.

It slowly dawned upon Nathan how little he knew about the men he was expected to lead. While making his way along the line of soldiers patiently awaiting the next round of inspections or the order to pack up and move out, he tried to find some way of joining in on the easy banter that those still awake were engaged in. Like strangers in a big city who were unsure of the other's intentions, Nathan exchanged glances with the men who were expected to follow him wherever Captain King's orders took them. These troopers, the privates and specialists whose sole purpose in life was to physically gain and hold whatever ground their superiors designated, came from societies and cultures that were worlds apart from the one in which Nathan had been raised.

Throughout his life Nathan had never considered himself to be an elitist or thought that his childhood had been any different than that other American children experienced. While it was true that the high schools he attended were dominated by military dependents, Nathan saw himself as just another kid. Some of his friends and classmates had fathers or mothers who were senior NCOs while others, like himself, came from families whose military member was a commissioned officer. And while it was true that some of the children from both groups went out of their way to exclude those from the other group, Nathan didn't have the time for such pettiness.

The soldiers who made up his platoon, however, came from a world Nathan knew little of. Their experiences, their views, and their manner of dealing with things were as different and as unique as their personalities were. Robert Ortiz, a SAW gunner, had been born and raised in the border region south of San Diego, California. Until he was assigned to Company A, 3rd of the 517th Parachute Infantry Regiment, Ortiz had nothing in common with Kenneth Hyde, who hailed from Leominster, Massachusetts. Yet there they were, sitting side by side on the tarmac of an Air Force base in North Carolina, arguing about the merits of Ort's Ford as opposed to Hyde's Chevy. Though he had no interest in the subject, Nathan decided to stop and listen in for a moment. He did not mean to interrupt their lively debate. There wasn't anything he could add to it one way or the other. To Nathan cars were little more than a tool designed to carry people from one place to another. His sole purpose in stopping was to burn up some of the excess time he had on his hands in the only manner he had available.

It was Ortiz who took note of his new platoon leader first. With the same instincts that had been bred into him whenever an authority figure took notice of him, Robert Ortiz stopped what he was doing and allowed his face to reconfigure itself into an expression of guarded defiance. Following suit, Hyde's easy smile was replaced by a frown that served notice to anyone who saw it that he was a man not to be trifled with.

This sudden transformation startled Nathan. Though he saw all the signs and read them correctly, the young officer was at a loss to explain what he had done to call forth such a reaction or how best to respond. His leadership training at VMI and Benning had prepared him to lead soldiers, not relate to them. For several long seconds Nathan looked down at the two soldiers trying to think of something witty, something lighthearted to say.

But nothing came to mind. What would these men consider entertaining? What could he say that wouldn't offend either of them or their comrades who were sitting to either side of them? Could he make fun of their current plight or the pending operation which was, for Nathan, still very much a mystery?

It was Ortiz, the bolder of the pair, who broke the impasse. "Hey, LT. What made you buy a Saturn?" he asked with a hint of mockery in his voice.

Having been spared the embarrassment of saying something that might not come across well, Nathan smiled. "Not my call. My mom and dad gave it to me as a graduation gift. They thought it would be safer than the one I had picked out."

"Oh," Ortiz responded, as if saying, "That's what I figured."

Hyde, never known for being able to keep his mouth shut, joined in. "Gee, is that why your daddy let you become a par-a-trooper?"

The double slight was not lost on Nathan. Where he could easily have laughed off Ortiz's snide remark and walk away, Hyde's comment was a direct challenge that could not be ignored. Still, Nathan had come to appreciate that such slights were to be expected and not worth endangering his relationship with his men over. "Well," Nathan replied with a forced chuckle, "I suppose we all turn out better than our daddies expect, don't we?"

With a hoot, Ortiz turned to his friend and grinned, as if to say, "he got you."

Having been bested by his companion and anxious to change subject, Hyde looked up at his lieutenant. "Sir, you're an educated man. Can you tell me what all of this is about? I mean, I don't much listen to the news and when I do it seems like the people who are supposed to be running this country are more interested in calling their opponent names than telling us what they're really up to. Sometimes I get the feeling that they're trying to hide what they're doing from us."

Relieved to be on familiar ground, Nathan twisted about in an effort to shift the gear he wore as he considered how best to explain the complex issues and politics that had led up to the confrontation in Idaho. "Well, it seems the governor of Idaho, as well as other like minded governors and politicians, want to reform the way the Federal government goes about its business without rewriting the Constitution."

"Can they do that?" Ortiz asked. "Can the President rewrite the Constitution?"

Nathan shook his head as he smiled at the SAW gunner. "As much as he'd like to, the President does not have the power to. In fact, that's one of the big debates that's been going on ever since the movement to rewrite the Constitution began to gain serious media attention. No one seems to know for sure who has the authority to rewrite the Constitution. Congress can amend it, as they have many times in the past. But to simply pull out a clean sheet of paper and start from the beginning," Nathan stated as he shook his head, "no one knows."

Hyde thought about that for a moment. "Don't you think it's about time that someone figured that out and wrote a new one? I mean, the one we have now doesn't seem to be working all that well. And it is kind of old."

Somewhat surprised by this comment, Nathan looked at Hyde. "While I admit the people who run the country could do better, why do you think we need to change the entire Constitution?"

With a shrug and a shake of his head, Hyde considered his statement. "I don't know, sir. I guess sometimes I get the feeling that no one who's connected to the government much cares about us little people until it's election time. Even then the only people they seem to chase after for their vote are minorities, old folks, gays, and tree hugging hippie freaks. People like Ortiz and me are ignored until it comes time to pay taxes or they need someone to send to Bosnia."

With his elbow Ortiz gave Hyde a jab. "Hey, amigo. Flash traffic. I'm a minority and there ain't been no politicians hangin' around my house looking for my vote."

While Hyde returned Ortiz's smirk with an expression that would have made a Doberman cringe, Nathan seized his chance to end this discussion and move on. Yet he couldn't do so without answering, at least in part, Hyde's original question.

"Like you, Hyde, there's a lot of people who are tired of how this country is being run. They feel disenfranchised and forgotten. They have come to think that the time has come to change how our leaders are selected and how the government goes about its business. Some believe that the only viable solution is to start all over again. Others want to go back to the way they think things used to be. A few are happy with the way things are or are simply afraid of change. I can't say for sure which is the best way to go about making things better. Solutions to those problems, as they say, are way above our pay grades."

Hyde smiled as Nathan turned away. "I hear ya, sir. Airborne."

Relieved to have extracted himself from that discussion without making a fool of himself, Nathan continued to make his way down his portion of the company line. As he did so, it dawned upon the young officer that it must have been circumstances like the one he had just walked away from which nurtured the aloof, often cold manner that his father assumed whenever he was thrown together with new and unfamiliar people. The more he found himself being confronted by new situations, the more he came to understand the man with whom he had spent most of his life.

GOWEN FIELD, BOISE, IDAHO · NIGHT, OCTOBER 30

It had been a long time since Lieutenant Colonel Nancy Kozak had found herself worrying about what her troops thought about her or looking for ways to relate to them. Such concerns, especially at times like this, were of no importance to her. Rather than bridging any gaps that existed between officer and enlisted, Nancy's mind was occupied with the problem of securing a site that was too large, too open, and too isolated with a force that was too small.

While her former duties within the directorate for training resources had often taken her out to the small ammo storage site that adjoined Gowen Field, her current responsibilities required that she look at the scattered bunkers and surrounding terrain through new eyes. Even now, in the harsh glare of the overhead lights, she watched as her handful of National Guardsmen dug in and prepared for a long, nervous night. Before reporting back to her superior Nancy decided to avail herself of one more opportunity to survey the dispositions she had made.

Carefully she made her way up the steep side of one of the dirt-covered bunkers from which she would be able to see everything. To the west was Gowen Field itself, a sprawling National Guard base. The buildings, motor pool sheds, maintenance facilities, fences, and combat vehicles were nothing more than a jumble of dark silhouettes set against a dark western sky. Here and there she could see the form of a fellow Guardsman pop up as he or she went about working on an Abrams tank or Bradley fighting vehicle. Like Nancy and her small detachment, the soldiers over in the main portion of the installation were part of the advance party, a handful of selected mechanics, full time Guardsmen, quartermaster types, and officers called in to open billets, prepare vehicles for issue, inventory stocks of fuel, and order perishable rations for the rest of the troops assigned to their units.

As yet a general call up had not yet been initiated. "The governor," quipped a personnel officer she knew at base headquarters, "doesn't want to send those people in Washington the wrong message. Of course, being the cautious soul that he is, he's not taking any chances. That's why we're here."

Those words came back to her as she looked to the northwest at the part of Gowen Field that adjoined the Boise Municipal Airport. While a commercial jet airliner descended onto the runway in the distance, Air National Guardsmen could be seen in the foreground performing their preflight checks of the A-10 ground attack aircraft under the harsh lights of their portion of the airfield. GO Thomas had once commanded the squadron that those aircraft belonged to. For a second Nancy wondered if he was actually over there. No, she told herself in the next second. He's far too smart a man for that. If anything he'd be where he could best influence the situation or restate for the umpteenth time the righteousness of his cause to the throng of cameras and reporters who followed his every move. With a shake of her head, Nancy discarded any thought of that sordid aspect of the crisis and continued her inspection.

Together with their Army counterparts who were busy tending a flock of AH-64 attack helicopters parked nearby, the Air Guardsmen's activities belied the contention that the governor was being cautious. Though Nancy understood that what they were doing was little more than rattling their governor's saber as part of this strange and dangerous political kabuki dance, she had no doubt that the omnipresent eyes of hosts of television cameras scattered about Boise beaming these images across the nation were painting an entirely different story. Even now she could see a news van parked out on West Gowen Road. With satellite relay equipment that was far more sophisticated than anything the Idaho Guard had, the crew of that van was shooting some background footage which would be spliced into a twenty-second news piece for later use. The final, edited videotape would not portray the fact that the equipment being filmed was not fully manned, or that most of the pilots for the attack helicopters sitting ominously at the ready had not been called to the colors. Nor would the dubbed-over voice convey the apprehension she and her fellow guardsmen felt as they went about their duty. All that the rest of the nation would see were the men and women of a rebellious state arming themselves to their teeth with sophisticated war machines.

Not wanting to dwell on that matter, Nancy continued to rotate in place slowly. To the west there was very little in the track of land that lay between West Gowen Road and Interstate 84. The closest structures, sitting about a half mile from where she stood, were a pair of rust stained oil tanks. She had never paid much attention to them. Making a mental note, she reminded herself that it might be useful to know what, exactly, was stored in those tanks. After all, it could prove embarrassing to let fly a warning shot in their direction in an effort to ward off the curious or malicious only to start a conflagration. Now there would be something for the media sharks to gawk at, she chuckled. In her mind, the dark humor that most combat veterans seemed to enjoy conjured up the image of a diminutive blond newscaster, with makeup and hair freshly touched up standing out on the road as the oil tanks burned behind her. With microphone in hand and an expression that portrayed the appropriate look of dread and concern, the journalist would report to the world with an audible quiver in her voice, that the opening shots of the second civil war had been fired and that she, the brave, stalwart, and ever vigilant defender of the fourth estate, was there to report it, live.

Continuing her study of the perimeter for which she was responsible, Nancy faced to the south. It was from this quarter, along West Gowen Road and the open range beyond, that Nancy felt they were most vulnerable. Both the main post to the west and the Air Force facility to the north afforded the ammo storage site some degree of protection. While a threat from those directions could not be ruled out entirely, Nancy decided she had little to fear from that quarter. Any intruder choosing either of those approaches would have to pass through a number of barriers, gates, check points, and other obstacles that had been set up to keep the curious and uninvited at arm's length. With the exception of a hundred meters or so of dead space and a singe chain-link fence topped with barbed wire, nothing separated Nancy's ammo bunkers from the public road that ran along the southern boundary of Gowen Field.

That in itself would have been bad enough. The lay of the land beyond the road, however, conspired to make her position quite precarious. The ammo bunkers where she stood sat in a slight depression, with the West Gowen Road running along the higher ground. On the far side of the road, the land leveled out. This created a vast blind spot. Even on top of the tallest ammo bunker in the site, Nancy could not see any farther than the road itself. Intruders coming across the open range beyond could crawl up to the road unobserved. From there they would be free to set up whatever weapons they had and dominate the entire facility by fire.

It was this peculiarity of terrain that dictated the disposition of Nancy's small command. She had few options. She could choose to defend the bunkers close in, which would mean surrendering control of the higher, dominant terrain. Or, she could extend her perimeter and establish one or more positions along the road in an effort to deny that ground to a hostile force. This would mean that her limited manpower would be stretched precariously thin. It also meant that any posts along the road would be isolated. Even a lightly armed force coming up along the road or from across the open range to the south would be able to pin those positions and isolate them.

There were advantages to this last course of action besides the most obvious one. Two positions, each with a machine gun, set on the high ground on the southern side of the road would be able to sweep the entire length of the West Gowen Road in either direction for a considerable distance. She could even establish roadblocks if greater security of the entire Gowen Field complex became necessary. Those same troops, using those same positions, would be free to parry any threat that came up from the south simply by shifting their fields of fire in that direction. If anything, the kill zones thus created would overlap, which would permit her people to cut any intruders to ribbons if an attacker were foolish enough to press their attack.

Having never been one for half measures and always looking to capitalize on any and all advantages that came her way, Nancy Kozak had opted to extend the perimeter. In fact, she had assigned eight men and women and two of her three machine guns, a full third of her puny force, to the two positions along the road. The easternmost was designated post number three. It covered the area from the oil storage tanks to a point off to the southwest. The Guardsmen who manned that post would rely on an M-2 heavy barreled machine gun. Though that venerable old weapon had an incredibly low rate of fire, no one would argue with its stopping power. Anything with skin thinner than the hull of a Bradley fighting vehicle was fair game to the half-inch slugs that the M-2 could spew forth at a rate of 450 a minute. Even a close miss, as many a former foe could attest, was more than enough to quickly zap an opponent's resolve and determination.

The other position, post number four, was fifty meters to the west. Its three occupants were backed up by a much more conventional M-60 machine gun. Even now, Nancy could see the unique silhouette of that gun as its crew continued to work away at improving their position by piling sandbags higher.

• • •

From behind her the sound of dirt being ground underfoot distracted her. Looking over her shoulder she saw Staff Sergeant William Lightfoot making his way up to the top of the bunker to join her. Even before he reached the top he called out. "Last of the troops have eaten, ma'am. All they're waiting on is you."

Nancy smiled. "And I imagine you, too."

Lightfoot stopped and looked up at her. "Well, yes, of course."

Nancy shook her head. "Old habits are hard to break, aren't they."

Lightfoot nodded in agreement. "The Corps learned me well. Officers and senior NCOs don't eat till the troops have had their fill."

"And what," she asked, "is the mess hall filling our troops with tonight?"

"Shrimp gumbo over rice," Lightfoot responded as he continued his climb to the top.

Recalling the pitiful offerings that the regular Army passed off as meals when she had been on active duty, Nancy exclaimed, "God, I love the Guard."

Coming up next to her Lightfoot didn't answer. Instead he did as she had just finished and surveyed the entire circumference of their perimeter. Only when he was satisfied that all was in order did he speak. "Well, I don't imagine that we'll be eating so high on the hog if the rest of the personnel stationed here are called out."

"You think the governor is going to do so?" she asked, as all traces of a smile disappeared from her face.

While keeping his eyes fixed on the five man position in order to assess their progress, Lightfoot shrugged. "I suppose that depends on what those people in Washington do. As I see it we're just window dressing, nothing more."

Glancing over to where the news van was still filming, with bright lights and great fanfare, Nancy didn't need any further explanation. The nation, and in particular the President and his senior advisors, would be bombarded with images of uniformed Idaho Guardsmen busily preparing tanks, infantry fighting vehicles, self-propelled howitzers, attack helicopters, and ground attack aircraft. The President's spinmeisters wouldn't have the option of shrugging off the governor's earlier actions as little more than a temper tantrum or a political stunt. Through the actions of Nancy and the small cadre of Guardsmen at Gowen Field, the Governor was announcing that a line had been crossed. The intrusive and often overbearing manner with which the Federal government treated state and local governments had gone too far this time. In a speech meant to buck the people of Idaho up and put things in perspective, the state's Attorney General had called Gowen Field Idaho's version of Lexington Green. "The men and women of our state's National Guard," he announced before a battery of news cameras, "stand ready to resist the tyranny of the Federal government and arrest the erosion of our Constitutional rights."

A shiver ran down Nancy's spine just thinking about how Thomas Jefferson Osborn had delivered that staement. When she had first sighted the weapons and personnel, she had thought that their most likely targets would be over zealous members of right wing militias. Up until that speech, Nancy had not given any real thought to what could happen if other, more powerful forces were brought to bear. Now, however . . .

"Getting cold, ma'am," Lightfoot stated in his deep, sonorous voice.

Nancy looked over into Lightfoot's face, half hidden by the shadow of his helmet. In his eyes she imagined that she saw his thoughts. Thoughts that were as foreboding as hers. Thoughts they both believed were best kept unstated. "Perhaps," he continued after a slight pause, "this would be a good time to get down from here and claim our share of that gumbo."

After a moment, Nancy Kozak cleared her throat and whispered, "Yes. Let's do that."

Nathan had barely managed to doze off when he felt someone slap the side of his helmet. Pissed at being wakened
in such a manner, he jerked his head back and looked up
to confront his tormentor.

With his face inches from Nathan's, First Lieutenant
Randy Wahler grinned, from ear to ear, as was his habit.
"How's the ride so far, J. O.?" he shouted in order to hear
over the roar of the C-141's engines.

The first words that came to Nathan's mind by way of
response were not the ones he used. Still unsure of where
he stood with the company executive officer, Nathan
chose, instead, a more tactful response. "Oh, pretty good,
I guess."

Having read Nathan's expression and sensed the internal
conflict, Wahler's grin widened. "I figured as much."

"Any particular reason," Nathan asked, "you felt the
urge to wake me?"

Looking about, Wahler judged that there was sufficient
room on the crowded nylon seat behind him to squeeze in
between two of Nathan's troopers. "Excuse me," Wahler
shouted to the soldiers even as he began forcing himself
into the space they had yet to make for him. The company
XO ignored the vicious looks hurled at him by the soldiers
on either side of him. Instead, he turned his attention back
to Nathan. "The CO wanted me to go over things with you
one more time."

Nathan, having been required to regurgitate the concept
of the operation and plan of execution multiple times before departing Pope, was miffed. It was like being home
all over again. First his father would tell him over and over
again what he was expected to do. Then his mother would
ask Nathan just before he left or she departed if he understood what his father wanted done. Biting his tongue, Na-

than struggled to push aside the most unchristian thoughts he was harboring toward his company commander and pay attention to what the XO was saying. Going over things, one more time, a voice of reason in the back of his head whispered, couldn't hurt.

"Our company has the mission of neutralizing those National Guardsmen already assembled at Gowen before the bulk of the battalion comes in."

Nathan smiled. "Neutralize." What a wonderful, simple, and useless term. What exactly it meant in terms of what they were expected to do to the Guardsmen was still a question that Nathan's tired mind had yet to resolve.

"If we're successful," the XO went on, missing Nathan's cynical smirk, "the rest of the battalion will land conventionally and taxi over to the portion of the airport where the Idaho Air National Guard is. We'll link up there, secure the entire airport, and await further developments."

"And if Idaho's finest decide to resist," Nathan enjoined, "we secure the drop zone we're going into and hold it till the aircraft carrying the rest of the battalion close up for a mass jump."

The grinning XO nodded. "You got it LT. Any questions?"

"Yeah," Nathan ventured. "Wouldn't it be better if we also landed at the airport instead of jumping? I mean, after all, we're already supposed to be coming into Boise using the flight plan of an air express carrier. At six A.M. no one is going to pay much attention to us until after we're on the ground. And even then, by the time they sort themselves out, we'd have had a chance to drop ramp, scramble out, and be all over 'em."

Leaning forward, Wahler punched Nathan's chest-mounted reserve parachute playfully. "Now there you go, lieutenant, thinking again. Don't you have faith in our national leaders in Washington and the august members of our division staff?"

Nathan shook his head. "No."

"Shame, shame," Wahler mockingly scolded. "I'm going to tell Captain King you're being naughty."

Knowing how much Wahler hated King and feeling a

bit bolder than he had previously when dealing with the more senior officer, Nathan laughed. "Yeah, right. Now be off with you. I need to catch up on my beauty sleep."

Reaching behind Nathan, Wahler grabbed the exposed red nylon straps that supported the jump seat Nathan was nestled into. With a grunt and a heave he pulled himself and his massive bulk of parachute, personal gear, and weaponry up into the standing position. "Adios, amigo," Wahler stated with a smile and a wave. Before leaving, he leaned down again. "We're not sure what's in the oil tanks on the other side of the road from where you're supposed to be landing. Could be anything, so do your best to avoid 'em. Use them for reference only."

"Yeah, yeah," Nathan waved. "Your platoon, *Lieutenant*," Nathan stated in a voice that was a mockery of his company commander's, "will sweep through the ammunition storage site and secure them as quickly as possible. Once that is accomplished you will continue onto the Air National Guard facilities with the bulk of your unit."

Again Wahler flashed his winning smile. "You got it." Then, without further ado, he turned and began to make his way back to his place next to the door. When it came time he would be the first to exit the aircraft.

With the executive officer gone, the soldier next to Nathan looked at his platoon leader. "You really think that we're going to be able to pull this off without firing a shot, like the company commander said?"

Nathan looked at the soldier, trying to decide if it was best to tell him what he actually thought, or simply regurgitate the party line that King had passed on during his briefing of the company. But before he could, one of the troopers who had been displaced by Wahler threw his two cents in. "Hell, yes," he shouted above the steady drone of the jet engines. "They're weekend warriors, for Christ sakes. There'll not be a clean pair of underwear in Boise when we hit the ground."

Turning his attention to this confident soldier, Nathan listened as the man went on.

"Listen, I've seen those good ole boys train. I drove the battalion commander this past summer when he and some of the officers went to evaluate a Guard unit at summer camp. Given detailed directions, those yahoos couldn't open a case of MREs without the help of the regular Army."

"They're not going to be serving us chow when we get there," the soldier next to Nathan reminded his friend.

Frustrated by his companion's rebuke, the trooper across from them ignored the comment. "All I'm trying to say," he went on, "is that even if they wanted to they're not going to be able to stop us. If anything they'll do more damage to each other if they choose to resist."

Screwing his face into a blank expression, the soldier next to Nathan came back with a response made popular by an old *Star Trek* movie: "Resistance is futile."

Angered, the soldier across the way gave his companion the finger. "Up yours," he said, then turned away as he tried to settle himself into a comfortable position again.

With this debate closed Nathan looked over at the man next to him, hoping that the young soldier had forgotten why he had brought the subject up in the first place. The trooper didn't seem at all interested in continuing the discussion. Instead he folded his arms over his own reserve parachute, and let his head go back until it came to rest against the high backed nylon seat. Nathan decided to follow suit. It would be a busy morning, he told himself. With nothing to do now but wait till the pilot flashed the ten minute warning, he decided go back to sleep.

CHAPTER **13**

Off to the east the sun was starting its slow, tortuous ascent. For Chester West, on duty at post number four, the sun's appearance that morning would come none too soon. Standing upright, he stomped his feet and rubbed his arms in an effort to warm up. From a dark corner of the pit a woman's voice, interrupted by a cough brought on by the early morning chill, called out. "Quit blundering about like a puppy with a bladder problem. You're keeping us awake."

"I'm cold," West whined.

"Maybe that'll teach you to bring your parka next time," Fran Meranno replied.

"I didn't know we'd be out here all friggin' night," West snapped.

"And all the next day," David Tillman chimed in. "Sergeant Lightfoot warned us that this was our new home till all this blows over."

"That'll teach you to keep yapping when the colonel's briefing us," Meranno concluded before she rolled over and pulled the blanket she was wrapped in over her head.

"Man," West called out to no one in particular as he looked up and scanned the pale, early morning sky. "This bites. This really, really bites."

Off to the west the glint of the still unseen sun caught the silver skin of an incoming aircraft. Finding his fellow Guardsmen had little sympathy for his plight, Chester West turned his attention to the lone aircraft slowly approaching Boise. "Man, I don't know where you're going," he whispered to the plane as his teeth chattered, "but I'd give anything to be on board you right now, enjoying warm coffee and . . ."

From his corner David Tillman threw a clot of dirt that smacked West in the leg. "Shut up, man," Tillman pleaded. "We're trying to get some sleep here."

Knowing that it would be his turn soon to be relieved and not wanting either of them seeking revenge by keeping him awake, West grudgingly complied. With nothing to do, he turned his attention back to the aircraft that continued to bore in at a leisurely pace.

At the control center of the Boise Municipal Airport a controller was also watching the aircraft on his radar screen. Designated Global Express 901, the cargo aircraft began to concern the controller when, at the last minute, the tiny green triangle that represented it veered sharply to the left and off the required glide path. Putting his coffee down, the controller keyed his mike and spoke with the same even tone he used regardless of what the situation was. "Global 901, this is Boise control. You are wide of the glide path. Immediately come to a heading of one oh five and decrease air speed by fifty knots."

Letting up off his push-to-talk button the controller watched for the aircraft to comply. After waiting five long seconds for a response, and seeing no change in the aircraft's erroneous course, the controller again keyed his mike. "Global 901, this is Boise control. You are wide of the glide path. Immediately come to a heading of one oh oh and decrease your speed. Acknowledge, over."

Again there was no response over his headset. And while the controller saw that the green triangle with the designation "G901" did turn, he quickly realized that it had not come around far enough. After seeing that the new projected glide path of the aircraft was south, and parallel to the runway, the controller could feel his anxiety level ratchet up a few notches. As distressing as this new development was, at least the altitude readout under the G901 on his screen wasn't changing. Instead of continuing its descent, Global 901 was now holding at an altitude of just under one thousand feet above ground level.

Vacillating between anger and panic as his commands

were ignored, the controller keyed the mike a third time. "Global 901, this is Boise Control. You are not lined up with the runway. Your current glide path will take you well south of it." Then to cover his bases he added, "If you have an emergency please state the nature of your emergency and any assistance you require."

The controller's supervisor, watching a screen on the other side of the room, overheard this last part. Panicked, she dropped what she was doing and moved over to where the controller speaking to Global 901 was waiting for an answer. "Has he declared an emergency?" she asked.

Frustrated, the controller leaned back in his seat and waved a hand over the screen in frustration. "He hasn't declared shit. He just keeps coming on, ignoring me all the way."

For a second the supervisor lingered as both she and the controller watched the green triangle designated "G901" continue to slow down while maintaining a course south of and parallel to the runway at an altitude of one thousand feet. Drawing in a deep breath, the controller finally broke the silence. "We'd better notify emergency services," he stated flatly. "I think we have a problem here."

With no need to see or hear more, the supervisor left the controller's station, rushed to her own, and initiated a warning that was not at all appropriate for the true emergency that was unfolding before their very eyes.

Aboard the aircraft emitting the code normally allocated to Global 901, Captain Andrew King stood before the open door. With his hands firmly planted on either side of the opening, King looked out toward the dark horizon. To his left a jump master stood ready, listening to the voice of the pilot over his headset as he stared intently at the bright red light over the C-141's open door. Behind King and on the aisle across from where he stood, the soldiers who made up 1st and 2nd Platoons of Company A, 3rd of the 517th Parachute Infantry were crammed together. Throughout the cavernous aluminum fuselage the wind, affectionately known to paratroopers as the "Hawk," howled and whipped about, drowning out all efforts to speak and be heard. This left King's troopers with no choice but to look up toward the rear of the aircraft or stare intently at the parachute of their companion before them.

This moment, when all was ready, when every muscle in the bodies of King's well-conditioned paratroopers was taut and straining with anticipation, each man was left with nothing but his own thoughts. For some those thoughts extended no further than the next five minutes. For others, like King, their minds were alive, open to images that were as boundless as the wide open Idaho horizon before him.

This, King told himself as he felt the invigorating rush of the cold morning air whip past his face, is my moment. Everything I have done, he told himself, all the suffering and humiliation endured as a boy, is about to be rewarded. It was no accident that his company had been selected to make the jump. No. He was convinced the honor of leading this assault was one that was rightfully his. *He* was the best of the best. He always knew that. But now everyone would. Why else had his company been selected to lead the way? While the others would share in the glory and acclaim that would surely come their way, *they* would be filmed walking down the ramps of their transports, much as leg infantrymen would. Only *his* company would do it the way that God intended paratroopers to do it, out the door at a thousand feet and into thin air.

"STAND BYYYYYY!" the jump master yelled, emptying his lungs in an effort to overcome the howls of the Hawk.

As if a switch had been hit, all thoughts of future glory disappeared from King's mind. In their stead the plan his company was about to execute quickly played out. 1st and 2nd Platoons were with him on the transport using Global 901's flight plan. They would hit the ground, form up, and rush the National Guard facilities where the bulk of Idaho's combat vehicles were stored. The rest of the company, led by the XO with 3rd Platoon would follow two minutes later in a C-141 squawking out the identification code for a cargo jet. They would land farther to the east, form up, and overrun the small ammo storage site located there. Without stopping, 3rd Platoon would then continue on to secure the AH-64 attack helicopters and A-10s that were the pride of the Idaho National Guard. When all initial objectives were in hand and both assault groups had linked up, the entire company would go forward and secure those sites and facilities that would permit the rest of the battalion, now coming on fast, to land.

There was no time left for King to finish out his review of the operation. The instant the red light over the C-141's open jump door blinked off and was replaced by a flashing green glow, the jump master slapped King's arm. "GO!"

Without thought or hesitation Andrew King grabbed the side of his reserve, tucked his chin into his chest, and stuck his left foot out into the howling stream of wind that was screaming down the side of the Air Force transport at better than two hundred knots an hour. In a flash he was gone, followed by the paratroopers of 1st and 2nd Platoons.

The British were on their way.

In an open bay, under the combined lights of the maintenance shed and motor pool, Master Sergeant Glenn Sours sat on the edge of an M-1 turret and looked down at the tank's exposed engine. He was tired. Two dejected mechanics stood at the rear of the vehicle with their heads hung low and their hands shoved into the pockets of their greasy coveralls. Like the great Sphinx, the tank sat there silent and unwilling to yield up the secret of its mechanical problem.

Pulling a rag from his pocket, Sours wiped his hands without taking his eyes off the engine. He hated to admit defeat. He hated to throw his hands up, turn his back, and walk away from a problem. Yet he knew there were times when all his years of experience, all his intuitiveness when it came to things mechanical, could not overcome a problem that was not yet ready to be resolved. Balling up the rag as tightly as he could, Sours threw it at the engine below him in a final fit of rage. And like his efforts to date, his ineffectual missile unraveled in flight and fluttered harmlessly down upon the engine.

"You're mocking me," the old mechanic bellowed at the engine as if it could hear him. "You're hell bent on making me look like a fool in front of the colonel, aren't you?"

The two mechanics on the ground said nothing. They didn't even smirk at their supervisor's angry taunts. Both knew how their sergeant worked. Both understood the deep and uncompromising pride he took in keeping the great, lumbering, iron beasts running. And both shared his frustration when they were unable to. So the two men stood by in silence and patiently waited for their master sergeant to make his next move.

Unsure himself whether it was wiser at this point to admit defeat and catch a few hours' sleep or keep plugging away, Sours turned away from his tormenter and looked up at the early morning sky. Off to the southwest, now clearly visible in the faint predawn light, an aircraft came into his field of vision. Seeking to clear his mind the tired old non-commissioned officer watched the plane as it made its way to the east.

Feeling every ache and pain that his forty-eight year old body could generate and not thinking about anything, Sours didn't recognize the parachutes he saw for what they were. At first he thought his eyes, too tired to focus properly, were playing tricks on him. Blinking as he shook his head, Sours craned his neck forward and forced himself to focus on the plane and the tiny mushrooming dots that it was leaving in its wake. When it came to him what those strange images actually were, his eyes popped wide open, like the olive green canopies of the paratroopers he was watching.

Snapping his head about, he looked down at his two companions. Expecting him either to say they were going to throw in the towel or announce triumphantly that he knew what to do, they were confused by the stream of orders he spewed out without pausing for a breath. "Tim," he screamed to the taller of the two, "grab your rifle, beat feet to the tank we finished up on earlier, and crank it up.

Harry, get on the phone to the duty officer and alert him, *NOW!"*

Not at all sure what those actions would do to resolve the mechanical problem with the vehicle they were currently working on, the two men stayed where they were, looked at each other, and then up at Sours.

Only after seeing the perplexed looks on their faces did Sours bother to point to the sky. *"PARATROOPERS!"* he shouted. "They're coming after us!"

For a moment the two younger mechanics stood rooted to the spot. With jaws agape, they watched as dark images of men and parachutes filled the southern sky. For a second time, Sours shouted down at them. "Move you idiots. We need to get over there before they're assembled."

The taller of the two hesitated. "I don't have ammo. That tank doesn't either."

Not waiting, Sours started to dismount the tank that he had been working on. "They don't know that," he shouted over his shoulder, pointing up at the paratroopers. "All they'll know is that we're bigger then they are and that we can turn them into hamburger." When his feet hit the ground the old man moved with surprising speed and agility, spinning about and barking as he went. *"MOVE!"*

※

From his position behind the XO, Nathan Dixon couldn't see much, beyond the mound of gear and parachute that hung from Randy Wahler. With static lines hooked up and equipment checks completed Nathan had nothing left to do but sway with the gentle rocking motion of the C-141, stare at Wahler's parachute, and go over the tasks assigned to his platoon one more time.

As hard as he tried to do so, other, more frivolous thoughts kept intruding. Instead of mentally walking through the entire plan of execution, Nathan could not help but think of how lucky he was. After all, he had been with the unit less than a month and here he was, making a jump that many a trooper who wore the patch of the 17th would never make. Though they were going into a permissive, or non-hostile environment, all the elements were there. The excitement, the anticipation, the knowledge that in mere seconds, he would be stepping off into the vast unknown in the company of some of America's finest fighting soldiers. His own father, as seasoned a veteran as they came these days, had not participated in his first major operation until he had obtained the rank of major. This, Nathan told himself, was what he had dreamed of, what he had . . .

Suddenly, Wahler was gone. One second, there was an overstuffed parachute container in Nathan's face, and the next, nothing. Startled, Nathan looked into the eyes of the jump master. *"GO, GO, GO!"* the man yelled frantically as he thrust his right index finger forward in a vain attempt to get Nathan's attention. With as much of a leap as his one hundred and fifty pounds of equipment, weapons, and parachute would permit Nathan lurched forward, swung his body and its heavy load into the open door and bombed out of the aircraft.

In a blinding flash he was sucked out and away from the transport. For several long seconds he found himself enveloped in a world of wild, violent jerks that was silent save for the rush of the wind and his own labored breathing. Falling away from the transport, Nathan strained to keep his body in the tight, chin down position he had been taught at Airborne school. Remembering to count long after he was out and away, the young officer started where he thought it should have been if he had initiated it at the door. Belatedly, he braced himself for opening shock.

That wonderful and traumatic sensation came almost as quickly as he thought about it. All over his body he could feel the stiff nylon harness, already cinched incredibly tight, squeeze him even more. This meant that things were going as they should. The static line and deployment bag, connected to the parachute by several strands of twine, had been snapped, freeing Nathan from the C-141 and allowing his canopy to fill with the trailing remains of the slipstream that the now distant transport continued to shed as it made its way slowly to the east. Though he was sorely tempted to look up and behind to see if his canopy was still deploying, Nathan kept his chin firmly planted on his chest and continued his slow, arduous count to ten.

He never finished it. Instead, when he felt his feet swing down under him, and the violent bucking ride come to an end, Nathan assumed all was well. Reaching up with his hands he grabbed the taut risers that gathered in the numerous parachute suspension cords that ran down from the skirt of his parachute and joined them to his harness. With risers firmly in hand, Nathan craned his head back and looked up. Above him he saw his fully inflated canopy illuminated by the early morning sun. How anything so ugly could look so glorious was a wonder to him. He spent a second, a most wondrous and valuable second, looking up at his parachute. "God," he all but shouted as he silently fluttered down. "I love this."

Reality brought this private moment of rejoicing to an abrupt end. Sounds that were familiar, yet totally unexpected, turned Nathan's head away from the his blissful descent and back to the hard, uncompromising duty that being a soldier demands.

Free of his harness and with rifle in hand, Andrew King looked about and took in everything that was going on around him. While the last of his soldiers to hit the ground were still wrestling with their collapsing parachutes, others were already flinging their grossly overweight rucksacks onto their backs or trotting over to where their squad leader stood waving his hand over his head. As best he could see no one seemed to be injured or unable to get up. That, King told himself, was a blessing. A nagging problem that was as old as airborne warfare itself was the terrible fact that the mere act of landing often took its toll. Though usually only sprained ankles or an occasional broken bone, a casualty, regardless of what caused it, was still a casualty.

"1st Platoon," a voice bellowed, "Over here, now." Locating the source of that order, King hoisted his own ruck up and headed in that direction. He would initially go with the 1st Platoon as they made their sweep of the motor pools. From there King planned on moving over to 2nd Platoon, whose primary objective was Gowen Field's headquarters and admin building located on West Guard Street. Since there was only a small chance that the Adjutant General of the state was there, King considered the task of securing the armored combat vehicles of greater importance. Hence, he placed himself where he felt the critical blow would be made. Denied the means of waging war, a general and his staff would be useless.

King was better than halfway to where the platoon leader of the 1st platoon stood surrounded by a growing number of men when a vaguely familiar sound broke the otherwise still morning air. Instinctively Andrew King's ears perked up. Even before his conscious mind was able to sort out what was generating the high pitched whine that appeared to be growing closer, King's subconscious had already raised the alarm and quickened his pace from a slow trot to a steady run.

Master Sergeant Sours managed to violate just about every safety rule and regulation as he moved the M-1 tank through the motor pool. How his driver managed to navigate past scores of vehicles and buildings without hitting a one was nothing short of a miracle. With Sours standing high in the commander's hatch, the lone M-1 tank burst out of the motor pool and onto West Gowen Road. There, it had one final brush with an accident as a car drove into the ditch instead of taking on the massive steel beast that jumped out in front of it. The only time Tim slowed was when he came to the ditch on the south side of the road. Even then, Sours gave him a sharp reprimand over the tank's intercom. "Kick it in the ass," he kept shouting as he searched the flat, open pastures beyond. Excited by the situation as well as by Sours's demeanor, Tim jerked the throttles on his steering "T" bar forward, throwing Sours backwards as the tank picked up speed and leaped the ditch.

When the tank was on flat ground, Sours scanned the horizon. All across the plain he could see individual figures moving about, forming themselves into clumps. In his haste the National Guard master sergeant had not worked out the details of how he, Tim, and the tank were going to prevent the paratroopers from assembling and moving on the motor pools. They had no small arms ammunition. Only selected Guardsmen manning the gates or assigned to other security duties had been issued a single magazine each. On board the tank the closest thing to a weapon was a length of pipe, known as a cheater bar, that slid over the end of a wrench in order to add leverage when tightening track bolts.

The one thing the tank did have was a functional engine that drove two tracks, each consisting of over two tons of steel and rubber. These, Sours hoped, combined with the vast bulk of the tank, would be enough to buy time for his fellow Guardsmen to respond to the alarm he had raised. By charging about the open range which offered little cover to the paratroopers, Sours planned to keep them from forming up and pressing their attack. It wasn't much of a plan. But it was the best he could come up with. He, like the paratroopers he was turning the bow of the tank toward, was committed.

Like most plans there was a flaw in the one which Sours settled upon. It was a common one. In deciding what he was going to do, Sours assumed that the paratroopers out there were operating under the same handicaps and constraints that the Idaho Guard was working under. Specifically, the lack of ammunition on the Guards' part and their attitude concerning using deadly force.

Neither Sours nor anyone else at Gowen Field had any idea that they had been called out for anything more than adding a bit of credibility to the governor's position. After all, the very thought that Idaho could stand up to the military might of the United States was little more than ridiculous. And since they were no more than props for the war of words being waged between the governor's mansion and the White House, no one in the Idaho Guard chain of command saw any need to issue anything resembling a full, basic load of ammunition.

Yet even if that ammunition had been issued most Guard junior officers and NCOs knew, in their hearts and souls, that the reasons for using that ammunition against anyone simply weren't compelling. The governor had made a political statement, he had kept the Idaho Six from being extradited, and that, the Guardsmen figured, would be that.

Andrew King's paratroopers, on the other hand, were not constrained by a lack of ammunition or an unwillingness to use deadly force. They were professional soldiers. They did as they were told, a trait Andrew King valued above all else and took every opportunity to reinforce. Pumped up by the indoctrination they had been exposed to from day one in the Army, a fair number of King's young paratroopers looked forward to the day when they would be afforded the opportunity to use the tools of their trade. Even King's own pep talk conspired to set the stage. "We're going there to do a job," King had told his men before they had boarded the transports. "There are people in Idaho who have chosen to raise their hand against our flag," he informed them in a manner that he hoped would fire them up. "Those people need to be shown that treason, in any form, *will not be tolerated*." Exposed to all these forces as well as a volatile mixture of adrenaline, testosterone, and fear the prospect of battle generates, it was little wonder that the soldiers of Company A hit the ground primed and ready for a fight.

Barging into this supercharged atmosphere were Master Sergeant Sours, Tim, and a tank that was, to every paratrooper who saw it, the most ominous and deadly creature they had ever laid eyes on.

From where he stood, King could clearly see that the rogue tank was hell bent on disrupting his company's efforts to form up. In the growing light he watched in disgust as a cluster of four of his highly trained paratroopers threw down their ruck sacks and scattered to either side of the tank as it careened madly about the open range. It was like watching a cat scatter a nest of rats. Dismayed by this unexpected turn of events and what King took to be the cowardly behavior of his own men, the young company commander turned to the leader of the 1st Platoon. "Baskas," King growled, "pull your people together and stop that damned thing." King considered adding, "before someone gets hurt," to his order, but didn't. Clearly he could see with his own eyes that whoever was controlling that tank didn't give a damn about the safety of his men. Therefore, he didn't give their safety a second thought.

For a moment, 2nd Lieutenant Baskas stared at King, then over at the tank as it took up the pursuit of a gaggle of paratroopers. "How, sir, do you suggest I do that?" Baskas asked innocently.

King exploded. "I don't give a shit how you do that, *Lieutenant*. Just do it, *NOW!*"

After throwing a weary glance over to his platoon sergeant, Baskas gave King a quick, halfhearted salute before taking off at a run in search of a member of his weapons squad.

In his race to find members of his weapons squad before the rampaging tank found him, Baskas came across two of these troopers clawing at a container. "You two, what are you doing?" he shouted as he trotted up behind them.

"What in the hell does it look like, LT," one of the excited young paratroopers shot back. "We're trying to get this CLU out and ready."

Baskas paused. The CLU they were busily digging out of the drop bag was the command launch unit for a Javelin antitank missile. While Baskas's first thoughts had been of securing a SAW with which to scare off the tank, it struck him that an antitank guided missile would be better. "How soon," Baskas asked, "before you're ready?"

The same outspoken Javelin gunner turned and looked at his platoon leader. "We'd be ready a whole lot quicker," he snapped, "if you'd lend a hand and get a missile ready."

Ignoring the chastisement and seeing the sense in the soldier's response, Baskas slung his rifle over his shoulder, dropped to his knees, and joined in the scramble to get the weapon up and operational.

><

The panic that had driven Master Sergeant Sours was fading. In its place a sort of euphoria began to overcome him. While somewhere in the back of his mind this bothered him, the veteran Guardsman didn't have any time to sort out his feelings. It took his full undivided attention to keep Tim from running over the paratroopers they were chasing. It wasn't that Tim was evil. It was just that the young man, like Sours himself, was caught up by the excitement. "Idiot," Sours yelled into the mike hanging in front of his face as he hung onto the edge of the tank commander's cupola. "After they start running let 'em go. There's no need to keep hounding them."

Down below in the hull of the tank, Tim listened and grinned as he jerked the steering T one way then the other in a effort to throw up as much loose rock and dirt as he could. "Okay, Sarge," he shouted back, ignoring his supervisor's orders and taking off after a paratrooper who looked as if he were getting ready to fire his rifle at them.

Sours, too, saw the man and turned to watch him more closely just in case the paratrooper did anything uncalled for or foolish, like shoot at them. It wouldn't do to allow things to get totally out of hand, Sours thought.

With his attention focused squarely on the lone paratrooper, Master Sergeant Sours almost missed the sudden flash of a missile being fired off to the right. Though he didn't quite know what was happening, he instinctively snapped his head around. For a second he watched as an object trailing flame and spewing smoke came at him. Even before he fully understood what exactly he was looking at, Sours was shouting to his driver to start taking evasive maneuvers. "Cut right, Tim, *NOW!*"

Tim heard and understood the order. But he didn't make the turn. The paratrooper they had been headed for had opted to flee rather than fight by making a flying leap, to the right, out from in front of the tank. Not knowing of the danger that Sours was seeking to avoid and fearing that a sharp right turn would crush the fleeing paratrooper, Tim held his course for a second longer than he should have.

Like a deer caught in the headlights of an oncoming car Sours watched the incoming missile. Other than execute some fancy maneuvers he had no idea what to do. "Tim," the maintenance sergeant yelled. "Turn the damned tank. We have a . . ."

When Tim finally did comply he did so with a vengeance. The resulting jerk to the right threw Sours off balance and to the left. Grabbing the tank commander's hatch in an effort to keep from losing his footing, the master sergeant barely saved himself from slipping down into the turret. This effort, however, demanded his full attention, leaving him unable to keep track of the missile.

For a moment the Javelin gunner lost sight of the tank he was tracking. The violent turn had thrown up a huge wall of dust. While he hadn't anticipated this maneuver, he wasn't thrown by it. Smoothly he ended his steady tracking and laid his sight onto the center mass of the dust cloud. Though he wouldn't be able to aim for the track as he had been ordered to, the gunner was confident that the guided missile would make its way through the thin veil of dust and smack the National Guard tank in the ass.

As if by sheer will the missile was enveloped by the cloud of dust just as the gunner controlling its flight had predicted, and found a mark. It didn't strike low, in the suspension system. Instead it smacked the top of the engine compartment. While the detonation of the Javelin itself was rather unspectacular, the effects that its warhead had on the turbine engine, spinning at max RPMs, was.

Nathan had barely had time to gain his feet before a flash off to the east, where the bulk of the company was assembling, caused him to pause. Looking up and over in that direction, he saw the pillar of black smoke shoot straight up just as the sound of the Javelin's detonation reached him.

Behind him one of his troopers was also watching. "Oh, shit, man," the trooper exclaimed, half concerned, half in awe. "They're using mortars on us."

Looking around, Nathan saw other soldiers in his platoon had stopped what they were doing and were staring. "It's not artillery or mortars," Nathan yelled confidently, not really thinking about the effects of his statement. "Someone just killed a tank."

The mention of the word "tank" caused those paratroopers who had heard Nathan to pause. Those who had not already done so stopped what they were doing and looked over at the angry black pillar of smoke rising against the pale morning light. Even Wahler was transfixed by the sight and what it represented. In the silence surrounding him, Nathan could make out the faint crackling of the flames as they consumed the stricken vehicle. A paratrooper holding his hands up over his eyes shook his head. "Don't think it was a tank. Bradley, maybe, but not . . ."

Nathan was looking around as the man's voice trailed off. Though the event was far afield and hadn't touched them, its importance had managed to rattle his platoon. "So," Nathan found himself muttering, "this is what leadership is all about." Taking a moment to ratchet up his own courage, Nathan summoned up his most commanding voice. "It doesn't matter what it was," Nathan snapped. "What's important is that we get off this drop zone and seize our objective before the Guard has a chance to sort themselves out. Now, get yourself squared away," he yelled as his flashing eyes swept the area where his men stood gaping at the burning M-1, "and get a move on. There's work to be done."

Seeing Dixon's statement as a verbal reprimand, Randy Wahler took up the challenge. "Right," he choked, as his eyes turned toward the north, where their objective lay. "Lieutenant Dixon, finish rallying your platoon. I'll take your 1st Squad and start for the road overlooking the ammo site. I'll set up a base of fire and wait for you."

Though he was miffed that the XO was inserting himself into the running of his platoon, Nathan said nothing. This was neither the time or place for a turf battle between two officers. Besides, with two years' experience as well as being the second in command of the company, Wahler was more than within his rights to do so. With a nod the young platoon leader bid the company XO adieu and turned to get his other squads formed up and on the move.

From his position along West Gowen Road, Chester West stared at the pillar of smoke. Stricken with the same nervous apprehension that had given Nathan Dixon's platoon such pause, he all but forgot about the paratroopers who were busily assembling on the broad, open plain that lay to their south.

Fran Meranno, the senior enlisted soldier there, hadn't. As a mother of two she had learned how to subordinate one's own fears and apprehensions and concentrate on what was important. At that moment a thin raggedy line of paratroopers advancing on their position with weapons up and at the ready was, by far, of greater concern to her than a burning vehicle way over to their right. "CW! Crack open the ammo and get it over here," she shouted as she and David Tillman scrambled to tear the cover off the M-60 machine gun. With a shake of his head, West looked over at them, then out at the paratroopers who were now less than two hundred yards from them and closing fast.

"Ah, shit," West groaned. "You don't think . . ."

"Shut up, West," Fran snapped, "and give me the ammo."

While the anxious female Guardsman dropped down on her knees and flipped open the cover of the receiver West tore his eyes off the paratroopers, reached down and grabbed a box of 7.62mm four-in-one link. Turning, he handed it to Tillman, who cracked open the metal container, jerked a one hundred round box out and frantically tore it open. West stood up as Fran took the end of the belt of ammo she was handed, laid it across the open receiver of the machine gun, and slapped the weapon's cover closed. With nothing to do West watched with growing alarm as the paratroopers continued to close on their position like a wave rushing in from the sea.

Troopers on either side of Randy Wahler saw the silhouette of a Guardsman suddenly rise up out of the ground and turn toward them. None waited to see if he was armed or a threat before they dropped down onto their stomachs, brought their own weapons up, and snapped off the safeties. Caught off guard, Wahler looked at his men, then up at Chester West who stood less than hundred yards away from him. Dropping to his knee, Wahler brought his own rifle up and paused. The inevitable question, asked by so many who find themselves in an awkward position raced through Wahler's mind. "Now what?"

From the recesses of his racing mind a part of the operational briefing popped to the forefront. Standing up, Wahler forced his face into what he thought was a most appropriate expression, and yelled out at the lone Guardsman. "We are members of the 17th Airborne Division. Drop your weapons and put your hands over your head."

When the figure did not respond, Wahler considered repeating his demand, but then abruptly stopped when he saw the movement of two other guardsmen. As a paralyzing chill ran down his spine, the company XO watched as a machine gun was manhandled around into position to sweep the area where he and 1st Squad were standing.

Pausing in her efforts to reposition the M-60 from where it had been overlooking the road to where the line of paratroopers had appeared, Fran Meranno looked up at West. "Get down, you damned fool," she shouted. Not bothering to see if her boastful companion had complied, Fran turned her attention back to the gun. Dave Tillman had already taken the traverse and elevation mechanism off the tripod's cross bar so that the weapon could be more easily rotated across the field of fire. Ready, Fran wrapped her hand around the trigger grip, leaned her right shoulder into the gun's short stock, and brought her left hand up. She rested it, as well as her right cheek, against the weapon to steady it.

Looking down at her and Tillman, West realized that they were as serious as the paratrooper yelling at him. Assessing that his chances of survival were better with his fellow Guardsmen, West dropped down to the bottom of the pit and curled up as tightly as he could against the side of their fighting position.

Having expected that the Guardsmen facing them would heed his demand to lay down their weapons, 1st Lieutenant Wahler was unprepared to deal with the situation he now faced. Quickly he glanced to either side. To a man, the members of Nathan's platoon whom he had commandeered were lying prone with their weapons at the ready and safeties off. As the seconds ticked by, they lay there, watching the sandbag position and waiting for Wahler's next command. Appreciating that someone had to break the deadlock he now found himself in, but not yet ready to give in to the impulse of firing on his fellow countrymen, Wahler forced himself to stand up as straight as he could and lower his weapon. Swallowing, he cleared his throat, and started to yell.

Trained to operate her assigned weapon in a strict sequence until each step was second nature, the impact that her next action would have never occurred to Fran Meranno. Reaching up, she grasped the gun's bolt and jerked it back.

The crisp, sharp sound of the M-60's action being worked cut through the stillness that had settled over the paratroopers and the forlorn Guardsmen. It should not have come as a surprise to anyone that someone reacted in a manner that was inappropriate.

A shot rang out. From somewhere along the skirmish line that flanked Wahler, a paratrooper's trigger finger jerked when he heard the sound of the machine gun's bolt being worked. With a shocked expression on his face Wahler looked to his left, then to his right just in time to see the entire line erupt in a raggedy volley.

In the pit Fran saw the bright muzzle flashes and understood what they meant. Without giving the matter any conscious thought, she flipped the safety of her weapon off, leaned into the gun, sighted down the barrel, and squeezed the trigger.

Standing upright and totally unprepared, 1st Lieutenant Randy Wahler caught the full force of Fran's first burst square in the groin. He was so close to the machine gun that his flak vest did little to slow the 7.62mm bullets as they tore clean through the young officer. The paratroopers on either side of him, focused on the target in their sights, paid no attention to what was happening to the company XO. Ignoring the fine red mist that drifted down upon them, they fired their own weapons as quickly as they could. What had started as just another deployment exercise for them had, in a matter of seconds, become a matter of life and death.

CHAPTER **14**

The initial spattering of fire quickly grew into a continuous rattling of musketry. Caught off guard by this Nancy
Kozak threw the telephone receiver she had been holding
down without finishing her sentence. Pushing past an
equally stunned Guardsman who had been standing behind
her, she made for the door of the small shed that served
as a command post. She no longer needed to seek guidance
or clarification on the rules of engagement. Her people
were being attacked. They were out there struggling to
defend positions that she had selected and put them in.
This was not the time to debate right or wrong. This was
not the time to step back and consider who were the good
guys and who were the bad guys. This was the time to do
what she had been trained and ordered to.

Once outside she came across a number of confused
Guardsmen milling about. Without pausing to explain, Kozak ordered them back to their positions and stand by.
What exactly she wanted them to stand by for was unclear.
The Guardsmen she had shoved aside in her efforts to get
out of the shed stuck his head out of the doorway and
yelled that Sergeant Lightfoot was at Post Number Four
where the Cal. 50 was located. Coming to an abrupt halt,
she turned toward the road. She could clearly see the back-
side of the position where Fran Meranno and her people
were fighting for their lives. Spinning about she yelled
back to the Guardsman in the shed, "Tell him to support
the M-60 position from there as best he can. I'll be with
him in a minute."

Without so much as a nod the Guardsman disappeared
back into the shed to relay her order, leaving Nancy free
to continue her sprint to where the fighting was. But she

hadn't managed to take more than a couple of steps, before a sergeant in charge of one of the positions facing to the west called out to her. "There are a lot of people moving around in front of my position. What should I do?"

Stopping a second time Nancy looked over to where the sergeant was pointing in an effort to see who they were and if they were a threat. Unable to do either from where she stood, she shot a worried glance back to the position under attack. With Lightfoot in the other position, and the M-60 pit holding its own, she quickly determined that it was more important at that particular moment to sort out the new threat. Without another thought she pivoted on her heels and made for the western side of her perimeter.

To the south Nathan Dixon was also reacting. Whatever shock he felt upon hearing the sudden outburst of gun fire was quickly pushed aside. Having caught fleeting glimpses of the defensive perimeter protecting the ammo storage site while still drifting down under his parachute, Nathan determined it would be best to take whatever force he had at hand and swing around to the left to hit the Guard positions from the west. Coming from that direction he would not have to face the larger, more menacing National Guard position that anchored the southeastern corner of the site. With Wahler and the 1st Squad providing a base of fire as he had set out to do, Nathan would be free to maneuver and overwhelm each of the Guard positions in sequence. In coming up with this plan Nathan was totally unaware that Wahler was already dead. But even if he had known he wouldn't have changed his plan. The 1st Squad already was doing what Wahler had intended it to do.

When the leader of the 2nd Squad reported that his men were ready, Nathan nodded. Turning to Gandulf, the young platoon leader instructed his plainspoken NCO to finish gathering up the rest of the platoon and follow as quickly as he could. With that 2nd Lieutenant Nathan Dixon was off.

• • •

To the west King stood in the center of his small command group staring off to the east. Everyone around him could tell that he was becoming concerned about how the overall situation was developing. Only his radiomen didn't hesitate to interrupt his thoughts. "Captain King," the RTO called as he reached up with the hand set.

Without taking his eyes off the distant firefight that his 3rd Platoon was involved in, King took the handset, squeezed the receiver end up under his helmet, and pressed it against his ear. It was the 2nd platoon. They had landed nearest to the road that separated them from the National Guard motor pools. In a voice that betrayed his mounting apprehensions, the lieutenant of that platoon reported that he could hear more armored vehicles starting up. As best he could determine there were twenty to thirty armored vehicles moving about. He went on to tell King that he was deploying his platoon as best he could, but doubted if he could hold back a determined, mounted attack on his own.

With his full attention now focused on what he considered to be a more immediate crisis, King turned his back on Nathan's distant firefight for the moment. Lowering the radio's hand mike, King looked to where the 1st Platoon was now assembled. Even with them he would have fewer antitank missiles than the National Guard had tanks and Bradleys. With that in mind he cast his gaze back over to the east. Squinting in the early morning sun in an effort to see what Dixon's platoon was doing, for a brief moment he considered recalling them. Just as quickly, King dropped that idea. Even if the 3rd Platoon were able to break off their engagement now, he reasoned, they would never make it over to where he stood in time to make a difference.

Over the radio King heard the 2nd Platoon leader calling for instructions. Drawing in a deep breath, King brought the mike up. "Break contact. Fall back to 1st Platoon's position. I'll meet you there, out."

Without waiting for acknowledgment, King handed the

mike back to the RTO and started off in search of the leader of the 1st Platoon. His primary mission of securing the National Guard facilities was now clearly beyond his grasp. The best he could do, he reasoned, was secure the drop zone and hope that the remainder of the battalion could rig for a jump while in flight and join him before he was overrun.

The movement of Guard vehicles in the motor pools across from where King's 2nd Platoon had been frantically burrowing into the ground was far less menacing than it appeared to the anxious para-troopers. In truth the danger the platoon leader reported was not a coherent effort with the aim of crushing King's scattered company. Rather the chaotic movement of tanks, Bradley fighting vehicles, self propelled guns, and personnel carriers was the cumulative result of individual Guardsmen bent on saving their vehicles from capture.

Of all the people racing about the motor pools of Gowen Field only one major had anything resembling a plan. Yet even if that major managed to carry out his design, Captain Andrew King and Company A would still not be in danger. The major was collecting every armored vehicle he could lay his hands on for the purpose of parking them on the Boise Municipal Airport's runway. Just as paratroopers get nervous when tanks wander out into their drop zones, aircraft tend to be reluctant to land when large, heavy vehicles are sitting about on their landing strip.

Still, King's decision to suspend his efforts to press his attack against the motor pools based on the information he had in hand was sound. Even if he had a solid appreciation for the chaotic state that the Guardsmen were then in or the fact that they had next to nothing by way of ammunition, King's overriding orders to avoid open hostilities with Guard units influenced his decisions. This, coupled with his desire to preserve as much of his precious company as he could, drove him to accept the smaller solution.

With nothing more to do while he waited for his 2nd Platoon to abandon its forward positions and withdraw to where he was, King looked over at the smoldering hulk of the Guard tank sitting in the center of his drop zone. Even from this distance he could see the motionless body of a Guardsman hanging out of the commander's hatch. Blood had been spilt. This was no longer a show of force. This was a battle, a real kill and be killed battle. And from where he stood, Andrew King started to imagine that it would be his company that would wind up being killed.

✕

Trailing behind his platoon leader, Nathan's radioman was doing all he could to catch up with the determined young officer. Like every RTO, he not only had to carry his own personal equipment, weapon, ammunition, and gear, he also had to haul the twenty-two pound AN/PRC 119 radio along with its spare batteries, extended antenna, and other associated items. Though he was as fit as any other man within the platoon, he was unable to maintain the pace. In the process of trying to do so, the RTO crammed the radio's hand set into a rear pocket of his trousers lest it fall off his web gear and drag behind him. Before doing so he never thought to readjust the radio's volume. As was his practice, the volume was still set on low to prevent the squawk of an incoming message from betraying his position in the early morning quiet. This, together with his own huffing and puffing and the noise around him, drowned out King's efforts to hail Dixon.

✕

The alarm raised by the Guardsmen positioned along the western side of the ammo site's perimeter had proven to be false. It took time for Kozak to realized that the people her NCO saw running about were fellow Guardsmen. Most of them were pilots and ground crew of the Army Guard helicopters and Air Guard A-10s scrambling in an effort to get their precious machines off the ground and into action. The rest were trying to start vehicles parked near the ammo site. Where those vehicles were going was beyond

Kozak. All she knew was that there were no paratroopers endangering them from that quarter.

Warning the sergeant in charge of the positions along that portion of the perimeter to hold fire unless he was actually under attack, Nancy again turned to where the real danger lay. She had neither the time nor did she feel the need to explain anything else to that sergeant. In the rush of events Nancy Kozak didn't see an assistant store manager who only trained with the Guard thirty-nine days out of 365. She saw a sergeant E-5. So she ascribed to him the same attributes, experience, and expertise that she had come to expect from the professional soldiers she was more familiar with.

Fran Meranno had never seen herself as anything but a part time soldier. Her military occupational specialty as an ammo specialist meant that she did little more during her time with the Guard than storing and sorting training ammunition. Still, she had enough tactical savvy to appreciate the grim fact that she and her companions were in a very difficult situation. Even with the Cal. 50 machinegun hammering away at the paratroopers arrayed before Fran's position, her attackers showed no sign of giving ground. If anything their steady hail of fire directed at her position was beginning to take a toll on them. Within minutes David Tillman was hit in the arm. Though unwounded, Chester West had dropped to the bottom of their pit in search of cover and salvation.

In silence the three Guardsmen worked together to keep their M-60 going. Though scared witless, West was not totally ineffectual. While making no effort to use his own weapon, since doing so would mean exposing himself to enemy fire, he managed to overcome his terror and scrounge fresh boxes of ammo for the machine gun. Taking great pains not to expose any part of his body above the level of the battered sandbags that protected them, West passed the opened boxes to Tillman. Using his one good arm, Tillman in turn fed fresh belts of ammunition to the gun every time Fran Meranno finished one off and threw open the receiver cover. Any reservations about firing on fellow Americans had been washed away by Tillman's blood and the dogged, uncompromising determination of the paratroopers. It didn't matter that Fran didn't think she was hitting anyone. The only thing that was important to her was that they were keeping the paratroopers out there and at bay.

With their attention focused on the paratroopers to their front, the trio of Guardsmen were taken by surprise when a fresh hail of fire started pelting them from their right. Just when everything seemed to be in hand and under control, things took an ugly turn. Before Fran knew what was happening he was there, towering above her at the edge of the pit looking down on Fran, David Tillman, and an absolutely terrified Chester West.

Everything transpired faster than Nathan could comprehend. One moment he was charging across the last few meters of open ground for all he was worth and firing as he went. The next he was standing there, aiming his rifle at the surprised Guardsmen. For a fleeting second the young officer hesitated in the hope that the Guardsmen staring up at him would appreciate the hopelessness of their position and surrender.

Combat has a strange effect on soldiers. People caught up in a life or death struggle don't react as they would under calmer, less stressful circumstances. Just two days before, a major crisis for Fran had been finding the right pair of shoes for one of her children so he could play football. Now she suddenly found herself having to make decisions that she was in no way prepared to make. Reaction and fear, not logic, drove her response.

When she looked up and saw Nathan Dixon bringing his rifle to bear, Fran Meranno instinctively reached down and released the machine gun from its tripod. While still maintaining eye to eye contact with the new threat looming over her, she pulled her gun up off its mount and began to swing it toward Nathan.

Now it was Nathan's turn to decide. Now he had to make a choice. And as so many others had already done that morning he reacted rather than reasoned. Without the slightest hesitation Nathan jammed the butt of his M-16 into his shoulder, laid his sights square on the machine-gunner's chest and pulled his trigger.

As much as the firefight along the southern portion of her defensive perimeter concerned her, Nancy Kozak was unable to ignore her overall responsibility for the ammo site. Using all her will power, she fought back her urge to rush over to the fight and instead made her way back to the small command post that linked her detachment with Gowen Field's operations center. There she checked in, reporting her current situation as she saw it while trying to find out what was going on elsewhere.

The captain who took her report was unable to provide her with a clear picture of what was going on or offer her any guidance. Frustrated with having wasted her time, Nancy tossed the phone aside a second time in disgust as she turned away and made for the door. Though she still had no clear idea what was going on over at Gowen Field itself, she sensed that she didn't have the luxury of waiting for orders that might never come.

Once outside Kozak dashed between two of the ammo bunkers before turning toward the pit where Fran Meranno was. The guard officer didn't get far. When she had emerged from the shelter of the earthen bunkers she was confronted with a sight that stopped her dead in her tracks. Before her, silhouetted against the pale autumn sky on the horizon, she saw the image of a paratrooper standing at the edge of the machine-gun pit. Even as she watched, she saw him fire down into the pit as calmly as if he had been on a rifle range. Instinctively Nancy drew her pistol. It didn't matter that the range was a bit extreme for a pistol. At the moment she had no choice. She had to do something, even if it was in vain.

• • •

As quickly as it had happened, it was over. Nathan stared at the three National Guardsmen who only a moment before had been alive and scrambling before him. Now they just lay there, twisted and contorted in a single, bloody heap. Except for the spasmodic jerking of a boot and a dark red pool of blood spreading over the bottom of the pit, everything was still.

Panting from both his exertions and the excitement, Nathan felt lightheaded, almost faint. Slowly he lowered his rifle, oblivious to everything around him save a tinge of nausea working its way up his throat. No coherent thoughts passed through his mind, no instinctive reaction moved him. Instead he simply stood there, as still as the heap of corpses before him, looking down at what he had done.

Coming up from behind, his radioman didn't much care what had brought his platoon leader's mad sprint to an end. By now the company commander was yelling so loudly that the radioman finally heard King's muffled voice through his pocket. With mike in hand he reached out to Nathan as he covered the last few feet that separated them. "LT, the Old Man wants you," the RTO shouted. "He's howling mad and demands that you contact him immed . . ."

Quite unexpectedly the RTO stopped mid-sentence. Still feeling a bit shaky and slow in responding, Nathan was just beginning to turn toward the RTO when he felt that man's body slam against his. Caught off balance, the two of them went tumbling down.

Nathan hit the ground hard, sprawling over on his back as his rifle flew out of his hand and his helmet slipped down over his face and smacked against the bridge of his nose. In an instant Nathan snapped back to the reality that surrounded him. The sound of the .50 caliber machine gun off to the right and small arms fire cracking and popping all around cut through the mental fog that had engulfing him. At first he thought that he had been shot in the face. Almost hesitantly he pulled his helmet back on his head, placed his hand up to his face to feel for the wound, and pulled it away.

When Nathan saw no blood he was overjoyed. That elation lasted only a second. The ping of a near miss and a moan from his RTO told him that not everything was in order. Lifting his head, he saw his RTO, still clutching the hand mike, lying across his legs. The man had been shot. One look at the stream of blood flowing from the RTO's wound was enough to galvanize the young officer into action. Though he had no idea where the shot that had stricken his RTO had come from, Nathan instinctively knew that he was in trouble.

Taking care not to cause any additional pain to his loyal RTO or expose himself to enemy fire, Nathan worked his legs out from under the wounded man, grabbed him by the straps of his web gear, and pulled the RTO back behind the sandbags.

Hitting a second paratrooper who had come out of nowhere was of no comfort to Nancy Kozak. She had missed her mark. And not only had she not killed the bastard who had fired upon her Guardsmen, both had gone to ground. Looking about, Nancy quickly took stock of the situation within the ammo site as she tried to figure out how many of her own Guardsmen she could muster for a counterattack. The hesitation and confusion that had kept her from being effective were forgotten. While she still had no idea at all what was happening outside her little perimeter, she appreciated the fact that she was the senior officer on the spot, and as such it was up to her to do something before more of her Guardsmen died.

✕

For most of the year Nelson Reeves was a corporate executive. Whenever he was handed a problem, he threw his all into it. His employer expected it of him and his own ethics demanded nothing less. This total dedication to succeed could not be turned off when Reeves donned the uniform of the National Guard and took up his duties as the commander of an armored cavalry squadron. He put out one hundred percent, one hundred percent of the time and demanded the same from everyone in his command. Through a deft understanding of his people and the particular nature of the Guard system, Nelson Reeves got what he wanted.

In addition to his drive Reeves had a knack for organization. He had used that talent to get the current governor elected and he used it on a daily basis to keep GO Thomas's sprawling business concerns growing and prospering while Thomas ran the state. This morning his skill for sorting order from chaos would prove to be the decisive factor in breaking the impasse between the paratroopers south of West Gowen Road and the Guardsmen scurrying about in the motor pools north of that road.

Reeves didn't spend much time at the headquarters building. He knew it was impossible to influence the situation from there at a time like this. The Guard colonel appreciated the fact that soldiers, even in the age of high tech weapons and sophisticated communications, still need to be led in person.

One of the first people Reeves happened upon as he made his way through the motor pools was the major who had been marshaling vehicles to park on the airport's runway. The major didn't belong to his cavalry squadron but the two men knew each other. Calmly Colonel Reeves listened to the harried major as he explained his plan. The colonel nodded in agreement with the concept but stated in a tone that belied his own concern for haste that it was more important that the threat presented by the paratroopers already on the ground be dealt with first.

In a manner more befitting a father giving advice to a troubled son, Reeves redirected the major's efforts. He instructed the major to deploy some of his tanks and Bradleys along West Gowen Road to act as a threat and keep the paratroopers from crossing it. While that was going on, the major was to dispatch those vehicles with full crews and machineguns on board to the ammo bunkers. There each of them were to pick up several boxes of small arms ammunition for their weapons. Once those vehicles were finished with that, they would move out to the road to replace the tanks and Bradleys that were on guard but had not yet had a chance to draw ammo.

Saluting smartly, the major turned about and faced the commanders of the vehicles he had managed to gather. Stepping back, Colonel Reeves watched and listened as the major appointed an officer to lead each ad hoc unit of tanks and Bradleys and assigned them each a specific task. Excited that they would be doing something that made sense and eager to get on with their assigned tasks, these subordinate commanders set out to implement the major's directives.

With that sorted out and in motion, Reeves took the major by the arm and gave him further guidance. The corporate exec turned colonel explained that it was his intent to use the major's vehicles as a screen behind which he would have the freedom to organize proper combat units. "Buy me some time, Major," Reeves admonished, "until we can put together a coherent force that will be able to conduct a proper, well-organized counterattack."

The major hesitated. "But what about the follow-on forces, sir? There's got to be another wave coming this way sooner rather than later."

Reeves smiled. "Hear that?" he asked as he cocked his ear over to where the Air National Guard A-10s were parked. "Those jet engines whining to life belong to our brothers in blue. While I was making my way through headquarters I dropped a bug in the ear of the senior Air Guardsmen on duty. They'll deal with any more uninvited guests."

"Are they armed?"

"Of course not. Like us, the A-10s are going to bluff their way to victory."

"Do you think they'll fall for it, I mean the pilots of the incoming transports?"

In a flash the smile that Reeves had been sporting disappeared. "That's not your concern, Major. Now, get a move on, Major, and make it happen."

Like his troopers, Andrew King had been watching the ominous massing of combat vehicles across the road from where his company was frantically digging in. While none of the Guard tanks or Bradleys had yet to cross the road as the lone M-1 had, it was clear that such a move would come sooner or later.

Only the continuous rattle of small arms fire to the east where the XO, Dixon, and the 3rd Platoon had landed diverted King's attention from the growing menace before him. Frustration upon frustration piled up as King's RTO announced sheepishly that he was unable to contact anyone over there.

Without taking his eyes off of the eastern horizon, King snapped, "Damn it! Keep trying."

It didn't take Nathan long to figure out that the position he had managed to seize single handedly was going to have to be abandoned. When the Guardsmen in the other pit along the east-west road found out that their companions had been overrun, they had shifted the fire of the caliber .50 machine gun and begun hammering away at him. The sandbags that had refused to yield to the small arms fire of Nathan's 1st Squad were being shredded by the huge half inch slugs that ripped the nylon bags open and kicked up clouds of sand all over Nathan and the wounded RTO. Looking about, he caught sight of the squad that had followed him. Like the 1st Squad they were pinned by fire.

To make matters worse, the fire that was being directed Nathan's way from the center of the ammo site was increasing at an alarming rate. What had started as a few stray shots was now becoming quite heavy. It was obvious that his efforts to get around the exposed flank had been for naught. The minor success he had achieved had been canceled by the quick reaction of the Guardsmen holding the ammo site.

The appearance of armored vehicles coming his way from the National Guard facilities to the west provided the last incentive Nathan needed to vacate the machine gun pit he was in. Whether they were coming to aid the Guardsmen or were simply headed that way in order to draw ammunition didn't much matter. Sooner or later they would be diverted to where he was.

Looking back at the pit where the caliber .50 machine gun was, Nathan watched and waited. One blessing about that weapon was that its bullets were big and each ammo box contained only fifty rounds. Though a well-trained crew could make the switch quickly, once a box was empty it took time to reload, time Nathan intended to put to good use. After stripping as much personal gear off himself and the wounded RTO as he could, Nathan waited for his chance and prayed that he guessed right.

✕

In the local air traffic control center taken over by excited Air National Guard controllers, the officer in charge didn't have much difficulty in figuring out which of the incoming aircraft were commercial flights and which belonged to the follow-on force. After having his controllers wave off all commercial traffic, the officer in charge attempted to contact the pilot of the lead Air Force transport.

The commander of those transports was Colonel Edward Macky, an officer with over twenty years of service. At first he refused to respond. With the paratroopers in his cargo bay beginning their pre-jump preparations and ten minutes to go before he was over the DZ, he was not about to back down. He had his orders, orders that he had every intention of carrying out.

That resolve did not last long. At Boise the OIC in the air traffic control center took care to ensure that the Air Guard A-10s based there came up on the same radio frequency that the FAA required all aircraft in the Boise area to monitor. With growing alarm Macky listened to the commander of those A-10s as he called the tower for permission to taxi onto Boise's main runway and prepare for takeoff. In a calm voice the controller granted them permission to proceed. Once the A-10's announced that they were set, the controller passed on a heading and altitude that the A-10s were to take once airborne. The air crews of all of the inbound C-141s monitoring these exchanges didn't need a navigator to tell them that the heading the A-10s had been given was an intercept course.

Ignoring the sweat beading up on his forehead, Macky asked his navigator how far out they were. Along with the navigator's response that they were still seven minutes away, Macky could hear the voice of the leader of the A-10s acknowledging permission to take off, followed by a lusty, "Here we go, boys." In his mind the Air Force colonel could picture the sinister looking ground attack planes thundering down the runway with their throttles wide open and their pilots easing back on the stick till their aircraft leaped up off the ground and became airborne. Though he wasn't familiar with the flight characteristics of the A-10s, he had little doubt that they would be able to make one good pass at them before his transports reached the designated drop zones. As bad at that was for his aircraft, it meant that the A-10s would be back in time to catch the paratroopers while they were helplessly suspended from their parachutes during their descent.

Macky's copilot sensed what was going though his commander's mind. "What now?"

Macky wanted to call back for instructions. He wanted to ask a more senior officer for orders, or guidance, or recommendations. But there was no time. Over his headphones he could hear the commander of the A-10s instructing his pilots to tighten up once they had reached twelve hundred feet.

"Six minutes out, sir," the navigator stated dryly.

The decision, Macky realized, was his and his alone. No one could make it for him.

"Commander of Air Force transports west of Boise, this is Colonel Terrance Smith, Idaho Air National Guard." Aboard the transports the crews tensed up. "Bring your aircraft to a heading of one eight zero," the A-10 squadron commander ordered without waiting for a response, "and take your aircraft out of Idaho airspace."

For a very long second he hesitated. Then, drawing in

a deep breath, he began to issue his orders. "Eagle flight, this is Eagle One. Break right, break right. Bring your aircraft to a heading of one eight zero and form up on me. Cease all preparations for the drop. Repeat, cease all preparations for the drop."

✕

As soon as they heard Macky instruct his transports to turn south, the pathfinder team that had gone in with King's jump relayed the news of the aborted jump. King immediately understood the significance of that message for he had watched the Air National Guard A-10s as they catapulted into the sky and raced off into the western sky. The company first sergeant and the leaders of the 1st and 2nd Platoon stood by in silence as they watched their commander look off to the north where the Idaho Guardsmen continued to mass vehicles, then to the hills south of where they were. Everyone knew what was going through their commander's mind. Each prayed that their hard charging commander would make the only decision that made sense while there was still a chance to get away.

After taking a deep breath, King turned to face his assembled leaders. "There's nothing more we can do here." With that having been said, the young company commander brought his map up in order to study the graphic representation of the ground that lay before him. When he was ready he looked up at his waiting subordinates. "There's a quarry of some type to our south," he stated in a low, carefully controlled voice. "We'll head for that and reform there. 1st Platoon will take the portion of the perimeter from twelve o'clock to six, 2nd Platoon, six to twelve." No one took note of King's efforts to fight back the despair that was welling up inside of him as he spoke. They simply listened to his orders. When he was finished, King looked about. "Any questions?"

No one said a word. Then, as a new spasm of small arms fire erupted to the east, the first sergeant asked the question that was on everyone's mind, "What about 3rd Platoon?"

Slowly King turned to look over to where a third of his company was fighting for its life. He had no way of knowing whether the failure of his XO or 3rd Platoon to respond was intentional or due to their situation. What he did know was that to stay where he was with those portions of his company he did have control over, while waiting for a response that might never come was foolish. The only bright spot in the whole disastrous affair was that 1st Lieutenant Wahler was with the 3rd Platoon. Though the XO didn't much like him, King knew he was a professional. Wahler would know what to do.

Turning his attention back at his assembled leaders, King gave the order to move out. "All right, gentlemen. It's time to go. 1st Platoon, move out as soon as you can. 2nd Platoon will follow. Any questions?"

When none were forthcoming, King nodded. "Good. Now let's get going." With the traditional hand salute initiated by King, the officers of Company A, 3rd Battalion, 517th Parachute Infantry broke up their meeting and scrambled to execute King's orders without giving the plight of the 3rd Platoon another thought.

CHAPTER 15

Patiently, Nancy Kozak waited in the State Adjutant General's outer office. Like a dozen other staff officers and commanders of support units, she was there to provide data in her particular area of expertise to the senior Guard commanders meeting with the governor and Adjutant General. She had already been called in once to give a quick breakdown of the ammunition stocks within Idaho as well as an update on additional munition that had been promised to them by the Montana and Wyoming Guard. While her news that short falls of some critical munitions could be filled by fellow Guardsmen from neighboring states was greeted with cheers, Nancy viewed the prospect of an escalation of the crisis with a growing sense of alarm. There was something, she kept telling herself, wrong about what they were doing.

To some degree this feeling stemmed from the exhaustion and listlessness that often follows combat. She had been there. She understood the mental trauma that tagging and bagging the bodies of her own dead generated. She knew the images of soldiers who had died on her watch would be with her for a very, very long time. This she accepted. She was, after all, still very much a soldier.

More troubling to her was the nature of this crisis and the face of her opponent. In the First Persian Gulf War her enemy had been foreigners. The Iraqis were different, culturally, religiously, and politically. She couldn't relate to them, making it much easier to view them as something other than human. The men who had stormed her positions that morning, however, had not been people whose ways were strange to her or who spoke a foreign tongue. The paratroopers were fellow Americans, no different from her or the Guardsmen she commanded. Under other circumstances the paratrooper she had shot could have been serving under her. That she had been forced to shoot him for no other reason than the fact they were on opposite sides of a political issue was unsettling.

The opening of the door leading into the Adjutant General's office, followed by a flood of commanders and senior staff officers from that room, signaled the end of their meeting. Pushing herself against the wall that she had been leaning against, Nancy studied their faces as they filed by. A few, she suspected by their downcast expressions, shared her apprehensions and concerns. Others clearly showed that they were delighted with themselves, the position of importance that events had catapulted them into, or the manner in which the people in units they commanded had performed that day. Most, however, wore masks that hid their personal feelings and any concerns they might be harboring over the situation they now faced.

The last two people to come through the door were the adjutant general and the governor. GO Thomas was wearing a brown leather aviator's jacket and a blank expression. Nancy wondered what was going on in that man's mind. He had once been a warrior, just as she had been. He had once taken an oath of office that was no different than hers. How then, she wondered, had he been able to precipitate this crisis? Had he misjudged the response that would result from his actions? Or was there more to this? Something more calculated, something . . .

Nancy's face must have betrayed the contempt that was welling up in her, for GO Thomas slowed his pace as if he were about to stop and ask what was troubling her.

Not wanting to deal with this sort of confrontation, Nancy averted her eyes and quickly pushed her way past him. It would take more than a few witty sound bites to justify the events of that morning. Whatever their reasons, Nancy knew that there wasn't a person present who would be able demonstrate to her satisfaction that the course they seemed so hell bent on following was worth the price so many would have to pay.

• • •

It had been years since GO Thomas had felt as alive as he did at that moment. Walking through the crowded corridors of the state National Guard headquarters, the businessman turned governor basked in the hearty handshakes and congratulations that were being heaped upon him. For him it was a return to the good old days when he was seen as the first among equals, a warrior leader, a conqueror.

While GO Thomas had not foreseen any of this, he was not at all averse to taking advantage of the situation. Despite his official title he was still an opportunistic businessman at heart. He knew that whatever profit there was to be harvested from the conflict now unfolding at his very doorstep needed to be seized immediately. He had spent too many years building up financial and political clout throughout the western states in an effort to position himself for national office to let a simple matter of unfortunate time sidetrack him.

With the support of the people of Idaho as well as many across the nation who shared his political views, GO was convinced that he would be able to use this incident to achieve his lifelong aspirations. So long as the President continued to blunder as he had that morning, Thomas knew he would be free to justify just about any action he took while winning the majority of the nation over to his side. The only thing that he would need to be careful about over the next few days was keeping his distance from those elements that could discredit his cause. Already a number of militia leaders and other fringe elements had made it public that they were ready and willing to support his stand. GO reminded himself that he would need to make doubly sure that his Attorney General understood the importance of keeping an eye on the militias and right wing radicals. GO appreciated the speed with which national leaders and the media could turn away when someone became identified too closely with extremists.

As important as that issue was, it would have to wait for the moment. Walking out of the building, GO could all but feel the warm glow of the media spotlight. Journalists and camera crews, kept at bay by a single strand of barbed wire strung up around the headquarters, sprang to life when they saw him. Like a pop star he paused, flashed his famous smile, and absorbed every ounce of the excitement and glory he could manage. With studied ease, he pulled a set of aviator style sunglasses from a pocket on the sleeve of his jacket, flipped them so that the arms sprang open, then coolly brought them up to his eyes while scanning the crowd. Only one thing could top this, he told himself as he looked at the mob of journalists. There was only one more victory that he needed in order to make this one of his more exciting and fulfilling days.

At first he didn't see her. GO had expected to find Jan Fields in the forefront of her colleagues waiting to interview him. She was, after all, noted for her aggressiveness when it came to getting the story du jour. He had been counting on this drive. It was therefore a bit disconcerting when he was unable to find the prize that he felt justified in claiming.

He had all but despaired of finding her when he saw the world famous journalist out of the corner of his eye talking to a Guard officer. Though he had no clue who that officer was or why she was wasting her time interviewing him, GO was determined that he would correct Jan's lapse in judgment. Buoyed, he gave the noisy crowd another broad, confident smile, a quick wave, and turned to make his way over toward Jan.

Neither the cameraman nor the sound tech took Jan's erratic behavior that morning calmly. In turn they attempted to draw her into one interview or shot after another. When she failed to respond without explanation, they would ask plaintively, "Well, what do you have in mind?"

Distracted by an unseen force, Jan never answered. Instead she would simply turn and wander away. Not even the frantic calls from the headquarters of World News Network shook her out of her uninspired and unproductive meandering. Only one thing could end them, one thing that Jan was almost afraid to find.

In the hope of being able to shoot some footage that might be of use as Jan stepped up to a Guard officer, the cameraman hoisted the nation's eye on breaking events and prepared to film once Jan cued her. But the suddenly absent minded journalist never gave her the now familiar flip of her hair and quick, over the shoulder glance. Instead she stood before the Guard captain with her back to the camera. Peeved, the cameraman let the lens dip down as she cast her compatriot a look of disgust.

Had the cameraman been a mother and had she known that Jan had a son who was a member of the nation's only airborne capable division, perhaps she would have understood Jan's distraction. But Jan never allowed herself to become too familiar with her crew, preferring to keep them at arm's distance. In the past this had served her well, permitting her the freedom to replace any member of her team as soon as they became sloppy, unprofessional, or uncooperative.

But the flip side of this meant that when Jan was on assignment she was very much alone. Other than her nightly calls to Scott, she didn't have someone with whom she could share that day's joys and triumphs, or tragedies and despair. This practice helped her maintain her image as a dedicated and unflappable journalist, a professional with no conscious thoughts except getting the story. Just when she could have used a little understanding and someone to lean on, she found that she had no one who could help her.

For their part, her crew followed her without comment. Working as a pick-up crew for a national celebrity, neither the cameraman nor sound tech felt comfortable pushing Jan. After all she was the one with all the national awards. Besides, until that morning her coverage of events in Idaho had been flawless and occasionally quite spectacular. So if Jan's behavior seemed to be a bit erratic at the moment, she could be forgiven. Having watched other artists at work, the cameraman suspected that Jan might be onto something. "Patience," she kept telling herself, "patience."

• • •

Frustration continued to build up as Jan's efforts to find out if her son had been one of those who had made the jump that morning failed. No one she spoke to was able or willing to provide her with the identity of the airborne unit that the Idaho Guard was facing across the open prairie just yards from where she stood. Like everyone else in Boise, the public affairs office of the Idaho National Guard had been caught completely by surprise. The best she could do there was talk to a harried sergeant when she had called them. "Lady, there's me and one lieutenant to take questions from a million of you folks. Please, be patient, take a number, and wait your turn. When we're ready to pass on some information that's worthy of a press release, you'll be the first to know."

It wasn't in Jan's nature to take an answer like that and go meekly off to a corner to sit quietly and wait. Falling back on her habit of ferreting out information, Jan scurried from one officer to another followed by her news crew. On one hand the cameraman and sound tech were a handicap, causing all but the most verbose to back off when they saw her coming. By the same token her press credentials and crew permitted her to stay within the confines of Gowen Field when everyone who wasn't in uniform and didn't carry proper ID was being booted out beyond an exclusion area surrounding the scene of that morning's confrontation. So Jan continued her quest with crew in tow, going from one person to another, asking the same question: "Do you know the unit designation of the paratroopers you face out there and if so, what is it?"

The latest victim of this inquiry was a tall cavalry captain who had just exited the building. He was in the process of explaining to Jan that even if he was privy to that information, it would be wrong for him to tell her without proper authority, when GO Thomas came up. Flashing the same smile that he had given her at all their previous meetings, GO interrupted the captain. "It just wouldn't be a crisis worth that title if Jan Fields weren't covering it, now would it?"

Ignoring GO's pitiful attempt at humor, Jan turned away from the captain and stepped up to the governor. If anyone could answer her question, it was this man. Already at wits' end and not worried about appearance, Jan asked him if he knew who it was the Guard was facing across the empty prairie to the south.

Having been an astute observer all his life, GO quickly noted that neither the cameraman nor sound tech had rushed forth with equipment in hand to record his response. If anything they seemed to be perturbed, almost angry at what Jan was doing. Yet there was concern in Jan's face, real, unrehearsed concern that GO had not seen in any of his previous meetings with this woman. Though he didn't quite know what to make of this, GO sensed that he was being handed a blue chip.

"Well, Ms. Fields," the governor stated in his smooth, winning style, "I am sure that information is available somewhere. I'm just not sure who would have it."

Though angered by the flippant manner in which GO Thomas was treating her question, Jan swallowed a caustic remark that was on the tip of her tongue. Instead she pushed her pride aside and did something that was uncharacteristic. Never having understood the true motivation behind the exclusives that GO Thomas had granted her in the past, Jan forced a smile as she reached out and touched GO's hand. "I'm wondering, Governor Thomas," she asked in a voice that was far too sweet for a person in her position, "if you could help me find that information."

The touch of this woman's hand on his sent a shock through Thomas that left him speechless. He hadn't expected that. He thought that he was going to need to work her, as he worked his employees, in order to motivate her to doing his bidding. But instead she was reaching out and all but offering herself to him. It was, he imagined, just as it should be. Jan, a most beautiful and dewy-eyed female, was presenting herself to him, the man of the hour.

For a moment the two stood there staring at each other, each trying to figure out what to say next in order to further their own very separate and very diverse goals. As was fitting, it was GO who recovered his balance first and responded. "I would love to help you, Ms. Fields, but unfortunately there are people waiting for me at the State

House. However," he quickly added, before Jan's disappointment permitted her the opportunity to pull her hand away, "I'll be most happy to see if the State Adjutant General's office can secure that information for you."

Continuing to hold her forced smile as well as GO's hand, Jan thanked him. "I would appreciate that very, very much. You can reach me at . . ."

GO winked. "Oh, I know. I have your mobile phone number." He smiled and with his free hand tapped a pocket where he kept his notebook.

Jan thought nothing of this as she gave his hand an extra squeeze. That she would get what she wanted was all that mattered for the moment. Letting go, she watched as the governor headed over to where a military sedan was waiting. She continued to watch as the sedan pulled away. For the first time that morning a genuine smile came to her face as she saw the silhouette of GO Thomas seated in back bring a cell phone up to his ear. "Yes!" she softly muttered. "Yes!"

If her anxious crew had heard her private elation, they showed no sign of it when she turned toward them. Taking a minute to compose herself, Jan looked them over. "Well, boys and girls," Jan stated in a cheery voice that surprised her jaded associates. "We have a job to do and a story to cover. Now," she stated firmly, "let's get to it."

Jan's demeanor would not have been quite as cheery if she had been privy to the phone message GO actually passed on to the Adjutant General's chief of staff. Though the chief of staff didn't have any idea at that moment what units of the 17th Airborne were out there, he did understand an order when he heard one. As soon as he hung up he called the public affairs officer. "Under no circumstances," he told the frazzled lieutenant who was still desperately trying to hold down the fort, "are you to release the designation of the Airborne unit until I tell you to do so. Is that clear?"

With half a dozen other phones ringing madly on vacant desks in the Idaho National Guard public affairs office, the lieutenant gave his superior a crisp "Yes, sir," and hung up as soon as he could without giving that order a second thought.

The lead F-16 Falcon made one more slow orbit of the base, piloted by Brigadier General Lee Deacon. He found he could not resist the temptation of saying farewell to the air base he had commanded for almost two years before he pointed his aircraft toward the setting sun. As he watched the other F-16s form up on him, he could not escape the feeling that this would be his last mission. Even if he were successful in completing the task he had been given, the Air Force general knew that he would never again be able to face fellow Americans without having them look at him and think, "Here is a man who bombed his own countrymen."

The order to attack and destroy Idaho's Army and Air National Guard aircraft had been issued by the Chief of Staff of the Air Force himself. Like Deacon, the Chief understood that there were certain orders one does not have a minion pass on. Each man found it impossible to delegate the responsibility for giving that order unless he, himself was involved. In the case of Deacon, this meant leading the attack himself. "When we go in," he told his stone faced pilots at the mission briefing, "I will make the first pass. I will draw the first blood." Then, lowering his head, Deacon found himself muttering, "And may God have mercy on my soul."

The crackle of a squadron leader's voice brought Deacon back to the here and now. "Mace One—this is Blue Mace Leader. Target area is in sight. Over."

Deacon shook his head. The woman who was leading the F-16s designated as Blue Mace was not the commander of the squadron that made up her flight. That officer was headed south toward the Nevada border with other personnel from Mountain Home not flying the mission. When word of what they were about to do leaked out, the squadron commander had presented himself to Deacon in his office and laid before the general the silver eagles that represented the squadron commander's rank and the wings that stood for his vocation. "I have no doubt," the squadron commander stated as clearly as his emotions would permit him, "that the orders you have received are valid. I cannot, however, bring myself to raise my hand against my fellow countrymen." After rendering a final salute, the former squadron commander pivoted about and left Deacon's office, passing a dozen other aviators who were lined up outside and waiting to follow suit.

Deacon had warned the Chief of Operations back in Washington that some of his pilots would decline the order he was about to issue. "Frankly," he told the senior general, "if I were not in command here, I am afraid I would find it hard to follow myself. But . . ." Deacon never finished his comment. There was no need to.

The glint of the setting sun off the dome of Idaho's capitol building stood out like a beacon. Quickly Deacon's eyes cut south to the runway of the municipal airport. His targets would be to the left, or south of that. Some of the A-10s would be on the commercial runway, on alert or dispersed, instead of at their normal location adjacent to the Army National Guard facilities. He also suspected that a few of the AH-64 attack helicopters would be up and about, hunting down the forlorn paratroopers farther to the south. All of this, plus the frantic activity at the Idaho Guard base, would make hitting their targets while causing minimal collateral damage all but impossible.

Swallowing hard, Deacon pressed his transmit button. "Blue Mace leader—this is Mace One. Stand by. I am going to make one pass and take a look at what's what." With that, the Air Force general dipped the nose of his aircraft and aimed for the cluster of maintenance buildings, barracks, and motor pools of Gowen Field.

Though he had expected that they would encounter some ground fire, Deacon had imagined the response would be slow in coming. When it did, he had hoped it would be sporadic and ineffectual. He was therefore quite taken aback by the maelstrom of small arms fire that rose up to greet him as he started his run. For the briefest of moments, Deacon was mesmerized by the image of bright orange orbs that came arching up toward him. These were tracers. Given the normal mix of tracers versus ball ammunition, there would be four unseen bullets coming his way for every tracer he saw.

That this was happening was only logical. It had been anticipated. Not all of the pilots who declined this mission did so because the thought of firing on their fellow Americans violated their personal morality. There were those among them who not only supported the stand that the governor of Idaho had taken, but were willing to do what they could to help further the budding rebellion. So the appearance of Deacon's aircraft, boring down on the men and women of the Idaho Guard, was far from being a surprise to the forewarned Guardsmen.

With a blink and quick shake of his head to clear his vision Deacon forced himself to look past the hail of incoming small arms fire and refocused his attention on the ground targets. Catching sight of an A-10 making its way from a taxiway onto the main runway of the municipal airport, Deacon abandoned all thoughts of making a quick look-see pass. Instead he jiggled his joystick and turned to line up for an attack on the Guard aircraft.

As a wing commander Deacon never had the opportunity to log as many flight hours as he would have liked. Not that he was alone. All but a handful of the pilots in the peacetime Air Force racked up the flight time they needed to stay truly proficient and combat ready, let alone satisfy the insatiable desire to punch holes in the sky that all pilots possess. Yet Lee Deacon was able to bring his F-16 around and start his gun run with ease. For several seconds, the ground fire that had been so disconcerting disappeared from his consciousness. He became fixated on his target. Every thought, save pressing home his attack, vanished from the wing commander's conscious mind. There was only the A-10 below, struggling to grab some open sky and Lee Deacon, a brigadier general in the Air Force, a husband of twenty-eight years, the father of three, grandfather to five, and a man who had become by order of the President of the United States an angel of death.

When it came, the decision to fire was easier than Deacon had feared it would be. In fact he started firing without really having to think about it. It came instinctively. The process that combines target, a pilot's actions, and machine into one continuous, closed loop operating almost without thought, took control. Nothing could break that loop. The hideous tapping of bullets ripping through the control surface of Deacon's aircraft, the bucking that shook the F-16 as its cannon cut loose, or the recorded warning blaring in Deacon's ear to tell him that he needed to pull up failed to brake the Air Force general's concentration. For a moment there was no wing to command. There was no ground fire. There were no concerns over what would become of him when he had finished this mission. There was only himself and the A-10 he had selected for destruction.

Just as suddenly it disappeared. What had been a sophisticated ground attack aircraft ceased to exist. With a force that Deacon imagined he felt, the fuel and munitions of the Idaho Air National Guard A-10 tore the hapless aircraft apart. Like a man awakening from a dream Deacon pulled back on his joystick and sought to regain some of the precious altitude he had burned during his gun run.

It was then, as he began to ease his joystick back, that he realized he was in trouble. All at once the cockpit of his F-16 was alive with the squawk of warning buzzers and the glare of indicator lights that told him his aircraft had suffered mortal damage. With effort Deacon was able to bring the nose of his aircraft up until he had achieved level flight. Ignoring the chatter of his squadron commanders as they issued their orders to attack, Deacon allowed his aircraft to fly west, out of the battle, as he looked about the confines of his fighter to assess the damage.

Like a program running through a computer, Deacon went through the prescribed battle damage assessment as casually as if he were sitting in a simulator back at Mountain Home. As he came across a fault or system failure he made a mental note of it and moved on to the next item in the checklist.

Only when he was sure that he fully understood the condition of his aircraft did he attempt a maneuver beyond those that had been necessary to keep him airborne. As expected, the response of the F-16 was sluggish, almost hesitant. In some cases primary control systems had failed entirely or were not working properly. Noting a dangerously high engine temperature that he had no hope of controlling, the Air Force General came to the inescapable conclusion that he had but a few minutes before the sophisticated, multimillion dollar fighter would fall from the sky like a rock.

While he was easing his stricken aircraft around and couching it into a slow climb, Deacon made a quick estimate of how much longer he could stay aloft. When he had come to a reasonable answer, he then calculated how far it was to Hill Air Force Base. He could make it, he figured, but just barely and if he made no demands of his crippled F-16 beyond level flight.

But all thoughts of doing so faded as he approached Boise again. In his absence the men and women who had followed him had gone to work. Even in the distance, he could see pillars of thick black smoke rising up from the vicinity of Gowen Field. His lads were doing their job, he told himself. They were doing what he had ordered them to.

It was at that moment that Brigadier General Lee Deacon made his decision. Slowly, he pulled the joystick back in order to gain more altitude even though he knew that the additional strain of doing so would quicken the engine failure that was now but a matter of time. Once he had reached a practical altitude, Deacon leveled out and started to make a slow orbit around the Boise area. "Blue Mace leader—this is Mace One," he called when he was set. "I need a quick update on what's going on."

The response he received was not one he had expected. "Mace One—this is Blue Mace One. Blue Mace Three is down—I repeat—down. He took a Stinger and went down over the city. He had no control. I repeat, he had no control."

As much as he dreaded doing so, Deacon brought himself to search the area north of the municipal airfield. When he saw the column of smoke spewing forth from several buildings engulfed by sheets of flames, the Air Force general's worst nightmare was realized. Turning his eyes away, he struggled to fight back a wave of nausea that was slowly making its way up his throat. Even the thought that this would soon all be over was little comfort to Deacon.

"Roger, Blue Mace Leader," Deacon managed. "Give me an update."

"As best as I can determine, we've nailed all the A-10s on the ground," Blue Mace Leader responded. "But I'm not sure of the attack helos. Some were out south of Gowen. They scattered and went to ground as soon as you started your run."

Deacon surveyed the area as he gently brought his stricken F-16 over a bit, so that he could get a better view. He tried to sort out which pile of burning scrap had once been an A-10 and which ones had been AH-64s. But moving at a speed of over four hundred miles an hour several thousand feet up made this all but impossible. With the sun setting and ground fire stabbing menacingly up at him, Deacon came to the conclusion that there was no way that he could be sure if they had achieved one hundred percent success. Still, he didn't want to turn his back and fly off with the mission half finished. "Blue Mace Leader—this is Mace One. Do you think we can do anything more here? Over."

"Other than lose more of our own for nothing," Blue Mace Leader responded after carefully weighing her response against what she had seen, "that's a negative."

"Okay," Deacon announced. "Break off the attack and head your people to Hill."

With relief, Blue Mace Leader acknowledged Deacon's order and passed it on to her squadron. It was only when they had formed up and taken an easterly heading that Blue Mace Leader noted that her commanding officer was missing. "Mace One—this is Blue Mace Leader. Where are you?"

There was a moment's hesitation before Deacon answered. When he did, there was no mistaking the mental and physical fatigue that had overcome the Air Force brigadier. "I'm south of Boise, Blue Mace Leader. I'm afraid that my aircraft has taken a bit more damage than the flight to Hill would permit."

Alarmed, Blue Mace Leader ordered her second in command to take over as she brought her own aircraft about, in a sharp turn, and made tracks to find her commander. "Mace One—this is Blue Mace Leader," she called as soon as she had visual with him. "I'll notify search and rescue and give them your location as soon as you . . ."

"You will do nothing of the sort, Major," Deacon snapped before Blue Mace Leader could finish. After a moment of silence, during which Blue Mace Leader brought her aircraft up next to Deacon's, the wing commander explained. "I'm riding this one out, Major," he stated calmly.

Looking over, Blue Mace Leader saw her commanding general, oxygen mask unsnapped and flopped over to one side, reclined in his seat, staring out over the open Nevada desert. He wasn't making any efforts to bring his aircraft around to a heading that would take him closer to Hill and safety. Nor was he making any preparation to eject. He just sat there, ignoring his instruments and looking out over the open desert that was bathed in the striking shades of red and orange that only a western sunset can produce.

Though she didn't quite understand why he was doing this, Blue Mace Leader knew that nothing she said or did would change his mind. Finally, she broke the silence. "Sir, if you don't mind, I'd like to stay with you a while."

Rolling his head over to one side, so that he could see his uninvited, yet very welcome wingman, Deacon smiled. "I'd like that," he replied softly.

Unable to control her voice as she choked back a flood of tears, Blue Mace Leader didn't answer. Instead, she rotated her head to face her commander. When he looked over, and saw her facing him, she gave him a crisp hand salute. After Deacon returned it, the two F-16 pilots looked away from each other and resumed their flight across the barren western landscape in silence.

CHAPTER 16

Like a prairie dog emerging from his burrow to search about for waiting predators, Nathan Dixon pulled back the small section of camo net he was hidden under and stuck his head up out of his shallow foxhole. As difficult as it was, the young officer forced himself to ignore the pillars of black smoke rising up over Gowen Field. Instead, he scanned the horizon in all directions. Only when he was sure that they were in no immediate danger did he look back toward the northwest.

Having heard his platoon leader stir, SFC Gandulf pulled off his camouflage. Though he suspected that his lieutenant had already done so, Gandulf also looked about. When he saw all was clear, the senior NCO moved over to where Nathan was. Settling back on his haunches he surveyed the same scene Nathan was observing in silence. After counting the fires, the NCO finally spoke. "Looks like the Air Force really laid into the Guard."

Nathan nodded in agreement without taking his eyes off the western sky line. "I'll be happy if the only thing they accomplished was smashing those damned AH-64s and A-10s. Maybe then we'll have a chance."

The sound of their platoon leader and platoon sergeant speaking to each other in hushed tones brought more heads up. One of Nathan's more outspoken soldiers add his two cents. "Looks like the zoomies went after more than the National Guard."

Nathan turned toward Boise. A pillar of rolling black smoke rose above the twinkling city lights. Even at this distance he could see one of Boise's few high rise buildings engulfed in flames. Nathan drew in a deep breath. "That," he said to no one in particular, "is what people who do targeting refer to as collateral damage."

Gandulf chuckled. "For those of you who don't comprende, that means one of those smart bombs we're always being told about flunked its final."

This brought a round of nervous laughter to all those who heard their platoon sergeant's comment. Even Nathan, left for hours with nothing to do but lie quietly in a shallow hole while National Guard helicopters swept the area all afternoon, managed a chuckle. But that brief respite from his concerns and worries lasted but a moment. Looking away from the destruction that the Air Force had visited upon the civilians of Boise, Nathan once more turned his attention to the west. Drawing his binoculars out of their case, he brought them up to his eyes and began to slowly scan the horizon. Gandulf joined in this effort. When the old platoon sergeant caught sight of a cloud of dust, he pointed it out to his platoon leader. "Vehicles moving north to south at eight o'clock."

Nathan was already tracking them. "Three Bradleys. I make the range to be between two and three thousand meters."

"Closer to two," Gandulf replied.

"Their guns are oriented in different directions," Nathan added as he brought the binoculars down. "They're looking for us, or the rest of the company."

"You suppose," Gandulf asked, "King and the other two platoons made it to the hills to the southwest?"

Nathan turned his face toward the low, rolling hills Gandulf was speaking of. "If they pulled back when we did, I imagine they did. I didn't hear any firing after we broke contact." After a pause he added, "I'm going to assume that they did."

The conversation between officer and senior NCO wiped away any relief Gandulf's earlier comment about collateral damage had generated. The soldiers of 3rd Platoon were reminded once again that they were isolated, alone, and in a very precarious position. Nathan could almost feel their eyes on him. He imagined they blamed him for the loss of the platoon radio, damaged when the RTO had been hit. Though Nathan made it known that the radio was inoperative, the fact that he hadn't brought it back to prove to his men that it was literally shot left room for doubt.

Unlike Gandulf, Nathan had not been with these men long enough to win their full trust and confidence. He didn't have the credibility that permitted his men to accept everything he said as gospel. Nathan's father had spoken to his son about this problem. He lamented the sad fact that an officer's word was no longer viewed as his bond in the United States Army. "One of the more enduring legacies of the war in Vietnam," Scott often reminded his son, "was the sad fact that the officer corps ceased being something special and became nothing more than another career oriented profession." Then Nathan had not appreciated what his father was saying. Now, however, this sad truth hit home. Though Gandulf did all he could to make it known he was in full agreement with his lieutenant's actions, Nathan found himself wondering if even his senior NCO actually believed in him or if he simply did so because the situation demanded that he stand by his lieutenant.

Exacerbating this feeling of uncertainty over his leadership abilities and judgment was the fact that his platoon had been less than thrilled about his decision to evade the Guard by moving to the southeast. While this did take them away from Gowen and the National Guard vehicles that had begun to gravitate toward the ammo site, it also took them farther away from the rest of the company. Nathan had judged the risks associated with going south, then cutting to the west in an effort to rejoin the company were too great. They were just as likely to miss the rest of the company if it was also on the move as they were to find it. Yet the draw of joining their comrades was compelling to the men in Nathan's platoon. Even highly trained paratroopers feel safer and braver when they are surrounded by their fellow soldiers, especially if the alternative is following a brand new lieutenant into the unknown.

Gandulf did his best to ensure that there was no open dissension to Nathan's orders. What grumbling did bubble up during the move was quickly squelched, if not by Gandulf himself then by the squad leaders who always kept one eye on the platoon's senior NCO. While aware of what was going on, Nathan did his best to pretend that he didn't notice it. Instead he mustered up the bravest, most confident mask of command that he could affect and went about the business of being a platoon leader.

While watching the Guard vehicles roam the plains in the fading light, Nathan went over the decisions he had made up to that point. With his platoon pinned down, the XO dead, his RTO bleeding to death in his arms, National Guard tanks headed their way, and small arms fire hammering away at his position, Nathan quickly appreciated that his platoon's initial objectives were beyond their means. Given that terrible fact, the young officer opted to go for King's alternate plan. As quickly as he could, he rallied his platoon and pulled it back to defend their drop zone. As he saw it then, his inability to fully accomplish his first real world mission would not result in dishonor if, when the rest of the battalion arrived, they landed in a DZ that was safe and secure.

Yet even this simple task proved to be unattainable. As the hours ticked away and it became obvious the follow-on force wasn't coming, Nathan began to despair at even being able to fulfill this modest achievement. By then the Guard was beginning to sally out of their motor pools looking for them, making it impossible to go west in search of the rest of the company.

In theory, decisions made at platoon level use the same methodology that the President and his chief advisors use. Factors such as the mission, the opposition, the terrain upon which the operation will take place, and the troops available to execute the mission, are all taken into consideration. Options of how to best accomplish the mission in light of those factors are formulated and then considered using a technique known as "War gaming." Once this process has been completed, the option that best suits the circumstances and promises the best chance of success is selected for implementation. This is known as a decision cycle.

There is, of course, no comparison between the circum-

stances and conditions under which the President operates
and those faced by a platoon leader in the field. The President and his advisors execute their duties in a controlled
environment where everything from who is allowed to enter the room to the very temperature of that room is regulated. Information required by the President is presented
to him using a well established procedure that is designed
to provide the commander-in-chief with only that information that is deemed necessary. Even this information is
delivered in a package tailored to the President's own personality. With few exceptions the presidential decision cycle is designed to permit the commander-in-chief time to
think things over carefully before making a final choice.

A platoon leader, on the other hand, has all the same
requirements when it comes to making a decision yet none
of the advantages. This was especially true for Nathan
Dixon as he watched the Guard Bradleys roving about the
open range to the west. Nothing, save for what his platoon
did next, was truly within his control. He had no idea
where the rest of A Company was or what they were doing. Though he could see combat vehicles moving about,
he could only guess at what their intentions were. For all
he knew some sort of agreement had been reached between
the folks in Washington and the errant governor of Idaho.
Anything, at this point, could be possible.

About the only thing Nathan was sure of was the condition of his platoon. They were now into their second day
of almost continuous activity and motion. During that period of preparation, marshaling, forward deployment, and
insertion, few in his platoon had managed to catch anything resembling a worthwhile nap. Looking about, Nathan
could clearly see that his men were starting to suffer from
the loss of sleep and stress. Added to that was the peril
they faced and a future that was as unclear as it was ominous. The young platoon leader could almost read the un-
spoken question that their expressions betrayed: "What
next?"

Yeah, Nathan asked himself. What next? Slowly, the
young officer stood erect. After being scrunched up in a
foxhole all day it felt good to stretch out. Looking off to

the west he caught sight of the three Guard Bradleys he had been watching. Farther off to the northwest he saw other clouds of dust being thrown up by heavy vehicles in motion. There was a lot of heavy traffic over there, all of which he had to assume was unfriendly. Twisting his body about, he looked off to the east and then northeast.

The contrast between the flat, open land to the west and what he saw in the opposite direction could not have been any starker. His eyes were drawn to the bright, colorful lights of a cluster of factory outlet stores not far from where he stood. He was close enough to see cars and figures moving about. Beyond that was Interstate 84 and a scattering of homes where people, not unlike the families of his paratroopers, were settling down to dinner or to watch the latest news story concerning events that had unfolded in their backyards.

That thought triggered an urge in Nathan to make for the nearest residence, sneak up, and peek in the window in the hope of catching some news or information that would aid him in his decision process. King's order that all portable radios and such be left behind angered Nathan. What had made perfect sense just twenty-four hours before was now proving to be really dumb. "Isn't it just my luck," Nathan muttered as he let that thought shrivel up and die, "that I get the only platoon where the soldiers do exactly what they're told."

Gandulf turned to his lieutenant with a quizzical look on his face. "Excuse me, sir?"

Realizing that he had let his thoughts cross his lips, Nathan mustered up a sheepish smile as he shook his head. "Oh, nothing, Sergeant. It was nothing."

Not sure if he should press his lieutenant, Gandulf simply nodded. "I'm going to check on Smitty if you don't mind, sir."

There was another factor that Nathan had to take into account. His RTO was in bad shape. Though the worst of the bleeding had been stopped and he was resting comfortably for the moment, there was no way that his platoon could move swiftly and silently about while hauling a man as badly shot up as he was. Not only would it be cruel, but the slightest moan at the most inopportune time would compromise the security of everyone else in the platoon. Yet leaving him, even in the care of fellow Americans, went against everything that Nathan had been taught. Still . . .

"Sergeant Gandulf," Nathan called just as the platoon sergeant was preparing to head off toward the wounded. "When you check with the medic, see what he thinks about moving him."

Even in the gathering darkness Nathan could read the expression that distorted Gandulf's ordinarily deadpan features.

"I think we're going to have to move, and move fast," Nathan volunteered. "If we're to avoid being scarfed up by the Guard we have to. We wouldn't be doing Smitty any favors if we took him with us. If anything, it'll probably kill him." Nathan let that thought hang between them for a moment before he continued. "It's not like we'd be leaving him with bloodthirsty barbarians who didn't speak a lick of English or who have no compassion for their fellow human beings."

Gandulf's chin dropped until it almost touched his chest. "I know that, LT," he finally admitted. Then, he looked up at Nathan. There was a hint of anger in the sergeant's eyes. "But that doesn't mean I have to like it." With that, the platoon sergeant pivoted about and stalked off, leaving Nathan very much on his own.

He was tired. For the first time, Nathan realized what being tired and alone really felt like. Lifting his head he looked up at the clear fall sky. A slight breeze was stirring, just enough to send a chill through him. His father had been in situations like this, he told himself. His father had dealt with many hard decisions. Some of them were probably just as unpleasant and seemingly hopeless as this one. But his father wasn't here. He was. Second Lieutenant Nathan Dixon was going to have to face down this situation on his own. The thought that his ancestors, Ian McPherson during the Revolution, and later James McPherson in the Civil War probably faced far worse didn't do anything to brighten Nathan's outlook or lighten his load. Whatever decision he made would have to be based on the here and now, on what he saw and what he believed to be proper given the circumstances his platoon faced. Though the stories of the trials and tribulations of past McPhersons and Dixons might provide him with a modicum of encouragement, none of the family's past glories would do him a whit of good. He was the one who would have to decide, to order, and to lead.

When he had collected himself, Nathan scanned the horizon. Everything, from the activities of the Guard to the limited mobility of his foot-propelled airborne infantry, was taken into account as he considered his next move. In the end Nathan found he had but a limited number of options available to him that made sense or were practical.

As these thoughts rolled about his exhausted mind, Nathan found himself looking over his shoulder, away from the dangers that lurked off to the west. Instead, his gaze kept being drawn to the distant, dark mountains that lay northeast of Boise.

The air attack had struck like a Biblical bolt out of the blue. It had given the triumphant Guardsmen an unexpected slap in the face. For the people of Boise it had come as a shock. There was no need to turn on one's television to view the carnage that a crippled F-16 and two bombs had caused in downtown Boise. They only had to walk their streets or listen to stories of neighbors who had been in harm's way to realize that this had become something more than a disagreement between opposing political views. True war, a civil war, between themselves and their fellow countrymen had come to Idaho.

In the waning hours of the day, when even the sun abandoned the sky, the shock of the day wore off. In its stead many of the citizens of Boise, both Guardsmen and civilians, discovered that their bewilderment was transforming itself into anger. Within hours rage became the order of the day.

"How dare they," Jan kept hearing repeated over and

over. "How dare those bastards in Washington do this to us." For her part, Jan managed to maintain an air of objectivity, although she knew such a stance was fast becoming impossible to maintain. The sight of body bags filled with men, women, and children whose only crime had been to live in a particular place, along with the stench of death tends to evoke strong emotions in even the most dedicated journalist, drawing them to side of the conflict or the other.

Jan didn't need to wait for this to happen. She already had a personal stake in this crisis. Still, she did manage to rally and pull herself together and report the events of the day. "What we're seeing here today," she summarized in one of her broadcasts, "may only be the beginning of a downward spiral as what had been a war of words becomes, for the people of Idaho, a struggle for survival."

Using buildings in downtown Boise engulfed in flames as a backdrop, Jan described the attitude throughout the capital of the rebellious state. "The apprehension over 'What's next?' that had been so prevalent here in Boise after this morning's surprise airborne assault," she explained, "has given way to an overpowering desire to lash out." Cutting to a film clip of Guardsmen reporting for duty shot earlier in the day, Jan's voice-over explained that what had been a limited call up had turned into a full scale mobilization. "Few of the Guardsmen who had not been part of the first call up waited to be summoned. Though most of these men and women confess that they do not fully understand why this confrontation between their state and the Federal government came about, no one I've talked to after the air strike left any doubt as to where their loyalties lie. As one Guardsman explained, 'This is where I live. The politics of Washington and what happens there mean nothing to me. Idaho is my home. Everything I own and everyone I know is here. So I guess if it comes to it, this is where I will die, defending my people and their right to live their lives as they see fit.' It is with this sort of sentiment," Jan concluded, "that the Federal government must now contend. What was a struggle between politicians involving abstract, constitutional ideas has become a blood feud for the people of Idaho."

Jan's ability to pull herself together and get on with her job with an energy more akin to what the public and WNN were accustomed to was her way of dealing with her own fears and apprehensions. Standing off on the sidelines, doing nothing as she waited for word about her son, would have been nerve wracking. In the field where people and events were in continuous motion and time was a precious commodity, journalists could forget their fears, their apprehensions, and even their own identities as they became a part of the story that they were covering. For Jan, her ability to lose herself was a blessing.

Every escape from one's personal reality does have its price. This was especially true in a situation like this one, where the people and events were hitting, quite literally, close to home.

Besides the story concerning the mobilization of the National Guard and all state emergency agencies, Jan was working on another piece that was far more disturbing. Though not flaunted in the same manner by public affairs officers at either Guard headquarters or the State building, the appearance and incorporation of irregular military formations into the state's defensive force was gaining momentum. Journalists who lacked the intimate familiarity with the American military failed to pick up on this. At first even Jan didn't see it. But slowly, almost imperceptibly, she began to take note of men wandering about in nonregulation camouflage uniforms, toting weapons that were not standard issue. In the end it was the beards and bellies hanging over some of the belts that finally clued Jan as to who these odd apparitions were. "My God," she gasped when the realization finally hit. "The militias are here."

Unlike the other pieces she had done so far in Idaho, shooting this story proved to be difficult and to Jan's cameraman a bit scary. Unlike the Guardsmen, who were now well represented by articulate spokespeople, the militiamen had no central figures to speak for them. Long conditioned by harsh experiences with the media, the militiamen recoiled from the camera when Jan tried the direct approach. "Unless you want that camera shoved down your throat," one belligerent militiaman warned Jan's cameraman, "you'd best take that toy of yours somewhere else."

Having been in similar situations, Jan knew enough to back off. Instead she directed her crew to do their shooting and sound recording either from a distance or in a more circumspect manner. At the ammunition point, for example, she had her people stand just outside the wire with their equipment at waist level looking as if they were waiting for permission to enter. Instead, both the camera and recorder were running as the female lieutenant colonel in charge of the ammo point refused to issue ammunition to any militiamen without proper authorization. In reviewing the material later, Jan was thrilled to hear Nancy Kozak's voice come through loud and clear. "Look," the determined officer informed a particularly obnoxious militiaman, "I don't care who you are or what sort of authority you think you have. You're not getting so much as a single cartridge until I am presented with a proper requisition and authorization from the State Adjutant General to issue to non-Guard personnel."

Of even greater interest was the reaction of the militiaman, whom Jan recognized as Louis Garvey. "Oh, that won't take long, little lady," Garvey replied with a smirk, the type that would send chills down the spine of most mortals.

Jan could tell, even in the terrible light under which this segment had been shot, that Nancy Kozak was within a hair's breadth of giving way to her anger. Only the timely intervention of a tall sergeant between Garvey and Nancy prevented this. "If you're finished with your business," the Native American Guardsman told Garvey in the sort of voice that left little doubt it was a last warning, "then be so kind as to move along."

Garvey remained uncowered by either Guardsman. With a smile and nod, the militiaman casually informed his newfound foes that he'd be back.

Jan was in the midst of editing this piece when she received a call on her personal cell phone. She was so wrapped up in finishing the piece, she almost managed to ignore it. But a little voice told her that this might be important. Reluctantly, she gave in.

"Jan," an unexpected voice greeted her. "I was wondering if you wouldn't mind coming by my place. I have some information that would be of interest to you."

Jan's sound tech, who was doubling as the crew's editor, saw the expression on the journalist's face. Pulling away from the video editing machine, the sound tech gave Jan a worried look. "Trouble?"

Without removing the phone from her ear, Jan shook her head. "No, I don't think so," Jan whispered while holding her thumb over the holes of the mouthpiece. "It's Thomas. He wants me to come out to the governor's mansion."

"An interview?"

Jan waved her hand and shook her head again as she listened to the governor's smooth voice drone on. "No, just me," Jan whispered.

To the sound tech's surprise, Jan responded that she would be happy to accept his kind invitation. "Old GO," Jan explained after she clicked the cell phone off, "just might provide us with a few missing pieces, vis à vis the militia. Besides," Jan added as she tried to laugh off the invitation, "it beats having dinner with you two again."

The sound tech was unconvinced. "That depends on who the main course is."

With an expression that belied her own apprehensions, Jan tried to wave her overprotective sound tech off. "Oh, I've dealt with worse," the journalist mused as she turned back to continue editing the video before them.

The sound tech shook his head. Like everyone in Boise, he was becoming more and more convinced that nothing, no matter how outrageous, was now beyond the pale.

Hanging up the phone, Thomas tried hard not to show the strain he was finally beginning to feel. Looking across the room at the two men before him, GO grunted. "The militia will get their ammunition. Orders will be cut tonight authorizing the distribution of ammo and weapons not required by the Guard to those units you have certified and will need to augment the state police."

For the first time since he entered the governor's officer, Attorney General Osborn permitted a smile to crease his face. "I assure you, GO, only those units that I personally approve and which are willing to submit to state authority will be sworn in."

GO nodded. "Choose wisely, Tom," GO admonished his Attorney General. "The other governors in the coalition and our friends across the nation are already getting nervous over the manner in which things are going. The last thing we need is to have neo-Nazis, skin heads, and the KKK wrapping themselves in our banners."

Osborn stood up. "Like I said, I will personally see that only the cream of the crop will be added to the state rolls." With that, he turned to leave, but stopped before he had taken a step. "And that female officer at the ammo site?"

Frustrated by having to deal with such a trivial matter, GO raised his hand and waved it as if he were swatting a bothersome fly. "She's history. The Adjutant General himself has promised me that Lieutenant Colonel Kozak will be replaced."

"That's not good enough," Osborn came back. "I want her drawn and quartered."

Now it was GO's turn to let his determination show. Standing, he stared at the Attorney General for several seconds before he spoke. When he did, he used the tone of voice he reserved for those times when he wanted it known that there would be no further discussion. "Listen, Tom. I have no idea what this colonel did to you. Quite frankly, I don't care. What I do care about is the fact that this state is in the midst of a major crisis. The Guard needs every swinging Richard, male and female, if it's going to generate a viable deterrence to future Federal action. That colonel you've taken a strong disliking to may be a burr under your saddle, but she's one of the Guard's best and brightest. While the Adjutant General is willing to move her, he made it clear that he'll be damned if he's going to throw her to the wolves just to satisfy someone's bruised ego."

Sensing that he had pushed Thomas as far as he dared for now, Osborn raised his right hand in a gesture of peace and nodded. "Fair enough."

Only after he was in his car and the driver had pulled away from the governor's mansion did Osborn inform the other man riding in the backseat with him of GO's decision concerning Nancy Kozak.

Rather than being perturbed by this, Louis Garvey accepted the decision. "Well," he stated with a bit more glee than even Osborn found comfortable, "it looks as if we're going to need to tend to our own affairs."

Osborn cautioned his compatriot. "Don't let your authority go to you head and don't go getting yourself in trouble. Be patient. When the time is right and the people are ready, we'll be able to step in and take over. Until then, we need to be team players."

With the last of his visitors and staff gone, GO slumped down in his overstuffed chair and laid his head back. Sometimes even dealing with his most trusted subordinates could be an exhausting experience. It was almost as if he were the only man in the entire state who understood what was at stake. Why, he wondered, didn't anyone else appreciate that they had, within their grasp, the last great hope of curbing the oppressive power of a federal government run by corrupt politicians and mediocre bureaucrats? Why did men like Osborn insist on cluttering their minds with the petty concern of "getting even" instead of keeping their focus on the big picture?

As he picked up a drink he had almost forgotten about, GO chided himself for having underestimated the President. Instead of being rocked back on its heels by the failure of the airborne assault that morning, the administration had struck back with a ferocity that damned near brought the entire leadership of the state to its knees. It had taken every bit of GO's amazing character to keep his state legislature from running straight to the President, hat in hand, begging for forgiveness. "Doing so," GO pointed out in a heated meeting at the statehouse, "would end the states' rights movement in the country. What Lincoln started in the 1860s, and Roosevelt expanded upon in the 1930s, must be stopped here and now. We've drawn our line in the sand. I'm challenging each of you to be man enough to step up and defend our rights." In the end, GO won out, but barely. He had no doubt that at that very moment little men were holed up in secret meetings not far from where he sat seeking a solution that would save their own petty political careers.

GO looked around the room as he took a sip of his drink. It was well appointed with hand crafted furniture that he had commissioned. He liked this room. It was a place where a man could relax after a long day. But tonight the deep rich hues and natural wood tones that appeal to a man brought him no pleasure or comfort. At that moment he felt as if he were little more than an exhausted old man who was beginning to feel both his liquor and his age. He needed to purge himself of his concerns and apprehensions. The air of supreme confidence and utterly unshaken optimism that he had been able to maintain when dealing with the leadership of Idaho needed to be replenished. A passionate night with a beautiful woman would do him wonders.

He poured himself another drink. Perhaps the devastating air strike launched was all for the better. Every enterprise that had ever been worthwhile in his life had required hard work and perseverance. Revolution, he figured, was no different. Things took time, a commodity that was on his side. With just the right spin GO began to see that any advantage the President now held could be turned against him. Every story had two sides. This one was no different. After a good rest and a bit of recreation, he'd find a way to turn the Federal government's actions against the people of Idaho around to his favor.

⚔

A call from Scott turned out to be a mixed blessing for Jan. Using short, cryptic exchanges, her husband answered many of the questions that had been uppermost in her mind. "The lad is where he should be, where he'd want to be," Scott replied when Jan asked after Nathan. "You understand, don't you?" he asked in a very guarded manner.

Jan wasn't able to respond. The best she could manage was to shake her head while she struggled to calm herself. This news brought on tears that were as much from the tension that had been piling up as they were from the dread that had now become reality.

Scott understood what was happening on Jan's end of the line and tried as best he could to calm her. "Some friends of mine will be there early tomorrow to give him a hand," he continued, speaking slowly as he carefully selected each word. "I expect they won't have much trouble. The lad and his buddies don't have much to be moved."

Though Jan thought she understood what Scott was saying, she wished she could ask him to spell it out. But she didn't dare. She was well aware that their chat could very well have uninvited ears listening in. Whether they were on Scott's end or hers didn't matter. Both, given the circumstances, were likely targets for monitoring. So she had to content herself with the shreds of news that Scott was able to pass on using his own version of crypto-speak. "What about you?" Jan finally asked when she was sure of her voice.

"Busy," was all Scott came back with. When he didn't say anything for several seconds Jan wondered if she should press him with another question. But she didn't. She wasn't as practiced at this as Scott. Finally he filled in the silence with a nonsensical story about a fight between Jan's hyperactive Jack Russell and Scott's overly curious Abyssinian. Jan listened and was entertained but longed to speak openly to her husband. Since that was impossible, she forced herself to be satisfied with just hearing his voice.

Before he said goodbye Scott dropped his own news on her. "I'm having lunch with Bernie tomorrow," the major general stated in a rather nonchalant manner.

"Oh?" was the best Jan could muster, realizing that Bernie was General Bernard Poulengy, Chief of Staff of the Army, and a great supporter of Scott's career.

"He'll only be in town for the day," Scott quickly added.

"Well, don't forget to give him my best," Jan nervously replied.

"I will," Scott answered. "He knows he can depend on us to do our best when he asks."

This last statement sent a chill down Jan's back. She knew what that meant. In the First Persian Gulf War Scott had been pulled from a nice safe assignment to serve on Poulengy's personal staff in the forward area. When there had been trouble in the Balkans and Poulengy had been sent there to sort things out, he had asked Scott to join him. A visit by "Bernie" at a time like this meant only one thing. Scott was going to be involved in the President's next move.

When Jan didn't comment on his last bit of information, Scott decided it was time to end this call that would be, in the eyes of the Army Security Agency, highly suspect. "Well, I have a very busy night ahead of me and a bitch of a morning to look forward to. I have no doubt your day tomorrow will be just as rough."

Jan swallowed hard. "Yes, I expect it will be," she replied as she thought about the political fallout that would rock Boise once it was discovered that the paratroopers had been extracted. The Biblical retribution that an emerging radical element was demanding would be denied them and they would not be pleased.

But that was tomorrow. For now she turned her attention back to the only man she had ever really loved. "Scott?" she whispered softly, "I love you."

The softness of her voice and the sweetness of her sentiment brought a pang of regret to Scott. "I know," he whispered. "Take care, hon."

As she waited for her host to show himself, she found herself amazed at how quiet things were at the governor's mansion. The hushed, homey foyer of GO's personal residence stood in stark contrast to the chaos and pandemonium that was engulfing Boise. Had this been the home of anyone else Jan would have relaxed and surrendered to the mood her surroundings were designed to encourage. She was so lost in her own thoughts and concerns that it took several minutes before she realized that there was no one else about. After letting her in, the housekeeper had disappeared. "Well," she told herself nervously as she fiddled with the gold chain about her neck, "here's the lamb. Now where's the big bad wolf?"

When he appeared, GO Thomas startled Jan. He didn't enter the foyer through the oversize arch that opened into a formal living room. Nor did he descend the wide staircase that emptied out into the center of the foyer. Instead a door Jan had thought was a closet opened. Like a game show host making his entrance, GO came popping through the doorway. "I was told you were here," he stated crisply. "Sorry for making you wait."

Jan noted that his manner and appearance were in stark contrast to what she had seen earlier that day. In place of the flight jacket and aviator sunglasses he had sported then, GO now wore a light blue denim shirt and khaki slacks. His face was freshly shaven and every hair was in its place. As always he was sporting a smile. Only his eyes betrayed a hint of exhaustion and concern. As he took her hand and held it a bit too long, Jan noted that the confident gaze which had made him seem so strong, so commanding during their past meetings was absent. "I've not eaten yet," he stated as he continued to hold onto her hand. "I was hoping that I would be able to prevail upon you to join me."

Withdrawing her hand from his grasp with a jerk, Jan reached down inside and managed to pull out her award winning journalist smile. "It would be my pleasure."

GO led Jan to a small dining room adjoining the kitchen, one that she guessed was used more often than the large, formal one that they passed. "I'm not sure what my housekeeper left me," GO casually informed Jan as he pulled out her chair and held it for her. "But whatever it is, I am sure there's plenty for both of us."

Again, Jan flashed a forced smile. "Oh, no doubt."

Taking a seat across from her, GO waved his hand across the table filled with bowls and trays of food. "Help yourself. We don't stand on formality out here in the west."

With her elbows on the table and her hands joined under her chin, Jan returned his smile. "That seems to be the only thing you people are not willing to make a stand on."

Jan's unexpected barb caught GO off guard. For the first time that evening his well practiced smile disappeared. Looking across the table, he studied her disarming smile and wondered if her comment had been the opening shot of a confrontation or simply a witty retort. Hesitantly, he continued spooning food onto his plate as he let her last remark pass. "You should try the green bean casserole. It'll never win an award, but it will definitely leave you asking for more."

"Gee," Jan exclaimed as she reached for the bowl. "What an appropriate dish for you."

Her comment struck GO like a slap in the face. This second insult left no doubt that the first had also been meant as one. Still, he continued on without responding. "If there is something you don't see here that you'd like, please do feel free to ask."

Jan looked up at GO and smiled. "I am sure you thought of everything, haven't you?" before shoveling a forkful of salad into her mouth.

Realizing that she had no intention of giving him a break, GO decided the best thing he could do was to back off and hope that a good, home cooked meal and a glass of wine would soften the headstrong woman seated across from him.

While that was his plan, Jan had her own. Having found out pretty much everything she needed from Scott, the original purpose of her meeting with Thomas had evaporated. She now felt no compelling need to be polite to him. With people like Bernie Poulengy and her own husband involved, Jan figured the days of GO Thomas defining and guiding the confrontation between the Federal government and Idaho were numbered.

Still, she knew that it would be helpful to stay on the good side of GO if that were possible. So Jan resolved to moderate her sharpness as she ate. Besides, the guarded manner in which GO conducted himself during the balance of their meal told her that her initial digs had accomplished what she had wanted. The Idaho power broker had been put on notice that she had no intention of succumbing to his charms.

When they were finished, GO suggested that they adjourn to his study. With a nod of her head and a polite smile, Jan agreed and followed. The sight of a pot of coffee with whiffs of steam curling up from its spout told Jan that they were not exactly alone. Though she always made it a point to pay attention to what was going on around her at all times whenever she was in a situation like this, Jan hadn't heard or seen anyone. Whether having someone else about was to her advantage or not wasn't clear to her. So she kept her guard up. Watching, she noted where GO sat before she selected her own seat, one which was about as far away from Thomas as the arrangement of the room permitted.

"I said I'd look into the matter of who those paratroopers were," GO stated as he poured Jan a cup of coffee and handed it to her. "I've been informed by the State Adjutant General that the unit was a company belonging to 3rd Battalion, 517th Parachute."

Not sure how much GO knew about her personal life, Jan bent her entire will to ensuring that she displayed no reaction to this news. Instead she did her best to downplay its importance to her. "Just one company raised all the fuss that rocked Boise this morning?" Jan asked in a tone that was intentionally meant to be demeaning.

Truly caught off guard, GO wondered why she was going out of her way to piss him off. In the past she had been quite attentive, doing all she could to make sure that she stayed on his good side. Now, however, she was deliberately being confrontational and downright insulting. This not only came across as ungrateful, it was blatantly rude. Any thoughts of seducing this woman, no matter how tempting it might have been earlier, were quickly dissipating as the governor turned to deal with her as he dealt with anyone who was foolish enough to stand up to him. "You seem to be forgetting your history, Ms. Fields," GO replied sharply. "It only took a single shot to ignite our own revolution."

Jan didn't let GO's sudden change in demeanor upset her in the least. In fact she welcomed it, for it signaled an end to the tension she had felt since her arrival. By way of demonstrating that she was unimpressed by his show of anger, Jan took a sip of her coffee before looking up into GO's eyes. "It took far more than a single bullet being fired in anger to bring this nation into existence. It took men of courage, principle, and passion, promoting a better way of life, a better system of government, and high moral standards to make the sacrifice at Lexington and Concord count."

Lurching forward, GO leaned closer to Jan and made no effort to hide the anger he now felt. "Are you implying that what we stand for in Idaho is base and vile? That the people are unethical and their beliefs are of no account?"

"Oh, no," Jan replied softly. "I was only speaking of their leaders, not the people."

Jan's words set GO Thomas off like a rocket. "You want to talk about unethical conduct? You want to discuss a lack of principle and self-serving politicians? Look to Washington! Look to those fools on the Hill and the moron in the White House. They," GO spit out as he shook his finger wildly off in a direction that was supposed to represent the location of the nation's capital, "they are the villains, not us."

Maintaining her calm, Jan placed her cup of coffee down and folded her hands on her lap. "In over two hundred years, only once did a state feel its stand on an issue justified the use of armed force against the very institution that created it. What makes you and those you've managed to put into power think that you have the right answer? That your interpretation of the Constitution is the correct one, *the* only correct one?"

Angered and frustrated by a day that had seen so much of what he had worked for brought to the test, GO Thomas laid into Jan with a viciousness that was normally reserved for his most despised foes. "Those paratroopers landed in my home state, not the other way around. No Idaho

Guardsman set foot on Capitol Hill, gun in hand, threatening to pull down the government. No state official stood on the steps of Idaho's statehouse and tore the Constitution to shreds. We are the victims here, Ms. Fields, the people of Idaho and the very Constitution that this President and his lap dogs have worked to subvert since the day they took office."

Throwing her hands up and turning her face away in disgust, Jan returned GO's verbal volley. "Oh, please. Save your whining for the evening news and the weak minded who lap up whatever drivel you choose to feed them." Then she brought her head about and glared at Thomas. "You engineered this crisis. You manipulated people and events until the President had no choice but to respond in a deliberate and forceful manner. You knew that he could not ignore what you did. Yet you just kept pushing, and pushing, and pushing."

GO smiled. "You give me a great deal of credit."

"No," Jan replied as she stood up. "You give yourself too much."

With his face glowing red from the anger, GO jumped to his feet. "And where do you think you're going? We're not quite finished."

The moment of truth had come. GO's true colors were flying from the masthead and it was time for Jan to push her guile to its limits. "Am I to assume by your statement that I am not free to leave here?" she asked as calmly as she could. "Is the champion of personal liberties going to deny me my freedom?"

It took a second for GO to realize that he had allowed his anger to override his common sense. With his hands curled up in tight, white knuckled fists, he stared at Jan. As he did, the color in his cheeks drained and his rage turned into embarrassment. Finally GO averted his eyes, lowered his chin, and brought his right hand up to scratch his head as his face deformed itself into a series of anxious grimaces. When he was composed and had collected his thoughts, he looked up at Jan. "Oh God, Jan. I am so sorry. I . . ."

Realizing that she had gained moral ascendancy for the

moment, Jan decided that it was time to go. "Am I free to leave?" she asked again in a low, yet deliberate manner.

Still off balance, GO nodded, "Why yes, of course you . . ."

"Don't bother to show me to the door," Jan quickly replied as she snatched up her purse and headed for the exit. "I know the way."

Feeling the sting of his foolish behavior as well as exhaustion, GO let her glide past without a word. When she was gone he dropped into his seat. He was losing control of the situation, he confessed to himself. What had started out as a well orchestrated campaign to make things right was starting to go awry. And he had no idea what to do next.

CHAPTER **17**

The small Army jet, painted gloss white over gloss olive drab, rolled to a stop just feet from where Scott Dixon and his aide stood. There was no honor guard, no band, no gaggle of straphangers. The only other people waiting were two drivers, one for the Humvee belonging to the 4th Armored Division's commanding general and one for a sedan. Of the four, only the two drivers had managed a good night's sleep.

The door of the jet and the steps that folded down from it hadn't been locked in place before General Poulengy appeared in the doorway. Automatically Scott, his aide, and the drivers came to attention. Without fanfare Poulengy bounded down the steps and toward Dixon. "I wish," Scott stated dryly as he saluted the senior general approaching him, "that I could say it was a pleasure to see you again."

"I wish I could say the same," Poulengy snapped after returning Scott's salute, then pointed to the Humvee. "You mind if we take that? Just you and me?"

Scott raised an eyebrow, but shook his head. "Other than the fact that I am not licensed to drive it, I don't mind at all."

"Well, neither am I. But it's a pretty sure bet that no one's going to report me," the Chief of Staff of the Army replied.

Overhearing the exchange, Scott's aide spun about and supervised the exchange of the star plates on the vehicles. Having assumed that he would use the sedan, the plate bearing the emblem and four stars of the Chief of Staff of the Army had to be switched to the Humvee as protocol dictated. While this was going on Poulengy climbed into the driver's seat, where he sat for a moment as he looked about. "There's a starter someplace around here, isn't there?" he asked his nervous aide who stood next to him in the open door.

"I believe, sir, this is it," the aide ventured as his mind raced to recall the controls of the Humvee he had once known by heart when he had been a battalion commander.

"Yes. That looks like one," Poulengy stated without any embarrassment. He was, after all, the senior general in the entire United States Army with much on his mind. That he didn't know everything about every piece of equipment in that Army was to be expected. If anything, he used that failing to put soldiers he met at ease. It was his way of showing them that he was a human being like them and that he needed each and every one of them.

Poulengy cranked up the vehicle, shifted into drive, and took off. "I know the way, Scott," Poulengy said as he navigated around his collection of surprised aides who were still climbing down off the jet.

"Is this going to be a Chief of Staff of the Army to Commanding General of the 4th Armored Division discussion," Scott asked after they were on their way, "or a Bernie and Scott chat?"

Poulengy waited until he had brought the oversize vehicle to a stop at the entrance to the airfield before he turned to Dixon. He stared at his friend and trusted subordinate. "Scott," he stated flatly, "as of this morning your son is officially missing in action."

For several seconds Scott saw and heard nothing. In his mind's eye he beheld a wide eyed child of two sporting a broad smile as he tottered toward Scott's outstretched arms. As that image faded, Scott didn't ask Poulengy what had gone wrong with the extraction of the surviving paratroopers. He didn't curse the national leadership that had sent Nathan to Idaho. He didn't even blame himself, for he had, time and again, done everything to dissuade Nathan from pursuing a military career. Instead, Scott's mind reached out as if trying to capture and hold onto every memory of his son that it could gather.

After letting his friend recoil from his announcement,

Poulengy tried to explain. "After what happened to the Air Force yesterday I felt that it would be best if I told you in person. We still have no way of knowing who's on what side of this issue."

Slowly Scott turned his head and looked at Poulengy. He didn't take any note of the apprehension that showed in the senior general's face as he crept along the broad streets, steering wide to avoid other vehicles that scattered to make way for their Humvee. Only when he felt he could control his voice did he speak. "What happened?"

Poulengy explained as best he could while driving along. "Your son's platoon was separated from the rest of the company shortly after the drop. When the Guard reacted, and the company commander pulled back, his retreat took him away from your son's platoon. The CO of the unit, a Captain King, reported after the extraction that Nathan's platoon was heavily engaged almost as soon as it hit the ground. The commander of the 17th Airborne assumes your son's platoon lost its radio during the drop or in the fire fight. Regardless," Poulengy went on, "when the Night Stalkers went in last night, they were only able to locate the two platoons with King."

"Then where the hell are they?" Scott demanded.

"Well," Poulengy mused, relaxing behind the wheel for the first time, "we're pretty sure the Idaho Guard doesn't have them."

"How do we know that, sir?"

Poulengy glanced over at Scott and winked. "Water can flow two ways through a sieve."

Scott's puzzled expression prompted his superior to explain. "There are folks with the Idaho Guard who have remained loyal to the colors. Though they're not able to provide us with anything concerning what the state's political and military leadership intend to do in the long term, they are able to provide us with real-time information on activities, dispositions, strength, and composition of Guard units that have been mobilized."

"Do they know that they still have a platoon of our people in Idaho?" Scott asked.

"As best we can tell, no. Which is why," the Chief of

Staff of the Army replied as he swerved to avoid a soldier who stood in the middle of the road, saluting as he stared dumbstruck at a four-star general driving a Humvee, "I waited till I got here to tell you. Eventually word will get out. But," Poulengy stated as he stopped the Humvee at a stop sign and looked over at Scott, "I want to keep that information close hold for as long as I can. Not just for your son, but for all of his men."

Behind them the driver of a two and a half ton truck, unaware of who was driving the Humvee, leaned on his horn when Poulengy didn't continue through the stop sign fast enough. "Scott," Poulengy continued as he finally began moving again, "with all the uncertainty as to where everyone's loyalties lie, normal operational security measures are useless. That is why I suggest that we just say fuck opsec. Let them see you coming. Stomp your feet. Pound your chest. Let the television film you every step of the way."

"Take care of opsec by ignoring it while intimidating the good citizens of Idaho along the way," Scott summarized.

"Exactly!" Poulengy exclaimed. "Perhaps the vision of your juggernaut barreling down on them will give the moderates in Idaho an excuse to break ranks with the radicals and settle this before you need to come to blows with their Guard."

"And if they don't?"

The senior general didn't answer at first. Instead, he concentrated on his driving. When he did respond, it was in a mournful tone. "Scott, that's why I picked you. I trust your judgment and discretion. I know without having to tell you that you'll apply just the right amount of force, at just the right time, to get the job done."

Scott wanted to thank his superior for the vote of confidence but didn't. Instead, another image interrupted. This one was of a ten-year-old-boy, turning to face his father after hitting a baseball for the first time in a real game. Instead of running for first base, the boy flashed his father a smile. Scott remembered that he had yelled at Nathan that day for being so stupid and not taking off for first at a dead run. *God*, Scott thought to himself, *why had I done that?* Nathan had been so proud of what he had just done and he had wanted to share that pride with his father. With eyes welling up with tears, Scott couldn't keep himself from muttering, "How, dear God, could I have been so stupid?"

To a man the staff of the 4th Armored Division was blurry eyed and a bit slow on the uptake. For many, it had been a grueling all nighter with scarcely enough time for those fortunate enough to live close by to run home, shower, shave, and throw on a fresh set of BDUs. Those who lived off post made do with a shower at the post gym. Since they were professional soldiers, they took this all in their stride. Every one of them understood that on a scale of sacrifices that soldiers were obliged to accept, loss of sleep was way down near the bottom.

Even if the division hadn't been responding to a crisis, a goodly number of people in the 4th AD would have spent the night preparing. A visit by the Chief of Staff of the Army anywhere outside the Beltway is, to put it mildly, an occasion. Normally weeks of planning and preparation crammed with briefings, dress rehearsals, and walk throughs preceded the Chief's visit. Often whole units were stood down from normal training activities in order to keep anything like training for combat from interfering with the visit. And while it is true that the United States Army didn't invent the term "dog and pony," over the years generation after generation of Army staff officers have honed that ritual until it has become something of a fine art.

Even faced with incredibly short notice and the amount of planning that needed to be crammed into the few hours between notification and the Chief's briefing, Dixon's staff could not shake this legacy. The conference room was all but spit shined and set up under the watchful eye of the Division sergeant major. For every staff officer who was crunching numbers, gathering intelligence, or assessing the feasibility of various courses of action, there was another of equal rank running about making sure the route the Chief would take to division headquarters was policed, checking that projectors and such were functioning, and other such foolishness. Scott never cared much for that sort of thing, and he always took great pains to make his thoughts on the subject known. But such was the nature of the beast that now, even at a time when issues such as national unity and civil war hung in the balance, the men and women who would determine if their nation remained a united one were unable to make the adjustment overnight.

Off to one side Bob Felden watched his staff go through their paces with the eye of a Broadway producer. That analogy was far nearer the mark than Scott cared for. Like all participants at such staged events, each of the primary staff officers and their deputies, brigade commanders and their operations officers, and selected support and combat support battalion commanders were in their assigned seats, arranged in accordance with Army protocol. Poulengy sat center stage at the head of the table, listening to the operational plan that Scott Dixon, seated to his left, had pulled together.

Everything about the plan had Dixon's signature on it. Like many commanders who had once been operations officers themselves, Scott could not simply pass his guidance on to his planning staff and leave them be. When it came to those operations that really mattered, Scott was in the thick of it, ably assisted by his G-3 and one of a handful of school trained planning officers known throughout the Army as "Jedi Knights." Though the curriculum at Leavenworth's School for Advanced Military Studies did not dwell on the domestic employment of the United States Army, Major Matt Kawalchek, the G-3 Plans Officer, rose to the occasion. Step by step Kawalchek took Poulengy through the phases that would move the 4th Armored Division from its peacetime garrison north, through three states, and into Idaho, ready to do battle if and when that was necessary.

For his part the Chief of Staff of the Army listened to

Kawalchek's presentation and nodded when the officer turned to him and sought approval with his eyes, an expression, or tone of voice. And though he listened intently, other thoughts and concerns crowded the four-star general's busy mind. Over the years Poulengy had come to expect near excellence from whatever Scott Dixon did. He had also had come to appreciate the hard fact that the Army was producing fewer and fewer officers like Scott Dixon, soldiers who truly understood their profession. While Poulengy would be the first to admit that Army officers were technically proficient in an increasingly technical bureaucracy, he also realized that the Army, like its sister services, was no longer developing a sufficient number of generalists, soldiers who could be depended upon to do just about anything with practically nothing on a moment's notice. So it was with satisfaction that the Chief of Staff of the Army listened to the energetic young major walk him through the operational plan that had Scott Dixon written all over it from beginning to end.

"The deployment and marshaling of the division in Wyoming, which is the hard part of this operation, will be briefed in greater detail by the G-4 Planner," Kawalchek pointed out near the end of his briefing. "Once we're on the ground and formed up the rest will be a relatively straightforward combat operation."

At this, Poulengy responded. "That's always the case, Major."

Unsure whether this last comment was an admonishment or praise, Kawalchek paused, looked across the room at the twin sets of four stars perched on Poulengy's shoulders, and gave the general a weak but polite smile before he continued. Such interruptions were rare, for Kawalchek was thorough.

When the major had finished his spiel and before the division G-4 Planner started his, Poulengy took the opportunity to remind Scott and his staff that this was not a normal operation. "Remember, people," he stated gruffly as he looked about the room, "what you are talking about. You, and the troops out there," he said as he pointed toward the window overlooking the cluster of barracks and motor pools, "will either be bringing a civil disturbance to an end or engaging in the first major campaign of this nation's second Civil War. Either way, those 'other people' marked in red that your fancy blue arrows are going through are your fellow countrymen, no matter what they believe in."

This somber reminder cooled the enthusiasm that the faultless briefing by Kawalchek had generated and put the G-4 planner on the spot. His plan would be the toughest to sell, for in it were some demands that Scott was sure would bring howls of protest from his fellow division commanders across the United States. "As the G-3 has already pointed out," the logistics planner stated as he opened his briefing, "getting there is going to be the trick. We not only need to marshal the necessary men and machines, we also have to establish a logistics base that is both secure and accessible by land and air. Right now, we're looking at Wendover, on the Nevada and Utah border."

"How far will it be," Poulengy asked, "from your division rear to Boise?"

The G-4 planner looked back at the map, then over to the Chief of Staff. "Just over five hundred kilometers by road, sir."

"That's quite a haul."

"Yes, sir, ten hours one way for planning purposes. But everything about this operation," the G-4 planner continued as he spread his arms out as if to encompass the entire map, "except the number of actual combat troops on the ground, is massive."

"That seems to include," Poulengy interrupted again as he glanced over the top of his glasses at a paper copy of the slides he had before him, "your requirement for heavy equipment transports." He looked back up at the G-4 planner. "Do you really expect me to gut the rest of the Army of its entire inventory of HETTs to support this operation?"

Sensing this was time for him to intervene, Scott took up the question. "We have no choice. Given the political climate in several of the states and communities that we will be traversing, I am constrained by the need to move entire units as entities. While rail would be cheaper, especially for the movement of the tanks and Bradleys, one act of sabotage anywhere along the unguarded route could very well bring an end to my deployment. I'd have a gaggle of dismounted tankers and mech infantrymen standing on the border of Idaho armed with nothing but strong language and menacing glares. By putting troops on buses and their combat vehicles on HETTs I can move them along the same route together. If, God forbid, someone along the way decides to join the mayhem we're suppose to be bringing to an end I will have the ability of fighting my way through."

The ease with which that last statement rolled off Scott's tongue and the look in his eyes sent a chill down Poulengy's spine. Scott understood perfectly well what was going on and what could happen. Unlike the idiots in Washington who had let things get out of hand, Scott and his staff were prepared to take anything head on.

"General Dixon," Poulengy finally stated as soon as he had managed to find his voice, "could I have a word with you in private?"

While everyone else in the room jumped to their feet and came to a rigid position of attention, Scott escorted the Chief of Staff of the Army to his office. When the door was closed and guarded by two nervous aide-de-camps, Scott and Poulengy took seats at opposite ends of the long leather sofa.

"Scott," Poulengy started as he rubbed his two hands together, "I've heard enough. Your plan is, as expected, sound."

"Then I'll get the HETTs," Scott asked quickly.

Poulengy looked down at his hands. "Yes, of course. In fact," he added, "when you gave me the heads up this morning about that I had my staff get on it. If things work the way I expect, some of the HETT units will be rolling your way by late this afternoon."

If this had been the only thing the Chief of Staff wanted to say he would not have not asked for privacy. Knowing his old boss better than most, Scott took the initiative. "You must appreciate, sir, that there isn't a man on my staff who does not understand the gravity of the situation which we face or the risks we will be running."

Looking up from his firmly clasped hands, Poulengy sighed. "It's not your staff I'm worried about. I suspect there isn't a man or woman in there that doesn't have less than ten years under his belt. For them and us it's the Army, first, foremost, and always."

"It's the soldiers you're concerned with, isn't it?"

Poulengy nodded as he sat upright, then stood. Pacing, he tried to explain. "The bulk of your enlisted men and women are in the ranks for any number of reasons, few of which have anything to do with a deep, burning devotion to patriotism. That's not to say," the Chief of Staff stopped midstride and faced Scott, "that they're not good soldiers. God knows they're some of the best I've ever seen. But," he continued as he picked up his pacing where he had left off, "the majority of them are still tied to their homes, their families, and their communities in a way old timers like you and me aren't."

Reclining, Scott took up the thread that Poulengy was slowly playing out. "You're concerned that when my people come eyeball to eyeball with the governor of Idaho's people, some of the lads will flinch."

With his brow deeply furrowed Poulengy returned Scott's stare. "You know they will, Scott. What happened to that fighter wing out of Mountain Home Air Base yesterday cannot be written off as an aberration. This morning the Chief of Staff of the Air Force was in the Sec Def's office jumping up and down swearing 'never again.' Scott," Poulengy added in a lower tone, "we can't afford to be embarrassed like that. If you get there after all our huffing and puffing and find out you don't have enough men to kick the door in, '*We, The People,*' are screwed."

While he had been hammering out the actual plan of operation, the same concerns Poulengy was expressing had never been far from Scott's mind. He had tried to think of ways of sidestepping the issue, to ignore it. But if the shooting started, he knew that some of his soldiers would, out of respect for their own homes and countrymen, hesitate, if not turn. That there was a great deal of sympathy throughout his division for many of the principles that the people of Idaho now represented was no secret.

After a long silence, during which the two men abandoned themselves to their deepest, darkest thoughts, Scott stood up, went to the door, opened it halfway, and motioned for his aide. Snapping to, the aide bounded over to him and leaned forward so Scott could whisper in his ear. When his general was finished, the aide went over to his desk, hit the speed dial for the 2nd Brigade, and relayed Scott's instructions.

The post gym, normally occupied by a handful of off duty soldiers shooting baskets at this time of day, was alive and crowded with soldiers of the 4th Armored Division's 2nd Brigade. Because that brigade was the farthest along in their annual training cycle Scott had selected it to be the lead element for the divisional deployment and advance into Idaho. They would deliver the main effort that would originate in Utah and follow an axis of advance defined by Interstate Highway 84. The division's 1st Brigade would stage in northern Nevada. That brigade would move north along two widely separated routes that would link up with the main effort at Twin Falls, Idaho, before heading into Boise. In that manner the Idaho National Guard would find its flank turned if they tried to stop the Second Brigade at any number of choke points along I-84. The division's National Guard round-out brigade, which normally was included in all real world contingency planning and operations, hadn't even been notified.

The men and women who would drive Poulengy's mailed fist down the throat of Idaho were at the gym conducting what the Army referred to as a POM, short for preparation for overseas movement. While it was true that they were not going overseas, all the items necessary for such deployments were just as necessary now. Dog tags, ID cards, pay options, shots, dental records, and other administrative personnel actions that the soldiers would be unable to tend to while in the field needed to be checked and taken care of before they left Fort Carson. Among the items that were being verified were the addresses and phone numbers of next of kin and, of course, the correctness of all options made by the soldier on his or her Serviceman's Group Life Insurance policy.

When Scott and General Poulengy arrived, Second Brigade's 3rd Battalion, 68th Armor was going through the process. The commander of this unit, a normally unflappable lieutenant colonel, was beside himself as to what to do. The division commander's aide had simply informed the brigade's executive officer that both the CG and the Chief of Staff of the Army would be at the gym in five minutes. While the sudden and unexpected appearance of the division commander was something every commander on Fort Carson had grown to live with, the idea of having the Chief of Staff of the Army "casually" drop in and mingle with the troops was enough to age any CO five years.

The entourage that the commander of 3rd of the 68th Armor met at the door was small and quite solemn. Dixon didn't waste time on social pleasantries. "Colonel," the tight-lipped division commander ordered, "assemble your men. I need to address them."

The battalion commander and his company commanders immediately scattered through the gym barking orders like sheepdogs gathering their flock. Scott, followed by Poulengy, found a place where he could be seen and heard by the troops when they assembled. Quickly, five mass formations began to take shape as soldiers automatically sought the guide who marked where the front rank of their company was anchored. When formed, the battalion commander, with his principal staff officers behind him, stepped out in front and presented himself. "Sir, 3rd Battalion, 68th Armor is formed."

Scott had told Poulengy nothing, though the senior general suspected he knew what his star pupil was about to do. He had, after all, trained him. For his part Scott hesitated a moment. With his feet spread shoulder width apart and his two hands behind his back he surveyed the sea of faces staring at him. Every now and then he paused as he looked into the eyes of one of the soldiers he was about to send into battle. The only noise that could be heard in the crowded gym was the hum of a soda machine in the corner. When Scott finally began, he did so in a low, but commanding voice, "Listen up and listen well, people."

"Several days ago," he stated in a loud voice that carried well beyond the rear rank of the battalion, "The governor of Idaho expelled all federal officials from his state. He followed this action with a statement that he would no longer accept the authority of the Federal government as supreme. Yesterday a unit of the 17th Airborne Division was dropped on the outskirts of Boise with the mission to reimpose that authority. In the course of that operation shots were exchanged between members of the 17th Airborne and the Idaho National Guard, resulting in casualties on both sides."

Poulengy could see that Scott was struggling with the realization that one of the casualties could be his son. Silently, the senior general found himself whispering under his breath, "Keep it together, Scott."

Inhaling, Scott averted his eyes by looking up at the ceiling, blinking them as he did so in the hope that a tear forming in his right eye would dissipate. When he was in control of himself again he looked back down at the troops, fixing his gaze on one of the hundreds of young, anxious faces watching his every move.

Ready, Scott continued. "Last night the paratroopers were extracted from Idaho, leaving no Federal troops in Idaho. Today, by order of the Chief of Staff of the Army, in response to a directive approved by the President of the United States and acting in accordance with the power invested in him by the Constitution, the 4th Armored Division has been placed on alert for immediate deployment to Idaho. You, the soldiers of this battalion and your sister battalions, have been given the mission of returning Constitutional authority to the state and people of Idaho, *by force if necessary.*"

The last part of Scott's statement was deliberately accentuated for both clarity and impact. As he paused to let that thought soak in Scott continued to scan the faces of his soldiers. "People," he barked suddenly, "I intend to execute those orders. They are valid orders. They are orders passed down to me by my duly appointed superiors. As an officer in the United States Army I am pledged to defend and uphold the Constitution, against all enemies, foreign and domestic. We are the guardians of that Constitution. We are expected to defend it, regardless of our personal thoughts, feelings, or sympathies. We all came into this Army with the understanding that someday we would be asked to place ourselves in harm's way. People, that day is at hand."

Again Scott paused. When he started again, he did so with a softer tone in his voice, one more akin to a father talking to a son. "I would be a fool," he stated flatly as he rocked back on his heels and bowed his head down for a moment to look at the toes of his boots, "to expect each and every one of you to snap to, salute, and blindly follow me without question or without reservation. The people we are going against, after all, are our fellow countrymen. They are Americans. Some of you are from Idaho. No doubt, some of you share the views of the governor of that state and fully support his stand. It has to be difficult for you, standing out there next to your fellow soldiers and friends, wondering what, in God's name, is the right thing for you to do. Once before soldiers just like you were faced with the same question, the same moral dilemma. Like them, you will have to decide if you will stand by the colors that you have sworn allegiance to or with your state, your community, and your people back home."

For the first time, Scott could see genuine looks of concern on some of the soldiers' faces and hear feet shuffling about. When he started again, he did so using his stern, no nonsense general officer tone. "People, we have one chance to get this right, one chance to go out there and settle this matter. I hope to do so without bloodshed. I hope that the leaders of Idaho can come to an understanding with the President of the United States before we commence operations in that state. But I cannot base my actions solely on such hopes. I must prepare for the worst. I must prepare and deploy this division, you and your fellow soldiers for war, civil war."

Poulengy winced when Scott said "civil war." In all his orders and briefings, he had taken great pains to ensure that his staff did not use that term. Anything and everything, from "reasserting Federal authority" to "suppression of domestic unrest" had been used. Unable to gracefully intervene, he allowed Scott to continue uninterrupted.

"When I go north *with the division*, I want only those soldiers who are *willing* and *able* to do their duties, without mental *or moral* reservations to go with me," Scott stated crisply, clearly, emphasizing selected words. "I do not want any man or woman here, or anywhere else in this division, to go if they feel that they will be unable to execute my orders and the orders of their superiors without hesitation and without reservations. To do so would not only be a disservice to your nation and your oath of induction, but would also place your friends, your fellow soldiers here in this battalion and in your company, in jeopardy. Hesitation, for whatever reason, is death in battle. I am therefore asking all of you who have serious doubts about your ability to do your duty to step out of ranks and voluntarily remain behind."

For the first time muted voices and whispers could be heard in the ranks. Scott, unsure of what was about to happen, glanced at Poulengy, who was no longer able to mask his own growing concern. Unsure what, exactly, to say or do, Poulengy averted his gaze. Looking back at the battalion, Scott figured that since he had gone this far, he had nothing more to lose. "At ease," he stated calmly in an effort to hush the mumbling.

When silence returned, Scott continued. "If you elect to remain behind because of moral and ethical convictions I promise you that you will not suffer any adverse administrative actions for doing so." Looking down at the battalion commander, Scott fixed his gaze on the worried colonel. "I am ordering you, colonel, not to interfere with the decision of those who cannot, in good conscience, go north with the division. Do you understand?"

The colonel, all but glowing beet red, popped to attention and thundered, "Yes, sir."

"This applies to your officers, and senior enlisted as well. Do you understand?"

"Yes, sir."

"If I hear, by whatever source or means," Scott continued, almost barking his orders by now, "that you or any of your officers or NCOs stood between a soldier under your command and his conscience, I will take appropriate actions against you under the uniform code of military justice. Do you understand?"

Shaking, the battalion commander shouted a last, raspy, "Yes, sir."

Scott looked about over the sea of faces again, drew in a deep breath, and ordered, "Carry on."

As the battalion came to attention and saluted, Scott and Poulengy filed out of the gym. They left behind them a somber collection of soldiers, young men and women about to make the most difficult decision of their lives.

CHAPTER **18**

The deployment of a division is a major event. Even the 17th Airborne, the nation's most flexible and combat ready division, needed time to prepare itself when ordered to pack up and move out lock, stock, and barrel. Normal twelve-hour work days become eighteen-hour-plus marathons as unit equipment is prepped and moved to marshaling sites. Soldiers who had not done so must find time to pack their personal gear before drawing their weapons and fall in for endless inspections and equipment checks. On top of these combat-related chores each and every member of the division has a personal life that he or she must place in order. Spouses need to be filled in on family matters such as car or mortgage payments coming due in the near future. BDUs that are still at the cleaners have to be picked up. The tube of toothpaste a father took out of his deployment bag when the family ran out one night requires an immediate replacement. All these countless tasks must be tended to almost simultaneously, creating a collective frenzy as officers and enlisted bounced back and forth between the execution of their assigned duties and personal obligations to family and self.

Not everyone is equally affected. The last soldier to leave the post does not turn out the lights and lock the gate. Inevitably every unit has a number of personnel assigned to it that are nondeployable. These people can include newly arrived soldiers who have yet to inprocess and draw equipment as well as those pending imminent discharge or retirement. Personnel with medical conditions, whether it be a broken ankle or a serious case of pregnancy, who would be unable to execute their assigned duties are left behind. In addition there are millions of dollars of equipment that are not required by a unit in the field. This includes items such as beds, wall lockers, office desks, computers, and the other odds and ends that cannot be neatly folded up and stuffed into a rucksack. So a small hand-picked cadre collectively known as the rear detachment, complete with a chain of command, is left to tend to these housekeeping duties as well as respond to the emergency needs of family members of deployed soldiers.

The selection of who stays behind to tend the home fires is left up to unit commanders. Where possible they select those qualified to execute these duties from personnel who would have to stay anyway. Often there are not enough officers and NCOs with an injury or an administrative hold to man the entire rear detachment. When this happens, the balance of the force is taken out of the unit's hide. Since the Army occasionally permits commanders to use their common sense, few units opt to dip into their small pool of stars to flesh out this skeleton force. Most commanders bypass their stable of reliable performers as well as those who have been rated as average or mediocre. In fact many a commander simply turns his list upside down and starts with those who used to be at the bottom. The end result is that the security and maintenance of the home installation, its station property, and the families of the servicemen are left in the hands of a collection of soldiers best described as the sick, the lame, and the lazy.

At the headquarters of the 2nd Brigade, 17th Airborne this select group included a master sergeant who had a medical record thicker than the novel *War and Peace*. He would be working for a chemical corps captain who was legendary for his ability to wander off and get lost. Like their counterparts all across Fort Bragg they sat at their assigned desks at Brigade watching the frantic comings and goings of outbound staff officers and NCOs. At the moment their sole task in life was to answer the phones. If a call came in that concerned the operation in Idaho they were under strict orders to grab the nearest officer and hand the phone over to him. They were to handle all other calls, especially from family members with questions or those looking for their spouses.

Since the brigade sergeant major was still in the area the master sergeant was unable to set up the small TV he had hidden under his desk. So he was left with nothing to do but read worn and torn magazines that had been left in the drawer of his desk by previous duty officers and NCOs. He was in the process of stirring himself from his seat in preparation to go off in search of a cup of coffee when the phone rang. For a second he looked at it with a scowl and let it ring again. Glancing over his shoulder, the master sergeant watched to see if his captain was making an effort to pick it up. When the phone continued to ring without that officer making any effort to answer it, the sergeant picked up the receiver. "2nd Brigade," the master sergeant stated in a voice that was more of a growl than an announcement.

He listened attentively but made no effort to pick up a pencil to transcribe any of the information he was being given by the caller. Instead, he merely nodded his head and grunted. After several minutes the master sergeant hung up.

He was about to renew his quest for coffee when he noticed that the Chemical Corps officer was standing next to him. "Anything important?"

The sergeant made a face. "No. Just a prank call."

Bored out of his mind and looking for some sort of diversion, the captain smiled. "Oh? What did this one say?"

The sergeant chuckled. "The guy said he was a platoon leader from Alpha, 517th and that he and his platoon were still in Idaho evading National Guard and militia patrols. He said he wanted to talk to the brigade ops officer or commander to report his situation."

"Well," the captain asked innocently, "did you remind him that Company A had been extracted two days ago?"

The sergeant was about to say, "I didn't tell them shit," but thought better. The brigade sergeant major had a nasty habit of showing up just when an NCO in his brigade was doing something the sergeant major disapproved of, like cursing in front of an officer. Instead the master sergeant shook his head. "I didn't tell him anything, sir. It was probably some colonel's kid getting his jollies off. No point in encouraging those people."

The captain shrugged. "I suppose. Well, in any case," he muttered as he pulled a crumpled beret from a pocket, "I'm going down to the PX annex for a few minutes and get some munchies. Can I get you something while I'm there?"

The master sergeant managed to hold back a groan as he did little to hide his downcast expression. To this particular captain an excursion of a "few minutes" could be anything from fifteen minutes to several hours. So much, the master sergeant thought as he watched the chem corps officer stroll out the door, for his fresh cup of coffee. Putting all thoughts of the phone call out of his mind, he slumped down in his seat, picked up one of the magazines, and opened it.

IDAHO CITY, IDAHO • MORNING, NOVEMBER 2

For the longest time, Nathan Dixon held the receiver of the pay phone while he stared at it in confusion. What was he doing wrong? The movies always made it look so easy. When Clint Eastwood found himself unable to contact someone by conventional means all he did was call back to base using his calling card and report in. Hanging up the receiver, Nathan shook his head. "Well," he mumbled to himself as he turned away from the phone, "It's true. I'm no Clint Eastwood. And this isn't Hollywood."

Walking away from the battered public phone, he looked over at the convenience store across the parking lot. For a moment, he entertained the notion of going in and buying something. A soda or maybe a hot dog that had been cooked on those heated rollers until every drop of moisture had been sucked out of it. Anything, Nathan thought, that would let him forget the plight of his platoon, if only for a second.

Turning his back on the small store and service station

that sat on the fringe of civilization, Nathan started his long trek back into the brown, barren hills that towered above Boise. There was much to think of while he made his way along the narrow, twisting road. Few of the thoughts that ran through his mind were thrilling. Most concerned the soldiers in his platoon and what to do about the gawdawful predicament he had placed them in. Using skills the young platoon leader wished he could have remained ignorant of, members of his platoon were able to "procure" a radio and a supply of batteries for it. While Sergeant Gandulf passed it off as justifiable and necessary, the idea of stealing and pillaging from American civilians, even if they were in rebellion, was a hard pill for Nathan to swallow.

But swallow it he did. Soon he himself was joining in when it came time to find some civilian clothing. "Even with all my patches and insignia removed I have the feeling I wouldn't blend in very well," he explained.

The paratrooper who had led the raid to liberate the radio smiled and nodded. "I know exactly what you mean, sir."

Nathan had given the man a hard look, one that soldier reveled in now that his platoon leader had come over to what his soldiers were calling the dark side of the force.

Kicking a stone as he walked along, Nathan fumed at the realization that their mini-crime wave would need to be expanded in a big way. With their rations all but gone he had no choice. It was either that or turn himself and his entire platoon in.

The sound of a truck making its way along the road brought Nathan to a stop. Instinctively he jumped into the ditch and flattened himself out. The red baseball cap, dark blue jacket, and blue jeans he'd fleeced didn't exactly blend in to the tan and brown rocks around him. Though the ditch was deep and no one would be able to see him from the road, Nathan reached down and pulled a knife out of the ankle sheath one of his squad leaders had lent him.

He remained in that ditch until the sound of the truck's engine had faded. Picking himself up and dusting himself, Nathan looked about. The time was fast approaching when he wouldn't be able to play it safe. The feeding of his men was going to demand that he'd have to start taking more chances. Otherwise, his men would turn away from him and go off on their own in search of food, safety, and a purpose. So long as he tended to their basic needs, Nathan reasoned he would be able to keep them together and under control.

Perhaps, he thought as he picked up his long trek back to where his men waited, he would even be able to do something useful when the Army returned. Many a battle had been decided by the sudden and unexpected appearance of a small, well disciplined force that had no business being where it was. Maybe, Nathan mused, he could even salvage a military career that was well on its way to being the world's shortest.

BOISE, IDAHO · NOON, NOVEMBER 2

Like clockwork the Adjutant General's executive officer came out of the AG's inner suite of offices and looked over to the desk where Nancy Kozak sat waiting. "Here's the morning mail for the governor," he announced with a broad smile.

Putting a copy of *USA Today* down, Nancy looked up at the bright, cheery major. She made no effort to return the smile. "There's a personal note for the governor," he added quickly. After handing her the sealed envelope imprinted with the "Eye Only" stamp, the major stepped back and retreated into his office without another word. A courier didn't need any additional instructions, especially when that courier had more combat experience than the entire staff of the AG's office.

Folding the newspaper Nancy laid it in a half-open drawer, retrieved her neatly blocked BDU cap from another drawer, and gathered up the bundle of envelopes containing reports and summaries considered too sensitive or important to send over to the governor's office via fax or e-mail. It never ceased to amaze Nancy how much paper existed in an age that was dominated by computers and office automation.

In the parking lot she found her driver right where she had left him that morning after they had made their run to drop off reports and summaries generated by the night shift. Staff Sergeant Lightfoot was already well into his second Clive Cussler novel when he saw Nancy coming. Setting aside the dog-eared paperback he adjusted himself on the seat of the well worn and over-mileage National Guard sedan as he prepared to make another run. Lightfoot had followed Nancy Kozak over to this assignment not because the duty required an NCO of his grade or experience. His transfer came after he vocalized his opinion of her relief in terms that could best be described as colorful and unvarnished. Since it was determined that she would need a driver, the state sergeant major stuck Lightfoot with the officer to whom he seemed so loyal.

Lightfoot's devotion to her came as something of a shock. She hardly knew the man. She had worked with him only on those occasions when her previous duties had required her to spend time at the ammo site. What it was about her that had impressed this quiet and dedicated Guardsman was beyond her. But she didn't complain. Even if few words were exchanged, his companionship was the only bright spot in the whole sordid mess.

Opening her door, Nancy tossed the stack of envelopes and papers onto the seat. Pausing, she caught the sight of a pair of bearded militiamen fondling their newly issued M-16A2 rifles. Wearing new camouflage shirts that couldn't be buttoned over their midsections if they tried and black baseball caps inscribed with their militia unit motto, the two sported toothy grins. As she watched she could feel her anger rising.

Turning her head away, she climbed in. Sergeant Lightfoot, who had been watching the two on and off, grunted as he started the car. "Looks like it's going to be a great day for Bubba and Billy Bob," he stated flatly. "I wonder what they'll be hunting tonight?"

"Whom," Nancy corrected him. "You meant to say 'whom,' I'm sure."

Lightfoot looked over at her. "I think you and I already know the answer to that."

"Well," Nancy sighed as Lightfoot pulled out of the crowded parking lot, "I'm sure the Governor knew what he was doing when he armed those folks. How did he put it?"

Lightfoot quoted the governor's pronouncement, word for word, from memory. "Against all the enemies of this state, its people, our cherished Christian values, and those God-given freedoms and liberties that were laid out in the Constitution of the United States and its first fourteen amendments."

"Which, I guess, doesn't include me since women didn't get the right to vote until the nineteenth amendment," Nancy added as she started to go through the envelopes looking for the one containing the latest INSUM, or intelligence summary.

Having no desire to continue down this dark, depressing path, Lightfoot tried to lighten the mood. "Well, Colonel," he stated blandly, "I want to be there when those good old boys take away your shoes and chain you to the stove."

Looking up from the report she was reading, she laughed. Patting the 9mm pistol strapped to her web belt, she grinned. "While I'm not saying they'll fail, I can assure there'll be a few more geldings in this state by the time they're done."

Squeezing his knees together, Lightfoot grimaced. "Ouch! Just the thought of that is enough to bring tears to my eyes."

Nancy wasn't paying attention to his response. Instead something in the INSUM caught her eye. After looking up quickly to see where they were, she pointed to a convenience store on the right-hand side of the road. "Pull in there and find someplace away from everyone."

Not asking why, Lightfoot hit the turn signal and made a New York right hand turn as he crossed from the far left lane in front of a pickup truck. Ignoring the horn blasts and the blasphemies hurled at them by the driver of the truck, Lightfoot drove to a spot where there were no other vehicles. After he had slipped the car into park, he turned to his colonel, who was furiously scanning the report on her lap. "What's up, Colonel?"

Instead of answering, she asked for the military map of the area they always carried. When he handed it to her she looked over at him. "Do me a favor and get me a Diet Coke and a big, steaming cup of coffee."

Realizing that officers tended to have some "peculiar" habits, he didn't question her request. Sliding out of the sedan, he left her while he went in to pick up her soda and coffee as well as one for himself. By the time he returned she was poring over the map.

He hadn't even managed to get himself settled before she turned to him. "If you found yourself here," she asked, pointing to a spot on the map, "and decided that you needed to escape and evade a mechanized force, where would you go?"

With the need to balance the hot coffees and soda, it was several moments before Lightfoot was able to take up the map and study it. As he did that Nancy took her coffee, pried open the drinking spout, and fished the "Eye Only" letter out of the stack of envelopes and reports that sat between them. Holding the back of the letter above the open spout, she let the rising steam hit the glued flap of the envelope of the confidential correspondence between the State Adjutant General and the governor. Slowly she began to move the rest of the envelope flap along the plume of steam until the flap began to give.

Looking up from his map study, Lightfoot watched his colonel for a moment. "I'm sure there's a good reason why we're sitting here, violating several articles of the Uniformed Code of Military Justice."

While continuing to work on the letter, Nancy explained. "Some of the folks who are in the Guard also work for the phone company. Knowing full well that there'd be efforts to pass information out of the state via phone lines and cell links, they have set up a program that sorts all outgoing calls from Idaho and list those calls made to certain area codes. Given that list the COMSEC folks working with intelligence are able to pick out calls made to military installations and federal agencies within those area codes."

"Okay," Lightfoot responded as he watched Nancy place the cup of coffee down. "So what's that got to do with escape and evasion and reading the Governor's mail?"

"Oh, the two are separate issues," she said as she carefully pried up the flap of the envelope so as not to tear it. "But the INSUM mentioned that several calls were made from a pay phone outside of Idaho City this morning to the headquarters of 2nd Battalion, 517th Parachute Infantry as well as its brigade headquarters at Fort Bragg."

Lightfoot instantly made the connection between this tidbit of information and her request to consider where he would go if he was trying to escape and evade. Turning his attention back to the map, he renewed his evaluation of the problem with greater enthusiasm. Meanwhile Nancy pulled the letter from the envelope and began to read it.

"Here," Lightfoot announced as he laid his finger on the map. "I'd go up here, northeast of town into the mountains away from everyone where I could hide but not so far away that it would take forever to come back down."

Nancy looked over from the letter to where he was pointing. "Okay, good. But where, exactly, do you think they are?"

Lightfoot looked over at his colonel. "Doesn't that letter say?"

Taking care to fold the letter as it had been, she put it back into the envelope. "I was hoping that it would give me a hint but it's not about the phone calls. It seems the AG agreed with the conclusion the Intel folks put forth in the INSUM."

"Which was?"

Nancy looked up at Lightfoot. "They stated that there is no reason to suspect that there is any significance to the random calls made to those particular numbers. Unless further calls are made to the numbers at Bragg from the same locations, additional analysis of the information is unnecessary."

"But you think otherwise," Lightfoot stated.

"Given what I've told you, don't you?" she came back.

Shrugging his shoulders the staff sergeant looked out the windows, scanning about to see if anyone was giving them anything more than a passing glance. Satisfied that they were still being ignored, he turned back to Nancy. "Those paras are an energetic and imaginative collection. And they're tough, dedicated, and not ones to roll over and play dead when the chips are down."

"So you agree with me," Nancy beamed.

"Even if I did, Colonel, may I ask what that has got to do with us? After all, they are on the other side," Lightfoot reminded her.

Looking into Lightfoot's eyes, Nancy hesitated. Her eyes narrowed. "Are they?"

Lightfoot didn't need to consider his answer. "No, I guess not," he whispered. Then, he added as he shook the map at her, "What do we do about them?"

Now it was Nancy who turned away and took a quick look around while she considered his question. When her eyes came back to Lightfoot, she cocked her head to one side as she licked the glue which had rehardened and pressed the envelope flap back down. Only when she was satisfied with her efforts to hide all traces of her tampering did she respond.

"I expect that they'll be running low on rations by now. And if they're using a pay phone to call, it's a cinch they don't have a secure means of contacting their higbers," Nancy reasoned.

Lightfoot nodded his agreement to her assessment but said nothing.

"It would be wrong for me," she stated slowly as she looked into Lightfoot's eyes, "to involve you in this, but . . ."

"I'd be mightily displeased if you excluded me," he stated before she could finish.

Smiling for the first time, Nancy continued. "Well then, here's what we do. After we're released tonight we find a Hummer no one is using, load it up with rations, fresh water, and anything else you might think is useful. Then we take off looking for them. Between the two of us I think we'll be able to sniff 'em out."

As they pulled out of the parking lot, Lightfoot asked Nancy what had been in the letter. She shrugged. "Oh, nothing important. The AG was simply expressing his concerns over what the Attorney General is doing. General Saunders wanted to make sure," she explained to her co-conspirator, "that the governor understood how he feels about arming the militias. It seems that he doesn't quite trust them."

Lightfoot looked over to Nancy. "That's a surprise. I thought Earl and all those good ole boys were bros."

She shook her head, "That doesn't seem to be the case." Not knowing what to make of this aspect of the strange state of affairs to which she was now part, Nancy let this thought drop as she reached for the map. Despite her confidence, she appreciated that it would be difficult, at best, to find a platoon of paratroops that was determined to stay hidden. They would need a healthy dose of luck if they were to succeed.

$$\times$$

BOISE, IDAHO · EVENING, NOVEMBER 2ND

Using techniques perfected during Operation Desert Storm, the Adjutant General of the State of Idaho conducted a televised update every evening for the benefit of the media and his own political aspirations. A sharp, young female officer wearing too much makeup and sporting a hairdo that would have been totally out of place anywhere else in the military started the update. She listed the activities of those Guard units which had been mobilized, significant incidents, and other concerns. All in all the data and information provided by this perky briefing officer was rather pedestrian and, under other circumstances, would have been passed off as totally unnewsworthy.

But this briefing was being held in Boise, Idaho by the military representatives of the "embattled" citizens who had stood up to the "tyranny" of the Federal government. For journalists who had never covered an armed conflict before this was their ticket into the big time. This was "their war" where they would be able to demonstrate their abilities to capture all the agony, all the sorrow, all the drama of war while placing themselves in mortal danger. It didn't matter that this was a civil war involving their fellow countrymen. This was the news event du jour. Everyone who was anyone or wanted to be someone was there, sitting in their assigned seats and listening to a National Guard spokesman rattle off a laundry list of mundane events and occurrences.

Jan Fields was among them watching, listening, waiting. After a shaky start, she had managed to rise to the top of the media pool. Even now, as the State Adjutant General himself came up to the podium to address the gathering of journalists he cast a nervous glance over in Jan's direction. Major General Earl Saunders was not an easily intimidated man. A person doesn't achieve political office such as his unless he has both the intestinal fortitude and savvy to play hardball politics with the best of them.

But dealing with the cream of the nation's press corps was something that Earl Saunders was not prepared for. Handling a room full of journalists who had the ethics and manners of starved piranhas was far removed from dealing with local journalists. Leading them was Jan Fields. She had a knack for hammering him or his spokesmen with hard, no-nonsense questions. For a while she had been threatened with revocation of her newly printed press pass and warned that she was in danger of being escorted out of the state. Jan not only laughed in the face of the state trooper who had given her that notice, but turned the event into a major story. "It seems," she had stated in that piece, "that the freedoms the governor of this state claims he and his people are fighting for are not the same freedoms that other citizens of the United States have come to enjoy and expect. Freedom of speech and freedom of the press in this embattled state has come to mean buy into what GO Thomas believes in or get out of Idaho."

This sort of reporting left her out of the loop when it came to securing interviews with key state officials. But it also gave her a sort of immunity that she was quick to take advantage of. When she saw that the state officials had abandoned all thought of throwing her out of Idaho for fear of alienating the nation's media, she dug her spurs in deeper, asking those questions that no one else in the vast media pool had the guts to put forth. Overnight she once more became the darling of the World News Network. It also elevated her to the position of the unofficial leader of the Boise journalists. Inevitably her fellow correspondents would wait to see what issues she would tackle before they committed themselves. Once it was clear what she was after they would pile on like hyenas feasting on a carcass as they asked their own follow-up questions.

Doing his best to ignore Jan's intense stare, Saunders read his prepared statement. Like the update that his comely spokesperson had delivered before him, the general's comments contained little in the way of news. If anything, they mirrored the sentiment that had been expressed by the Governor and his Attorney General. "As has been pointed out," he stated in a blustery manner that put her in mind of a used car salesman, "the men and women of this state's National Guard are prepared to defend their homes, their families, and their rights. From Eastpoint on the Canadian border over by Montpelier next to Montana, they stand ready to fight if that becomes necessary. Of course," he added as he affected a politician's take on a sincere smile, "they would all prefer a more peaceful, less violent resolution to the impasse between this state and the Federal government. I can assure each and every one of you that the minute the Federal government agrees to the reforms set forth by Governor Thomas and supported by numerous other governors and national leaders, we will put aside our arms and gladly go home."

Sensing that this was the perfect time to bring up the subject that she wanted to take on that day, Jan shouted out without waiting for any sort of acknowledgment. "Does that include the members of the unorganized militia groups that you have been arming?"

Having come to expect this sort of outburst from that bothersome woman, Saunders ignored Jan's question. Instead, he looked down at his notes as if he were seeking his place while he struggled to contain the anger he felt welling up. He was about to begin where he had left off when a reporter from the *Washington Post* jumped up out of his seat and took up Jan's question. "What about the militia, General? Will they go home without a murmur if the political differences between your governor and the Federal government can be worked out through negotiations?"

For several long seconds the Adjutant General glared at the newspaper correspondent in an effort to force him to recant and take his seat through sheer force of will. But the reporter would not back down. He withstood the general's silent anger. Another voice, this one from a correspondent from the local public radio station, broke the deadlock. "What about the status of the militiamen, General? A growing number of our listeners are become concerned that their numbers in and around Boise are increasing as more Guard units pack up and move out to defend the state's borders."

Looking about the room, Saunders considered blowing off the question by stating that this issue would be addressed at a later date, but thought better when his eyes fell upon Jan Fields. Her firm, confident expression and pose told him he would have no luck dodging this bullet. As had become her habit, she had managed to whip the natives up into a frenzy, leaving him no easy or graceful way out. With a frown he launched into a disjointed response that didn't seem to please anyone. "The militia units that have been accepted into service are being assigned law enforcement and security duties. As such they take their orders from the Attorney General, who is coordinating those efforts for the governor. While the National Guard has the duty of providing them with small arms and excess equipment not needed by Guard units, the militias do not fall under my control." Then, in an effort to head off other questions on the matter, Saunders quickly added, "Any further questions concerning the militias should be directed to the Attorney General's office or the newly appointed commander of that force."

A TV journalist from the back of the room shouted out a question concerning the identity of this militia officer.

"If I am not mistaken," Saunders mumbled as he grew tired of the subject, "the man's name is Louis Garvey. He's being given the temporary rank of colonel in the state police, but I do not believe he is answerable to them."

Now it was Jan's turn to come back with another question. "General Saunders," she called out as soon as there was a lull. "It seems that I recall hearing that Louis Garvey was under investigation by the FBI when the offices of that agency were closed down in this state. If that is true, and Mr. Garvey is connected to the bombing of the Federal building in Kansas or the Wyoming incident, aren't you concerned that the inclusion of people like him will bring discredit to your cause?"

Saunders sighed. "Ms. Fields, I have already said that any further questions concerning the militia or the people connected to it need to be directed to the Attorney General. I am sure you will find that when you do so, he will be able to provide you with all the information you need. Now," he stated crisply as he prepared to bring this briefing to an end, "if there are no further questions, I'd like to thank you for your patience. Good night and good-bye."

CHAPTER **19**

Dixon's aide-de-camp stood off to one side with other secondary staff officers watching their commanding general pace back and forth much as a caged leopard does in a zoo. Scott ignored the staff officers, just as he ignored the clouds of dust being thrown up by the unloading of tanks from heavy equipment transports. Busy tending to their vehicles, the soldiers were equally oblivious to the presence of their commanding general. Their full attention was riveted on the task at hand. They were lucky, Atwater thought to himself. The tankers and their officers would parade past Dixon like bit actors in a play and then disappear from view.

Atwater, on the other hand, was seldom out of his general's sight. His duty as an aide required that he be within arm's reach of Dixon twenty-four hours a day. Normally this was not too difficult to deal with. Everyone on Dixon's staff managed to find their own particular way of living around the clock in the close proximity to the proverbial five-hundred-pound gorilla. Colonel Bob Felden did what he could to help by keeping the general busy or shielding his staff officers when possible. But Felden could only do so much. He also needed to have some time for himself away from the man he served. This was especially true when the CG had worked himself into a perpetual state of agitation.

The source of his irritation under ordinary circumstances was easy to determine. Sometimes it was simply bad staff work. At other times it was a blatant display of ineptitude, a condition frequently displayed by young officers serving on the general staff for the first time. With amazing regularity one of these young lions sent Dixon through the roof by shrugging his shoulders and trying to explain away an omission by pointing out that a particular task wasn't in his job description.

On this day there was no simple explanation for Dixon's dark mood. As best Atwater could discern, there had been no single incident that had provoked his commanding general. If Felden knew who or what had put a burr under Dixon's saddle, he wasn't saying. Like everyone else, the division's chief of staff was riding out the storm as best he could by keeping out of his commander's way whenever possible. "The old man is under a great deal of pressure," was all Felden offered by way of explanation when soothing bruised egos and ruffled feathers. "Remember, we're on the verge of doing something that no American commander has had to do in over one hundred and forty years. We're marching on our fellow citizens with the intent of engaging them in combat."

Though that prospect was daunting and distasteful to him, Felden and the others were not privy to the real reason behind Scott's obsession with getting to Boise as quickly as possible. Just how long he could keep the fact that the Army still had a platoon of paratroopers running about loose somewhere in Idaho a secret worried him. Military spouses, used to seeing their partners disappear off the face of the earth for long periods of time without a word had, to date, said nothing. This was aided by the fact that the balance of Company A of the 517th Parachute Infantry had been collected up and packed off to an isolated stretch of the Idaho border. The 17th Airborne Division's chain of command assisted by creating a deception plan. According to that story, Nathan's platoon had been detached to perform security duties elsewhere after being extracted. Given the wild and unprecedented nature of the current operations, no one questioned this lie. Like the men and women in Scott Dixon's division, the soldiers of the 17th Airborne had more than enough to keep their minds occupied.

Had circumstances been otherwise, Scott would have been able to push aside his personal concerns by throwing himself into dealing with the enormous pressures and responsibilities he was confronted with. But the more he tried, the more he found that he could not set his son's plight aside. As the commander of the main effort to restore Federal authority in Idaho, he and the men and women under his command controlled his son's chances of survival. If Scott's staff had known this even the dullest of them would have understood why a man known for his calmness under pressure was coming down on them so hard. His intolerance of the slightest hint of a delay would have been excused. Even his verbal abuse of officers whom he deemed to be slovenly in the execution of their assigned duties would have been tolerated. But no one knew.

From the commanding general's Humvee, Scott's driver shouted to Atwater that there was a call for the CG from the Chief of Staff. Looking over to a cluster of other officers that included Colonel Felden, Atwater made a face. Puzzled, the aide pointed at the division chief of staff. "Colonel Felden's over there."

The driver managed to restrain his urge to shout out, "Duh!" Instead the tactful enlisted soldier explained that it was the other Chief of Staff, "the one with all the stars."

This animated Atwater. Without delay he made his way to where Scott was pacing. Coming up to his superior Atwater snapped to attention, saluted, and waited for Scott to notice him. When his commanding general stopped his pacing and looked at the young captain, Atwater chirped, "Sir, General Poulengy is on the horn for you."

Looking over to the Humvee, Scott returned Atwater's salute before making for the Humvee with a deliberate pace. When he arrived there, he took the hand mike. Covering the mouthpiece, he looked at the driver. "How about checking with the folks over at that mess truck and seeing if there's something decent to munch on."

Knowing when he was being told to piss off, the driver gave Scott a crisp, "Sure thing, sir," and took off on his fool's errant.

When he was alone Scott settled into his seat, cocked his helmet over to the side of his head so that he could place the receiver up to his ear. "Dixon here. What's up, sir?"

Poulengy was already on the phone. "I've got some good news for you from Campbell, Scottie," the senior general stated cheerfully. "Though Dougie isn't thrilled with parting with two of his precious infantry battalions and the helicopter assets to support them, they're on their way to you."

Scott managed a smile. "It's good to see that even in today's Army four stars can still prevail."

"Well, even my folks agreed with your assessment."

"That's a first," Scott shot back.

Ignoring the slur on the Army staff at the Pentagon, Poulengy continued. "It seems the main build-up of National Guard units continues to be around Twin Falls."

"They hold the center position there. They can either stand fast, and make us come to them or, if one of my brigades gets too far ahead of the other they can sally out of their positions at Twin Falls and whack it," Dixon stated coolly as he closed his eyes and visualized a map of Idaho in his mind. "Either way I expect they'll do their best to snipe at us as we move north in the hope of eroding support for military action through the slow, continuous bleeding of the division."

"My public affairs officers are already having to deal with that," Poulengy replied. "Our friends in the media are asking the question, 'what price submission?' The editorial page in one of the papers here today is calling for the President to give peace a chance."

Now it was Scott's chance to moan. "Where, sir, have we heard that one before?"

"Let's just hope we have no need for a bloody new wall in Washington when this is all over," Poulengy stated slowly.

That thought brought the subject of his son back to the forefront of Scott's thoughts. "Any word on the platoon?" he blurted.

Poulengy didn't need to ask Scott which platoon he was talking about. There was only one that this particular division commander would bother the Chief of Staff of the

Army with. "No, Scott, 'fraid not. We've had a Guardrail aircraft over Boise continuously scanning every possible frequency the unit might be on. So far, nothing."

Scott knew better than to ask if anyone had attempted to broadcast a message to Nathan's platoon. While the Idaho Guard did not have an appreciable electronic warfare capacity available to it, there was no doubt that they were monitoring every likely means of communications that Federal conventional and special operations forces would be likely to operate on. To go about broadcasting indiscriminately in the hope of soliciting a response would be inviting disaster.

"Scott," Poulengy responded when his friend didn't say anything, "Nathan's a good kid. And he's a paratrooper. Those boys train for this sort of thing."

Scott sighed. "I know, sir. But this is my son we're talking about."

"You're human," Poulengy stated bluntly as he switched to a more formal tone of voice. "I understand your concern. But I also know that you're a professional. As hard as this is, I know that you'll be able to put your feelings aside and do what you have to in order to bring this thing to a quick and acceptable conclusion."

"I appreciate the vote of confidence," Scott replied. "I'll do my best." Scott, of course, didn't tell his superior that he was unable to relegate the safety and welfare of his son to the dark recess of his mind. He couldn't bring himself to admit that he saw his every action and that of his division as being his son's only hope. To do so would create doubt in his superior's mind and could, if he wasn't careful, lead to his replacement. The thing that Scott feared most at that moment was being taken away from his division, the instrument of his son's salvation.

After covering other topics, Poulengy wished Scott luck and hung up. By then, Scott's driver had returned bearing a box containing two meals. "All they had was lasagna, sir."

"Didn't we have that for dinner last night?" Scott asked as he made a face.

"Yes, sir," the driver replied quickly. "And we had it for breakfast yesterday."

As he took the plate of semi-warm sauce-covered glob, Scott sighed. "Remind me to remind the G-4 to remind the Headquarters' company commander to do a better job at ration breakdown, will you?"

The driver settled into his seat and grinned as he prepared to feast on the Army's version of Italian cuisine. "Oh, you can bet that I will, sir."

With that taken care of, Scott sat in silence as he mechanically ate his meal. With each bite, he couldn't help but think that, given a chance, his son would die for the very food that he and his driver were annoyed by. Such is the Army, he told himself. Such is life.

NORTH OF BOISE, IDAHO · NIGHT, NOVEMBER 5

Staff Sergeant Lightfoot slowly drove along the unimproved road in blackout drive as Nancy Kozak, holding a thermal viewer to her eyes, looked for something, anything, that would give away the paratroopers. Lowering them in an effort to give both her arm and her eyes a rest, Nancy muttered, "You know this is totally screwed up."

"How so, Colonel?" Lightfoot asked as he strained to see the road ahead.

After three nights of coming out in search of the paratroopers, Nancy found that she was beginning to have second thoughts about what they were doing. Turning to face her companion, she looked across the radio console that separated them. "I've been thinking about this, Sergeant Lightfoot. If we're right, these are the people who tried to overrun us at the ammo site. They're the ones who killed . . ."

"Colonel," Lightfoot stated flatly, "don't go there. They're American soldiers, just like you and me. They were doing their job, just like Fran, Chester, and Dave. That things got so screwed up between us and the people in Washington wasn't our fault. And it isn't theirs. What happened, happened. All we can do now is act upon those beliefs that each of us hold dear."

Nancy remained silent. They had been over it all before. In her heart she knew what they were doing was right. Still, as she went back to her search for the paratroopers, she could not escape the fact that this was definitely the strangest situation she had ever found herself in.

She was just getting her elbows in a comfortable position so that she could keep the thermal viewer propped up when a sharp black blob appeared in her field of vision. The thermal sight was set so that cool objects, including the ground, appeared green. Anything that retained or gave off heat became a progressively darker shade of green until items that were very hot showed up black. Blinking her eyes, Nancy concentrated on the suspect object. She was getting tired. After having put in a full day of playing postman for the Adjutant General, the pair had spent the previous two nights wandering about the hills in search of the paratroopers. After another long day, they had picked up where they had left off. Aware of the effects of exhaustion, Nancy took great care to ensure that her eyes, burning from hours of viewing the world through the thermal sight, weren't playing tricks on her.

When she saw the object bob about and she was sure that it wasn't her or the movement of the vehicle, she knew. "Slow down," Nancy ordered in a low voice as she attempted to focus on the heat source she had detected.

As the Humvee slowed, the object she was observing disappeared behind a rock that was somewhat warmer than the rest of the steep rocky slope that rose up on either side of the dirt road they were on. This action, so familiar, convinced Nancy that they had found the paratroopers. "Stop," she commanded as she quickly scanned the area to either side of the rock.

"Think it's them?" Lightfoot whispered above the hum of their vehicle's engine.

"I think so." Then, after scanning the area a bit longer, she lowered the night sight. "There's only one way to find out, I guess," she whispered, more to herself than Lightfoot as she continued to scan the area with her naked eyes.

Lightfoot started to reach for his rifle with one hand and the door handle with the other when he felt a hand on his arm. Turning, he looked into Nancy's eyes. Even in the darkness, he could clearly see them. "This was my idea," she stated in a tone of voice that officers use when they don't expect to debate. "I'm the senior officer on deck. Like they say, there's a reason why I get paid the big bucks."

Though he was uncomfortable with this, Lightfoot made no effort to dissuade her. Instead, he pulled his rifle out of its holder. "Watch yourself, Colonel."

Nancy understood both his actions and his reply. "You can be sure of that." Without another word she opened her door and dismounted.

Once on the ground she paused in order to get her bearings and allow her eyes to adjust to the dark. Though very useful, night vision devices do tend to screw up one's unaided night vision. As she waited Nancy looked up the rocky hillside to where she thought she had seen someone. While the distance wasn't that great, the climb would leave her vulnerable since she would be bent forward and paying attention to her footing as she went. Anyone who wanted to jump her or knock her back on her ass wouldn't need to do much at all. One good smack with the butt of a rifle would send her tumbling back to where she started.

Still, she had no choice. Otherwise everything they had done up to now, including three nights of efforts and a great deal of "borrowing and procuring," would be in vain. Drawing a deep breath Nancy lurched forward and began her ascent. Back in the Humvee, Lightfoot moved over to the passenger side where he could keep an eye on his colonel.

Slowly, Nancy pressed on. After every few steps she stopped and looked ahead as she caught her breath. The sweat that beaded up on her brow was as much from the anticipation of the unexpected as it was from her physical exertions. Efforts to listen for any sounds were a waste of time. Her own labored breathing masked any sounds that she wasn't making herself as well as giving anyone out there an easy way of keeping track of her progress. Looking at the ground immediately to her front, she tucked her head down and continued her climb.

By the time the Guard officer finally reached the rock outcropping where she thought she had seen something, there was no one there. A quick scan of the area above her didn't reveal any clues as to where the person had gone. Dropping down on one knee, Nancy took a closer look at the ground. Perhaps, she thought, she could find a boot mark or a discarded food wrapper that would confirm or deny that there had been someone there.

From his perch overlooking the abandoned listening post, Nathan watched the dark figure get down on one knee and start looking closely at the ground. "He's looking for footprints," the squad leader crouched next to Nathan whispered to his platoon leader.

"More likely he's looking for candy wrappers that Belden is always leaving behind," countered Gandulf, who was lying on the ground on the other side of his platoon leader.

Though he heard those comments, Nathan said nothing. Instead he watched the figure slowly poke about the abandoned outpost. Nathan's mind was alive with questions, concerns, and thoughts as to what to do next. Nothing in his three-month basic course at Benning or his four years of ROTC at the Institute had addressed a situation like this. Easing his way back down behind the berm he and his two NCOs were using for cover, Nathan turned to Gandulf. "Well, I'm open to suggestions."

Like his platoon leader, Gandulf was at a loss. "If it was a combat patrol, that person rummaging about down at the OP would have someone with him for security?"

"Remember, Bob," the squad leader whispered, "these are Guardsmen. Since when have you seen a Guard unit that could walk and chew gum at the same time."

Gandulf wasn't impressed with the junior NCO's logic. "I don't recall many of those folks we ran into the other day having a problem coordinating their trigger fingers."

Seeing that their banter was going nowhere and catching on fast that both sergeants were as bankrupt as he was when it came to brilliant ideas, Nathan raised his hand. "Enough."

To the squad leader this pronouncement came as a shock, much like the one a father experiences when his son stands up to the old man for the first time. Gandulf, on the other hand, was pleased. *Finally!* he said to himself, *the lad is growing a backbone.*

"Whoever it is doesn't have a backup, at least not close," Nathan concluded.

"But they sure have a lot of radio antennas on that Humvee," the squad leader added.

Nathan shrugged and waved his hand as if he were wiping an imaginary blackboard. "Be that as it may, they're out here looking for someone, possibly us. Why else would they be creeping along the road in blackout drive scanning the hills with a night vision device?"

Under ordinary circumstances the squad leader would have made a wisecrack. But their miserable plight, which seemed to be growing worse by the day, and Gandulf's hard gaze kept his tongue in check.

Turning to Gandulf, Nathan drew in a deep breath. "At the moment, there's only one thing that makes sense to me, Sergeant Gandulf. And unless you can come up with a compelling reason not to, I'm going to go down there and see what that person wants."

Gandulf merely nodded. "We'll cover you from here, sir."

Having expected some sort of argument or at least some sage advice, Nathan hesitated. When he figured that his battle-hardened platoon sergeant didn't have anything in his bag of tricks that could be of help, Nathan drew himself up and prepared himself for what was to be his next, and possibly his last, major command decision.

The sound of rocks cascading down the hill alerted Nancy to the fact that she was not alone. Snapping her head up, her eyes darted about, searching the darkness in the direction that the sound was coming from. Crouching low, she threw herself up against the rock. When the sound of footfalls ceased, she pushed herself away from the rock and continued to look about.

"Hold it right there," a low, menacing voice commanded. From where she stood, Nancy could not detect a hint of fear or hesitation in the voice that came at her from out of the darkness. Perhaps these telltale traits of human nature were being filtered out by her own fears, for Nathan Dixon, standing awkwardly on the side of the hill with his rifle held at the ready, was anything but comfortable with this particular situation.

Moving away from the lee of the rock, Nancy drew herself erect, cleared her throat, and called out into the darkness. "I am Lieutenant Colonel Kozak. Advance and be recognized."

The familiar name and the feminine voice dissipated some, but not all of the tension Nathan felt. Emboldened, he responded with his own challenge. Though it seemed a bit Hollywoodish, he couldn't think of anything better. "Are you friend or foe?"

Still unable to see who she was talking to, Nancy called out in a low voice, as if fearful of being overheard, "If you're the 17th Airborne, then we're friends."

Though still not quite ready to drop his guard completely, Nathan decided that it was time to make a bold move. Lowering his rifle, he continued to make his way down the side of the hill to where the female colonel stood. When they were but a couple of meters apart, Nathan cradled his M-16 in his left arm and saluted the dark figure that now seemed far less imposing than it had just seconds before. "Second Lieutenant Nathan Dixon, Company A, 3rd of the 517th Parachute Infantry at your service, ma'am."

A smile lit across Nancy Kozak's face. She was, she realized as she brought her own hand up to return the lieutenant's salute, back where she belonged.

The appearance of Nancy and her sergeant in a Humvee loaded with rations, fresh water, and new radio was a turning point for Nathan. Up to then he and his platoon had

no purpose, or function in life. The only thing that had
kept the platoon together had been their training, their discipline, and a collective fear of the unknown. Which of
those three elements was the strongest, Nathan had come
to discover, varied from man to man. How long he could
have depended on them to sustain his unit when everything
from hope to rations had run out was a question he now
knew he would never have to answer.

"For now," Nancy stated in a tone that made it clear
that she would brook no debate, "you will lay low with
your platoon. Until we have a clear mission for you or a
situation arises that provides us with an opportunity to do
something meaningful it's best that no one in Idaho know
that you exist."

Gandulf looked up from the pouch of food he had been
busily attacking while he was listening to Nancy. "So," he
stated after swallowing a mouthful of beans, "we're going
to be the joker in the deck."

Nancy looked up at him and smiled. She loved sergeants
like that, men who knew what the score was and didn't
need a lot of guidance. "Yes, that's right. This platoon is
sort of like the Trojan horse, but without the horse."

For the first time in days, Nathan and his collected
NCOs chuckled. They were back in the game. Looking
about in the darkness he could see those men who not
standing watch were relaxing as they dug into their second,
and in some cases third, bag of MREs.

All was not, however, sunshine and roses. While watching his men file by the Humvee and draw their initial rations from Staff Sergeant Lightfoot, Nathan was annoyed
when one of his troopers stopped in front of the National
Guard NCO. "Why did you guys shoot at us when we
landed the other day?"

Lightfoot, though caught off guard by this, wasn't at all
hesitant with his response. "Why did you people come at
us like you did?"

Taken aback, the paratrooper looked at Lightfoot for a
moment. "Well hell, we were ordered to, that's why."

"You think that makes what you did right?" the Idaho
Guardsman countered, making no effort to hide his anger.

"Does that justify you and your company barreling in on my hometown like we were some sort of Third World country?"

Unnerved, the paratrooper didn't quite know what to do. His platoon sergeant, however, did. Stepping up behind the trooper confronting Lightfoot, Gandulf grabbed the soldier's collar and yanked him away. "Visocsky! You're a fucking idiot!"

The paratrooper, now more concerned that he had gotten his platoon sergeant upset, bowed his head. "I wasn't causing trouble, Sarge. I just wanted to . . ."

"Piss off this man who has risked his life to bring you food?" Gandulf shouted back. "Annoy a person who has made the gut wrenching decision to turn against a state that he calls home in order to stand up for a nation he believes in?"

Clutching the bag of rations he had just received, the soldier looked at Gandulf, then over at the angry Guard sergeant. With his head tucked between his shoulders, the paratrooper shuffled past his platoon sergeant. Looking up at the big Guardsman, the paratrooper extended his right hand. "I . . . I'm sorry. I didn't mean . . ."

The mournful tone of the man's voice was enough for Lightfoot. Reaching into the open box of rations, Lightfoot grabbed another and shoved it into the paratrooper's hand. "Don't worry about it, kid. Now move along. You're holding up the line."

Though he had been alarmed at the time, Nathan was glad that this sort of thing had happened early. It cleared the air and put what the colonel and Sergeant Lightfoot had said into its proper perspective. It wasn't until all the rations and water had been passed out, their next meeting arranged, and a wish list compiled for Sergeant Lightfoot to fill for the platoon that Nathan managed to get Nancy off to one side. "I can't tell you how relieved I am that you have taken charge. I had no idea what I was going to do."

"Lieutenant," Nancy said flatly without the slightest hesitation, "until I ran into you, *I* didn't know what I was going to do. Fact is, I still am not sure what to do with you."

Nathan waited for her to explain. But she never did. Instead, she gave him her final orders. "Stay low, keep out of harm's way, and be on time for the next rendezvous."

Snapping to attention, Nathan saluted. "Yes, ma'am."

With that Nancy returned his salute, climbed into her Humvee, and drove off. Only after they were back on the road and headed into Boise did she allow herself to relax.

CHAPTER **20**

In the beginning, no one took note of them. They didn't come storming onto the stage in a dramatic manner as the 17th Airborne had the previous week. Nor was their mobilization trumpeted by their leaders in the same way that the Adjutant General of the Idaho National Guard had boasted when his units were called up. Instead the unorganized militiamen simply started showing up.

When the Idaho National Guard left their armories and marshalling areas for the state's borders, the bulk of the journalists followed. Jan Fields, however, was not among them. "The crucial decisions will be made here," she told World News Network in Washington, D.C. "While some lucky camera crew may get some great shots it's the politicians and key players in Boise and Washington that will give meaning to the military operations out there, not vice versa. And since you pretty much have your end of the story covered, I'll stand fast here and handle this end." Unable to assail her logic, the executives at WNN assigned other crews to cover the Federal buildup along the border and Idaho's response.

Jan's decision to stay in Boise was not totally motivated by her desire to remain close to Idaho's political movers and shakers. Much had to do with a growing revulsion she began feeling over the manner in which her fellow journalists were reporting the crisis. In the aftermath of one of the Adjutant General's evening briefings, Jan stood off to one side watching and listening to a gaggle of her peers as they stood before their cameras and filmed their post-briefing comments. Amazed and appalled by what she was hearing, Jan began to shout at them. "Don't you people know what's about to happen here? Don't you understand that the Army is going to roll across the plains and crush everything and everyone in its way? This isn't a Super Bowl game where everyone goes home alive and the loser gets to try again next season. And those people out there," she screamed as wide-eyed journalists looked on in silence, "aren't Third World fanatics. They're Americans, fighting for the very soul of this nation."

Fortunately, the collection of correspondents and camera crews had been so taken aback by Jan's behavior that no one thought to turn their cameras on her. When her own cameraman commented on this later that evening, Jan lit into her. "I wish they had. These people and the zombies that waste their time watching them need to pull their heads out of their collective ass and wake up to what's going on up here!"

After that no one said much of anything when they were around Jan. They just left her alone, free to dwell on whatever thoughts she chose to center on as they drove about Boise from one interview to another. It was during these drives that Jan began to take note of the increasing number of militiamen. At first she said nothing. Only when she sat up and forced herself to count the number of indifferently uniformed and rough looking characters running around in pickups and SUVs painted in wild camouflage patterns that she appreciated what was actually happening around them.

With nothing to do on the morning of the sixth, Jan decided to drive around in a nondescript rental with her cameraman. Using a hidden camera, Jan went from place to place looking to see if her hunch held up. At the state capital they cruised about the grounds, taping as they went. Next, they circled the executive mansion and other offices belonging to the state executive branch. When they were finished there Jan drove over to the Federal Court House, taken over by the State of Idaho after the expulsions of federal officials. Finally they ended their circuit by going south to Gowen Field, which was now almost totally vacated by the Idaho National Guard. At each location the evidence Jan found supported her supposition.

While a thin veneer of state troopers remained at their posts guarding key state buildings and facilities, Jan's cameraman was able to capture glimpses of militiamen loitering about in the background. At one point Jan even had her park their car next to a state police car they spotted in the parking lot of a convenience store. Since she was a westerner and Jan's face was too well known, the two switched roles. While Jan hung back in the car working the camera, the cameraman went into the store with a recorder in her pocket. Through the window Jan watched her impromptu plant buy a soda, then wander over to where the troopers were chatting with the store's proprietor.

After listening in for a few seconds while pretending to read the headlines of the daily paper, the cameraman joined the conversation. "You guys must be putting in some hellacious hours these days."

The younger of the two troopers looked at the cameraman and smiled. "Ah, it hasn't been too bad. The militia boys the Attorney General's been mobilizing have been a big help."

The older trooper sneered. "Bullshit. They're a nuisance. I have to spend just as much time keeping an eye on them as I do on my regular duties."

The cameraman leaned over the counter and propped herself with one elbow. "Oh?" she mused innocently. "I'm surprised to hear that they're slacking off and not pulling their weight. I'd have thought they'd be all charged up and anxious to do their part."

"Well, my bud does have a point. They just might be doing too much."

Picking up that point, the older trooper explained. "Slowly but surely we're being replaced by them. While we're being sent to man road blocks along the border, they're being left here to safeguard the governor. The way I see it," he stated as he straightened up and reached into his pocket to fish out some coins to pay for his coffee, "this is a case of calling on the wolf to guard the hen house."

"The governor doesn't seem to have a problem with it," the young trooper countered as he grabbed a sweet roll from a rack and threw it on the counter.

The older trooper shook his head. "The governor doesn't seem to have a choice."

Annoyed, the younger trooper threw down some change to pay for his sweet roll and chased after his partner. "Now there you go again, getting on GO Thomas's case. What is it with you? You think after standing up the whole United States Army he's going to roll over and play dead for some half ass militia types?" the young man asked as the pair disappeared through the door.

Later that night as Jan and the cameraman sat in their van matching the recording the cameraman had made with the tape Jan had managed to shoot, she realized that she was on to something. Though she suspected that she already knew what that was, it was far too early to go public. She'd need more time and a hell of a lot more evidence to support her theory before she came out with the story. Besides, a little voice in the back of her head told her that she'd have but one chance to get this right. While the National Guard and the State police had rules of engagement that they were required to abide by, Jan knew that the people she was preparing to go against didn't.

THE IDAHO-UTAH BORDER, SOUTH OF STONE, IDAHO • EVENING, NOVEMBER 7

The scene where Interstate 84 crossed from Utah into Idaho was becoming familiar to Scott and the officers who accompanied him. The orange and white barriers that blocked the road with rolls of razor wire stacked before them didn't strike Scott as being all that different from similar barriers he had seen in Germany before unification, or in the Persian Gulf, or the Balkans. When observed from a distance the heavily armed police pretty much looked like their German, Iraqi, or Serbian counterparts. It was only when one took the time to study them more closely that the differences stood out. It was the little things that struck Scott, like the words "State Police" on the side of the patrol cars, or the shape of a Guardsman helmet and his weapon that set the hairs on the back of his neck to standing.

Lowering his binoculars, Scott surveyed the entire area once more before the last light of day disappeared. "Do you think," Scott asked Clyde Emerson, "they know what's about to happen to them?"

The commander of the 4th Armored Division's 1st Brigade didn't answer his commanding general right off. Instead, he finished making his own visual reconnaissance. When he was satisfied that nothing had changed since his last visit to this spot, Emerson lowered his binoculars. "Despite all the training you had prior to your first taste of battle, did you really understand what combat was like until after it was over?"

Scott sighed. "No, I guess not, Clyde. But that was different. I was a combat soldier, a trained professional. Practically everything I had done up to that point had prepared me for that moment. And the people I faced were professional soldiers, too. They knew what they were doing. They knew what was at stake."

Arching an eyebrow, Emerson regarded his superior with surprise. "And you don't think those folks down there understand what they're doing?"

"No," Scott growled. "They think they do. They think they're standing up for rights they believe have been stripped away from them by some insidious plot to destroy America from within. But in truth I don't think they appreciate the horrible fact that they're nothing but pawns in an obscene power game being played out by men who don't give two shits about them."

"If that's true, sir, what does that make us?" Emerson asked innocently.

Scott didn't answer. He couldn't, for it was a question he had asked himself a dozen times a day and had yet to find a suitable answer for. Instead he looked out over the vast empty desert and listened to the howl of the night wind. Finally Scott turned to the commander of his 1st Brigade. "Are your lads up to this?"

Though he had gone over it before, Emerson felt it wouldn't hurt to hit the old man with his reservations once more. "Well, I feel like I'm being sent in to fight a fire without my pants on. Throwing one battalion forward while the second one hasn't finished off-loading and the 3rd Battalion still in transit is, in my opinion, a tad bit risky."

"Nonsense," Scott replied. "We're not going to hit any serious resistance until Twin Falls, and maybe not even then. The battalion from the 11th Air Assault I gave you together with the air cav troop and attack helos should be more than enough to sweep aside any ambushes the Idaho Guard throws across your line of advance. With luck the battalion that's still in transit from Carson can roll right through here without pause and continue on almost to Twin Falls before you need to off-load them. That'll give you a fresh battalion, ready for immediate pursuit."

The brigade commander charged with delivering the roundhouse punch along I-84 said nothing. Like everyone else, he was aware that his division commander was acting out of character. But he also appreciated the fact the situation that they faced was unlike anything any of them had ever imagined, let alone confronted. So he was tolerant of Scott's short temper, his incessant demands to hurry, and his frequent visits to see how things were progressing. Emerson imagined that his commanding general was simply anxious to bring this nasty little affair to a decisive close as quickly as possible.

"So," Dixon repeated his question, "are your people ready?"

"The lead battalion is 2nd of the 13th Infantry. It has three company instead of the normal four," Emerson stated dryly. "That's due more to reduced manning levels and poor recruitment than the loss of those who felt they couldn't participate in this operation," he quickly added. "Tank platoons have three tanks instead of four, infantry platoons can only put a dozen or so dismounts out on the ground, and 155mm artillery battery in support has but six guns."

Impatient, Scott snapped. "I know the numbers. What I want from you," he demanded, stepping in front of the startled colonel, "is a simple yes or no. Are your troops ready to close with and destroy the enemy by the use of fire, maneuver, and shock effect?"

For a second, Emerson wasn't sure if he was more shaken by his division commander's conduct or the question he posed. "The enemy," after all, were fellow Americans. Despite their political views, despite the fact that they stood less than a kilometer away armed to their teeth, they were Americans. That he would be leading his command forward against them in less than six hours was still, to Emerson, akin to a bad dream.

But Scott's agitated expression, his flaring nostrils, and his penetrating eyes told Emerson that all of this was in deadly earnest. Blinking, the brigade commander swallowed hard. "Yes, sir. My command is ready to execute its assigned duties."

"Thank you, Colonel," Scott replied coldly before walking away.

BOISE, IDAHO · EVENING, NOVEMBER 7

Finished with her final run for the Adjutant General, Nancy Kozak made her way down the steps of the building to where Lightfoot sat waiting. Odds were he was asleep, she told herself as she trudged along. She didn't blame him. Once she was back in the sedan she'd be doing the same. "So long as you sleep when we're parked," she told her trusted NCO, "and I sleep when we're moving we'll be okay."

Their courier runs by day and clandestine rendezvous with the paratroopers at night were taking their toll. Neither managed more than three hours of sleep per night. She knew this pace could not be sustained indefinitely. They'd have to start skipping nights, she told herself as she made her way to where she had left Lightfoot. They were behind on their sleep debt and it was fast approaching the time they would need to repay it.

Lost in her own thoughts and quite oblivious to the coming and going of the people about her, the sudden appearance of a woman right in her path startled Nancy. She came to an abrupt halt and looked up at the other female.

"I'm so glad I managed to catch you, Nancy," the older woman exclaimed in a voice that seemed a bit too cheery.

"Hello, Jan," Nancy stated mechanically. "What can I do for you?"

Looking about as if she were trying to see if anyone was paying attention to them, Jan Fields lowered her voice. "We need to talk."

Suddenly it sank into Nancy's exhausted mind who she was talking to and what she wanted to talk about. Wide awake now, the younger woman grabbed Jan's arm and made her own survey of the people who were about. "Ah, yes. Of course. Over here," Nancy stammered as she began to drag Jan over to the shadows of a nearby building. Only after they were safely tucked away out of sight and where no one could hear them did Nancy let go of Jan's arm and face her.

Fortunately for the Guard officer Jan spoke first. "I know that you probably can't answer all my questions, and I really don't want you to do anything that would compromise yourself, but I need to find out what is going on with the militia groups. Since the National Guard units have started their deployment it seems that the number of militia types in and around Boise has multiplied."

Stunned, Nancy stared at the journalist. Having wondered whether it would be better to tell Jan the truth about her son or lie, the Guard officer was caught complete off guard by the questions Jan was now pelting her with.

Jan misread Nancy's expression. The journalist immediately thought that she had blundered. Drawing back, she desperately tried to extract herself as quickly as possible. "Please understand," the journalist stated as fast as the words would come. "I appreciate your dedication to duty and the sense of loyalty that you feel toward your adopted home state. Scott's the same way, you know," she explained.

"Yes," Nancy found herself saying, "I know." In the meantime, the Guard officer found herself wondering if she could use Jan and her press credentials as a means of establishing contact with the Federal forces that now encircled Idaho. But just as quickly as that thought jumped to the fore, Nancy discounted it. It wouldn't be right to endanger Jan like that. Besides, the relationship between Jan and Nathan, not to mention the one between those two and Scott Dixon, might create unforeseen complications. *No!* Nancy told herself. Keep your mouth shut.

"It's probably best if we both forgot about this. Don't you agree?" Jan volunteered.

Still not sure what to say, Nancy simply grunted and nodded. "Yes, sure. Of course."

Then as quickly as she dared Jan left Nancy and made her way to where her crew was waiting for her. While she knew that not every idea a journalist had paid off, it still annoyed her to no end when one of hers flopped as badly as this one had.

Out on the street, two men sitting in a parked car watched Jan walk away from Nancy. "Which one do we follow?" a lean militiaman asked his buddy.

"The one we were told to follow, fool," his bearded companion sneered. "The bitch in BDUs is nothing but a high paid postal worker. Followin' her isn't worth the effort."

"Well, maybe the female colonel gave the reporter something?" the lean militiaman insisted. "Maybe she's passing secrets."

Starting the nondescript sedan they were sitting in, the bearded militiaman shook his head. "What difference does that make. So long as we keep an eye on the journalist and make sure she doesn't get too far out of line everything will be okay."

When they saw Jan disappear around the corner, the bearded one pulled away from the curb, flipped on his headlights, and followed her.

From the shadows where she was still collecting her thoughts Nancy took note of the strange behavior of the car across the way. While she caught only a brief glimpse of the car's occupants, their appearance, and the questions that Jan had hit her with, added a new concern that Nancy Kozak had to deal with.

CHAPTER **21**

With night as their cloak a covey of predators raced north toward the imaginary border that separated the United States from the rebellious state of Idaho. Perched high upon their armor plated seats, the crewmen flying the attack helicopters scanned the horizon for prey. The weird green glow emanating from sights and instruments before them gave their features an unworldly appearance that matched the sinister profile of their aircraft. To the airborne controller of an E-3A AWACS orbiting two hundred kilometers away, the AH-64s of the 4th Armored Division appeared as little more than computer generated symbols on his screen. To those whom they were hunting, the Apaches would become Death incarnate.

Designed as an antitank weapon, the AH-64 Apache has proven itself to be quite adept at killing just about everything. This airborne merchant of death is found in one of two organizations. When assigned to an attack helicopter battalion the Apache is a sledgehammer. Its operational range of five hundred kilometers provides a division or corps commander the ability to deliver a smashing blow against enemy ground units long before those units can be deployed. Closer in, Apaches of the attack helicopter battalion can create a breach through which the division's tanks and mech infantry can pour or plug a hole in the division's own line. All in all this unit is the most flexible weapon a division commander possesses. Scott Dixon's 4th Armored Division had one of them.

While the AH-64 remains just as capable when employed with the air cavalry, the manner in which it is operated changes. As a member of the air cav team, the Apache is a rapier, used to deliver a killing thrust with speed and precision. Unlike its counterparts in an attack battalion, the air cav Apache is more concerned with doing the sneaking and peeking for the division's killers. In this role, the forward-looking infrared sights, better known as thermal sights, and a daylight TV sighting system are often more important than the helicopter's weapons. The same range and speed that allows the attack helicopter unit to penetrate into the enemy's rear areas to wreak havoc allows the AH-64 equipped air cavalry troop the opportunity to flit about and find out what their foes are up to. On this particular evening Dixon's two air cav troops were looking for mischief.

In the traditions of the cavalry the air troopers of the 1st of the 9th Cavalry were leading the way north. In the wee hours of November 8th the pilots of Charlie Troop, 1st of the 9th Cav, were working with lighter, more nimble scouts. Flying in excess of 130 knots and never more than fifty feet above the ground, they crossed into Idaho unseen. The National Guard of that state lacked their own early warning network, leaving them dependent upon the spotty coverage radar at commercial airfields provided them. The air troopers knew of this weakness and exploited it.

Though only darkness raced up to greet the troopers of 1-9 Cav, they were not flying into the unknown. For days Air Force E-8A J-Stars surveillance flights had kept track of all ground movements throughout southern Idaho. Together with electronic intelligence gathered from Army EH-60C Quick Fix helicopters, most of the ambush sites Scott Dixon feared had been pinpointed. Armed with the fruits of this collaboration, the 1-9 Cav went forth, not to play blind man's bluff with the Idaho Guard but to operate upon it with all the precision of a surgeon.

WEST OF ROGERSON, IDAHO · EARLY MORNING, NOVEMBER 8

Struggling to stay awake, Private Anthony Kelo, Idaho National Guard, rocked back and forth, shifting his weight about on the gunner's seat he was perched upon. While the other Guardsmen who manned this lone M-3 Bradley scout enjoyed a fitful sleep down below in the vehicle's troop compartment, Kelo blinked his eyes and kept watch over a stretch of US 93.

Together with the second Bradley in their section, their mission was to engage and destroy vehicles of the Regular Army's advance guard when it came. In effect they were a speed bump. The state police manning the roadblocks at the state line farther south would raise the alarm when the Army crossed the border. "The moment the Feds start north, the folks at the roadblock will make one radio call," Kelo's platoon leader told them, "and then get out of the way. We'll have maybe thirty minutes' warning before the lead elements of the Regular Army reach us. When they do, we'll be the first serious resistance they meet. We," he said with a grin, "get to draw first blood."

The look on his platoon leader's face and the tone in his voice worried Kelo. The men and the women of the Idaho National Guard were not given the opportunity to stay behind if they had doubts about their mission. It was more than the simple fact that the Idaho Guard had precious few soldiers. Rather, no one thought of asking the soldiers in the ranks if they agreed with what they were doing. It was assumed by officers who had been carefully selected by their political leaders that their subordinates shared their sentiments concerning important state issues. To a degree those officers were correct. Most of the members of the 114th Armored Cavalry Brigade, Idaho National Guard, did.

But sharing a view does not automatically translate into unquestioning loyalty to a cause, even if it is a just cause. As days had dragged on and the TV images of Regular Army tanks, self-propelled guns, and Bradley fighting vehicles being moved to the borders of their state bombarded them, more and more Guardsmen questioned their personal commitment to their state's chosen course. With his platoon leader's words still rattling about in Kelo's exhausted mind, the vigilant Guardsman kept watch.

Even if Kelo had been fully alert he wouldn't have seen

the Apache as it jockeyed into a firing position. With the aid of a light scout, the Apache slithered through a dry streambed until the observer in the scout, watching both the lone Bradley and the attack helicopter, determined that the Apache was where it should be. With a crisp, "Okay, you've got him," the scout handed the target off and eased down to watch.

Slowly the pilot brought his Apache up and clear of the river bank. The gunner had switched from his helmet mounted sight to the heads down sight that sat between his knees. With a methodical precision forged during hours of training and repeated battle drills, he scanned the area before him. When his sight reticule was superimposed on Kelo's Bradley, he flipping the safety of his 30mm cannon to the off position. Pausing, he keyed the radio. "Mike 34, this is Mike 33. Set and ready," he announced.

In his helmet, the voice of the gunner in his sister gun ship came back. "Roger that, 33. I'll be with you in a second."

That, of course, was a figure of speech. It took the Apache with the call sign Mike 34 almost a minute before he was in place and, like Mike 33, ready to engage. In the meantime the gunner in Mike 33 watched his prey. Bumping up the sight's magnification, the gunner wondered if the lone figure squirming about in the Bradley turret had any idea what was about to happen to him.

"Mike 33, This is 34. Set and read. Let's rock and roll."

Oddly, Private Anthony Kelo was alerted to the fact that his recon section was under attack when he saw the gun flashes and stream of tracers directed against the other Bradley three kilometers away from his. The initial burst of 30mm HE and armor piercing rounds that flailed the ground next to his track almost went unnoticed. It took him several seconds to realize that he was more than a spectator to the opening shots of a ground invasion of Idaho. He, like his companion across the way, were now participants.

The sting of debris and shrapnel kicked up by the volley that barely missed his left track was the first hint of the mortal danger Kelo was suddenly faced with. Instinctively he turned and looked around. He was facing the rear of the track, still trying desperately to sort out what was going on when he saw a shower of bright burning orbs with long, sharp tails coming right at him. Though he opened his mouth to scream, no sound came out. Whether it was an instinctive reaction or simply the buckling of his knees, Kelo sank down into the illusionary safety of the Bradley's cramped interior.

Even before his butt hit the turret floor the other members of the scout vehicle were awake and shouting. "Jesus, Anthony! What the hell is going on out there?"

Inside the track the ping of hot metal and rocks kicked up by the detonation of another burst of 30mm HE and armor piercing rounds to the right of the Bradley could be heard. "Attack!" Kelo stammered. "We're under attack."

The track commander said nothing nor asked any further questions. Making his way past the other men of his crew, he snaked his way into the turret, pushing Kelo out of the way as he did so. *"LARRY!"* he yelled in the direction of the driver's compartment. "Crank this bitch up and get ready to haul ass!"

The driver was already awake and in the process of starting the vehicle. "Where to?"

Looking up at the open hatch, the track commander thought twice about sticking his head out. But he had no choice. If he didn't do so they'd all die then and there. Drawing in a deep breath, the track commander shot up into his seat and through the open hatch.

Once outside he jerked his head this way, then that. The sound of the other Bradley, already on the move, could be heard above the rumble of his own vehicle's engine. The track commander squatted down on his seat and turned to Kelo. "Toss me my CVC!"

Looking about frantically, Kelo spotted his commander's combat vehicle crewman's helmet, grabbed it and shoved it into his commander's waiting hands.

Pulling it on, the track commander keyed the radio and called to the other Bradley which was out there trashing about. "Bravo Two Two, where are you going?"

When the commander of the other track responded, he

didn't bother with call signs. "I'm getting the hell out of here. Those are Apaches out there!"

Since the track commander of Bravo Two Two was also the section leader, Kelo's commander saw no choice but to follow. Besides, it was clear that their little ambush had been blown. There was no point in staying where they were. "Okay, Larry," the track commander shouted over the vehicle's intercom, "get us outta here, and fast."

The driver didn't need to be told twice or given any further guidance.

From their attack positions, the Apache crew watched the two Bradleys scramble for the deserted highway and make their way north as fast as their Cummins four stroke turbo-charged V-8 diesel engines could carry them. The gunner sighed. "There they go."

The pilot chuckled. "How about giving them a good send off."

"Why not. Since we're not supposed to kill 'em if we can help it, at least we can scare the piss out of them." With that, he lay his sight on the center of mass of the trail vehicle to permit the tracking system to compute the target's rate of lateral movement while he ranged. When he was ready, the gunner moved the aiming dot off target and onto the road immediately behind the fleeing Bradley. Mashing the trigger, he let fly another burst that missed the Bradley by a hair, just as the other bursts had.

This last burst was a wasted effort. Everyone, from the track commander who was keeping his head as low as he could to the men crouching down inside, never heard or saw the Apache's parting shot. To them, there was no shame in their flight. It was, Kelo thought as he struggled to collect himself and settle in one of the padded seats in the crew compartment, the smartest thing they had done in days.

BOISE, IDAHO · MORNING, NOVEMBER 8

The timing of a major attack takes many things into consideration. The period between two A.M. local and four

A.M. is particularly favored. To begin with most military organizations that have to maintain twenty-four-hour operations usually do so with two shifts. Normally the best and the brightest members of the staff find themselves assigned to the day shift. The second shift is often reserved for the junior members of the staff or those staff officers whom section chiefs don't want around when the boss is under foot. Routinely the deputy of a staff section is the senior man on deck at night, although some staff section leaders like having a strong number two close at hand throughout the day. In that case the number three man leads the night shift.

The second factor that comes into play during the golden hours of two to four A.M. is the body's natural rhythms. Early Homo Sapiens lacked the keen hearing, acute sense of smell, or sharp night vision needed to become a night predator. This forced primitive man to hunt by day and seek the protection of caves, fire, or numbers at night when they slept. Thousands of years of evolution cannot be undone at the snap of a finger or by order of the commanding general. Nor can people accustomed to sleeping at night reverse their cycle. That leaves personnel relegated to the graveyard shift vulnerable to physical and mental exhaustion as they fight with their biological clocks.

Hand in hand with this is the fact that the key decision makers, staff section leaders and senior commanders, are tucked away and enjoying the most restful and deepest sleep of the night. Though junior officers are left with a certain degree of authority and often disgustingly long lists that prescribe what they are to do in the event of an emergency, serious decisions cannot be made until the principals are back at the helm. This takes time. The officer in charge has to come to the conclusion that the situation warrants disturbing his superior. Then the call must be made or someone dispatched to awaken the poor old sod. Most people need a bit of time to collect their wits after being awakened from a sound sleep. Add to this is the act of dressing, since few senior commanders look good in boxer shorts and they know it.

All of this is repeated at each level of command that news must travel through before decisions can be made and sent back down. The result is a lag in response time, something that Scott Dixon understood and used to his advantage.

⚔

The military is not the only organization that suffers from these sorts of problems at night. National news agencies, whether they be the print media or broadcast journalism, also have similar staffing and response problems. Word of an operation that started at midnight in Idaho would not begin to make its way into the news cycle for an hour, maybe two. That meant that the ground offensive against Idaho by the United States Army would not hit the eastern news centers until three or four A.M. at the earliest. Even then the shreds of information coming in would be fragmented snippets that were all but meaningless. It was a factor that no modern commander can easily ignore.

Jan had been witness to some of her time's grimmest and most disturbing events. She had enjoyed the dubious pleasure of attending an execution that was staged especially for her. In Africa she had suffered the misfortune of being the first to stumble upon the scene of a massacre that had taken place days before. And when covering one of America's own wars, she had once found herself holding the hand of a young soldier who pleaded with her to stay by his side so that he wouldn't die alone. All of these things were kept locked away in her memory where they were not permitted to intrude upon her work.

None of these memories seemed to disturb Jan's sleep. Not even the fear of being eclipsed as one of the nation's top media personalities by a spry young thing with blond hair, a manufactured smile, and perfect skin robbed Jan of her sleep. Instead, the one recurring nightmare that could trigger a cold sweat involved Jan hearing the phone ring in the middle of the night and being unable to rise and answer it. While some might find this rather silly, the panic that Jan felt whenever she heard a phone cut through the haze of her slumber was very real and very disturbing. For even if it wasn't a replay of her nightmare, it meant only one of two things, neither of which were good. The first was that something had happened to Scott or Nathan. The second was that a story had broken while she was asleep and that she was already behind the curve.

Tonight a call from the Washington office of WNN informed her that it was the second of these. This, Jan told herself as she dressed after calling her crew together, she could handle. What worried her was not what she would find in Boise. The dark thoughts that plagued her all concerned her husband and son. Somehow she knew the two people she dearly loved would soon be in the thick of the fighting that was sure to come.

The morning briefing in the National Guard headquarters pressroom was a far cry from those of previous days. The spokesman, a young female captain that Jan thought was too perky to be taken seriously in any other role, gave only the sketchiest of details concerning actions from their side of the lines. Journalists like Jan who were tapped into news agencies that had people covering the Federal operations were quickly able to compare notes, spot discrepancies, and ask for clarifications or explanations. The Guard officer could provided neither. She had a prepared statement from which she could read, a few sketchy notes she had made while talking to the Adjutant General's executive officer, and nothing else. "You must understand," she repeated time and again after she sidestepped a question for which she had no answer. "The situation is still quite fluid. The time lag that exists between reports generated in the field and good information reaching here is considerable. I am sure that we will have more for you later."

To a generation raised on news broadcast live as events unfolded, the spokesman's words sounded like a dodge. Things, they all told themselves, must be going badly. Otherwise, the briefing would have been more upbeat and full of stories of incredible victories against overwhelming forces. Not finding anything of value at National Guard headquarters, the journalists scattered throughout Boise like rats seeking a meal. All of them, Jan included, scurried to those inside sources that they had carefully cultivated over the months. It was time to tap them and tap them hard.

OFFICES OF THE GOVERNOR, BOISE, IDAHO · NOON, NOVEMBER 8

Standing at his window, GO Thomas looked down into the street at the crowd of milling journalists and their entourage of technicians. A line of indifferently uniformed militiamen manned the police barricades and kept them at bay.

A cynical smile lit his face. All they were looking for was something to throw out to the rest of the nation, something to fill air time. They wanted a story, any story, no matter how grim or disastrous.

From behind his back, Thomas brought a piece of paper bearing the State Adjutant General's seal and looked down at it. Any one of them, he told himself, would do anything short of murder to see this. Some, he suspected after having watched their antics all these months, might even be tempted to try that.

Ignoring the tumult below, Thomas began to reread the letter, hastily drafted two hours before. *"You have received further updates, I am sure, since I drafted this note,"* the Adjutant General stated by way of a preamble, *"so I will not waste time on the particulars of our situation here in Twin Falls. Rather I find that it is necessary at this time to explain to you my actions and plans for the immediate future.*

"I can assure you, the men and women under my command will give a good account of themselves if called upon." Thomas paused, as he had the first time he had read the note and considered the Adjutant General's use of the word "if." A plain spoken man, Major General Earl Saunders chose his words with the same care that any other political appointee did. So the word "if" spoke legions.

"Having said that," the letter continued, *"it is my duty to point out the grim facts of life to you, the chief executive officer of the State of Idaho and head of the Idaho National Guard."* Again, he stopped and considered the passage he had just read. What Saunders was doing, GO snickered, was reminding him that he, ultimately, would be held accountable for all decisions, political and military, that were made during this crisis. The Adjutant General was laying the groundwork for the "simple soldier just following orders" defense. Not that Thomas could blame Saunders. If there was a reasonable explanation that he could manufacture and rely on, he'd also be polishing it up.

Allowing the letter to drop down to his side, Thomas moved away from the window over to his desk. When he reached it he looked down at a plaque sitting off to one side. It was a simple mahogany block of wood upon which a set of shiny aviator's wings was mounted. How much easier it would be, he found himself thinking, if I were nothing but a simple pilot again. Then he could leave all the heavy thinking to others, as he had during the war in the Gulf. Things, he mused, had been so easy back then.

Lifting the Adjutant General's letter, he picked up where he had left off. *"I have at my disposal two maneuver battalions supported by a couple of batteries of artillery, the two AH-64s that survived the air attack, and combat engineers. With these I can delay the advance of the Federal forces and even stop their advance for a while if I choose my ground well. But militarily, there is no way that we will be able to prevail. In the Twin Falls area alone I face six tank and mech infantry task forces, two reinforced self-propelled artillery battalions, an attack helicopter battalion, a cavalry squadron minus one ground troop, and two air assault infantry battalions. Added to this are electronic warfare units, electronic and signal intelligence units, and other combat support elements that I have no way of matching or countering. In the hands of a general with the skills and reputation that Dixon possesses, this force can go anywhere and do anything.*

"Given the above facts, I have made several decisions that I am acting upon unless I receive orders from you to

the contrary." Here it comes, Thomas thought to himself. Saunders is creating legal wiggle room. *"It is an unwritten rule that when a defender comes to the realization that defeat is inevitable, he does as little as possible to anger the attacker. After all, one cannot inflict crippling losses on a foe one moment and then expect mercy from him. Eventually my Guardsmen will have to lay down their arms and spend time as prisoners of war."* A shiver ran down Thomas's spine. Turning his face away from the letter, he looked about the quiet, well-appointed office he had occupied for so long. Everything in this room was as it had been the day before. Everything spoke of power, authority, and dignity. The great seal of the state of Idaho hung on the wall behind his desk, just as it had the day he had walked into this office. These symbols, together with the media coverage and political posturing of the last few months, had hidden from him and his closest advisors just how shaky their state's independence was. Even in the aftermath of the aborted assault of October 31, everyone, including Thomas himself, fancied that some sort of amiable accord could be reached with the Federal government.

Now, however, with Federal forces actually rolling through Idaho with guns blazing, there could be no hiding from reality. Looking back at the letter, Thomas shook his head. It was clear that Saunders had awakened to the truth. Now it was time for him to do so as well. *"All reports indicate,"* his letter went on, *"that Federal forces are avoiding bloodshed whenever possible. I see this as a good sign and have ordered our Guardsmen to do likewise. Naturally that means I will need to abandon our positions here around Twin Falls almost immediately.*

"This brings me to my next decision, one which I am certain you will find no fault with. Regardless of the outcome of this conflict, the people whom we are sworn to serve will still be here when all is said and done. They will need to continue with their lives under whatever conditions the Federal government imposes. It would, therefore, be ruinous to their future prospects if I executed the barrier plan I had briefed you on earlier. The destruction of highways, bridges, and the communications net-

work would do little to hinder the advance of Federal forces. Instead, it would place an unnecessary hardship on our fellow citizens. Therefore I have ordered that all prepared demolitions be disarmed and removed as time permits. Those which cannot be removed will be left unexecuted and clearly marked. Again, the people who are coming to crush our rebellion will, in a few short days, be our fellow countrymen once more."

Carefully, Thomas folded the letter and placed it in a pocket of his suit jacket. Walking back over to the window he looked at the undiminished crowd below. This time, his eyes didn't fall upon the sullen journalists and their accompanying technicians. Rather he stared at the oddly uniformed militiamen who kept both the journalists and him in check. The common sense that was guiding Saunders's actions would not go over well with those people and the men who were their self-appointed leaders. They would not go back into the political and social shadows from which they had emerged as gracefully as his Adjutant General was preparing to do. These men were dangerous men, Thomas told himself. They were not pledged to serve the people of the state of Idaho. They fancied themselves to be patriots dedicated to principles that they believed could only be defended by making a blood sacrifice. Just how much blood it would take to convince these men that this was not the time or place to save the nation they claimed they so dearly loved was unknown.

What had become clear to Thomas during the past week was that men like Thomas Jefferson Osborn would not permit him to simply roll over and give up the fight. Osborn had made sure of that. Again looking around his office, GO Thomas now saw that room not as a power base from which he would be able to catapult himself into the White House, but rather as a gilded cage, a prison that he had created himself.

✕

ALONG INTERSTATE 84, EAST OF BOISE, IDAHO • EVENING, NOVEMBER 8

By now Nancy Kozak had the routine down. Since neither the governor nor Adjutant General used any special seals on the letters she hand carried between the two, she had found a printer that could replicate the font used to address the envelopes those letters were sealed in. Using the exact type of envelope, Nancy had produced a number of them with the appropriate addressee on it. So she was now free to rip open the envelope knowing that she could simply stuff the letter into one she had produced, seal it, and pass it on with no one being the wiser.

With her penlight in one hand and the Adjutant General's letter in the other, she read the contents aloud to Sergeant Lightfoot. "It would seem General Saunders is going to make his stand in the vicinity of Glenns Ferry."

Lightfoot thought about that for a moment. "You know the spot, Colonel. It's where the interstate runs along the side of a mountain. To the south there is a great flat expanse on the other side of the Snake River. Rising up on either side of the flat are two mesas."

Putting the Adjutant General's letter aside, Nancy reached for a map and flipped it over until she found Glenns Ferry. "I see what you mean. It would be difficult, at best, to swing a force to the north, but not impossible."

"A handful of people who know the ground," Lightfoot injected, "would play hell with that effort."

Nancy nodded. "Yes, they could. And anyone going south of the Snake River will need to come down off of the eastern mesa and cross the flat open area fully exposed to anyone sitting on top of the western mesa."

"Our fellow Guardsmen would have all day to pick their targets as the 4th AD looked for a good place to get up onto the western mesa," Lightfoot continued.

Nancy continued to pore over the map, studying the terrain in detail, looking to see how she would execute such a maneuver. In the process of doing so she came upon the name of the flatlands that lay between the two mesas. Putting the map down, she slowly turned her head and looked out the window. Having been a professional officer, she didn't believe in signs or omens. Ancient Roman generals had. Her hero, Joan of Arc, had. Still, she could not deny that there was this thing called Fate which defied all logic. "Do you know the name of that place between the mesas?" she asked.

Lightfoot nodded. "Yes ma'am, I do." Taking his eyes off the road for a moment, he met her stare. "Deadmans Flats."

The rest of the trip into Boise was made in silence.

THE GOVERNOR'S OFFICE, BOISE, IDAHO · EVENING, NOVEMBER 8

Making her way through the now familiar corridors, Nancy was not paying attention to anyone or anything along the way. She was in a hurry. Nathan Dixon and his platoon would be chomping at the bit to get back into the action. They needed to be restrained now that the Army was on its way. What she would do with this platoon was still a big question. In and of itself, it was not a very powerful force. In a standup fight it could do little. What gave Nathan's platoon so much potential was the element of surprise its appearance at the right time and place would create. The big question for her was where that time and place was.

She was about to turn the corner and enter the suite of offices where the Governor resided when she ran headlong into an unexpected barricade of desks. Coming to an abrupt halt, Sergeant Lightfoot bumped into her from behind.

"Where you goin'?" a militiaman wearing shiny captain's bars demanded.

Nancy looked up at the man. "The governor's office,"

she responded sharply. "I have dispatches for the governor from the adjutant general."

Advancing, he reached his hand out. "Turn them over and I'll take care of them."

Stepping back, Nancy clutched the map case in which she carried the letters and reports. "These are for the governor's eyes only. I have been ordered to hand them over to no one except the governor or his . . ."

The militiaman closed the space between them. He was now joined by two other militiaman who had roused themselves off chairs they had been lounging on. "I said hand them over," the militia captain barked.

From behind her Nancy heard Sergeant Lightfoot step back as he released the bolt of his rifle. The sharp, distinctive snap of the M-16 bolt ramming a round into the chamber, followed by the ominous click as Lightfoot flipped the safety off, echoed through the corridors. "The colonel has her orders," Lightfoot stated in a low voice that put one in mind of the rumblings of an earthquake.

For a moment the two parties eyed each other. Though they outnumbered Nancy and her NCO, the militiamen could not discount the pair's determination or unpredictability. After a moment, the militia captain stepped aside. He said nothing as Nancy passed.

Once in the governor's outer office, Nancy allowed herself to relax. "What is going on here?" she inquired of an aide to the governor whom she recognized.

Noting the vicious stares that the militiamen were giving her through the open door, the aide shook his head. "If it wasn't clear who was running this operation before, it should be now. We've not only become prisoners in matters of policy, but I am afraid," the aide whispered, "we're captives in our own office."

"When did this take place?"

After nervously glancing around, the aide drew closer. "Right after it became known that the Guard was pulling back from Twin Falls without a fight. The Attorney General came storming in here and told the governor in no uncertain terms that consequences be damned. The Guard was going to fight. While that argument was going on, they came," the aide said, lowering his voice as he tilted his head toward the militiamen outside. "Within fifteen minutes, the 'stand fast' order was issued in the name of the governor."

Having read General Saunders's letter, she now understood everything. Just to make sure that she wasn't mistaken, he asked whose idea it had been to issue that order. "Was it Thomas or the Attorney General?"

The aide's reaction was just as telling as his answer. Pulling away, a look of horror lit his face. "The governor was on the verge of calling the President when Osborn arrived. If the governor had his way, this whole nightmare would have been over by now."

Without changing expressions Nancy reached into her map case, pulled out the items she was responsible for delivering, and handed them over to the aide. "If there's nothing else, we'll be on our way."

While the aide was checking the correspondence he had been handed, Nancy pivoted about and left the office. The militiamen at the barricade in the corridor didn't do anything to hinder her exit. They did, however, watch her every move.

When they reached the outside and were sure that there was no one within earshot, Lightfoot came up next to his colonel. "Are we going to drive by Gowen Field and draw more rations before we head up into the hills?"

Nancy was about to respond when her eyes fell upon Jan Fields standing at the foot of the steps with the other journalists. In an instant she knew where and how she would employ Nathan and his platoon of wayward paratroopers.

CHAPTER 22

It had been understood from the beginning that the military would have no responsibility when it came to the actual reassertion of Federal authority over Idaho as that occurred. This arrangement suited Scott Dixon just fine. One meeting with the officials sent from Washington to oversee this process was enough to convince the commander of the 4th Armored Division that he wanted no part of their program. Following the example of many a wise American commander who had preceded him, Scott stayed out of the politics and concentrated, instead, on his primary task. While the Idaho Guard had given, it remained unbroken. Correcting that state of affairs now became the focus of the 4th Armored Division.

But before his division could tend to this, Scott was faced with the need of ordering an operational pause. With its logistical network still stretching back into Utah and Nevada, the division's support command needed time to reel it in and establish forward support bases in preparation for the next phase of the operation. Though he wanted to press on before the Guard had an opportunity to collect itself, Scott knew instinctively that he had no choice in the matter. After a rapid and all but unopposed advance, the 4th AD came to a halt just west of Twin City. In many ways this pause was a blessing, for it gave the commanders of his combat units an opportunity to gather in their widely dispersed command and pull some badly needed maintenance on their vehicles. It also afforded commanders and soldiers alike an opportunity to catch up on some badly needed sleep.

Besides the hard-nosed military necessities that drove this operational pause, Scott appreciated the fact that there was also a physiological element in play. The news teams that were following in the 4th Armored Division's wake were filming the quiet, almost passive acceptance of the return of Federal authority to Twin Falls and regions to the east. These images sent a powerful message to the rest of the state. The absence of retribution or animosity from either side gave members of the Idaho Guard something to think about. Scott's pause also permitted their political leaders time to reassess their current position, evaluate options available to them, and contemplate the consequences that they would face if they continued to maintain their chosen course.

That this time was not being used wisely by the leadership of Idaho was not fully appreciated by anyone outside of Boise. Even there only a select group understood the political reality that prevailed in the state. While it was widely known that there had never been more than a handful of people who influenced the state's agenda, no one knew that the introduction of the militia groups into the equation meant that there were now even fewer running the show. Had Scott known just how radically the political landscape in Idaho had changed, he would have had second thoughts about stopping when he did.

The first hint that the situation they were facing had changed came on the afternoon of November 9. Scouts sent forth to locate the Idaho Guard and encourage a resumption of their retreat had been fired on. In one incident a platoon of the 1st of the 9th's ground troop had become involved in a heated fire fight with a Guard outpost not far from Glenns Ferry. This skirmish had resulted in the campaign's first serious confrontation and the realization that bloodshed could not be avoided.

By the evening of November 9th it had become clear that the Idaho Guard had ceased their retreat. Taking up positions in the vicinity of Glenns Ferry, the main combat units of the Guard's 114th Armored Cavalry Brigade began to dig in. Probes of those positions by 1-9 Cav in the early morning hours of the 10th were thrown back with heavy losses. Faced with this development, Scott called his senior commanders and staff together to assess the situation and prepare for the next phase of the operation.

This gathering took place on the western edge of Black Mesa, just south of Interstate 84. From there they could survey the ground that the division would have to cross in order to come to grips with the 114th Armored Cavalry. None of the professional soldiers gathered on Black Mesa much liked what they saw. They hadn't been encouraged by their preliminary map reconnaissance after a warning order had been put out earlier that morning. They were even less inspired now that they had been afforded the opportunity to see the ground itself.

"To the north of the Snake River and I-84 is Deer Haven Mountain," the G-2 stated as he pointed out that feature to the assembled officers. "It severely restricts maneuvers in the quarter. An effort to go around Deer Haven along US 20 would only result in a major bottleneck some forty kilometers northwest of Glenns Ferry as it passes between Bennet Mountain and Anderson Branch Reservoir. To the south," the G-2 continued as he turned to face the wide stretch of flatlands at the foot of Black Mesa, "the problem is quite different but equally daunting. First we must descend this mesa into the valley below. Once down there numerous dry streambeds that cut across our axis of advance will restrict the speed with which we can move forward. After crossing the valley the ground maneuver elements will be funneled into a limited number of egresses leading out of the valley and up onto the high ground. Added to these daunting physical characteristics is the fact that the enemy knows this land far better than we, has had time to prepare himself, and will be able to see just about everything we do."

Finished, the G-2 turned to Felden and nodded as he waited for his commanding general to either dismiss him or ask questions. Folding his arms tightly across his chest, Scott said nothing as he stepped forward to the edge of the mesa and gazed off across the flats below. He knew what he wanted to say. He knew what had to be said. He was just waiting until the last possible moment to do so in the vain hope that an alternative to the plan his staff was already preparing would reveal itself to him. Though it seemed more and more unlikely with each passing hour, Scott even found himself hoping that the Guard units arrayed against his division would pack it in and either resume their retreat or lay down their arms.

As these thoughts ran though his mind and the gathered multitudes stood behind him watching his every move the only sound that disturbed this strange silence was that of the winds coming up from Nevada as it howled across the foreboding landscape. Even when his chief of staff cleared his throat in an effort to gain his attention, Scott stood with his back to his commanders and staff as he maintained his silent vigil.

His mind now moved on to an issue that was never far from his conscious thoughts. Someplace out there he had a son. Where he was, what he was doing, and how long he could last were questions that were beginning to cloud his judgment more than he dared admit even to himself. Scott found that it took every ounce of willpower he had to focus on his duties and keep from using his position as a division commander to pursue a purely personal agenda. He was even beginning to question his decisions. As he listened to the wind Scott wondered if his insistence on attacking the Guard here and now was because that was the sound military course to pursue, or if his drive to press forward was being motivated by his need as a father to do everything within his power to save his son regardless of the cost.

Unable to resolve this conundrum, Scott finally turned around, let his arms fall to his side, and faced his officers. "People," he stated in unusually sharp voice, "we came into Idaho huffing and puffing and threatening to blow the National Guard down. Until now we have gone out of our way to avoid bloodshed in the hope that somehow our political leaders could find a less violent way to end this."

Scott paused a moment as he glanced over his shoulder and looked back at the Guard positions one more time. In the distance he could see clouds of dust being thrown up by earth moving equipment digging defensive positions along the lip of the mesa across the way. They were still there, he told himself. He had no choice. He had no other option. They had thrown down a gauntlet at his feet and now it was his duty to pick it up and accept the challenge as well as all the consequences that doing so would entail.

Looking back at his senior commanders and staff officers, Scott gathered himself up. When he spoke his words were as sharp and cutting as the wind. "Tomorrow we attack. We will cross the flats before us, ascend the high ground over there, and smash all opposition before us. In doing so I want nothing held back. I want every weapon, every soldier, every resource within this division brought to bear against the enemy. Let no one hold back. Let no one hesitate. When we go forward, we go with but one purpose in mind, to crush the Idaho National Guard."

He paused to allow this thought to permeate itself throughout the collective consciousness of his assembled leaders. When he was ready to continue, Scott looked over at his G-3. "While we could do as you suggest and swing south, I doubt if the Guard would sit over there and allow us to bypass them. They have interior lines. As soon as they figure out what we were up to they will shift around to face us as we try to maneuver on the outside track."

"We can still split the division," Lieutenant Colonel Joe Brown, the G-3, offered. "One brigade here would be more than enough to hold most of the units we now face while leaving the second brigade free to swing south and around their open flank."

Scott shook his head. "No, Joe. Not this time." Looking at all the staff principals and brigade commanders gathered before him, Scott explained. "Up to now we have succeeded in making this a bloodless coup. If the governor of this state and the commander of those Guard units over there really wanted to keep it that way, they would have kept on going west. But they didn't. For whatever reason they stopped. They stand there because they have decided to call our bluff."

Brown looked down at the ground for a moment. Lifting his eyes, he looked at his commander. "Sir, we're not playing poker here."

Folding his arms across his chest, Scott nodded. "We've talked about this before. We knew that this could happen. I understand your trepidation. I understand your reservations. Believe me, I share every one of your concerns, your fears. What we are about to do will stay with us for the rest of our lives. Unlike previous battles we have found ourselves in, there will be no glory tomorrow. I do not expect that there is a man standing here now who will leave here proud of what we are about to do. But do it we will. Come tomorrow when I give the order to move out I expect each and every one of you to put aside any personal feelings you have. I expect you to go forward and crush the enemy. That is your sworn duty. That is what you have trained for all your life. And that is what I am ordering you to do."

Pausing, Scott looked into the eyes of each of his commanders. When he spoke again, his tone was less strident. "I pray that tomorrow will bring an end to this terrible chapter in our nation's history. I pray that what we do here will convince others to seek more peaceful means of resolving their political differences. Whether or not either of those comes to pass will very much depend upon how well you execute your assigned duties."

When he finished no one spoke. Only the sad, mournful howl of the wind whipping across the land broke the stillness. With everything of importance having been said and no one able or willing to add to it, the gathering dispersed. Brigade commanders returned to their units to pass on their warning orders and begin their own precombat preparations. Staff officers scurried back to the division's main command post to finish pulling together the well coordinated plan of operation that would, in less than twenty-four hours, hurl thousands of combat troops and hundreds of combat vehicles and aircraft into battle.

BOISE, IDAHO · AFTERNOON, NOVEMBER 10

The change in attitudes of the officials was palatable. Where there had been copious amounts of bombastic rhetoric flowing freely through the streets of the state capital, there was now silence. Press briefings were now curt, stifling affairs where questions were unwelcome and went unanswered. Most disturbing was the fact that no one of any account such as the governor, lieutenant governor, the Adjutant General, or the State Attorney General was seen in public. With the increased presence of militiamen manning key points throughout the city, speculation began to spread among the press corps in Boise that there had been a shift in power. While few believed that there had been a coup in the formal sense, no one who had been following the ebb and flow of events in Idaho had any illusion as to who was now calling the shots.

As a result of this change in the manner in which the affairs of state were carried out in Idaho, solid news of any value was now all but impossible to obtain in Boise. Still, journalists like Jan Fields stayed and did the best they could. "Rather than despair," Jan told her crew, "think of this as an opportunity to excel."

In her usual fashion, Jan's cameraman, Angela Carter, tried to have the last word. "Thank God we weren't on the *Titanic*. 'Cause if we had been, I'm sure you'd have tried to talk us into staying behind in order to get an exclusive with Captain Smith as he watched the last of the lifeboats lowered away."

Jan smiled. "Ah, yes. And you would have done it, wouldn't you?"

Angela said nothing. Though she had found herself in situations that were far more dangerous than the one she now faced, she didn't believe in taking unnecessary chances. There were far too many militiamen roaming about for her liking. Though the press credentials she carried offered her a degree of protection, Angela Carter decided it was time to call upon an old friend of hers.

Perseverance did pay off on occasion. As night fell upon Boise prematurely because of an oncoming storm, GO Thomas, flanked by militia officers, emerged from the capitol building and made his way down the steps to his waiting limousine. Jan and her crew were waiting. Lunging forward past militiamen, Jan shoved a mike in Thomas's face and yelled out the first question that came to mind. "Governor Thomas, have you ordered the National Guard to stand fast and resist Federal forces?"

It was the sudden appearance of the woman he had once so desperately wanted to seduce rather than the question or her actions that caused GO Thomas to pause and face the journalist he found so alluring. For a moment he stood there, looking down into the warm and inviting eyes as he recalled how close he had come to possessing her. Here was his chance, perhaps his last to put an end to this insanity. With his armed escort off balance, GO Thomas wondered if he could say enough to make it known that he was no longer running the state, that all he wanted to do was end this terrible nightmare.

While the governor hesitated, Jan continued to press forward. Clearing her throat, she repeated her question. "Is the National Guard going to fight? Or is this short-lived rebellion of yours about to come to an end?"

Thomas's hesitation to seize the opportunity Jan had given him permitted the militiamen around them to intervene before he could do any damage. While one man grabbed the governor by the arm and pulled him toward the limousine, two others pounced on Jan and her crew. One militiaman took the butt of his rifle and smacked it into the cameraman's midsection, sending her to her knees. Another stepped between Thomas and Jan, using his body to physically force the journalist back.

Enraged by the actions of the militiamen and angered that he hadn't acted sooner, Thomas tried to make his way over to where Jan was fighting to get free of her assailant.

From the limousine an arm holding a pistol emerged. Jamming it into Thomas's back Osborn ordered Thomas to get in. "Give it up Governor, or she dies right here and now."

Again Thomas hesitated. By now he had become convinced that Osborn was capable of anything. Ashamed, but seeing no good alternative, Thomas acquiesced.

• • •

Once they were safely in his limousine, Osborn turned to Louis Garvey. "It's time we thinned that herd," the Attorney General stated in a menacing manner that he used when he didn't want the person he was addressing to disagree. "That one," he went on, alluding to Jan, "would be a great place to start."

When Osborn had brought up the subject of muzzling the media before, some of the militia leaders had objected to such a move. Now, however, with the Federal forces closing in and their role in dictating policy secure, Osborn felt he could make his move.

In the seat across from him, Thomas glared but said nothing. It was, after all, his fault that harm was about to come to that woman. Just like it was his fault that the very state he loved was about to be torn apart by a country he had once served.

BOISE, IDAHO • EVENING, NOVEMBER 10

As she waited for the governor's nightly letter to the Adjutant General, Nancy looked around the outer office and made a few mental notes. While someone had been nice enough to bring a cot in for the governor, the aides and assistants who stayed by his side had to make do with one sofa and their chairs. Nancy saw this as a lucky break. No cots meant less clutter and furniture to trip over later. She also noted that the militia officers had posted only one man in the outer office to keep an eye on the staff who had access to the governor. While she had no idea what he was instructed to do in an emergency, Nancy doubted that he would pose a serious problem.

Emerging from the governor's office, an aide handed Nancy the nightly letter for Adjutant General. She held it at arm's length for a moment and studied the envelope. While the font used to address the letter was still the same, Nancy wondered just how much of the content of the letter was the governor's and how much had been generated by someone else. Well, she thought to herself as she stuffed the letter in her map case, she'd read enough of the governor's work by now to figure it out.

Leaving the office she made her way to the barricade manned by the militiamen outside the office in the hall. Hesitating, she looked around. One of the militiamen noted the look of concern on her face and chuckled. "Your driver's taking a leak."

From somewhere around the corner the sound of a door being kicked open could be heard, followed by the distinctive footfalls combat boots make on highly polished tile floors. When her driver came around the corner he was still buttoning his fly. He finished this task just as he came up to the militia checkpoint. Looking at Nancy, he smiled. "Ready whenever you are."

Though she was angry, Nancy said nothing. Instead she gave the driver the nastiest look she could manage, pivoted about and started for the stairs. Looking over to the militiaman, the driver rolled his eyes as if to say, "women." The militiaman returned the driver's glance, but for a different reason. He was sizing up this new man, trying to determine his mettle. Though not nearly as physically imposing as the Indian, this new man had a sharp lean look that reminded the militiaman of a bird of prey.

With a nod, the driver in the National Guard uniform waved. "See you later."

Once outside Nancy turned on her driver. "That was dumb," she snapped. "I told you to stay put while I was in the governor's office. The next time I give you an order," she continued when they reached the Humvee, "I expect you to follow it. Is that clear?"

From the driver's side Nathan Dixon looked through the open door of the Humvee at the peeved lieutenant colonel who had led him through the capitol building in order to familiarize him with it. "Colonel," he stated with a plaintive tone of voice, "I had to see what was around the corner. I needed to know if there were more militiamen about."

After throwing herself into her seat and crossing her

arms, Nancy looked up at Nathan. "If you wanted to know that then you should have asked me, damn it!" After a moment her expression softened. "You get one 'atta boy' for initiative and one for thinking. But the 'aw shit' for not doing what you were told cancels both. Now, let's get going. We have some people we need to pick up."

Realizing that she wasn't too upset, Nathan climbed into the Humvee and cranked it up. It was going to be a long night, and there was much that remained to be done.

As is often the case in military operations, kinks develop in the plan at the most unexpected and inopportune time. The plan that Nancy Kozak was in the process of pulling together was no different. After driving into the parking lot of the motel where Jan Fields and company were staying, she instructed Nathan to park the Humvee behind the building where the distinctive shape of the vehicle and rumble its diesel engine made would be less likely to be noticed. She didn't want to draw any more attention to them than necessary. Dismounting, she made her way to the front of the building.

She was about to turn the corner when she saw a van, hand painted in a motley camouflage pattern, parked in front of the office. A militiaman with his rifle slung over his shoulder and his arms folded across his chest was leaning against the front of the vehicle. His head was bowed as if he were dozing. Drawing back, she watched as half a dozen thoughts began running through her mind.

After several minutes the doors of the motel opened amidst a babble of voices. One gruff voice was shouting commands. Nancy recognized the female voice that was protesting. Pulling back a bit farther she pressed herself against the side of the motel.

Escorting Jan Fields and the two members of her crew were a pair of armed militiamen shoving them toward the van. Upon hearing them approach, the militiaman who had been leaning on the van sprang to life and made for the driver's side. Not waiting to see more, Nancy eased away from her hiding place, turned, and sprinted for the Humvee.

Upon reaching the Humvee, Nancy leaped into the passenger side. "Pull up to the side of the building."

"What's up?" Nathan asked innocently as he slipped the gear shift into drive.

"Just shut up and go. Don't go around the corner until I tell you," Nancy barked.

Without another word, Nathan complied.

By the time they reached the corner of the motel the van had already pulled away. Across the parking lot she caught sight of its taillights as it was waiting to pull out into the late night traffic. "Follow that vehicle," Nancy ordered. Again, Nathan complied without comment. While not quite sure what was going on, the young officer had come to trust this female lieutenant colonel. When the van lights lurched forward, he moved out.

The Humvee followed the van through the sprawl of Boise's south side. At first, Nancy thought that the van was headed for Gowen Field, where the militia had taken over several of the empty Guard buildings. But the van kept going south across Interstate 84 past Gowen and into the open prairie south of Gowen where Nathan and his platoon had landed. "They might be headed for the state penitentiary," Nancy stated more as a mental note to herself than to inform Nathan. But when they passed the penitentiary without the van showing any sign of slowing down or turning, Nancy said nothing.

"What's south of the penitentiary?" Nathan asked as he kept the taillights in sight.

"Nothing. Just the desert."

It was then that Nancy came up with her plan. It was a desperate one but the only one she could think of at that moment. "Move up closer to the van," Nancy ordered. "When you're right behind them hit your horn and flash your lights."

"What are we going to do, Colonel?" Nathan asked without taking his eyes off the van that they were now gaining on.

Without taking her eyes off the van, Nancy shook her

head. "I'll let you know as soon as I figure that out."

When they were almost on top of the van's rear bumper Nathan leaned on the Humvee's horn and flipped the headlights on and off. The van's driver immediately hit his own brakes and started to pull off onto the side of the road. Nathan followed suit, making sure that he stayed behind the van. When both vehicles were fully stopped on the narrow shoulder of the road both Nancy and Nathan remained in the Humvee and watched as both the driver and front seat passenger of the van threw open their doors and climbed out. Turning to face the colonel, Nathan again asked, "Now what?"

Nancy's response to his question was nonverbal but understood. Slowly she reached down with her right hand and drew her 9mm pistol from its holster. Bringing it over to her lap, she grasped the slide with her left hand and jerked it back. After slowly letting it return forward, she flipped the pistol's safety off. Only then did she turn to face the young paratrooper. "Wait for me."

Nathan didn't need her to spell out what their next move was. Picking up his M-16, Nathan worked the bolt to chamber a round, then flipped the safety off and onto the three round burst setting.

Nancy drew in a deep breath. "It's show time," she stated calmly before dismounting. As she did so she took great care to keep her drawn pistol down and close to her side.

Blinded by the Humvee's headlights and unsure of what was going on, the two militiamen ordered Nancy and Nathan to halt. "Stand where you are and identify yourself," the wary man who had been in the front passenger seat shouted out.

Knowing that her voice might tip them off as to who she was, Nancy said nothing. Noting her hesitation and the increased nervousness of the militiamen, Nathan responded instead. "There's been a change in plans," Nathan said with the deepest voice he could manage. By now the two militiamen had reached the rear of their van. When the pair stopped at either end of the rear bumper and turned toward the source of the voice, Nancy saw her chance.

Without hesitation she brought her pistol up, held it at arm's length and pointed at the militiamen on the passenger side. She made no announcement, gave no warning. She simply squeezed off two quick rounds at the militiaman before her as fast as the pistol recycled and chambered the rounds.

Naively, Nathan had expected her to say something first like "freeze" or "throw down your arms." So he was as surprised as the driver of the van when she just opened fire. In unison, both men turned to face Nancy, then to the body of the militiaman now lying on the ground in a pool of blood. Fortunately Nathan recovered first. With an ease that he had perfected on the rifle range, Nathan brought his weapon up to his hip, drew it tightly into his side and let fly a three round burst. The driver screamed, dropped his automatic rifle, and grasped his midsection as he fell to his knees and toppled over.

Remembering that there was a third militiaman in the van, Nancy ran to the side door, grabbed the handle, and jerked it open. To her surprise she saw Jan staring wide eyed at her cameraman as she held a snub-nosed pistol under the chin of the other militiaman. Looking over to Nancy, the cameraman smiled and wiggled the gun, causing the militiaman to grimace. "I always carry my little friend when it looks like things are going to get stupid," the cameraman explained.

Jan shouted at the cameraman, as much in surprise as anger. "Don't ever do anything like that again! Do you know how much danger you put us in?"

Looking around, the cameraman chuckled. "You mean like this?"

Unmollified by Angela Carter's explanation, Jan was about to lash out at her again when she heard a familiar voice coming through the open door of the driver side. "Hi, Mom! What's up?"

Anger turned to shock, then surprise, then to joy as Jan pushed her way past Nancy and out of the van. Mother and son came together in a huge bear hug in the van's harsh headlights. "Oh, God," Jan stammered through a stream of tears that ran freely down her cheeks, "I was so worried about you, Nate. When I heard . . ."

Taking her head in his hand and gently laying it upon his chest, Nathan tried to calm his mother. He couldn't remember ever seeing her so shaken. Of course, he had never been in a situation like this with her.

That thought caused him to step back and look down at Jan. "Mom," he stated in a plaintive voice. "I need to, ah . . ."

Recovering some of her composure, Jan shook her head. "I understand."

Coming up to Nancy's side, Nathan saw that the cameraman and sound tech were already in the process of binding and gagging the militiaman in the van. Pointing over to the wounded one on the side of the road, he asked what they would do about him.

The two of them walked over to where the militiaman lay kicking and thrashing about in pain. She looked at Nathan, then down at the man. Nathan had done a good job on the militiaman. All three of his shots had found their mark just below the man's heart. In the headlights of the Humvee parked behind them, she could see the bloody froth gurgling up every time the man drew breath. He had a sucking chest wound. Without expert assistance, he would soon die as blood filled his lungs and he drowned in his own blood.

Nancy looked around. To leave him would be cruel. To take him even crueler. Yet to drop him off at a medical facility would jeopardize their enterprise. Never one to turn her back and walk away without doing something, Nancy made her decision. Without a word she aimed her pistol at the wounded man's head and squeezed off two rounds. When the twitching stopped, Nancy looked over at Nathan. Standing across from her the airborne officer stared at the body for several seconds before he slowly lifted his gaze and met her cold eyes. "War is hell and life's a bitch, Lieutenant," she explained. "Learn to live with it or find yourself a new vocation."

Without another word, Nancy flipped the safety on her pistol, slipped the warm weapon into its holster and walked to where Jan was still standing. "I don't suppose you have your camera and the equipment you need to broadcast live with you, do you?"

Jan, shaken by the execution she had just witnessed, shook her head. "No."

Nancy sighed. "Well, I'm not going back to recover yours. That wouldn't be smart. Do you know another news team you can trust who would be willing to take a chance to do something important?"

Tearing her eyes away from the body lying on the road, Jan thought for a moment as she gathered her wits. "Yes, I do. Sam Anderson. He owes me big time."

"Do you know his phone and room number?" Nancy asked quickly.

"Yes I do. He's out by the airport."

"Good." By now Nathan had returned to his colonel's side. "I'm sure you two have a lot to talk about. Hop in the back seat of the Humvee, Mrs. Dixon, and go with us. We'll find a phone that you can call your Sam Anderson on. I'll have the van follow us. We can always use another vehicle."

Nathan looked at his shaken mother, then at Nancy. "I don't think it's a good idea to have my mom go with us, Colonel," he stated.

Surprised, Nancy looked at the young officer. "And why not, Lieutenant?"

"Well," Nathan explained with a straight face, "my mom always gets nervous as hell and screams a lot when I drive."

It took Nancy a moment to realize that Nathan was joking. But instead of becoming angry, a hint of a smile managed to curl the edges of her lips. This was a good sign. While he might not approve of what she had just done, Nathan wasn't rattled by that or the entire action. He would do well in the coming days. "Okay, Lieutenant, let's stow that wit and get rid of these bodies. We have work to do."

Nathan nodded. "Yes, ma'am." Then he turned to his mother, who was glaring at him.

"You're just like your father," she snapped.

Nancy looked over to Jan. "I'm glad he is."

CHAPTER **23**

The storm that had been threatening throughout the early evening finally broke shortly after midnight. It wasn't a particularly vicious storm. But it was more than enough to make the pitiable existence of soldiers on both sides more miserable.

For the air assault troopers of the 11th Division this was especially true. Strapped into their seats, they were lashed by the wind and pelted by the rain it carried through the open doors while their Blackhawks zipped about just above the ground. Within minutes all were beaten into near despondency, until all thoughts of where they were going and what they would face once they got there all but disappeared. Some longed to hit the ground if for no other reason than to end this wretched journey. Others saw their arrival at their objective as an opportunity to strike out at someone and make them pay for subjecting them to this sort of suffering.

In the cockpits the pilots were quite literally flying on the edge of their seats. Taking an aircraft into enemy territory was in and of itself a nerve-wracking experience. Doing so at night, through a storm, as part of an elaborately synchronized plan, only adds to the already considerable stress. One pilot in each Blackhawk wore night vision goggles in order to keep an eye on what was going on outside of the cockpit, both on the ground and in the sky around them. He not only had to fight the physical elements that conspired to blind him and the terrain he was skipping over, he also had to resist the urge to slow down or put a few extra feet between his aircraft and the ground racing by before him. The other pilot monitored the conditions of the aircraft itself. Hunched over he watched the instruments in front of him. In silence he prayed that none of the warning lights he kept glancing at would flicker on. Together they did their best to ensure that they delivered their human cargo at the appointed time and place.

In the darkness not far ahead of these northbound helicopters were the scattered platoon fighting positions of the Idaho National Guard. The Guardsmen defending the eastern edge of the mesa overlooking Deadman's Flats who could do so had taken shelter against the storm long before the first raindrop fell. Those left with the task of manning outposts or standing watch in the commander's hatch of their vehicle had little to do but wrap themselves in layers of clothing and suffer in quiet misery. During this lonely vigil many reflected upon their plight and the future that was, at that moment, as cold and foreboding as the night itself.

For ten days they had done all that had been expected of them. They achieved far more than many had thought themselves capable of. They had put up a brave front. United, they had stared down Washington's political elite. Now, with the Regular Army preparing to call their bluff, most felt it was time to do the only thing that made sense. Even the most radical Guardsman standing watch expected their governor to declare victory, make peace with the Federal government, and send them home.

Few of the sons and daughters of Idaho manning the line that night were aware they were about to be called upon to make the ultimate sacrifice. Even fewer appreciated that this gesture was not being made at the behest of the people they had elected to lead them. None of them were fools. Like so many other forlorn souls caught between two clashing ideologies, the members of the Idaho National Guard were out there doing their duties because they had made a commitment, trusted their political leaders, and believed that they were doing what was right. Whether this dedication was based upon a strong personal conviction to a particular code of ethics or beliefs, or simply because they didn't want to look bad in the eyes of their fellow Guardsmen was unimportant. What did matter was that this small band of citizen soldiers were out there ignoring the elements, Federal authority, and some would say common sense.

The weather, the time of night, and the dispersion between units robbed the moment of the drama it so richly deserved. Perched upon a specially fabricated seat in the open cargo hatch of an ancient M-113 armored personnel carrier, Scott Dixon watched the western horizon and waited for the appointed hour. Within minutes, he would lose control over the battle. The plan that he had set in motion was about to slip from his fingers. Once initiated the fight would be carried on by his subordinate commanders, men and women he had done his best to train and prepare for this very moment. That this trial was coming at the expense of their fellow citizens did not matter. Neither Scott nor the soldiers of his division could allow it to matter. They were professionals, fighting for a people and a set of principles that all believed far outweighed the petty concerns or reservations of the individual. What mattered to the major general sitting on the edge of a windswept mesa and the men and women who had followed him to this place was that every one of the actors in this vast tragedy did their job and did it well. Failure to do so would not only mean that some of their number would die for naught, but that those who survived would have to do it again.

In battle the weather is neutral. The staff of the 4th Armored Division could not have counted on it to provide cover for the air assault. This task fell to the heavy guns of the division. At precisely zero three hundred hours the massed guns of Scott's artillery brigade unleashed a synchronized barrage that would mask the final approach of the Blackhawks carrying the soldiers of the 11th Air Assault Division. In addition to the task of suppressing the Guardsmen during the insertion of the heliborne troopers, the storm of fire would severely limit the Guard's ability to respond to the attack that would follow.

The first volley of improved conventional munitions hammered selected Guard positions. Each artillery projectile dispensed dozens of small bomblets over the targeted Guard positions. This continued for several minutes as the helicopters touched down, disgorged their passengers, then took to wing again and fled south. All was done according to a time schedule, making it critical that the air assault element be punctual and the artillery be accurate. Errors of mere minutes or a few dozen meters could be disastrous.

When the air assault element had completed their disembarkation, the guns lifted and shifted their fires to other Guard positions. This fire was meant to be suppressive, a bombardment engineered to prevent those elements from interfering with the destruction of key Guard units and vehicles by the air assault troops. While this phase of the attack was in progress, the 4th Armored Division's mounted ground maneuver elements would break out from concealed attack positions and charge across Deadman's Flats as quickly as their vehicles could carry them. The tankers and mech infantry of lead elements were to aim for the gaps in the Guard's defenses that the combined efforts of the artillery and air assault troopers had carved out. Once the lead units had climbed the steep mesa and established a foothold, follow-on forces would pass through and begin the methodical process of crushing what was left of the Idaho National Guard.

Not all would go as planned. The most junior commander in Scott's division knew this just as well as their commanding general. Some Guard units would not be affected by the artillery fire. Not all the platoon positions targeted by the air assault troopers would be overwhelmed before the 4th Armored's tanks and Bradleys came into the range of the Guard's tanks and Bradleys. So unit commanders at all levels had contingency plans. More often than not these plans involved a number of their M-1A1 tanks. Following the lead elements or set on commanding ground the gunners and the tank commanders of units assigned to watch over the advance would scan the far horizons through their thermal sights looking for trouble. When they saw an enemy vehicle that looked as if it were moving into a position from which it could place effective fire on the lead elements, the over watching tanks had the task of silencing it. While they could not count on getting off the first shot in every case, all were determined that they would fire the last.

SOUTH OF HAMMETT, IDAHO • 0305, NOVEMBER 11

With the helicopters finished and away, Sergeant First Class Samuel Decon looked around and called for a sitrep from all his squad leaders. When he had heard from the last, he reached for the handmike from his RTO. After a quick check with his company commander, he took a second or two to orient himself on the ground. When he was ready he gave the command to move out.

Decon could see the impacts of artillery up ahead marking the location of the Guard tank platoon that his platoon was charged with attacking. The artillery would force those tankers to button up. Even after the artillery lifted and shifted, Decon hoped they would be more than a bit rattled. He knew *he* would be. With luck, the fifteen year veteran told himself the guns would kill one or two of them. Regardless of what the red legs did, it was the mission of his platoon to eliminate the tanks sitting astride one of the trails leading up onto the mesa, and clear the way for the 4th Armored Division.

Except for the squish of mud under boot, Decon's platoon made their way through the gently falling rain in silence. Like the air assault troopers who followed him in loose squad clusters, Decon couldn't totally close his mind to personal thoughts. At the moment he found himself debating whether it would have been better to have a second lieutenant platoon leader with him at a time like this or, as was the case, lead the platoon himself.

He was of two minds on the subject. In garrison an

officer was handy. They took care of all the paperwork, went to the old man's meetings, signed for the platoon's equipment, and listened to the more lame excuses malingering soldiers concocted. In the field they were another matter. While it was true well-trained second lieutenants managed to hold their own and even helped by handling critical tasks like reporting and planning, a poor one reminded him of taking a rambunctious two-year-old into a crystal shop. Sometimes it was only the lieutenant's own demise that saved the platoon from serious damage.

Up ahead the leader of the platoon's point element signaled that he had the Guard tanks in sight. Gesturing for everyone to stay put, Decon made his way to where the men of the point element lay prone in the fresh mud. "Three tanks," a buck sergeant whispered as he pointed them out. "Two there and one over behind that dirt berm."

Technically there was a fourth M-1 on the position. But the weird angle of the gun tube and smoke curling up from the rear of the turret indicated that the 4th Division's artillery had earned their pay for the night.

"Have you seen any sign of the crews?" Decon asked.

"Negatory," the buck sergeant replied. "Not hide nor hair of 'em."

"Okay," Decon whispered. "I'm going back. I'll send the squads up one at a time. Direct one squad to each of the remaining three tanks starting on the left. Join your squad when the last squad comes by."

The sergeant nodded, then eased himself back down to keep an eye on the platoon's prey. Decon made his way back to where the platoon waited. There was little he needed to tell the squad leaders. What they were there for and how they would accomplish their mission had already been discussed. All Decon needed to do was point to where the buck sergeant waited and wish them luck. Decon joined the last of his squads, the one that would take out the tank behind the berm.

Within minutes they were in place. Decon watched as the squad leader he was with placed his tank killers. Because the platoon had only two Javelin antitank guided missile trackers this squad had to rely on the lighter, less sophisticated AT-4 LAW, short for Light Anti-tank Weapon. While capable of penetrating fifteen inches of armor, and much improved over the Vietnam era LAW, the AT-4 lacked the punch of its more lethal brothers, the Javelin and the TOW. Since one shot cannot be counted on to achieve a kill, the leader of the third squad had four of his men, all armed with AT-4s, line up in a semicircle behind the tank they were about to ambush. On his command he would direct them to fire in sequence. Should that still fail to do the job, each of the tank killers had a second AT-4 that he would ready once his first rocket had been expended.

Set, the squad leader gave Decon the high sign. Now Decon's moment had arrived. Judging that the other squads had more than enough time to get into place and set up their Javelins, Decon signaled to his RTO for the hand mike. He keyed it even before he had it up to his ear. "Bravo Six, this is Bravo Two Six. Set and ready."

"Roger that, Two Six. Stand by to execute."

With nothing else to do Decon listened to the company net. His company commander was growing impatient as he tried in vain to contact the leader of his third platoon. Impatiently he looked down at his watch. Finally, with his exasperation coming over the radio loud and clear, Decon's CO called him. "Bravo Two Six. I have negative contact with Bravo Three Six. Have you seen him? Over."

Decon keyed the mike. "Negative."

"Have you heard any firing off to your right?" the company commander asked.

Decon again keyed the mike. "Negative."

After a short pause, the company commander came on. "Okay, we can't wait any longer. Two Six, when you are finished, beat feet over to where Three Six was supposed to be. If he is there, give him a kick in the ass. If he's not, take out the tanks he was supposed to. Acknowledge, over."

Despite the severity of the situation, and the pressure that his company commander was under, Decon couldn't resist. "This is Two Six, I acknowledge one kick in the ass to Three Six, over."

In the silence that follows, Decon could imagine the look on his young company commander's face as he swore at the hand mike he held. Then the CO came back on. "Bravo Two Six, Bravo Two Six, stand by to execute, over."

In a flash, the leader of the first platoon came back. "Bravo One Six. Stand by."

Then Decon keyed his mike. "This is Bravo Two Six. Standing by."

After a brief pause, the company commander came back. "Fire when ready, out."

Tossing the hand mike to his RTO, Decon pointed to the squad leader. "Fire!"

Without hesitation, the squad leader began the task of killing his fellow countrymen.

SOMEWHERE ON DEADMAN FLATS, IDAHO •
0318, NOVEMBER 11

Up ahead Captain Martin Aguilar could barely see the tanks of his second platoon and the Bradleys of the attached mech infantry platoon with his naked eye. After making a quick scan of everything to his front, he glanced down at the GPS mounted in the ring of his cupola. With his left index finger Aguilar hit the DISPLAY button on the GPS, then checked the location it gave him with the map that he had secured on a covered board fastened to the rear of his machine-gun mount. Letting go of the cupola ring, he thrust his right arm in front of his face and checked his watch. "We're slow," he told himself as his body swayed about to compensate for the rocking motion of his tank. "We should be at least two hundred meters farther west by now."

Nervously he looked over his left shoulder at the M-1 that was lurking fifty meters to rear of his own tank. It was the colonel's tank. As if he didn't have enough stress to deal with, the commander of Task Force 3-68 had chosen to go forward with his company. From the beginning things had not gone well. First there had been the traffic snarl on the trail they had used to move off Black Mesa. Then there was the discovery that the ground they had to cross was more broken than anyone had anticipated. And on top of all of that, the rain had all but stopped. This left Aguilar's vehicles, heated by their exertions, silhouetted against a ground that had been cooled by hours of rain.

Turning back to face the front Aguilar slumped down. Such things didn't matter to the old man who was fond of reminding his officers that the maximum effective range of an excuse is zero meters. Accomplishing the mission on time was all that mattered to him.

Though a modern warrior, Aguilar never outgrew the superstitions he had grown up with. He had been taught as a boy not to speak badly of the dead or wish for something that you might not like. He always did his best to maintain a positive attitude for fear that negative thoughts manifested themselves into evil. Tonight, as his concerns began to worm their way from the recesses of his unconscious mind and palpable fears began to emerge, Aguilar found himself unable to restrain the foreboding sense of doom that grew with each passing moment.

Even before he was able to apprehend what was happening, a flash on the high ground up ahead caught his attention. With the speed of a bolt of lightning, a deadly streak of light tore through the night sky and slammed into a Bradley just off to Aguilar's front right. Like an eyewitness to an accident, Aguilar watched as the stricken Bradley shuddered, before tearing itself apart from within. Nine men, Aguilar told himself, had just died. The shock of this was even more disconcerting to the young captain since he had come to believe that catastrophic explosions in Bradleys weren't possible. Bradleys had every survivability feature that could reasonably be installed in a combat vehicle. Nothing, however, is one hundred percent. Chance in battle is part of every move, every action. For the men of Aguilar's stricken Bradley, chance took a hand by bringing the incoming round fired by the Guard tank into contact with the warhead of a TOW missile stored in the Bradley's squad compartment.

In rapid succession Aguilar keyed his radio and shouted a warning to his three platoons over the company net just in case someone was suffering from extreme tunnel vision and had missed the death of the Bradley. Next he flipped his radio frequency over to the task force command net and passed a quick spot report to his commander and the task force staff. Finally Aguilar ordered his own gunner to start looking for targets, though the gunner had been doing this all along.

All this took but a matter of seconds, fifteen, maybe twenty. In that time Aguilar saw another Guard tank open fire. Fighting an overwhelming urge to duck down into the safety of his own tank's turret, Aguilar watched to see where this one went. The relief he felt when none of the vehicles to his front were hit was short lived, as a third projectile launched from a different location was hurled down upon his command. They were in the shit, Aguilar told himself. And there was precious little that he could do except hope that the tanks behind him, tasked with suppressing Guard tanks, got the bastards, and soon.

Major Randy Medway, the operations officer of Task Force 3-68th Armor, was traveling with the tank company charged with overwatching the advance of the rest of the task force. Under ideal circumstance the overwatching element never moved while the maneuver element was in motion and exposed. But the distances that needed to be covered by the ground elements of the 4th Armored that night dictated that the overwatching tanks move forward, from time to time, behind the elements they were supposed to be protecting. Medway was in the process of making one of these moves when Aguilar's company was hit. He saw the same flashes and heard Aguilar's excited report. Medway didn't need to wait for anything more. Mashing down on the lever on the side of his crewman's helmet that keyed the radio, he shouted to the B Company commander, "Bravo Six, get those people up there, *now!*"

All around him, Medway watched as the tanks of B Company came to a halt even as their tank commanders slew the massive main gun toward the spot where the

Guard tanks sat. Almost as an afterthought he gave his own driver the order to follow suit.

Medway's tank was still gliding to a stop when his gunner yelled out. "Target identified!" Dropping down, Medway shoved his eye up to the commander's sight extension. Clear as day he saw the turret of an M-1 tank silhouetted on the horizon. The gunner had already laid the aiming dot and ranged to the target. Impatiently, the gunner called out again, "Target identified!"

Quickly, Medway glanced over to his loader. Private Cleeves sat on his seat, pressing himself against the turret wall with one hand on the gun's safety, ready to flip it to the off position when he heard the fire command. He returned Medway's stare. Whether it was the rain that had pelted them earlier or sweat from the same nervousness that Medway felt, Medway understood what the loader's expression meant.

Turning back to his sight, the task force S-3 looked at the turret of the Guard tank sitting there before him. This was for real, Medway told himself. That was a real tank, an American tank. And the round in the chamber of his own tank was equally real. He was still wrestling with all of this when Medway saw the turret of the Guard tank rotate to the right. He watched as the gun was depressed. The Guard tank was getting ready to fire, Medway told himself. He was going to kill another one of our tanks.

"GUNNER! SABOT! TANK!" The words thundered from Medway's mouth without thought, without effort.

Almost simultaneously the gunner responded "Identified" as the loader snapped a crisp "UP!", meaning that the gun was loaded, the gun safety was off, and he was clear of the main gun's path of recoil.

Without any further hesitation, Medway screamed his command of execution. "FIRE!"

The word wasn't out of Medway's mouth before his gunner was announcing, "ON THE WAAAAAAY!", as he pulled the trigger.

Inside the tank there was very little noise. There was a muffled "Boom" and a gentle rocking back as the 120mm main gun began its recoil. Quickly, the smell of acrid smoke entered the turret as wisps of burnt propellant spilled from the gun's open breach.

Even before this came to an end, the round they had fired found its mark. With no dust kicked up by the blast, the image of the Guard tank was visible to Medway as soon as his tank settled back down on its tracks. In his thermal sight the operations officer saw a shimmering glow obscuring part of the Guard tank's turret. It looked as if a blob of something very hot had been smeared on the target. Still, except for the weird mark, the Guard tank looked pretty much as it did before. Quickly Medway decided to put a second round into it, just to be sure. "*TARGET!* Re-engage!"

Again the other two members of his turret crew came back with "Identified!" and "UP!" And again, Medway gave the order. "FIRE!"

As before, the crew experienced something more like a nudge rather than a violent jerk as the main gun launched the next round. And again, Medway brought his eye back to his sight to see what the collective efforts of his crew and their tank had accomplished.

This time, there was no mistaking the effectiveness of their efforts. Sheets of flame shot up from the Guard tank while bits of the turret, most probably blow-off panels, twirled about like leaves in a stiff fall breeze. They had fatally crippled the opposing tank. "TARGET. CEASE FIRE!"

Medway continued to stare at the stricken Guard tank for several seconds. He felt no joy at what he had done. Rather than exhilaration, the only sensation the major experienced was one of stunned silence. In his own mind, he couldn't articulate his feelings. There was no way of quantifying them. All he knew was that there was something wrong. Pulling back away from the sight, he looked about the turret. Both his gunner and his loader were staring at him. The expressions they wore told him they, too, felt as he did. "Okay, crew," he finally said without ceremony, "let's get moving. Driver, move out."

As the tank lurched forward and picked up speed, Medway thrust his head out of the hot, humid confines of the turret. "God," he called out as he looked up into the night sky, "please don't make me go through that again."

With the last of the camouflage netting pulled clear and their preflight checks finished, Warrant Officer Keith Peters prepared himself. Together with First Lieutenant Bill Sarson, and the AH-64 that they crewed, Peters et al. made up exactly fifty percent of Idaho's remaining air power.

When Sarson looked out of the cockpit, he saw two members of the ground crew watching the aircraft they had so tenderly cared for prepare to lift off. For the first time in his life the Guardsman wished that he was out there on the sideline instead of sitting in an attack helicopter preparing to depart on a mission. After drawing in a deep breath Sarson gave his pilot the go ahead. "Okay, Keith, let's do it."

Slowly, Peters brought the helicopter off the ground a few feet and began to build forward speed. A lot of effort had been expended hiding this aircraft and its lone sister ship. After the Air Force attack both surviving Guard AH-64s had been hidden away in hangars. When it came time to take them to where the State Adjutant General expected the fight to take place, the pair of Apaches were loaded up on flatbed trucks, covered with tarps, and moved by road. Everything was done to protect them until they were needed.

From the small airfield the two Apaches would follow Little Canyon Creek south about fifty kilometers until they reached Glenns Ferry. There they would be dispatched to whatever part of the thin Guard line needed to be plugged. Sarson compared their mission to throwing a sponge below decks on the *Titanic* to sop up the water rushing in. Peters, an easygoing copier repairman who usually laughed even when Sarson's jokes were pathetic, could not find it in himself to muster a chuckle in response to his comrade's attempt at graveyard humor. Besides the ground crew, Peters was leaving his wife of eight years and their two children behind.

Two hundred kilometers south of Glenns Ferry aboard an E-3A Sentinel cruising at thirty thousand feet, a radar operator picked up Sarson's and Peters's Apache almost as soon as it left the ground. For a moment he watched the unknown contact as it snaked its way south through the canyon. Once the radar operator was convinced that he had a valid target, he initiated the alert. All pertinent data concerning the Guard Apache and its consort was passed on to the 4th Armored Division via a downlink from the E-3A. Within the 4th Armored Division word was passed to units scattered throughout the division, alerting them to the new threat. Out on the ground, air defense artillery teams armed with missiles and small caliber rapid fire cannons prepared to engage.

While Dixon's air defenders waited, Peters and Sarson entered the 1st of the 9th Cav's sector. Assigned to screen the division's northern flank from just such a threat, a pair of AH-64s from 1-9 Cav prowling along King Hill Creek heard the alarm. Like all young aviators who have taken to the air, the crew members of these Apaches carried with them the dream of coming head to head with an enemy helicopter in aerial combat. Those who have never flown likened this primeval warrior urge for one-on-one combat with a foe of equal skill and cunning to Snoopy's fanciful quest to defeat the dreaded Red Baron.

This wasn't the sort of thing that 1st Lieutenant Megan Kessler had been raised to aspire toward. Her mother had wanted her to be a medical doctor while her father had hoped she would make her mark in corporate America. So when it came, Kessler's choice of an Army career baffled both. Somehow neither understood that the keen sense of competition and pursuit of excellence that they had instilled in their daughter had pointed her toward the one profession where such attributes are pushed to the extreme.

It wasn't until Fort Rucker and the Army's School for Aviation that Kessler was infected by the Snoopy syn-

drome. Once it took hold, the idea of fighting another helicopter never let go. As soon as she heard that there was
an enemy helicopter entering their assigned patrol sector,
Kessler began looking for a way to place her section in
harm's way. After consulting her map and seeing that Little Canyon ran parallel to the one they were in, the first
lieutenant found she couldn't resist the urge. Fate was
tempting her with something no Apache crewman in her
boots could resist.

Without informing her troop commander, Kessler
skipped over into the narrow valley through which Little
Canyon Creek ran. The E-3A controller saw the two 1-9
Cav Apaches make the move and grinned as he watched
from his distant perch. "This ought to be good," he snickered as he pointed at the screen that displayed multi-
million-dollar machines flown by flesh and blood crewmen
as tiny computer generated symbols.

In silence, Peters pushed his Apache to the limit as he
weaved back and forth across the meandering creek they
were following. Speed, the cover of this canyon, and a
faint hope of surprise were their only allies that night. The
tense warrant officer was determined to make the most of
them.

In the front seat with his sights powered up, Sarson
clutched the handles on either side of the multipurpose
sight system. He didn't dare touch the joystick or the collective, though their dizzying speed and wild gyrations
tempted him to take a hand in the flying of the helicopter.
In time he would be free to take charge once they were
on the edge of the battlefield and ready to engage. Until
then all he could do was hang on, keep an eye open for
anything unexpected, and pray that they could do what was
expected of them without having to pay too dearly for it.

They were still a good ten kilometers from their first
firing position when Sarson caught a glimpse of something
ahead. Turning his head toward the sudden apparition was
no easy task. He had to counter every twist and turn and
dip that Peters imparted to their Apache as he sought to

make the best use of the terrain around them. So it took Sarson several seconds to get a clear image of the object that had suddenly popped up in his thermal sight. Even when he did the Guardsman hesitated since he had no idea where the other Guard Apache was.

From their firing positions Kessler suffered none of the handicaps that stayed Peters's hand. She had complete situation awareness. She knew where the other Apache in her section was. She knew where the opposing Apache would be coming from. Her aircraft was in a stable hover. And her weapons systems were armed, oriented, and functioning. So when the Apache manned by Warrant Officer Keith Peters and 1st Lieutenant Bill Sarson came screaming around the bend in the canyon five hundred yards in front of her, all Kessler had to do was lay the aiming dot on the approaching AH-64, range to it, allow the fire control to adjust the sight for range and ammo selected, and fire.

With a rate of fire of over six hundred rounds a minute it would take mere seconds to burn up the entire load of 380 rounds of HE and armor piercing 30mm ammunition Kessler's Apache carried for its M-230 chain gun. But she didn't need anything approaching that number of rounds to bring the Guard helicopter down. Tracking with the speed and agility that she had perfected on live fire ranges and countless hours in a simulator, Kessler kept her sights on target, pumping rounds into the Guard Apache as it went screaming past her. Seated behind Kessler, her pilot watched the engagement through his helmet integrated sight, bringing the aircraft around as the motion of the target required so that his gunner could continue to engage.

Both cavalrymen saw the Guard helicopter suddenly lurch up as if it were trying to climb before pitching over to one side and spinning about. For a moment Kessler thought she had failed. She thought the Guardsmen were coming about to engage. But then it dawned upon her that the Apache she had just finished hammering was in its death throes. In silence the Army aviator watched Sarson's and Peters's crippled Apache end its last flight by slamming up against the side of the canyon with a force Kessler imagined that she could feel. Neither she nor her pilot said a word or let out a cheer as the nineteen 2.75mm rockets and two Hell Fire missiles stored on the side of the Guard helicopter tore the stricken aircraft apart. Even before the last smoldering bit of debris floated down onto the cold wet ground below, Kessler ordered her pilot to turn away and head back to where they belonged. There was, in the end, no victory to savor, no joy in accomplishing something that most aviators will only be able to dream of.

SOUTH OF HAMMETT, IDAHO • 0345, NOVEMBER 11

As the tracks of his tank found level ground and gave Major Randy Medway his first unobstructed view of the high ground his battalion had been tasked to secure, he felt no great joy either. What relief there was in having survived the dash across Deadman's Flats was tempered by the knowledge that the cost of that accomplishment had been heavy. Captain Martin Aguilar's company alone had lost four of the eleven vehicles that he had led down off Black Mesa. Even worse for Medway was the fact that one of the derelicts they had left in the wake of their advance belonged to his battalion commander.

Though the old man was alive, he was unable to exercise command and control of the task force. That left tactical command in Medway's hands. The task force XO back at the command post on Black Mesa was in no position to command from there. And the time it would take him to cross over to where the task force was even if he had a combat vehicle with which to make the trip was prohibitive. So this left the junior major in command of Task Force 3-68 Armor as it began the next phase of the battle of Glenns Ferry.

With the Guard's main defense breached, it was time to roll up those battle positions that had not been taken out by the air assault troopers, the artillery, or the direct fire Medway and other fire support elements had provided during the ground assault. This had been foreseen and planned for in all the ops plans, from division on down. But since there was no way of knowing what Guard forces would still be active and where they would go once they began pulling away from their initial fighting positions, no one could formulate detailed plans or synchronize all of the units involved in this phase. This part of the fight was very much in the hands of the commanders who were forward with the division's lead elements. It was a battle of captains and colonels. Scott, stranded in his forward command post, could do little to influence its outcome. He could only redirect division assets when and where they were requested by his subordinate commanders and pray that their training, knowledge, and war fighting skills would see them through.

It was with no small amount of relief that Sergeant First Class Samuel Decon watched Major Medway's M-1 trundle off and head north to join a tank battle that was already being joined somewhere over there. Decon was exhausted, worn out from the stress, physical exertion, and nervous energy that are part of battle. A momentary feeling of joy that he felt over surviving that night's ordeal quickly passed when his eyes fell upon the dejected faces of the Idaho Guardsmen his platoon had gathered up. To a man they wore the same uniform as his people did, even down to the cloth tape embossed with "U.S. Army" that all soldiers wore over their left front shirt pocket. The men that they had been fighting and killing were fellow Americans. Walking over to the group, Decon took the canteen from its carrier, unscrewed the cap, and handed to one of the Guardsmen. "I hope this has been worth something to someone," the platoon sergeant mumbled.

The Guardsman accepted Decon's canteen but said nothing. It wasn't in his power to place value on their efforts or justify their sacrifices. Like Smith he was just an agent of his duly appointed superiors. Decon and the Guardsman were soldiers, no different from the thousands of soldiers scattered all about them. They had been called on to sort things out by placing their lives in mortal danger when those in positions of authority could not find words powerful enough to overcome their own pride or stubbornness.

CHAPTER **24**

Like a man returning from an all night drinking binge, Earl Saunders staggered into his office and threw himself onto the sofa. None of his staff followed him past the outer office where they drifted over to their old desks. Some simply sat down in their seats and looked around, not quite sure what to do now that the Idaho National Guard had all but ceased to exist. Others, taking off their helmets and field gear, made as if they were going to catch up on some work that still sat where they had left it. All responded differently to the morning's events. All had their own opinions as to whether what they had done had been right or wrong. Yet none thought of leaving the side of the State Adjutant General. While their sworn allegiance was to the state, each felt a strong personal loyalty to the general they served that somehow overshadowed all other considerations. For better or worse, the men and women who had been handpicked to be on Saunders's personal staff were going to stand by him, even in defeat.

Within minutes of his arriving, a phone rang in the outer office. Shaken from their own, dark thoughts, the staffers sitting around looked up at each other, then at the nearest phone to see what line the call was coming in on. As the phone continued to ring, one staffer after another looked about the room to see who would pick it up. Finally the executive officer shrugged his shoulders and grabbed the receiver of his phone: "State Adjutant General's Office, Lieutenant Colonel Hadley speaking, sir."

When he heard the response to his introduction, Hadley sat up. "Yes, sir. He is. Just a moment, sir. I will put you on hold and let him know you want to speak to him." After hitting the HOLD button, Hadley hung up the phone, got out from behind his desk and stuck his head around the corner and into his general's office. "Sir, it's the governor's office," the executive officer called out in a hushed tone.

Saunders didn't budge from his seat. "Put it on speaker phone."

Entering Saunders's office, Hadley crossed the room and hit the SPEAKER button. "Sir, you're on speaker phone," Hadley announced. "General Saunders is here."

From the speaker phone, a voice thundered out across the room. "Congratulations, general. You and your boys did well."

In silence, Hadley watched his general's face turn red from anger as he listened in silence to the attorney general.

"I want you to know that the sacrifice of your Guardsmen was not in vain. Their efforts have paid off exactly as we had hoped."

Saunders was seething with rage by now and unable to keep his tongue in check. "Just what in the hell kind of perverted logic brings you to that asinine conclusion?"

"Haven't you heard the news?" Osborn asked innocently.

"No, you fucking idiot!" Saunders bellowed as he jumped to his feet and bolted over to his desk. Leaning over the phone he screamed into it. "I've been watching my people die."

Still unshaken by the outburst, Osborn continued. "Well, if you take a minute and flip on the nearest radio or TV you'll see that we've won."

Stunned, Saunders looked at his executive officer. With a motion he directed the lieutenant colonel to turn on the TV in his office. Set on the World News Network station, the image on the tube was that of the President standing before the White House press corps. "How long do you intend to hold the 4th Armored Division back?" one of the journalists in the crowd shouted out above his peers.

Ashen faced and solemn, the President stared at the journalist. "As I said in my prepared statement, I feel the time has come for cooler heads to prevail and leaders on both sides of the issue to sit down and resolve this thing through reasonable and good faith negotiations. Peace and understanding are now the watchwords of our policy."

Flabbergasted and wide-eyed, Saunders slumped down in his seat. "I'll be damned."

✕

HAMMETT, IDAHO · NOON, NOVEMBER 11

The 4th Armored Division's forward command post had been set up and functional for the better part of an hour. Still, the commanding general had yet to make his appearance inside for an update or to consult with his staff. None of the hand-picked officers who manned the austere CP could blame their general. Given half a chance they would flee the crowded confines of the armored command post carriers to some place where they could vent their anger or sulk. Unfortunately for them, they had yet to reach a rank that permitted them the leeway to come and go as they pleased. Unable to escape, the majors, captains, and senior sergeants remained at their posts doing their duties in silence.

When he arrived, the division's chief of staff was not at all surprised by this sullen atmosphere. It was the same everywhere he went. Standing at the entrance of the tactical operations center, he looked about. When the G-3 saw Felden, he roused himself from his seat and sauntered on over to greet him. "Where's the general?" Felden asked by way of a greeting.

"Outside. He's pretty shaken by the insane orders that those jackasses in Washington have issued."

Felden was about to remind the G-3 that calling the President a "jackass" was inappropriate, but didn't. How could he fault a fellow officer for articulating something that he himself felt. Instead Felden walked over to the situation map. "We're still in the process of the collecting of Guardsmen," G-3 stated as Felden looked at the map symbols representing the various units in the division.

The division's chief of staff looked about the room. "I do not want to hear the term prisoner of war," he stated loud enough so that everyone present could hear. When everyone had stopped what they were doing and turned to face him, Felden continued. "They are your fellow countrymen. Remember that and conduct yourself accordingly." Satisfied that his message had been understood, Felden looked back at the map. "I need an update."

With a glance the G-3 cued a captain. Stepping forward, the young staff officer pulled out a pointer that was conveniently hanging next to the map and began the task of informing Felden of the location, status, and current activities of the division's major subordinate commands. When the update was finished, Felden nodded. "Well, at least we were able to secure Mountain Home Air Base before the order to halt took effect."

The G-3 grunted. "A troop, 1-9 Cav rolled through the front gate with five minutes to spare."

"No resistance?" Felden asked.

"None. After they broke contact, whatever was left of the Idaho Guard turned tail and headed west," the G-3 responded without any sign of joy in his voice. "Colonel Parkman has already been by here. She's been asking when she will be free to move some of her aviation maintenance and support units up there."

Felden nodded. "Check with 1st Brigade. As soon as they have closed on Mountain Home and secured the area give Parkman permission to start moving in there. But," he added, "remind her that the division support command is going to be moving in there as well. I don't want another turf battle between her aviators and Tim Bates's loggie toads."

The G-3 nodded. Then, he gave Felden a funny look. "Do you want me to inform the CG of these decisions or . . ."

Felden shrugged. "No, that's okay. I will."

Felden found Scott sitting on the hood of his Humvee. The commanding general was alone, staring off into the distance. Balancing the two cups of coffee he held, Felden made his way to the Humvee, reflecting how the gray, menacing sky suited the division's prevailing mood.

"I thought you could use some company," Felden stated as he came up to his commanding general and offered one of the coffees to him.

Taking the cup, Scott nodded, then went back to gazing west. "You know," he stated wistfully as Felden set his cup down and began to climb up onto the hood of the Humvee, "it was easier in the Gulf when we didn't know what was going on in Washington."

Settled, Felden grunted in agreement. "Easier for us. But I don't imagine the commanders of VII Corps or 3rd Army were thrilled when they received their order to halt just as we were about to crush the Republican Guard."

"Probably not," Scott agreed. "I can't see how anyone who has watched the men and women he commands die in battle not feel like shit after being stopped when victory was within their grasp." He checked himself before he added, "It's insane." Such thoughts were somehow unseemly for an officer of his rank and position. Besides, Scott didn't need to say that anyway. He knew his chief of staff well enough to appreciate that Felden probably felt the same.

The two senior officers lapsed into a painful silence. During that time they both sipped their coffee and allowed their minds to wander freely. There wasn't much they needed to do at the moment. Whereas the division's activities in the predawn darkness had been directed by the officers commanding the brigades, battalions, and companies of the 4th AD, dawn and the cessation of battle saw unit executive officers and the commanders of service support units move forward and take over. They tended to the wounded and began the grim task of recovering the dead. In units at all levels first lieutenants, captains, and majors oversaw the process of rearming and refueling in preparation for the division's next mission. Finally, Scott mumbled as he strained to look beyond the western horizon, "I've failed."

Expecting this sort of thing, Felden turned to face Scott. "You did everything expected of you. Without exception the soldiers of this division performed magnificently. The plan was executed with precision, your commanders seized every objective assigned to them, and we did what was asked of us. No one could have done any more than you did."

Struggling to hold back, Scott turned and looked at his chief of staff dumbfounded. *He didn't understand,* Dixon thought. *How could he.* He didn't know that Nathan was still out there. Felden couldn't appreciate how crushing the order to stop had been to him coming, as it did, just when he had been given an open road and a chance to go all the way.

Even now Scott found himself battling the rage he felt. How easy, Scott told himself, it would be to issue orders for a part of his division to sally forth and continue their advance on Boise. He was the commanding general of the division. While there would be open discord among his staff and commanders, Scott was confident that if he ordered them to do so they would execute such an order.

But years of training and conditioning restrained the emotional responses of the father. Scott knew doing so would be more than wrong. It would be a betrayal of everything that he stood for, that his beloved Army stood for. While it was fashionable in Third World countries for officers to use their troops for personal gain, such things simply were not part of the American fabric. From the earliest days of that institution, when George Washington refused to heed the call of his officers to place himself over his civilian masters, American Army officers had kept the faith. Generation after generation of Army officers had placed duty, honor, and country above all else. Scott Dixon, despite an anguish that was tearing him apart, could do no differently.

The grieving father was unable to respond to his chief of staff for fear of losing control of his emotions. Instead, he simply averted his gaze by looking back out over the western horizon.

ALONG MORES CREEK, IDAHO · EARLY EVENING, NOVEMBER 11

The collection of personalities gathered about in a tight circle in the center of the paratroopers' hide position was as unusual as the course of events that had brought them here. Among them were the journalists, Jan and a very nervous Sam Anderson. While their crews tried to mingle with Nathan's men, Jan worked on Anderson. "There comes a time," she was explaining to him after he had heard the plan, "when we have to stop being journalists and stand up for what we believe in."

Anderson shook his head. "I'm no coward. I've covered some pretty nasty stories. There were times when I sat in the shelter of a building watching tracers go screaming by and asking myself 'what in the hell are you doing here?' You know the feeling."

"Yes I do, Sam," she responded in a hushed, sympathetic tone. "And I know you did what I always did. You swallowed your fear and ran out in pursuit of the story."

"We're not pursuing a story here, Jan," the other journalist countered. "We're making the story. We're using our cameras and access to influence events."

Nathan, who represented the Federal government, couldn't resist the opening. "Yeah, sort of like Woodward and Bernstein did with the Watergate thing."

The New York–based journalist gave Nathan a dirty look. "That was different. They were only doing what good investigative reporters are supposed to do."

"And you," Nancy Kozak stated crisply, "are being asked to do what any good American, given a chance, would do." All eyes turned to the National Guard officer who stood with her arms folded and back to the wind. Though not particularly tall, she seemed to tower over them all. Even the normally skeptical Sergeant Gandulf accepted her authority without hesitation. "We're not asking you to kill anyone. All I'm asking you to do is your job. What you say after the governor makes his statement is up to you."

"How can you be sure the governor will roll over and call for an end to hostilities?" Anderson shot back as he rose to Nancy's challenge.

"I've read everything he has sent to the State Adjutant General since this crisis broke," Nancy explained. "I believe he had no intention of pushing this affair as far as it has gone. While it is true that he set the stage and is responsible for what's happened, given the opportunity to make things right I am convinced he will seize it."

"What happens," the skeptical journalist continued, "if he refuses? What do we do if we suddenly find ourselves stuck in the middle of Indian country with a hostile chief executive on our hands?"

"We hold him hostage," Nancy stated calmly, "and hope that someone in the chain of command takes advantage of the situation we will have created. With luck they'll ignore the President's stupid 'stand fast' order and come charging into Boise to rescue us."

At this, both Jan and Nathan exchanged glances. They guessed that Nancy Kozak was counting on Scott to do just this. Having served under him on several occasions she knew the professional views and habits of the commanding general of the 4th Armored Division, just as Jan and Nathan knew the love he had for his family.

For several minutes Sam Anderson said nothing as he sat cross-legged and hunched over studying his two hands which he held clutched firmly in his lap. Finally he looked over to Jan. "We share all credits on this," he stated. "And I get the first interview."

Jan smiled. Though she had always intended to do exactly what he had asked, except maybe the first interview, Jan appreciated Anderson's need to feel as if he were an equal and not just being taken along for the ride because he had the equipment and connections to make the broadcast.

"Then it's all settled," Nancy announced as she surveyed the gathering. Turning to Nathan, she began to issue her orders. "Lieutenant, I want you and your platoon sergeant to coordinate with Sergeant Lightfoot and come up with the load plan for the four vehicles that we have. It's going to be cramped, but I think we can do it."

"Any chance of getting one or two more vehicles, Colonel?" Gandulf asked.

The Guard officer shook her head. "While there's plenty of time, I do not want to jeopardize the operation at this point. All we need now is Boise police getting involved. Besides, we'll be going in at oh dark thirty hours. A lot of vehicles suddenly running around near the capital building just might raise an eyebrow or two. When we go in, I want total surprise."

"I need to contact my station in New York and let them know that I am alive and that I need to do a live broadcast," Anderson announced. "What time do you want the governor to go on?"

"Make sure you tell them nothing," Nancy warned the New Yorker. "Don't even give them a teaser."

Anderson put his hands up. "Oh, trust me. There's no need to worry about that. I know where my ass will be and what'll happen to it if someone screws up in New York."

"Good. Lightfoot and the squad with him will hit the lights at four twenty," Nancy explained, running through the high points of the operation once more as she answered Anderson's question. "I anticipate needing twenty minutes to clear the wing of the building the governor's office is in. When that's secure, I will give you twenty minutes to set up your equipment and establish the link with New York. It will also give the governor a chance to prepare his remarks."

"So you're looking at broadcasting at seven A.M. eastern?" Anderson asked.

Nancy nodded. "The primary decision makers will be in place in Washington or on their way. News and talk shows will be coming on and the folks in Boise will still be asleep."

Listening to the National Guard lieutenant colonel explain things like this made Nathan appreciate what his father saw in her. There was no trepidation in her voice or the slightest hint of doubt in her manner. Nathan wondered how long it would take him to become a professional like her.

Finished, Nancy looked around the motley collection of people whom she was convinced held the fate of her nation in their hands. "Any further questions?" In the fading light, she gauged the ability and confidence of each as she waited for someone to speak up. When no one did, she clapped her hands. "Okay, people. We have a lot to do and not a whole hell of a lot of time left. Let's get moving."

CHAPTER **25**

Vigilance is the order of the day. We must not allow ourselves to be lulled into complacency," Thomas Jefferson Osborn admonished in an address to his militia commanders. "We stand on the verge of achieving everything we have worked so hard for. I therefore urge you to redouble your guard."

While stirring, such words always seem to wear thin as the hands of the clock sink deeper and deeper into the wee hours of a new morning. By four A.M. the small detachment of militiamen standing watch at the side entrance to the capitol building had withered away to just two. The remainder of the detachment assigned to guard this portion of the capitol building were just inside the double glass doors, scattered about and curled up on the floor along the wall or slumped down on chairs asleep. With so much to do in the next few days, their leader reasoned that the Attorney General had precious little time to spend creeping about in the shadows in the hope of catching a guard dozing off.

When the National Guard Humvee pulled up to the side entrance not a single soul inside stirred. Its appearance was barely enough to rouse the two militiamen who were on duty. One of these sentinels was seated on the concrete steps off to one side with his rifle resting across his knees and his back against a column. The other was leaning against the building itself. The pair exchanged glances to see which of them would check the ID of the Guardsmen approaching them. "You go," the militiaman sitting on the step grunted to his blurry-eyed companion. "You're already on your feet."

Though there was logic in those words, the man who had been leaning up against the building still gave his friend a snarl as he straightened up. Without bothering to unsling the automatic rifle that dangled from his shoulder, the militiaman sauntered over to the center of the landing to wait for the Guardsmen to come to him.

Stopping one step below the waiting sentinel, Nancy Kozak flashed the most demure smile she could muster. Nathan Dixon continued to move on past the Guard officer and sentinel. Caught off guard by this, the militiaman in front of Nancy twisted about to keep an eye on Nathan. "Now hold on there," the militiaman called out. "Where you goin'?"

At the door Nathan stopped and looked in. Turning, he gave Nancy a quick nod before starting over to where the second man was sitting.

Becoming alarmed by their behavior, the militiaman before Nancy began to unsling his rifle. Nancy gave him no time to act upon his growing apprehensions. Before he understood what was happening, the militiaman felt a searing pain rip through his groin. Turning to face his assailant, he stared down at the National Guard officer before him. Her smile had been replaced by an intense expression. As the agony coursed throughout his body, the militiaman looked down in horror at the handle of the Ka-bar knife she held. It was already coated with blood gushing from the spreading wound. He couldn't see the blade, though he felt it as it continued to rip its way upward through his intestines and on into his stomach cavity. When he finally collapsed, the sharpness of the knife and his own weight carried the blade further along its murderous path.

The militiaman who had been seated on the steps stared at his companion. Unsure of what was happening he hesitated, a mistake that cost him his life. When he saw his colonel make her move, Nathan closed the remaining distance between himself and that man in a single bound. Shoving the man's head against the concrete column he had been leaning against, Nathan drove his drawn bayonet through the man's neck until the point of that weapon came to a dead stop against the column.

The blood of these two hapless militiamen hadn't even splattered the steps of the capitol building before a wave of paratroopers emerged from the nearby shadows. Rushing past Nancy and their platoon leader, they made for the door. The two point men of this assault pulled the doors wide open and held them for their companions. With bayonets drawn, the others rushed in. Once inside, each of the paratroopers selected their victims on the fly. While Hollywood tends to play up the value of bayonets and knives in commando and superhero movies, the Army itself doesn't feel the need to devote much attention to this primitive form of stealth technology. Just how the individual soldier goes about using it in combat is pretty much left up to the soldier himself. This was particularly true of the paratroopers in Nathan's 1st Squad. Though they got the job done, it was not accomplished in what one would consider a neat and professional manner. Two of the militiamen actually had an opportunity to squirm and make an effort to resist necessitating a second, third, fourth, and even fifth jab before the shock and pain of being murdered overwhelmed them. This all took time and made noise.

Having expected as much, Nancy made her way into the building as quickly as she could. She entered with her pistol drawn and ready. Nathan was at her side with his rifle up and planted squarely against his shoulder. Together the pair rushed down the long corridor past the 1st Squad as they finished their grisly work. Immediately behind the two officers came the 2nd Squad led by Sergeant Gandulf with the journalists in tow. When Gandulf came up behind Nancy, he whispered in her ear, "2nd Squad is up." These were the first words spoken during the raid.

Upon hearing this, Nancy nodded. "Looking good. Form 'em up and let's move out."

Jan made her way forward in the wake of the paratroopers. As she weaved her way around the spreading pools of blood she did her best to remain calm and collected. Focus, she told herself as she followed the trooper assigned to protect her. Focus on what you need to do when we get to the governor's office. She struggled to forget that it had been her son who had done this. She had to ignore the fact that they were all still in great peril, embarked on a venture that could go to hell in a heartbeat. "Think positive," Jan mumbled to herself again and again. "Think positive."

Forward and upward they went. Equipped with night vision devices, 2nd Squad took the lead. With weapons at the ready, they hugged the walls as they advanced. Still flanked by Nathan, Nancy walked down the center of the corridor a little farther ahead as she made her way to the wing of the building where the governor's office was located. All eyes were on her left hand, held up and even with her head. When she wanted them to move up the Guard officer simply waved her hand. They were so close and so attentive to her every move that she didn't need to wave it but a few inches. When she thought she heard something or she wanted them to stop while she moved ahead a bit farther for a look-see, she lowered her hand. The lower she dropped it, the lower the paratroopers following her crouched down and prepared for whatever was coming their way.

Nothing unexpected hindered their advance. Step by step they went on. Slowly they snaked their way up side stairs to the floor where the governor was being guarded by a dozen militiamen manning barricades made of desks and haphazardly reinforced by sandbags. Nancy had considered rushing these people as she had done at the door but decided against that. There would be too much risk. The militiamen would be alert and they would have the drop on them. There was simply too much corridor to traverse and no place for the follow-on force to hide as they had done outside. Instead of stealth and cunning she would rely on a straight up assault aided by surprise and darkness.

Before reaching the top of the stairs, Nancy stopped. Craning her neck, she looked over the top edge of the last stair. After checking her watch, she paused. They had two minutes before Sergeant Lightfoot was scheduled to hit the main circuit breaker. She had allotted him a five-minute window, from 0420 to 0425, to get set. If the later time had come and gone and the lights were still on, Nancy was prepared to fall back to her plan B, which was to pretend that she was delivering dispatches from the field. Since she had never done so at this hour, that option entailed greater risks. This was why it was plan B.

At 0419, Nancy turned and signaled the paratroopers behind her to lower their night vision goggles and turn them on. With her left hand, she removed her BDU cap, brought her night vision goggles up from around her neck where they had been dangling on a cord, and pulled them down over her eyes. Switching them on, she watched and waited.

No sooner had she gotten them in place than the bright, almost blinding green world before her suddenly dimmed to a tolerable level. Down the corridor and around the corner, she could hear voices babbling and confused shuffling about. It was 0420.

"Let's go," she commanded with a well practiced firmness and calm. Taking the last of the stairs two at a time, she went forward. The voices were growing louder, more distinct, and more frantic. Behind her the thump of rubber soled boots pounding the tile floor was deafening. To the end of the corridor she ran, never pausing or holding back as she neared the corner. They were committed. For better or for worse, no matter what lay around that corner they would have to take it on head first. There was no stopping, no turning back. Salvation and victory lay around that corner that was now mere meters away. Everything depended on what the paratrooper with her did in the next few seconds.

⚔

BOISE, IDAHO • 0440, NOVEMBER 12

It took Thomas Jefferson Osborn several long seconds to pass from the depths of his slumber to near consciousness. It took him even longer to appreciate the fact that it was the phone next to his bed that was the agent of this unwanted intrusion. Through the fog of semiconsciousness Osborn reached out and smacked the face of the phone panel in an effort to activate the speaker phone. "What is it?"

"Tom, this is Lou. They've hit the capitol building."

Still groggy but waking up fast, Osborn propped himself

up. "They're here? In Boise? I thought the tank division stopped at Mountain Home?"

"They did," Garvey explained. "I think the people here are Rangers, or Special Forces. They were able to clear the building before anyone knew what was going down."

"The governor?" Osborn asked as he threw his legs over the edge of the bed.

"Tom," Garvey stated, making no effort to hide his concern, "I think he's planning on making a public statement on television. One of the men who made it out of the building alive said something about the soldiers having journalists and a TV camera with them."

The Attorney General looked at the time. It was almost seven A.M. Eastern, a fact that Osborn appreciated was no accident. "God damn that two faced bastard," he screamed as he grabbed his pants. "I want you to get a hold of every swinging richard you can lay your hands on and stop him. You need to get in there and sort this thing out."

"How?"

"Attack, you fucking idiot," Osborn yelled. "I want you to force your way back in there and kill every last one of those bastards if it costs you every man you have."

THE CAPITOL BUILDING, BOISE, IDAHO · 0455, NOVEMBER 12

The first counterattack was a hasty, thrown together affair. They came on without any semblance of a plan, with no fire support whatsoever, and no clear idea what they were going against. With everything happening too fast for the amateur soldiers to deal with, they were slaughtered by the heavy fire raining down on them. In all the confusion none of them took note that the most devastating fire came not from the capitol building itself but from a building behind them where Sergeant Lightfoot and the 3rd Squad had taken up positions after knocking out then restoring power to the capital building.

From his vantage point Nathan watched as the paratroopers with him went about their task with ease and pre-cision. The militiamen below were cut down before a single man reached the other side of the street. "It won't take long before they figure out what happened," Nancy stated dryly.

"How soon before they try again?"

Nancy didn't give him an answer. She was too con-cerned about what was happening in a windowless con-ference room down the hall. Thinking that she had not heard him, Nathan repeated it. "Colonel, how long before they stage another attack?"

"If we're lucky," she replied, "it'll come after the gov-ernor has said his piece."

The success of their high-risk gamble depended upon creating the illusion that the governor was in complete con-trol and was speaking from a position of strength. Even the slightest hint that he was not, or that he was being forced to deliver his speech at gunpoint, would doom their entire enterprise. "Lieutenant," Nancy stated as forcefully as she could, "not a shot is to be fired from this building unless I give the order. I want complete silence while the governor is making his announcement. If you have to, use bayonets, fists, teeth, anything. But no shooting. Is that clear?"

Though he was confused by this, Nathan trusted Nancy and her judgment. There was a valid reason for this par-ticular order, one that he couldn't come up with on his own at that moment. So without further hesitation he nod-ded. "Roger that, Colonel."

Without acknowledging the lieutenant's cocky response, Nancy looked down at her watch. After taking one more look at Nathan's paratroopers and out the window into the street below she made for the room where Jan, Sam An-derson, and their combined crews were about to make a stab at playing midwife to history.

The scene that was playing out at the division tactical command post was not at all unusual. The well drilled procedures being used during the impromptu briefing for key commanders and staff officers on the unfolding situation in Boise had been practiced time and time again during numerous training exercises and simulations. Scott, the chief of staff, G-2, and G-3 listened intently to the briefing being delivered to them by the officers belonging to the night shift. Since the events in Boise did not involve any of the division's subordinate commands or was being reported by them, it was the G-2 who delivered the bulk of the hasty update which was both baffling and full of surprises. One bit of information that inadvertently slipped out was the fact that there was a long range recon section in Boise. "They infiltrated the city two nights ago," the intelligence officer informed the chief of staff when he asked about this. "They took up position on the rooftop of a hotel near the capitol building. It was from this source that we first got word that something was going on."

"Are these people still in place?" Felden asked.

The G-2 captain shook his head. "I don't think so, sir. A police SWAT team saw the value of the position our people were occupying and moved in. The last we heard from the LRRP team was that they were moving to their alternate position."

"How long before they're in place?" the G-3 asked in turn.

The briefer shrugged. "Negative knowledge, sir. Things are pretty screwy around the capitol area right now."

"Okay," Felden stated by way of getting back to the main issue. "So who's in there? And what do they want?"

Good commanders succeed because they plan well and are lucky. Great commanders make their mark because they intuitively know which opportunities to seize and which ones to pass on. Standing up, Scott walked over to the map, turned, and looked over at Felden. "It's a platoon belonging to Company A, 517th Parachute Infantry," he stated matter of factly.

Dumbfounded, Felden looked at the G-2, then the G-3 before turning back to gaze at Scott. He wanted to ask his commander how he knew that, but didn't. Besides, there being no time for such a question, Felden had been in the Army long enough to appreciate the fact that generals tended to know things that mere mortals weren't privy to.

Scott saw the look on his chief of staff's face but said nothing. Instead, he began issuing orders. "It is critical that we do everything we can to assist those paratroopers. Joe," he snapped, turning to the G-3, "crank up 1-9 Cav and order them to move out five minutes ago. I want two air assault companies saddled up and ready to pull pitch in twenty minutes. And put 1st Brigade on alert. They're to have at least two battalions ready to roll with fifteen minutes notice. G-2," he continued as he turned to face his intelligence officer. "Get an immediate update out to all units on the current situation in Boise as well as location and activity of all Guard forces between here and there."

"What do you intend to do, sir?" Felden asked guardedly.

Caught short by this question, Scott was still groping about for an appropriate response when an excited captain rushed into the room from the G-2 section next door. "Sir," she yelled to no one in particular. "I know you're in a briefing and all, but the governor of Idaho is making a speech. I think he's surrendering!"

**WASHINGTON, DC • 0705 (EASTERN),
NOVEMBER 12**

Though he was just as mystified by the turn of events that were unfolding before their eyes, the President knew a heavensent opportunity when he saw one. "Ed," he stated firmly to his chief of staff. "We must go to Boise today."

There was a silence as everyone present turned and looked at the President, then each other. Knowing that there would be those among his staff would do their best to dissuade him from doing so, the President stood and turned to face those assembled around him. "We have a chance," he stated slowly, "to go out there with our hand outstretched in friendship, ready to accept Idaho and its people back into the fold without prejudice, without re-crimination. A visit by me on this very day would go down in history as one of the bravest, most noble acts a serving president has ever made. Not since Lincoln traveled to Richmond days after its evacuation has an occupant of the White House had an opportunity to make a gesture like this."

Again, there was silence as his advisors held their collective breath and stared at their commander in chief, watching and waiting for a brave soul to step forth and explain to him that such a move would be ill advised. Not even his most gifted spinmeisters, however, could find either the words or courage to do so. Without further ado, the President walked over to his desk, took his place behind it, and began to draft an announcement that would one day be the cornerstone of his Presidential legacy.

**ACROSS FROM THE CAPITOL BUILDING,
BOISE,
IDAHO • 0510, NOVEMBER 12**

The scene inside the Tac CP that the SWAT team had hastily set up across the way from the besieged capitol building was as chaotic as the streets outside when the Attorney General arrived. On one side of the room stood a group of senior militia leaders glaring at an equally hostile SWAT team and state troopers on the other side. Between these two groups was Lou Garvey. He was nose to nose with the head of the SWAT team. "You can yell and scream all you want, you brainless shit," the SWAT officer growled, "but I am not going to throw my people out into the open in a half-assed attack. No one wearing a badge is going anywhere until we know exactly what we're dealing with."

Osborn cast a nervous eye toward the TV screen. Having finished his prepared speech, the governor was now talking with Sam Anderson. "Moron," Osborn shouted as he turned his full attention to Garvey and the SWAT team leader. "We don't have that kind of time. The enemy," he stated, pointing toward the door, "is over there, not here."

With his anger overriding his normally calm demeanor, the SWAT officer turned on Osborn. "When it comes to the lives of my people and the safety of the citizens of this city, your title and authority don't mean squat to me."

Enraged by this response, Osborn planted his hands on his hips and leaned toward the SWAT officer. "Just who in the hell do you think you're talking to?" he bellowed.

As he drew in a deep breath, the SWAT officer's eyes narrowed. "This insanity has gone on long enough." Then, before Osborn could respond, the SWAT officer pivoted on his heels and marched out of the rear door of the room. To a man his team and the state troopers followed, dragging their equipment along with them.

It took Osborn a second to recover. When he did he turned to Garvey. "Where's Saunders?" he snapped. "They have a few Bradleys and a tank or two left down at Gowen. Someone get me a phone." After one of his lieutenants scurried off to comply, Osborn gave Garvey his marching orders. "While we wait for them I want you to go in there and start rooting those sons of bitches out."

To his surprise Garvey hesitated. "Listen, Tom. It's starting to come apart. Everything we've worked for is slipping away and there's not a damned thing any of us can do. Don't you see that?"

The man who had done so much to engineer the Idaho rebellion wasn't about to stop. He had risked everything. To simply roll over and quit now was impossible. Convinced that he could still salvage his cause, Osborn pushed Garvey out of the way. "I didn't fail in Wyoming. I have no intention of doing so here." With that, he turned his back on his assembled leaders and went off to organize the next attack himself.

From across the room, Saunders's aide-de-camp covered the mouthpiece of the phone and called to his general. "Sir. It's the Attorney General."

Like everyone else, Saunders was in his office watching as GO Thomas expanded upon his decision to ask for immediate and complete reconciliation with the Federal government to a pair of journalists. Looking over to his aide, Saunders snarled. "What does *he* want?"

The aide asked and listened for a moment before covering the mouthpiece again. "The militia at the capitol building need support. He wants you to gather up everything you can lay your hands on and send it down there as quickly as possible."

Saunders didn't respond immediately. Instead, he looked back at the television screen as he considered his answer. "Sir," the aide called. "He's waiting for an answer."

Coming to his feet, Saunders gathered himself up and gave his aide a hard, cold stare. "Okay," he snapped. "Inform the Attorney General that we're coming."

After the aide hung up, the officers who had heard his pronouncement scrambled out of their own chairs in anticipation of the AG's orders. Saunders drew himself up erect as he prepared to address them. "Gentlemen, we've got one more ride to make together, a ride that will make all the difference. I believe you all know what needs to be done. Sound Boots and Saddles. We move out in ten minutes."

THE CAPITOL BUILDING, BOISE, IDAHO · 0530, NOVEMBER 12

The next effort to storm the capitol building was far better organized and led. They came at the building from three directions, each covered by a mix of riflemen armed with high powered rifles and automatic weapons.

In the room where GO Thomas and the journalists were sending out their live feed Nancy heard the pop, pop, pop of small arms fire. Raking her right index finger across her neck, she signaled Jan to cut their interview. Prepared for this, Jan raised her hand up to the side of her head as if she were listening to someone in a studio in Washington talking to her via a hidden earpiece. Then she looked into the camera in front of them. "I have just been given word that there is another story breaking, so we'll have to leave this interview." This announcement left the two news-rooms, Jan's and Anderson's, assuming that the person making the cut was the other journalist's producer. Turning to face Thomas, Jan forced a smile. "I would like to thank you for your indulgence, Governor." With that, she nodded and the camera clicked off.

When she saw that the live feed had been cut, Nancy pushed open the door and ran out of the room. Turning to Jan, Sam Anderson made a face. Jan pointed out the door the Guard officer had left open. "We do have a breaking news story. We just can't broadcast it yet."

Outside Nathan watched and waited. Within the first min-ute of the attack two of the paratroopers that were with him went down, serving notice to the others that the militia meant business this time. Pressing himself against the wall, he alternated between looking along the line of windows where his men waited anxiously for someone to give the order to fire and down the corridor to where he hoped

Nancy Kozak would soon appear. By the time she rounded the corner at a run screaming to open fire, the first wave of militiamen had made it across the street. Unfortunately for those that followed, her order to fire came just in time to catch them in the open. Having seen their companions make it without any problems, those poor souls had thrown caution to the wind and rushed forth. Their slaughter came as quickly and completely as it had for those who had made the earlier, failed attack. While this fire from the paratroopers brought on a renewed hail of gunfire from the militia positions across the street that cost Nathan another man, it served to isolate those foes who had made it into the building.

Seeing no sign of an immediate follow-up to the failed second wave, Nathan turned his attention to the militiamen who were now loose in the building. Not wanting to allow them to dictate the terms of the coming fight, Nathan yelled over to his platoon sergeant. "Sergeant Gandulf. You and 2nd Squad stay here and cover the governor and the journalists. I'm taking 1st Squad and going after the people downstairs."

Kneeling next to Nathan, Nancy thought about countermanding part of Nathan's order. Instead of letting him go, she wanted to take Gandulf and a squad to hunt down the intruders. After a moment of reflection, however, she recanted. It was his platoon. He seemed to be in control and his actions so far had given her every confidence that he could handle this situation. With a nod she wished him luck and watched half of her small command scamper off in search of prey.

From his vantage point Staff Sergeant Lightfoot could not tell if the militiamen who had rushed the building had been lucky in choosing a point of entry that he and the 3rd Squad could not cover or if the militiamen knew of their presence and had intentionally avoided them. Regardless, he saw that the squad with him was doing no good where it was. Turning to the squad leader, Lightfoot ordered him to gather up his men and follow him. They needed to clear the militiamen who were sniping away at the capitol build-ing.

Pounding down the staircase that led to the street, Light-foot and the paratroopers following him didn't stop to look around before spilling out into it. The National Guard NCO knew better. He understood that in a city fight it is important to look about before you move out into the open. But Lightfoot figured that everyone's attention was ori-ented on the capitol building. Knowing that time was tight he took a calculated risk. It wasn't until they were in the middle of the street, running for all they were worth, that he realized that he had made a terrible mistake.

The crew of a National Guard Bradley was also taken by surprise when they saw the cluster of heavily armed paratroopers suddenly appear in front of them. Unsure of who they were and what they were doing, the track com-mander and gunner held their fire. With momentum on their side this gave the paratroopers a chance to scatter. Even as the squad leader and Lightfoot dove into the same doorway for cover, the airborne staff sergeant caught sight of a second Bradley pulling up next to the first. "Now what the fuck do we do?" he shouted to Lightfoot as the two lay side by side and surveyed the situation.

Struggling to catch his breath, Lightfoot looked around. "My ancestors will surely curse me for saying so," he told his fellow NCO with a straight face, "but we better start praying for the cavalry."

Inside the capitol building Nathan and the squad with him caught part of a militia unit creeping up one of the back stairwells. Rather than opening the engagement with rifle fire, Nathan grabbed a grenade and held it up. Two para-troopers immediately behind him did likewise. When they were ready the three men pulled the pins from their gre-nades. Letting the spoon flip up and arm the grenade, Na-than counted to three before rolling his down the stairs as the other paratroopers chucked theirs up and over the side.

Not quite sure what was going on, the militiamen sneak-ing up the stairs stopped, squatted down, and looked to see what was making the noise they heard. By the time they saw the grenades it was too late.

It took several seconds for the reverberations of the detonating grenades to die away in the close confines of the stairwell and longer for the smoke to clear. When they saw no sign of anyone below making a second effort, the paratrooper next to Nathan chuckled. "Well, it seems like these boys don't have such a steep learning curve after all."

Nathan agreed. "Now all we have to do is figure out where the other little weasels will pop up. Let's move, out!" With that, he took off down the stairs.

One of the paratroopers with Sergeant Gandulf was the first to spot them. While dropping down from his firing position in a window to reload his weapon, the paratrooper noticed that the elevator doors halfway down the hall were being pried open. With a shout he warned the others, but not before a volley of grenades came sailing out though the narrow opening. Scurrying for cover, all but one of Gandulf's men found safety. Unlike the militiamen who had pulled back from Nathan's grenade attack, Gandulf and his men had no choice but to stand their ground. Ignoring the fire from across the street, the paratroopers rose up from where they had sought cover and blasted away at the partially open elevator doors.

Everyone had emptied a magazine's worth of 5.56mm ball into the elevator doors and narrow opening between them when a hail of gunfire from an uncovered fire exit farther down the hall swept through them, putting another paratrooper out of action. Diving back down onto the floor in an effort to find cover from the fire coming from that quarter Gandulf realized that they were in deep trouble. "Can someone find the lieutenant and tell him he needs to get back here?"

Nancy was on her feet in a flash. "Pull your men back and cover the conference room. Keep the militia away from there as long as you can. I'll find Dixon."

• • •

In the conference room Jan listened as the fighting grew closer. The sudden appearance of the paratroopers just outside the door did little to ease her apprehension. She understood that their defenders were preparing to make a last stand. Not knowing what else to do, Jan picked up a recorder she had borrowed from Sam's crew and crawled over to where Thomas was, where she shoved the mike into the governor's face. "So, Governor Thomas," Jan asked as if she were back in a Washington studio, "would care to comment on your plans concerning your political future?"

Nancy had managed to make it halfway down the corridor in her search for Nathan when a familiar sound from outside caught her attention. Dropping down, she crawled through the shattered glass that lay strewn about on the floor to the nearest window. Though she knew the sound growing louder by the second belonged to a Bradley, the Guard officer wasn't quite sure whose Bradley it was. Once she was at the window she peeked up over the edge of the sill in an effort to find out if the vehicles below was friend or foe.

It took but one glance to realize that infantry fighting vehicle making its way down the center of the street belonged to the Idaho Guard. Buttoned up and ready for action Nancy saw it for what it was, the final blow. Even as she tried to figure out some way of saving as many of the paratroopers and journalists as she could, Nancy couldn't tear herself away from the window. Ignoring the danger posed by the militiamen firing from across the street, she continued to watch the Bradley trundle down the street over the bodies of the dead and wounded militiamen who covered it.

He was making his way back to where he had left Gandulf and his 2nd Squad when Nathan Dixon also saw the Bradley on the street outside. Unlike Nancy he wasn't familiar with the tactical markings used by the Idaho Guard. He wasn't even sure how the vehicles in his own father's division were marked. So when the turret of the Bradley spun away from the capitol building and began raking the militiamen firing from the second floor of the buildings across the street with its 25mm cannon, Nathan naturally assumed it belonged to the 4th Armored. Overjoyed, he stood in an open window and gave a hearty yell. "I knew you'd make it in time. Give 'em hell, Dad."

He had no way of knowing at the moment that the general he should have been cheering was Major General Earl Saunders. As he was obligated to do, the State Adjutant General had risen up to defend his state and its constitution against its enemies.

EPILOGUE

Except for the two men standing behind podiums bearing the respective seals of their offices, the front of the room was barren. On the media side of the camera lens, the term "wall to wall journalists" was not an exaggeration when applied to the mass of journalists and their support crews. As predicted, the meeting between Governor Thomas of Idaho and President Chris Littleton had become an unparalleled media event.

In another room in the capitol building a number of selected dignitaries watched the proceedings on TV like millions of their fellow countrymen. Standing in the middle of the room, the President's chief of staff mused wistfully, "It's too bad he's already in his second term. This alone would have made him a shoo-in."

Though still exhausted from his efforts of the past two weeks, Scott managed a polite smile, but that was all. Such men, he thought as he tried to pay attention to the historical event unfolding, will never be able to rise above their own pettiness.

Bored by the words that he felt were little more than political posturing, Nathan nudged his father. "I hope you don't feel bad that I didn't wait for your division. At the time, I wasn't being very particular about who came down the street, looking to save me from myself."

Thankful for this opportunity to turn aside the dark thoughts that were troubling him, Scott turned to face his son. "Well," he replied, straight faced, "I hope you've learned something out of this."

"Yes sir, I have," the younger Dixon quipped. "Tanks are like American Express cards. Don't leave home without one."

Jan was satisfied to stand by in the back of the room and watch the proceedings from afar. She had done her job as a journalist, and done it well. It was time for someone else to tend to the business of taking the news of the day to their fellow Americans. Besides, she was more than satisfied with watching father and son chatter. It would be good to be back home again. With each passing crisis, Jan found that it was the things that she had ignored while pursuing a career that were becoming more and more important to her. Turning to Nancy Kozak, who had also opted to hang back and stand against the wall next to her, Jan asked if she was sure she was making the right move.

The former National Guard officer shrugged. "Well, your husband has warned me that General Poulengy can be a bastard to work for. But," she said as a smile began to appear at the corner of her lips, "I'll be glad to be back where I belong. I miss the Army. As stupid as many of its policies in peacetime are, as unforgiving as it is when it's finished with you, I love it."

Jan heard, in Nancy's voice, the same dedication to a thankless profession that she had once felt herself. Though she wanted to shake this younger woman by the shoulders and tell her to wake up, she didn't. As she saw it, eventually everyone wakes up to what is important and what isn't.

Turning her attention back to the TV screen, Jan watched and listened to the two politicians talk about the future. As she watched the men on the screen, she wondered if they too would wake up to what really mattered to the people they served in time to do something about it.

AUTHOR'S NOTE

This work of fiction, written in 1996, is not meant to be a cautionary tale or a call for action. It is only a story. Still, within my own lifetime, I have been witness to what can happen when civil discourse fails and radical elements of the citizenry feel that they have no other recourse but to take up arms against a government and society they believe has betrayed them. Less than a half an hour's drive from where I grew up in New Jersey, armored personnel carriers roamed the streets of Newark during some of the worst racial violence of the sixties, raking buildings with .50 caliber machine guns in an effort to suppress snipers. Three months before I matriculated at the Virginia Military Institute, National Guardsmen charged with enforcing the law fired on a body of rioting students at Kent State, killing four. To this sad list one can add Ruby Ridge, Waco, and Oklahoma City. So the idea that we Americans are immune to the sort of civil strife that rocks many a Third World country is little more than an illusion. We are, after all, the inheritors of a government that is founded on a document that states,

> "...when a long Train of Abuses and Usurpations, pursuing invariably the same Object evinces a Design to reduce them under absolute Despotism, it is their Right, it is their Duty, to throw off such Government, and to provide new Guards for their future Security."

As an officer in the United States Army Reserves, I took an oath. It is one I will never be able to turn my back on, for this country, our country, is without equal in the world today. It is not perfect. Nor are its leaders always as wise and as noble as we would like. But right or wrong, it is my country, one which I stand ready to defend, against all enemies.

Harold Coyle,
October 18, 2001

Look for

MORE THAN COURAGE
Now available

CHAPTER **1**

SYRIA • 18:05 LOCAL

By the time the sun began its final swift descent in the west it had been drained of all its harsh cruelty. The great solar orb that had the power to suck the life out of any creature foolish enough to show itself during the day was now little more than a harmless orange ball receding in the distance. Within minutes it would be gone from sight completely, giving the parched desert it ruled over by day a few hours' respite. Sensing the coming darkness, creatures of the night began to emerge from their holes and coveys. Even before the last long shadows of daylight were absorbed by the gathering gray twilight they would be out and about, pursuing those chores that were so necessary for survival in this harsh and most unforgiving land.

Those creatures that were native to Syrian Desert could only rely upon natural skills to track prey. When they managed to corner their quarry, they had to employ their own teeth, claws, venom, and sheer brute strength to bring it down and kill it. When times were hard and victims scarce, these same predators had no qualms about turning on each other in order to survive. Under the right circumstances, any animal will turn on its own for self-preservation and survival.

Not all the predators that populated Syria's barren landscape were indigenous. Few of the fourteen members of the U.S. Army Special Forces unit known as Recon Team Kilo thought of themselves as predators. None would have considered themselves to be the most dangerous ones in the area. But by any measure, they were. Unlike the creatures that crawled and slithered in the sands about the laager where RT Kilo's vehicles lay hidden, the Americans conducted themselves in a well disciplined, methodical manner that thousands of years of civilized warfare had distilled into something of a science. Aided by instructional memory and state of the art weapons that enhanced their own ability to seek, strike, and destroy, RT Kilo was the tip of the mightiest killing machine ever assembled.

Still, it was a fragile tip, one that was in danger of being becoming dull due to over use and prolonged exposure to a harsh environment and the stress of having to survive in a hostile and unforgiving environment. Its very existence depended upon adhering to the same laws of survival that all predators live by. The first law of survival is avoiding position and actions that threaten that survival. First Lieutenant Ken Aveno understood this principle very well, which is why he followed a strict routine when moving about within the confines of the team's laager while it was still light. He began by pulling himself up from the reclining position he had settled into hours before. Using the same cautious, almost hesitant motions that a prairie dog does when emerging from its burrow, the Special Forces officer paused to scan the trackless horizon through the broken pattern of the camouflage net that protected him from observation and the brutal daytime sun. Only when he was satisfied that it was safe to do so did he rise out of the shallow pit he had dug just prior to dawn that morning. He parted a seam in the tan net, stuck his head up through the opening like a swimmer breaking the surface, and continued to looked around now that his view of the flat, barren landscape was unobstructed. Satisfied that all was as it should be, he ducked back under the net and started preparing himself for another long night.

Slowly he slipped into the flak vest he had shed during the heat of the day, took up his weapon, and did his best to muster up some enthusiasm. With each passing day he was becoming acutely aware that the amount of effort he needed to motivate himself was increasing. It was as if he had only a finite reservoir of élan, a supply that this mission and his duties were depleting at an alarming rate.

Pausing, he shook his head. "Gotta keep it together," he mumbled as he adjusted his gear and glanced to his left and right, catching quick glimpses of other members of the team as they prepared for their nocturnal labors. To a man they moved in a deliberate manner that was purposeful while at the same time reflecting the same lack of enthusiasm he himself was struggling to overcome.

This concerned Aveno. He knew they were tired. But it was more than simple physical exhaustion that worried the young officer. They had been deployed for six weeks plus with no down time, no opportunity to kick back and simply rest and relax. Their area of operation and the nature of their mission required that they maintain an around the clock vigilance in a harsh environment that was taxing for even for the hardiest of them, physically and emotionally. The same fine grains of sand and grit that worked their way into the gears of their vehicles and the actions of their weapons, also found their way into every mouthful of food they consumed, breath they took, and bodily opening left exposed. The sand was a constant irritant. It could be tolerated. It could be joked about. But it was always there, like the unseen dangers that added mental stress to the physical duress that the desert inflicts upon any and all who reside there.

The result was an attrition that could not be stopped. Efforts to lessen the stress and gradual but steady erosion of each man's health could only do so much. Each member of the team had sufficient opportunities to rest, plenty to eat, and medical attention as soon as it was required. But nothing short of removing them from this milieu would restore both their full mental or physical well being. That this would not be happening any time soon only served to accelerate the ebbing morale and growing strain that was becoming more and more evident with each passing day.

When originally conceived, the plan allowed each Special Forces recon team three days to infiltrate along a predetermined route to its designated sector in Syria. Once it was in place the unit would spend two weeks gathering intelligence, observing known terrorist training camps and, if necessary, employing their laser designators when someone thousands of miles away decided that a target required immediate attack. At the end of this two week phase, when a new team was en-route the deployed team would extract itself. All of the preceding ten recon teams dispatched as part of Operation Razorback had started out following a schedule that placed them in harms way for just under three weeks. But like RT Kilo none of them, Alpha through Juliet, had been able to stay within this schedule. Each team had its deployment extended time and time again by unforeseen operational requirements as the war on international terrorism siphoned off already scare special operations resources to deal with other, more pressing needs. The days when a recon team's deployment in Syria was extended by a mere two additional weeks was now nothing more than a memory. Six weeks in place had become the norm, with eight not being unheard of.

It was not knowing when they would receive the word to disengage and head back to 'The World' that Ken Aveno suspected was most wearing on them. As he finished up tending his personal chores and prepared to turn to his assigned duties as the Team's executive officer, he wondered just how much the other members of the team were being affected. Though part of being on a Special Forces A team meant that rank was often ignored, Aveno was still an officer. There were conventions within the United States Army that even the camaraderie and professionalism of an elite unit could not overcome. As with any other officer, he depended upon two things when it came to judging the combat effectiveness of those entrusted to him: his personal observation of the men and his own physical and mental state. While not quite at the end of his rope, he could feel himself slipping and he suspected that the motivation and endurance of the others was ebbing as quickly as his own. Still, he remained confident that in terms of material, equipment and weapons, they were more than capable of executing their assigned duties as when they had begun their tour of duty.

Kilo was basically a reinforced Special Forces A Team, armed to the teeth with the best weaponry the lowest bidder could provide them. Most carried the venerable M-4 carbine, which was nothing more than a modified M-16A2. Those who had connections sported an MP-5, the weapon of choice for special ops types around the world. With a cyclic rate of 800 rounds per minute and a muzzle velocity of 400 meters per second, the German-designed Heckler & Koch MP-5 fired 9mm parabellum, full-metal-jacketed rounds, with a surprisingly high degree of accuracy due to its action, which fired the first round from a closed bolt position. In the hands of a highly trained professional it was a most effective instrument. Rounding out the category of individual small arms were 9mm pistols as well as one good old-fashioned Remington 870 pump-action shotgun.

To augment these personal weapons, RT Kilo's arsenal included a number of heavier weapons. Among the more impressive was the Barrette M-82A1 Caliber .50 sniper rifle, capable of firing standard 12.7mm cartridges. With a ten-power telescopic sight this rifle had a range in excess of 1000 meters, or a tad over six-tenths of a mile, allowing a good marksman to reach out and touch his foe long before that unfortunate soul became aware that he was in danger. The sheer size of the slug, one-half inch in diameter ensured that even a glancing blow was more than sufficient to ruin someone's entire day.

The crew-served weapons mounted on the unit's vehicles were the real heavy weapons. The Hummer that gave them the mobility to range far and wide also provided them with platforms for weapons that their Vietnam forebears could never have imagined humping on their backs.

Kilo Six, the Hummer used by the team commander sported an M-2 caliber .50 heavy barrel machinegun. Based upon a German World War One 12.7mm anti-tank rifle and classified in 1921, it was fast reaching the century mark with no end to its useful military career in sight. Like the Barrette, it fired 12.7mm ball or armoring piercing rounds. Unlike the sniper rifle, the M-2, known affectionately by its operators as the Ma Two, had a rate of fire that was 450 to 500 rounds a minute. Newer by a full half century was the M-19 40mm grenade launcher that graced the ring mount on Kilo Three, which was Aveno's Hummer. Capable of chunking out 60 baseball-sized grenades per minute up to a range of 1600 meters, its only major drawback was the limited number of rounds that could be held in its ready box.

Range was not a factor for the crew-served weapon affixed to SFC Allen Kannen's Hummer Kilo Two, which was the only all-enlisted humvee. Kannen, the team's senior NCO, fully appreciated what was probably the most unusual weapon for a Special Forces team—the tube-launched, optically tracked, wired-guided missile or TOW. The decision as to whether or not to include this long-range anti-tank weapon had been an issue hotly debated at every level of command that had a say in the organization, deployment, and operational control of the recon teams. In the end the choice had been left to the individual team commanders. Captain Erik Burman, Kilo's commanding officer, explained his decision to use the TOW by telling his people that when one goes wandering about in bear country, its not a bad idea to take along a bear rifle even if it's not bear you're looking for.

The only RT Kilo Hummer that did not have an over-sized weapon protruding from it was Kilo One, which belonged to the two-man Air Force Team headed by 1st Lieutenant Joseph Ciszak. Instead of a ring mount and crew-served weapon, Kilo One's hard shell was adorned with an array of antenna and a small satellite dish. Ironically, it was this innocent-looking vehicle that was responsible for all the devastation that RT Kilo had managed to rain down upon their foes during the past six weeks. The members of RT Kilo were hunters in every sense of the word but they did not do any of the actual killing. None of them had fired a single round since they had crossed the Turkish-Syrian border. Rather, it had been Lieutenant Ciszak and his collection of high-tech radios connecting him to his fellow aviators that did all of Kilo's killing. Using all the wonders of modern electronics and his trusty hand-held laser designator, Joe Ciszak was able to employ the full spectrum of conventional munitions available to the United States Air Force. Were it not for the need to provide security and locate hard to find targets, the Special

Forces A team would have been totally superfluous.

In and of itself this impressive array of weaponry and comms equipment had no real value. The most accurate firearm in the world is worthless unless it is used by someone who possesses both the training and the motivation to use it. Military history is replete with accounts of lavishly equipped armies being humbled by ragtag forces that won through a triumph of will and courage. The United States Army itself has seen both sides of this coin, once at its birth when it faced the best-trained army in the world and later in Vietnam when opposed by a foe who refused to yield to logic and the cruel mathematics of attrition. It is the willingness to soldier on and do one's duty in the face of daunting odds and seemingly insurmountable difficulties that often determined who is victorious and who is vanquished.

So the question of a unit's morale, even when made up of elite warriors, is always of the greatest importance. Lacking a definitive means of measuring this critical element and suspecting that the other members of RT Kilo were suffering from their protracted deployment in much the same way as he was, Ken Aveno found himself worrying how his morale was impacting those around him. Perhaps one day, he told himself, he would find a sure fire away of steeling himself against the slow, subtle corrosive effects of sagging morale. Perhaps when the twin silver bars of captain were pinned to his collar they would shield him from that demon and give him the strength to be the sort of soldier that everyone expected him to be. Until then he would have to muddle along, executing those duties that were assigned to him as best he could and keep morale from robbing him or his unit of its ability to carry on.

Climbing from the shallow hole that he had spent much of the day in, sleeping when the heat permitted, the executive officer of the small A team stretched his five foot ten frame for the first time in hours as he continued to looked around. There was not much to see. Each of the team's Hummers was hidden under tan and brown nets. It never failed to amaze Aveno how the squiggly strips of material laced through the squares of the knotted nylon nets managed to hide something as large as a Hummer and those who operated it. Yet he knew that from a surprising short distance, a net that was properly set up blended in nicely with the surrounding nothingness of the desert. From even further out, the nets and Hummers tucked underneath them simply disappeared, just like Team Kilo.

Shaking off his lethargy and anxious to get started before the faint light of early night was gone, Aveno chugged forward. As the XO he was charged with the maintenance and logistical affairs of Team Kilo. This required that he check each of the Team's specially modified Hummers on a daily basis to ensure that they were being maintained in accordance with established standards and ready for that night's operations. Unlike unit morale, this task had established standards and procedures that could be measured and relied upon. In the process of overseeing maintenance, he was also expected to keep track of current levels of ammo, food, fuel, and water. After six weeks this drill had become second nature, as routine as the setting sun. In fact it had become so routine that the young first lieutenant found he had to guard against complacency.

Each member of Recon Team Kilo was a professional in every sense of the word, men who had been in the Army long enough to appreciate the reasons behind Aveno's precombat inspections. Yet it still irked some of the enlisted men to have someone poking and prodding every nook and cranny of their vehicle and equipment day in and day out. They were after all the crème de la crème, the best of the best, professional soldiers who expected to be treated as professionals, not rank recruits. Only through quiet diplomacy and an occasional threat was Sergeant First Class Allen Kannen, Kilo's senior NCO able to keep their tongues in check. Still, not even he couldn't stop their every effort to let Aveno know just how much his daily inspections irritated them.

On approaching each Hummer, Aveno would call out to its driver, who was usually tearing down a camouflage net or checking out his humvee. The men assigned to the Hummer would greet him with whatever subtle sign of resentment they thought they could get away with. For his part, Aveno ignored this as he set about following a script that had been burned into his memory from repeated use. The routine never varied.

First, he unscrewed the cap of all water cans hanging on the side of every vehicle in order to check their contents. Then he'd crawl inside each door, pulling out any opened cases of MREs tossed in the rear and counting the number of meal packs remaining inside. After inspecting fuel gauges, and drawing dipsticks during his examination of the engine compartment of each Hummer, Aveno would drop to the ground and crawl under the vehicle checking the suspension. Everything had to be touched by him to confirm that every Hummer was functional and in order. Only the crew-served weapons, inspected by the commanding officer himself were ignored during this obsessive daily ritual that caused Kannen to secretly nickname Aveno, "Captain Queeg."

If Aveno reminded the enlisted members of the Naval officer who commanded the *U.S.S. Caine*, then their commanding officer was without question the Team's Captain Ahab. It had been the only other officer assigned to RT Kilo, Lieutenant Ciszak of the US Air Force who had graduated from Notre Dame with a BA in English who first made this comparison. One night, while he was waiting to direct an air strike, Ciszak turned to his driver, Sergeant Holton and commented that Captain Burman's single-minded dedication to duty, aloofness, and drive to accomplish every mission regardless of difficulty or danger reminded him of Melville's fictional captain, a processed man who prowled the seven seas on an endless quest. Amused, Sgt. Holton shared this observation with his fellow NCOs who immediately started using nautical terms whenever possible, including calling out "Thar she blows!" whenever they located a target they had been dispatched to find.

Ignorant of its origin, Captain Burman joined in on what he took to be a harmless attempt to liven up their harsh and monotonous existence. It was three weeks before Aveno discovered, through a slip of his driver's tongue, the true story behind the adaptation of seafaring clichés. Unsure of how Burman would take this piece of information, Aveno decided to keep that knowledge to himself. With the irritating sand and stress already eating away at Burman's nerves, Aveno knew that it wouldn't help to tell his commander that he was the butt of a collective joke.

Adding to the strain of their protracted deployment and the stress that living in the desert placed upon them was a gnawing doubt Aveno had concerning the value of their efforts. Like the Cold War that his parent's generation had endured, the current war on terror seemed to have no end. To many of his fellow countrymen, people to whom 9-11 was just another news story that was little more than a bad memory, the war on terror had become a distraction, a drain on national resources that some felt would be better spent on social welfare programs, education, or new roads. To them the idea of chasing terrorists and eradicating the threat they posed was a quixotic notion, a foolish dream that could never be achieved. Even Ken Aveno found himself wondering from time to time if it made sense to dispatch a group of highly trained professional soldiers like those belonging to RT Kilo to chase small cells of terrorists and call in bombers to drop high tech precision guided bombs on their tents when they were found.

This point was driven home every time a nation that was supposed to be an ally took a step to undo those small success that RT Kilo did manage to achieve. In truth, Aveno could find little fault in what the French and others were doing. He believed that if his own national leaders were not prisoners of their own rhetoric, they would be seeking some way of getting out of an open ended policy that was only costing American lives. Of course, such considerations were well above Aveno's pay grade. His personal mission was to follow orders and finish his current tour of duty with some degree of pride and sanity.

These dark troubling thoughts were in Ken Aveno's mind as he approached Kilo Six, Captain Burman's Hummer. Through the camo nets still draped over the vehicle, he caught sight of Burman perched upon the hood of his Hummer. This was a bad sign, for it had become something of a ritual for his commander to assume this particular posture when translating orders he had received during the day into detailed instructions. It was his way of announcing that the team had been tasked to go out into the gathering darkness once more and find something that a cabal of staff officers, ten thousand miles away, had suddenly taken an interest in. While most of these forays resulted in the discovery of targets that were subsequently bombed into oblivion, more times than Aveno cared to count the forays had turned into a snipe hunt, but one in which the snipe had sharp teeth and long, deadly claws.

Stopping a few meters away, he watched as Captain Burman pored over maps and scribbled notes on a pad lying next to him. It didn't seem right to the young officer that in this age of computers and high-tech wizardry success and failure in combat still depended upon illegible scribbling on a page made by a human being. It was like they were insulators placed within an increasingly high-speed system to keep it from overheating or spinning out of control. That there were fellow officers sitting in the Pentagon and at Fort Leavenworth trying to figure out how to eliminate those insulators was no great secret. Rubbing his irritated eyes, Aveno thought that the sooner those guys finished their work and made him obsolete, the sooner he would be free to pull pitch and turn his back on Syria, its people, and its fucking desert.

It was several minutes before Burman noticed that his executive officer was standing off to one side watching him. Determined to finish what he was doing before he lost the last bit of useful daylight, Burman ignored Aveno.

The task his team had been given that night was another routine mission. A Syrian ADA missile battery had become active some sixty kilometers southwest of where they were. As far as anyone knew there was very little in the region where the battery was located, and nothing of military value. The small villages scattered throughout the area dealt with camels and goats. Half of the population was still nomadic, real Lawrence of Arabia stuff, as SFC Kannen put it. Hence the reason for curiosity and concern by various intelligence agencies.

Though the operations order he had received made no

mention of it, Burman knew that someone back in Washington, D.C. was hoping that the barrenness of the area was an indication there was something worth defending hidden among the sun-dried brick huts and seemingly innocent expanses of nothingness. So Team Kilo was being dispatched to find out if it was just another cluster of terrorist training camps, or something more significant, especially installations involved in the development, testing, and manufacture of special weapons, the modern catchall phrase used to describe nuclear, biological, and chemical weapons. Everyone knew that facilities dedicated to this purpose existed somewhere in Syria and that the Syrians were doing their best to hide and protect them. But not everyone agreed on where they would most likely be found and how best to go about finding them. So even the relatively simple mission of locating and designating the Syrian ADA battery for aerial attack carried with it the implied task of uncovering any evidence of unusual or suspect activity that other intelligence resources had, to date, failed to detect.

Even so, the evening's mission was pretty much routine. As such Burman saw no reason to make a big fuss over the way it would be executed. When all pre-combat checks and briefings had been completed they would move out in a dispersed column. He would lead out with Kilo Six, followed by the team's senior NCO in Kilo Two and the Air Force liaison officer, or LNO in Kilo One. Aveno, who was still patiently waiting, would bring up the rear in Kilo Three. Once they were within striking distance of their objective the team would find a concealed spot from which Burman and Aveno would sally forth, either mounted or on foot to sniff out the exact location of their target while Kannen stayed back with Ciszak. How they would proceed depended on what they discovered during this preliminary recon. So other than mapping out their route of march, Burman saw little need for any additional detailed planning.

Having finished jotting a few notes just as the last modicum of light evaporated, Burman lay his map and pad aside and looked around. When his eyes finally did turn toward the dark shadow of his executive officer, he acted surprised. "I didn't see you standing there, Lieutenant Aveno."

Burman slowly eased his way off the Hummer's hood. "I imagine you're waiting for me to vacate this spot," he quipped, "so you can finish your appointed rounds."

"No rush, sir. I knew you were in the midst of putting together an order." When Burman turned to walk away without saying a word Aveno called out, "Anything exciting, sir?"

"Nothing to be concerned about, Lieutenant."

Aveno remained where he was, struggling to suppress the anger he felt welling up in him. The bastard was fucking with him. He was always fucking with him. It was as if they were still back at the Point, and Burman was still a first classman and Aveno was still a plebe. Since they were in different units and first classmen seldom took the time to bother with plebes who were not in their own company neither men had known each other then. Still, after all these years the psychological gulf remained.

There wasn't a man in the team who hadn't taken note of the "Me Tarzan, you Jane," attitude that Burman showed in all of his dealings with his number two. Aveno knew it wasn't personal. As best as he could tell, he had never said or done anything that could even remotely be considered improper or offensive to his commanding officer. Yet from day one the two had never really clicked. In Aveno's opinion Burman's policy of keeping him at a distance and his insistence on using proper military titles instead of establishing a more amiable relationship did not prevent the two from working together professionally. But it did create unnecessary friction. Like the fine grains of sand that he could taste with each bit of food and feel every time he blinked his eyes, Burman's manner was irritating and wearing. All Aveno could do was to endure, just as he endured the harsh and uncompromising desert. The same could be true for the rest of Team Kilo. For better or worse the fourteen men had to keep functioning and surviving until such time as the Fates smiled upon them and their circumstances changed.